THE BLUE HYDRANGEA

mirette hanley

felicitas press

ISBN: 0995685800
ISBN 13: 9780995685802

For Paul

PART ONE

CHAPTER ONE

April 2012

Destiny came calling one spring day, unannounced. She could scarcely believe her good fortune. No one in their right mind could call her lucky. Her life had been struck with tragedy. In an instant, her world had ended. Afterwards, she was never the same.

Yet, life had chosen to smile favourably on her that afternoon. At the time, she had been following the narrow woodland path upstream. A small wooden signpost signalled her arrival at Beat Two, and she had strayed off the footpath, walking silently onto the timber boardwalk. She stood at the edge of the casting platform, transfixed by the river. Unexpectedly, she blessed herself. It was a small, but heartfelt gesture. This was where he had died suddenly, eight months previously.

"May you rest in peace," she whispered. She remembered seeing his dead body on the boardwalk. First, she had felt disbelief, swiftly followed by a wrenching pain and then, regret.

On the other side of the narrow stretch of river was Doonmara Castle, rooted on a grassy slope littered with daffodils, with a backdrop of the Twelve Bens Mountains. The baronial style edifice had four linked irregular castellated turrets and a gothic porch. Her room, a corner suite on the second floor, overlooked the spot where she was now standing. Framed by hundreds of majestic trees, the river, renowned for its salmon catch, wound and weaved its way around the castle and lush greenery. The trees swayed in the April breeze. If you were going to die, this had to be the most beautiful and peaceful of settings. The thought had occurred to her more than once.

Rarely had the river been this low. There would be no fishing today or any day soon for that matter. The sun had made a guest appearance and the clarity of light was striking. She walked to the end of the platform and cast her gaze on the river below, where tiny fish, the size of small anchovies, but darker in colour, darted about purposefully, in water that was crystal clear.

Water grasses undulated side to side on a river-bed floor scattered with stones. She observed the long slender sheaves as they moved backwards and forwards, hypnotising movements that were slow and graceful. Fleetingly, the sheen of something hidden beneath the reeds caught her eye.

She squatted down, peering into the water to have a closer look. It seemed to her that the longer she watched, the less the grasses shifted, and she was sorely tempted to give up. Nonetheless, she remained fixed to the spot and was rewarded for her diligence, for as the reeds shifted, there was another brief flash.

This time, she was able to rule out several possibilities. It wasn't an old tin can, or silver foil, or a piece of broken glass, or metal. Was it a piece of jewellery? Patiently, she waited until the 'trinket' appeared again. When it did, her curiosity remained unsatisfied.

Afterwards, she never knew exactly why she had decided to wade into the river that afternoon. She could only put it down to a gut instinct. It was an impulsive decision and foolhardy too. The chance of her finding diamonds on the riverbed must have been remote at best, and she was bound to be disappointed.

She gauged the depth of the water near the reeds to be no more than two feet. The drop from the jetty was, perhaps, eighteen inches. Without hesitation, she took off her runners and then her socks, before rolling up her jeans as high as she could. A smattering of pearl pink nail polish adorned dainty feet. As she dipped her toes in, her body was assaulted with the sharp shock of freezing cold water.

A small cloud of mud descended as she anchored both feet firmly. She waited until the mud had settled.

She leaned forward, eyes downcast. Shoulder length, tawny-coloured hair tumbled around her face. It was a face etched with character. For the umpteenth time that day, she pushed her hair behind her ears. The look in her green eyes, which were framed by untamed eyebrows, was determined.

Cautiously, she moved her feet, taking baby steps and shifting her gaze until she found the spot. She reached down and separated the grasses gently; small handfuls at a time. Her hunch proved correct. A diamond ring, a solitaire, was nestling between small clumps of stones.

The enormity of her catch only hit home when she held the ring in her hands, and she drew a sharp intake of breath. Although dirty and muddied, it was truly breathtaking. The setting was old. Art Deco, she judged correctly. The solitaire had to be four if not five carats. The platinum band was filthy and she washed it carefully in the water before wiping it on her jumper. On closer inspection, she partially made out the engraving which read *Suri,* followed by a date that was impossible to decipher.

The magnificent solitaire glistened in the sunlight. It fit perfectly on the middle finger of her left hand, next to her own engagement ring.

Never before had she seen such an exquisite piece of jewellery. The diamond was emerald cut with a row of smaller diamonds mounted on either side. She examined the workmanship from every angle and waved her hand admiringly. How long had it been in the river, she wondered?

Her legs were icy cold and numb now, so cold that they stung. She hoisted herself back onto the jetty and quickly wiped her pale goose-bumped limbs with her socks.

The certainty of a warm welcoming turf fire was enough to lure her back to the hotel. Sure-footed, she made her return along the short-looped path. Her thoughts drifted back to the previous summer and to her stay at Doonmara Castle Hotel, a visit that she would never forget. That weekend had altered the course of Laura Hamilton's life.

She picked up her speed, head gently bobbing on a slight, slender frame, until she arrived at the small wooden gate on the avenue bridge. The lock was stiff and she rattled it for a few moments until it gave. She took a left turn towards the hotel.

＊＊＊

August 2011

Laura arrived on a Thursday evening in mid-August. A heavy downpour descended as she drove through the hotel gates. The castle loomed once she had turned the corner on the long avenue. Ahead, the mountains had taken on a purple hue against the dark grey skyline.

It had been raining intermittently that day. Noting that the inclement weather hadn't deterred visitors, she found a car space with difficulty, bypassing an invasion of hydrangeas in a myriad of colours taking up prime residence in the front garden.

Much to her annoyance, the only available space seemed to be the one furthest away. There had been a space directly outside the entrance, but the car in front had whipped it.

By the time she got to reception, she was soaked through. She waited in line as the family ahead checked in. The father turned to her while the receptionist busied herself with his credit card details.

"What an awful night," he said, effortlessly charming and well-spoken. He was a tall man and although a little over weight, he carried the extra pounds well.

"What an awful summer," she said, rubbing her hands rapidly to warm up.

"I was lucky with the parking," he said. "I'm guessing you were in the car behind."

"I was and not quite as fortunate!" She pulled at her wet hair. His was dry, tousled black flecked with grey.

His wife, Laura's age, a forty something pencil-slim brunette, and two children, a boy and a girl, were warming themselves at the fire. The son was young, no more than thirteen, his sister a little older.

Laughter generated from where they stood and for a moment Laura was envious. She was tempted to join them. There was a genuine happiness and spark about this family which even the miserable weather hadn't dampened. She was keenly aware of how her own circumstances were so different. She felt achingly alone in that moment. Her husband, Alex, had deferred his arrival until tomorrow.

"I'm flat out at work, Laura," he said. "I'll join you Friday afternoon."

Alex always came up with the same excuse. Her plans had been botched, despite the fact that it was her birthday today, and that she had planned the trip weeks ago.

Now, here she was in her favourite place on earth and alone. She longed to part of a tight knit family unit like the one in front of her.

'What's for you won't pass you by," her mother had told her that very morning.

"It has," Laura replied bitterly, and thought she must have heard every platitude known to mankind at this point.

Once, things had been very different. Once, their lives had been blessed with Rachel. Automatically, she pulled at the gold locket wrapped around her neck. She did that whenever she thought of Rachel, which was often.

Those were the golden years of Laura's life and never to be repeated, because Rachel, their beloved and only child, had died. Rachel, her darling daughter, whose scent she could inhale, and whose laughter she could hear. She could barely recall the sound of Rachel's voice and it both frightened and saddened her. But her child's laughter – a ripple of giggles and small squeals – that she could remember with ease.

Laura vividly recalled the first time that she had laughed after Rachel died. Laura had been driving and listening to the radio. Something the presenter had said on air had made her laugh. Immediately, she was horrified and consumed by guilt.

She had burst into floods of tears, so distressed that she had to pull the car over. She was a bad mother. How could she be happy and laughing? How could she not remember her child was dead? Laura had sat in her car, weeping uncontrollably. At the time, Rachel had been dead three years.

Rachel had been an affectionate child. Laura imagined now, Rachel's arms wrapping her close. What she wouldn't give for one of those hugs. Everything about Rachel remained indelibly imprinted in Laura's mind: Rachel's mischievous grin; her beloved face with its cherubic features; that mop of dark curls; Rachel's tiny hands and feet; and her little kisses. Rachel would remain forever Laura's little girl, as shortly before her fifth birthday, Rachel had died.

Laura had kept a lock of those curls. The solitary curl was encased in the locket around her neck. She had cut it from Rachel's hair when the child was dead. It had seemed like an act of brutality at the time, as if the very act itself might hurt Rachel, which was nonsense, because Rachel was lifeless. She looked peaceful, as if she were asleep. She wore a rose-pink party dress, and her favourite soft toys surrounded her in the small white coffin. In vain, Laura had willed the little figure to wake up.

Laura's reverie was interrupted with a jolt.

"Mrs Hamilton, it's nice to see you again," Maura, the receptionist, proclaimed with a beaming smile.

"It's lovely to be back," she said, recovering quickly. She had years of practise in similar situations. Few would have guessed at the heartache behind Laura Hamilton's smiles.

The receptionist found Laura's booking on the computer.

"We've put you in the River Suite as requested. I'll get Seán to bring up your luggage, Mrs Hamilton."

As if by magic, the porter appeared. Laura greeted him fondly. It was a small hotel, and she knew most of the staff by first name.

"It's in the boot," she said, and handed Seán the keys to her car.

He disappeared into thin air. For a stout man, he was incredibly nimble on his feet.

"Will Mr Hamilton be joining us this evening?" Maura asked.

"He won't be arriving until tomorrow."

Diplomatic to her finger tips, Maura simply nodded.

"The restaurant is especially busy tonight, Mrs Hamilton. Shall I make a reservation for you?"

"Would you, please, Maura."

The dining room overlooked the river and the view was magnificent. You could make a reservation but you could not pre-book any of the window tables. As a consequence, the window tables went early.

"You can head in whenever you like, Mrs Hamilton. Here's the key to your suite."

Laura took hold of a bedroom key that was attached to a clunky wooden key ring, engraved with the hotel's name on one side and her room number on the other. As she turned to leave, she collided into the guest who had checked in before her.

"My apologies," he said, flustered.

Laura decided that his blue eyes were his most attractive feature. They were pale blue. A dark blue rimmed the irises, which were an even mix of blue and white rays. Maura looked at Mr Russell expectantly.

"I'd like to organise a fishing lesson for tomorrow morning," he said. "Is that possible or have I left it a bit late?"

Laura was glad she had overheard. As an afterthought, Alex had asked her that very morning to book Conor, his favourite gillie, and it had slipped her mind completely.

"I can book you in now, Mr Russell."

"My son is joining me. We're both beginners."

"Then your best option is the fly fishing tutorial with John."

"That sounds perfect. Can you run through the itinerary with me, please?"

The conversation looked likely to continue for some time. Laura had eavesdropped enough. She would phone Maura later from her room and make the necessary arrangements. If John was taking the lesson, Conor might still be available.

She made her way to the River Suite, walking down endless corridors. The view from the corner suite room would be her reward.

Laura turned the key in the door and let herself in. She flitted past the narrow hallway to the sitting room. Cream and gold brocade curtains framed floor to ceiling windows which ran the entire length of the room. Laura went to the window. Outside, the rain was spitting on the river. The rich woodlands were spectacular, a veritable oasis of fauna, flora and trees. Even in the rain, the landscape painted a bewitching canvas.

Wallpapered in a sage green with an unobtrusive cream floral print, the room itself was tastefully furnished. A large couch, upholstered in a cream velvet fabric, was positioned in front of a mahogany coffee table. Laura had spent many an afternoon curled up on that couch with a book. There was a comfortable armchair. An old writing bureau occupied one wall and a large gilt mirror, hanging over an old fireplace, now rendered obsolete, dominated the other.

She heard a rap on the door.

"Come in," she said, opening the door and ushering the porter into the suite. As Seán went through to the bedroom with her bags, she went in search of her purse. Moments later, he joined her in the sitting room.

"Apologies for the delay, Mrs Hamilton," he said. "The family before you had a lot of luggage. Now, is there anything I can get you? Would you like a pot of tea sent up?"

"No thank you, Seán. I'm going to head down to dinner shortly."

"We've a full house tonight. We've been run off our feet all summer."

"You've had a good season then. I'm glad to hear that. I know business has been down in recent years."

"Too true, ma'am. Mind you, even when times were good, Doonmara never attracted the high fliers."

That had been one of the things that she and Alex had liked about the place.

"What's the fishing been like, Seán?"

"There were two salmon caught today. Mr Russell, the gentleman who checked in before you, asked me the very same thing, so he did."

"I overheard him book a tutorial."

"He's taking a lesson with his son. The family is from Lisbon."

Seán knew everything that was going on in the castle. Alex called him the Doonmara grapevine.

"I thought the father was Irish."

"More 'Oirish' than Irish if you get my drift. The wife looks foreign. Portuguese, I'd say. Mr Russell told me he has an old family connection to the place."

"Oh, that's interesting. My husband will be joining them on the river. Which reminds me, Seán, I must book Conor or I'll be in hot water."

"Do you want me to have a quiet word with him? He's in the bar."

The gillies often retired to the bar for an early evening pint after the day's fishing. Seán's role varied. Part porter and part concierge, he also occasionally tended the bar and stoked up the fires of which there were plenty.

"Would you, Seán? That will save me a job. The fishing was booked for half-three."

Laura smiled gratefully.

"Mr Hamilton has taken to the fishing, so he has." Seán showed no sign of budging.

The porter liked to have a natter with the guests, especially with Mrs Hamilton.

"Like a duck to water, Seán." It crossed her mind that her husband was at his happiest fishing. Alex would gladly spend the entire weekend fishing.

"He caught a salmon the last time he was here, if memory serves me right?"

"I never heard the end of it."

"He did well," he said, stating the obvious.

Laura smiled thinly.

"Beginners luck, Seán."

"Better not let him hear you say that."

"Oh, I'd be in deep trouble!"

The porter straightened up.

"All right then," he said. "If that will be all, Mrs Hamilton, I'd better get back to reception. They'll be sending a search party out for me."

Laura handed the porter a generous tip.

"It's always a pleasure to see you here," he said, after thanking her. "And God is good. Maybe Mr Hamilton will catch another salmon."

"God is good!" Laura repeated after Seán left, in a tone of voice that suggested otherwise.

He wasn't good to her. He certainly wasn't good to little Rachel. Laura was inclined to be morbid on her birthday. It was a day when she felt the loss of her daughter keenly.

Laura remained in front of the window staring at the river, the tissue in her hand already moist. It was easy to lose oneself in the canvas that stretched before her. She had felt increasingly insignificant since Rachel died, like a small dot on the land-scape. With each passing year, Laura faded more and more into the background. She felt like a ghost hovering on the edges of her own life.

As it turned out, Alex Hamilton didn't catch a salmon the next day. He had planned a perfect afternoon whiling away a few hours fishing. It was not to be.

CHAPTER TWO

"Did you book Conor?"

Predictably, that was the first question Alex asked when he phoned Laura later that evening. The rain pelted against the bedroom window pane. She fingered the duvet cover absently.

"He's slotted you in for half-three," she said.

"Good woman."

Laura hated that expression.

"I'm looking forward to trying out my new rod," he said, animated.

She had bought him a fishing rod for Christmas. She put a lot of thought into his presents. He hadn't enquired about her journey, or dinner. The conversation had been about the weather and the fishing, for the former affected the latter.

With a parting word, he redeemed himself a little.

"Good night. And Laura, Happy Birthday. I'm sorry I'm not with you. I'll make it up to you."

Laura was feeling lonely and empty, and for a moment, those few kind words dusted her in sunlight and warmth. She lapped them up.

"I'll hold you to that," she said.

She hung up, placing her mobile on the bedside table, before switching off the bedside light. The warmth disappeared when the phone call ended, and Laura drew up the duvet cover. The wind was up and from time to time she heard a whooshing sound.

Alex may have wounded her but she had forgiven him. She always forgave him, out of guilt, mainly. Laura was aware that she had pushed her husband out of her life years ago. Their marriage was a travesty. No wonder he'd thrown himself into his work.

She had dined alone on her birthday. At forty-three, she felt old, older than her years. As soon as Laura entered the restaurant, the restaurant manager made a beeline in her direction.

"I'm on my own, Jane," Laura said, greeting her with a perfunctory kiss on both cheeks.

Jane flinched. She didn't like to overstep the mark with the guests.

"A table for one, it is," she said. "Too late for a window table I'm afraid."

Laura had eaten in the restaurant often enough not to feel the slightest bit uneasy dining on her own. In a way, Laura had been alone since the day Rachel had died, because something inside Laura had shut down that day. Death could ricochet through a life, causing ravaging sorrow.

Laura was polite and she was friendly, but she was a shadow of her former self, the bubbly Laura so full of life and purpose. Some days, she barely scratched the surface of life.

Her fellow diners provided enough distraction, in particular the Russell family, seated adjacent to her table. Looking dapper in a pair of cream linen trousers, a navy blazer, and a striped pink shirt paired with what looked like an old school tie, Mr Russell radiated contentment on that August evening.

"That's the third time you've yawned at dinner," Laura heard his wife tease. "I hope we're not boring you." Her eyebrows rose playfully over chocolate-coloured eyes.

He laughed heartedly, baring very white teeth. Laura wondered whether he had them whitened. They looked unnaturally white.

"You, boring?" he reiterated. "No one could ever accuse you of that, Felicia. After eighteen years of wedded bliss, you still constantly surprise me."

"I'm very glad to hear that. How reassuring to know it has all been bliss."

Her husband chuckled. Her daughter sneered.

"Every single moment," he said. "But in all seriousness, I am a little tired. It's nothing that a good night's sleep won't remedy."

"It's been a long day. You probably need your beauty sleep."

Once, Laura and Alex used to banter like that. It seemed a lifetime ago. For a moment, Laura was nostalgic.

Felicia's English was excellent. She sounded British with no trace of a Portuguese accent whatsoever. Laura wondered whether Seán had got his wires crossed. It would not be the first time.

"And Harvey, you do look jaded," Felicia continued. "Come to think of it, you've been complaining of being tired for the last day or two."

Harvey! Judging by his accent, and his appearance at dinner tonight, and now his name, Laura conjectured that Mr Russell was indeed Anglo-Irish. She was in agreement with Seán on that score.

"We'll head to bed early tonight, darling," Felicia said. "Straight after dinner and let there be no argument." Long jade earrings dangled from her earlobes. They were arresting against her tanned skin. Her hair had been swept up into a messy bun and the style suited her. She exuded confidence.

"I know when I'm beaten," he said. "Early to bed," he mouthed gratefully.

"Mum, we're on holidays," their daughter whined.

She was olive skinned with a prominent jaw like her mother, the same dark eyes and heavy brows. You could see a slight resemblance to her father, but it was to her mother she most obviously owed her Mediterranean looks.

"You two are off the hook," Felicia said. She was wearing a coral, sleeveless V-necked silk dress which showed off ample cleavage. An emerald green pashmina casually draped her shoulders and a coral lipstick complimented her dress.

Jane had come over for a chat and Laura lost the thread of the conversation at the next table. A stalwart member of staff, Jane had been working at Doonmara Castle for the last twenty-five years. "I'm part of the furniture," she joked.

Jane raced around the dining room and to-night was no different. *No wonder she's whippet thin*, Laura thought. The restaurant manager worked too hard. She had never married. There was no room and no time for romance. Or so, Laura imagined. Who knew? Perhaps, Jane preferred to keep a professional distance from the guests and to keep her private life private. Laura could empathise with that. Laura kept pretty much to herself.

Jane had an edginess about her which manifested itself in the way she spoke. It was less apparent with those guests she knew well. She was more relaxed with 'the regulars'. However, a brittle voice belied a generous heart. Laura adored the walnut brown bread they served in the restaurant. On occasion, when the Hamiltons were leaving, Jane would meet Laura in the foyer, armed with a loaf carefully wrapped in tinfoil.

"A little something to remember us when you get home," she would whisper conspiratorially, pressing the bread into Laura's hands.

Jane liked to read crime thrillers in her spare time, a passion Laura shared. Sporadically, Laura would pass on books that she had read to Jane. This was one of those times.

"I've brought a couple of books for you, Jane. There's one I know you'll like," she told the restaurant manager."

Years previously, Laura had been dining alone in the restaurant with only a book for company. Jane asked Laura how she rated the book. Jane was reading the same Nordic crime thriller at the time, and that's how they both become aware of a shared interest.

Laura had known Jane for the best part of seven years. On several occasions, Laura had asked Jane to address her by her first name. Jane would smile politely but she never did.

Laura and Alex began visiting Doonmara the year Rachel had died. The beauty of the place comforted Laura. She seldom revisited places they had been to with Rachel. It brought back too many memories, making her painfully aware that Rachel was no longer with them, no longer making new memories to treasure.

Even though Laura was cordial, Jane thought that there was an air of mystery about the woman. Mrs Hamilton had an elusive quality and a reticence. She engaged with the staff, but Jane couldn't help thinking that Laura Hamilton was going through the motions. She lived in a world of her own. That had become apparent to Jane over time. Often, Mrs Hamilton looked sad.

Sometimes, it was hard to credit that she was married to a man like her husband. Alex Hamilton was the most handsome man Jane had ever set eyes on. You wouldn't have put a man like that with Laura Hamilton. Mrs Hamilton had let herself go. Jane would have expected Alex to have gone for someone more striking.

Laura had never spoken about Rachel to Jane, or to any of the staff. Nonetheless, Jane knew of Rachel's existence. Word got round. The Hamiltons lived in a small rural village. Jane had casually mentioned their name once to another couple from the same parish.

"We have guests from Cratloe who come here regularly," she said. "Alex Hamilton and his wife."

"We know the Hamiltons," the wife said. "Poor old Laura has had a dreadful time."

Jane's curiosity was aroused. She couldn't resist asking questions.

"Their little girl died. It was shattering for both of them, but especially for Laura."

For a moment, Jane felt bad that she had trespassed onto something so private.

"She was their only child. It was heart breaking," the wife said, and outlined what had happened.

At dinner that evening, the waiters danced around Laura. She was a popular guest at the castle. She remembered everyone's story. She hardly ever spoke about herself.

The Hungarian waiter came over to say hello and she asked after his family. "How is your little boy?" she said. "Is he starting school in September?"

"Have you set a wedding date yet?" she asked the Polish waiter who offered her a bread roll. He was engaged to the pretty Slovakian girl who cleaned the rooms. As was typical of lots of Irish hotels, many staff were non-nationals.

As Laura got up to leave, Harvey Russell acknowledged her. For a few moments, Laura engaged both parents in casual conversation. The Russells were having coffee at the table. Laura had chosen to have coffee in the lounge, in front of the marble fireplace with its blazing log fire.

"Did you enjoy your meal?" she enquired politely.

"Yes. The food here is very good. And what a beautiful setting this is," Felicia said, her eyes taking in the river view.

"Isn't it just," Laura said. She noticed that Felicia's coral nail polish was exactly the same shade as her lipstick. "Is this your first time staying in the hotel?"

"We were here once previously but years ago," answered Harvey. He gestured at his children. "These two hadn't been born."

"You've been here before, I take it," Felicia said. She noticed the attention that Laura had received at dinner.

"My husband and I are regulars. He enjoys the fishing. He's joining me tomorrow."

"My son and I are having a fly-fishing lesson tomorrow," Harvey said, and turned to look at his son. "We're looking forward to it, aren't we, Jack?"

The boy's face lit up.

"Good luck with that," she said, addressing the boy.

Laura exited the dining room leaving a trail of Shalimar perfume in her wake. Felicia recognised the scent.

"What a lovely woman," Felicia said to her husband.

"Very pleasant," he agreed.

Felicia had noticed her earlier in the restaurant. Although Laura had been chatty with the dining room staff, Felicia couldn't help thinking that the woman looked a little forlorn. She was attractive in her own way her but she was like a faded flower that had lost its bloom.

Laura dreamt that night, the same disturbing dream that she had been having for years. She is standing alone on a deserted shoreline at dusk. A hooded figure in a boat is drifting towards her but she can barely make out the bluish-grey form. As the boat draws nearer, she begins to see more clearly. The boatman turns to the side for a moment, revealing an aged face. To his right, is a small figure, partially hidden. His passenger is bundled in a heap and asleep surely, or dead.

The boatman has come to collect Laura. He is ferrying the souls of the dead across the river. He's tantalisingly close and calls her name. She takes a few steps backwards as if to distance herself.

Eventually, he turns the boat around and heads off without her. She watches until the boat disappears into the night. At this point, she inevitably wakes. *That night* was no different. Occasionally, she wakes up crying. *That night* she woke up with tears streaming down her face. His passenger was dead. His passenger was Rachel.

CHAPTER THREE

Alex Hamilton was turning in for the night. The fishing was confirmed. It was a recently discovered passion, and one that was giving him a great deal of pleasure.

Once, Laura had been his passion, and he had been hers. But things had changed and drastically. Rachel's death had seen to that.

Alex Hamilton was irresistible to most women, having the good luck to bear an uncanny likeness to the actor George Clooney. The one woman who was immune to his charms was his wife. Laura avoided any kind of intimacy altogether.

After Rachel's death, Laura began to drift away. She froze whenever he touched her. At first, he thought he understood, for she was awash with grief. They both were. He was considerate and patient. Time marched on, and Laura continued to recoil from any physical gesture. It was hard not to take it personally. Their sexual relationship had ended the day Rachel died.

There had been silence in the house the first year after Rachel's death. His wife barely communicated with him. She was deaf to his words. Alex would walk into a room and Laura would walk out. He wanted to know what was really going on beneath Laura's silence.

He could feel her pain but he was unable to help his wife. She would not let him in. She visibly shrank back from any contact whatsoever. He was even afraid to hold her hand. It drove him mad.

Once, during an argument, he blew up.

"You don't love me anymore," he said.

Laura hadn't replied. Instead, she got up and left the bedroom. Alex had followed her into the lounge. Bingo, the family dog, trotted behind him. Laura sat on the couch, Bingo immediately leapt up onto her knees. She began to gently stroke the animal.

"Even the dog gets more affection than I do!" he said, more hurt than angry.

"The dog doesn't want anything back," Laura replied coldly.

Laura's words echoed inside his head. His wife remained on the couch, focusing her attention on Bingo. Gravely wounded, Alex had stormed out of the house. In an effort to cool down, he went for a drive.

Bingo was the only recipient of Laura's love and attention because Laura was incapable of reaching out to anyone. Rachel had loved the cocker spaniel. He had been 'Rachel's dog'. Laura had been devastated when Bingo had died four years later.

At home, it got to the stage where Alex was afraid to say anything. Laura was full of anger and he never knew what might set her off. The first two years after Rachel had died, he tip-toed around his wife. Home became a prison. Laura's grief ran through every minute of their day. He felt diminished by her pain.

He had kept going the first year. He'd had no choice. There were hurdles to be met: the first birthday, the first Christmas, the first New Year's Eve, the first anniversary of Rachel's death.

The second year arrived and Alex realised that Rachel was never coming home. Not ever. Rachel's death really began to sink in. He found the second year more difficult.

That year Laura had taken to visiting Rachel's grave at night. Their daughter was buried in the village cemetery.

One night, Alex had woken up startled. He had heard the engine of Laura's car starting. He had leapt out of the bed, thinking that burglars were stealing the car. Then, he noticed that that his wife wasn't in the bed. It was Laura in the car. He checked the time. It was half two.

Laura returned two hours later. By then, he was frantic.

"Where were you?" he asked, trying to remain calm. He was sitting at the kitchen table. He had made a cup of tea but it remained untouched. Fearful of what she'd do, Alex had prayed to God to keep Laura safe. "I was so worried about you, Laura."

She looked pale and exhausted.

"I went to Rachel's grave," she said. "I needed to be with her."

"You're shivering, Laura. You must be frozen. Why don't you go back to bed and I'll bring you in a cup of tea?"

Alex was relieved that Laura had arrived home in one piece, and he said nothing further. What was the point?

After that night and every so often over the next two years, Laura would drive to the graveyard in the middle of the night. Sometimes, she would fall asleep on Rachel's grave.

Alex had lost Rachel. Now, he had lost his wife. Laura didn't love him anymore. Alex became convinced that Laura was punishing him for Rachel's death. Though she never said so, he was certain Laura blamed him.

He would stay with his wife regardless: "Till death do us part" as his father was wont to say. Alex felt he owed it to his wife to stay. Deep down, he too thought that he was responsible for Rachel's death.

He was unwilling to live the life of a monk, however. Not that he had been. Not for some years. Caroline, his current fling, had been on the scene for the best part of six months. Curvy with beautiful breasts and bee stung lips, Caroline had creamy silky skin and a mane of long, blond tousled locks. Caroline was the light relief in the world he occupied, a world full of shadows.

"You do know, you're the spitting image of George Clooney," she said the first time they met. Her manner had been flirty.

"Who's George Clooney?" he said.

She had laughed quietly by way of response. They were sitting in a Jacuzzi at the time.

"It's a nice hotel. Are you staying here?" she asked a few moments later.

"No. I'm a member of the leisure centre. Are you staying?"

"Yes," she said, straightening up, and giving him an eyeful of her breasts. They were barely contained in her skimpy, pink bikini top. The move was deliberate.

"What brings you to Limerick?"

"Work," she told him. "I'm a sales rep. I've started a new job and Limerick is one of my journeys."

They chatted easily and introduced themselves. The chemistry was instant.

"I'm cooked," he said eventually, getting up. "It was nice meeting you, Caroline, and good luck with the new job."

"Thanks."

"Who knows, we might bump into each other again."

"We might. I'll be in Limerick every fortnight. Or, we could meet for a drink?" she pressed. She stood up, intent on leaving also. She had a knock-out figure and she knew it. She looked at him unflinchingly. He was wearing his wedding ring but it didn't seem to put her off.

"Let's do that," he said, taking the bait.

They arranged a date. It was that easy. With his matinee idol looks, Alex never had to try too hard to lure the females of the species. Wedding band or not, they threw themselves at him. He had heard of web sites where married people could hook up with other married people for sex. Alex never had cause to resort to the web.

He remembered the first time he strayed. Rachel had been dead three years. He had felt bad, and he had come clean, begging his wife to forgive him. He had suggested they attend marriage counselling. Laura wouldn't hear of it. She had been averse to any kind of bereavement counselling too. It was as if she couldn't bear to be happy if Rachel was dead. That would mean that Laura had forgotten Rachel.

Laura hadn't hit the roof. To a degree, she seemed relieved. He thought he knew why. It alleviated any harbouring sense of guilt she might have felt. It helped to justify her actions. It gave her permanent ammunition to refute his advances. He wondered if the real George Clooney could work his magic on Laura.

After his confession, Laura didn't broach the topic further. Alex should have walked away then but he couldn't leave Laura by herself.

With each passing year, Alex felt as though he was slowly dying inside, fading away, like the colour from a photograph left out in the sun. Laura barely communicated with him for the second and third year either. To be fair, she was like that with everyone. She was overwhelmed with loss. Rachel had been the light of her life and his, but Alex's grief was forgotten.

He had tried to raise the subject of bereavement counselling again.

"Laura, I know we have a long road ahead of us," he began in earnest one night.

She had looked at him and said, "Alex, I'm not even on the road yet." Then, she got up and left the room. Rachel's third anniversary was a month away.

He ached to take away Laura's pain. He hoped that one day she would reach out to him. That never happened and he threw himself into his work.

And then, a year after that first extra-marital encounter, he strayed again. Though he still felt guilty, he was not prepared to forgo a sexual life, because it gave him a release, albeit temporary, from his own personal pain. He needed to feel something. Anything. It was an instinctive drive to survive.

His lapses were occasional. He thought that Laura was aware of his infidelities. He assumed she knew. She never questioned his whereabouts or his late-night business appointments. He tried to be discreet. In a kind of unspoken alliance, they motored along this rocky road.

After some time, an acceptance of sorts replaced Laura's terrible anger. These days, Mr and Mrs Hamilton were friends, certainly, but not bedfellows. Alex was a good provider, and he tried to be a good companion. There was little warmth at home and work became his main focus. It masked the loneliness.

He missed the loving embrace of his wife. Previously, they had enjoyed a good sexual relationship. It had brought them close. And my God, how he missed Rachel. Her death left a great void in his life.

It was ironic. Even though Rachel's death had effectively destroyed his marriage, his little girl was the glue that somehow bound him and Laura together.

"The death of a child will bring you closer together or tear you apart," his father had told him.

There was truth in what his old man had said. His unhappiness was apparent to his father, as was Laura's chilly manner. Once, she had been tactile with her husband. Not anymore. It had not gone unnoticed within the family.

Alex was cross with himself for messing up Laura's birthday. At the last minute, something had come up at work. He hadn't been lying about that.

It was time to end things with Caroline and move on. He had been with Caroline for too long as it was. But she was easy company and she didn't ask too many awkward questions.

Suddenly, he had a mental image of Caroline lips and what they were capable of. At that thought and in equal measure, he felt terrible guilt but enormous pleasure as he remembered in detail where those lips had been when last they met. She was an enthusiastic lover. And despite all the sexual bravado of their initial encounters, there was a kindness about her that was endearing.

Not that he had ever allowed himself to get close to Caroline, or to any of these women. It was all about the sex. Any attempts at a real closeness would have been a further step of betrayal, and one too many. Nevertheless, he had grown fond of Caroline.

It was his wife's birthday today and he had let her down. And then, to make matters worse, the first thing he had asked her about tonight was the fishing. How thoughtless was that.

"I'll make it up to you," he had said. "I promise."

He considered his words carefully. It was an empty promise, and one that he couldn't ever deliver, because he could never bring Rachel back. Once he had been a man of his word and a man of principle. He wanted to be that person again. If he continued this double life, he would end up without an ounce of self-respect.

He needed to get his life back on an even keel. If he left Laura, she might be forced to move on with her own life. She might embrace life again. God knows, he wanted that for her. Neither of them deserved the life they had settled for. It would mark the end of their marriage, but it might be the best option for both of them.

He would end the affair with Caroline. He needed to clear the decks. This summer had marked the seventh anniversary of Rachel's death. His little girl would have been twelve this year and on the cusp of womanhood.

It was time to draw a line. He wanted to start living again. He wanted to come out of the shadows.

⊨⊹ ⊹⊨

Rachel had died a week before her fifth birthday.

"It's a glorious day," Laura said gaily, early that morning, the day Rachel died. "Why don't we head down to Kilkee."

"That sounds like a plan," Alex said.

Rachel skipped around the kitchen in a pink sparkly dress. Laura had bought the dress for Rachel to wear at her birthday party.

"Do you like it, Daddy?" the child asked.

"Let's have a look," he said. "Turn around."

The child twirled.

"You look like a little princess."

Rachel gave her daddy a big smile in appreciation.

"It's my party dress," she said.

He had feigned ignorance.

"Whose party is it?"

"It's my birthday, Daddy."

"It's not your birthday. That can't be right."

Rachel was highly indignant.

"It is. Tell him," she said. "Tell him, Mummy."

"He's teasing you, Rachel," Laura said. "Bad Daddy," Laura whispered into Alex's ear.

Laura, Alex and an excited Rachel had packed up and headed off. Kilkee was a popular coastal resort in West Clare, about an hour's drive from their home in Cratloe.

"Are we there yet?" Rachel demanded on the drive. She had started swimming lessons and was keen to get into the water. "Mummy, did you bring my swim suit?"

"Yes, sweetie."

"The pink one with the butterflies?"

"The very one," Laura said. Everything was pink in Rachel's wardrobe.

"Did you bring the bucket for the sand castles?" the child asked.

"That's packed too."

"And the other thing?"

Laura smiled. Rachel could never remember the name for a spade.

"The spade is packed, Rach."

Alex had smiled at this exchange. Rachel's excitement was infectious. He was looking forward to their family day out.

"Good Mummy!" he said. "Mind you, I prefer when mummy is bad," he added in a lower tone, one that only his wife could hear.

Laura had smiled back. She knew exactly what her husband meant. Momentarily, she relived their love making that very morning, before Rachel had finally woken up. Rachel had slept in and they took full advantage. She could still feel his arms around her. Laura looked at him tenderly. God, he was a handsome devil. Best of all, he was her handsome devil.

"We're here," Alex said as they drove into the seaside town.

Rachel had squealed with excitement. It was a bank holiday weekend and that, coupled with the fine weather, had drawn the crowds.

"The place is heaving," he remarked to Laura as he scanned the beach.

"There's a spot, over there, Alex. Look."

He led the way. They parked themselves on the sand and set themselves up for the day. Alex laid out the beach towels. Laura undressed Rachel. The child attempted to put on her swimsuit.

"Lift up this leg, sweetie," her mum advised. Rachel tripped in her eagerness. Alex laughed.

"Stop laughing, Daddy. It isn't funny," she snapped back, which made Alex want to laugh even more.

"I'm sorry, sweetheart. Let's go paddling."

"I'm not a baby. I can nearly swim by myself."

"Of course you're not. Mummy told me how good you are at your swimming lessons."

"I'm ready, Daddy."

"What about your arm bands, Rachel?" he said.

"I'm not wearing them."

He looked at her sceptically.

"I don't need them anymore, Daddy."

Recognising that it was a battle that he wasn't going to win, Alex took her hand and they ambled off towards the sea. Rachel ran in and out several times and hovered around the water's edge. Alex scooped her up in his arms and walked out into the sea. She clutched him tightly, arms wrapped around his neck. He held her afloat as she tried to swim. Eventually they made their way back to Laura.

"I'm thirsty, Mummy."

Laura sat up. She had been taking advantage of their absence to sunbathe. She wanted to get some sun on her stomach. She'd had a C section, and she was conscious of the scar, even though it had faded with time.

Laura searched for the juice.

"Flip it. I've left the drinks in the boot of the car," she said.

"I'll go and get them," he offered.

"No, you're grand. In this heat, everything will be lukewarm by now. I'll run up to the shop and get some stuff. I could do with stretching my legs."

She slipped on her shorts and top and got up to go.

"Where are you going, Mummy?" Rachel said.

"To get some drinks, Rach. You stay here with daddy. I'll be back soon, sweetie. Do you want a bottle of water, Al?"

"Water is good. Make sure it's cold."

Off Laura went.

Alex had been building sand castles with Rachel when neighbours of theirs wandered over to say hello. Alex got engaged in conversation. He took his eyes off the little girl. When he turned round, she had disappeared. One minute Rachel was building sandcastles and the next, she was gone. He remembered the sound of the waves gently lapping and crashing against the shore.

CHAPTER FOUR

"Have fun, darling," she said grinning. Felicia was in bed but Harvey was up, showered and dressed.

"You betcha." He sat on the bed for a moment. "I'm looking forward to this morning," he said. "To think, my father used to fish here with my grandfather."

"Did they come here often?"

He shrugged his shoulders.

"My grandfather was a regular visitor but how often dad went I don't know. Dad clammed up immediately when I asked. We were watching a fishing programme at the time and I think it slipped out unintentionally."

"Their relationship was a very unhappy one."

Harvey bared his teeth in a grimace.

"It was pitiful," he said. "For most of my father's life their relationship was non-existent. That was the only happy memory that dad shared."

She squeezed his hand and smiled sympathetically.

"I can't fathom what happened," he said. "As Jack gets older I think about it more often. If our relationship ended up like that, I don't know what I'd do."

"Oh Harvey, that would never happen. Jack idolises you."

"Not always."

"His hormones have kicked in. He's a teenager." She saw Harvey glance at his watch. "Off you go and enjoy yourself," she said. "This will be a day to remember."

Harvey placed a parting kiss on her lips. Shortly after 8.30 am, he knocked on his son's bedroom door. He had phoned Jack earlier to wake him.

"Good morning," he said. "All set?"

"Yeah," Jack replied unconvincingly.

Harvey popped his head around the door. Anna lay comatose on one of two single beds. Felicia would have trouble getting her down to breakfast. The eiderdown had been kicked off the bed. It was lying in a heap on the floor along with her clothes. She was a messy creature, the opposite of her mother.

"She snores," said Jack, who didn't like sharing a room with his sister.

"So does her mother."

Jack was sleepy eyed. It took him time to come round in the mornings. In the dining room, a waiter passed their table carrying two plates laden with sausages, eggs, bacon and black pudding.

"They look the business," Harvey said. "I think we should seriously consider the full Irish. What do you think? We have a long morning ahead of us."

Jack nodded, visibly more alert, at the mention of food. His father was right. The fry up did look good.

"Was everything all right, Mr Russell?" Jane asked when they finished breakfast. He had barely touched his food.

"It was excellent. But I think my eyes were bigger than my stomach."

Harvey thought he might be coming down with something. He felt a little off-colour. He pushed the thought aside. Today was a special day.

"Are you all set for the fishing?" she said.

"Indeed we are, and looking forward to it," he said cheerfully. "We're heading out now."

Harvey and Jack made their way to the walled garden at the rear of the castle, next to the tennis court, where John was waiting.

"You may not become experts in one day," the gillie said, "but you'll come away with a good insight into the basics. First, I'm going to show you how to set up your tackle correctly. Then we'll look at casting techniques and at which flies to use."

"When are we fishing?" Jack said, unimpressed.

"Not for a while yet, Jack. We have a lot of ground work to cover first."

Jack's face was transparent and disappointment was written all over it. The gillie took heed.

"We'll head down to the river after 11," he said. "You can put your new skills into practise then."

John was rewarded with a big smile. The morning flew by. Before they knew it, lunchtime had arrived.

"We'll take an early lunch and rendezvous back in reception at 1.30," John said. "We're back at Beat Two this afternoon. You can leave your rods over there against the wall."

Jack practically skipped into the bar, his excitement palpable. Harvey watched with pride. It had been a wonderful morning, one that Harvey would treasure. Four generations of the Russell family had now fished at Doonmara.

"Do you think we'll catch a salmon, Dad?"

"You never know," he said. Privately, he thought that it would take a miracle but Harvey didn't want to dampen his son's spirits.

Harvey would have liked to have sipped at a pint of Guinness but decided against it. He was suffering from a touch of indigestion and he opted for a bowl of soup.

Before long, Felicia and Anna arrived, and in contrasting styles. Felicia was clad in a crisp white linen shirt and loosely fitting indigo jeans. Anna was wearing impossibly tight, faded skinny jeans that had been laddered across the knee caps, paired with a sweatshirt that featured an assortment of fruit. *Good grief, she's wearing a bowl of fruit,* he thought. He was wise enough to say nothing. Anna could be touchy. He recalled Felicia's comment about teenagers and hormones.

"What are you having?" Anna said, eyeing up her brother's toasted sandwich.

"The house special," Jack replied.

"I'll have what's he's having," she told the waiter. Anna recognised him. He had brought up the luggage to the room.

"Righty oh, miss. And for you, ma'am?" Seán asked

"I'll have the seafood chowder, please," Felicia said.

Sean bowed his head by way of acknowledgement. He went to put in the order, thinking as he did that Mrs Russell didn't sound Portuguese. Neither did the children. She was most likely British.

"How did this morning go? Felicia asked. "What's the verdict?"

"I'm completely hooked. I'll be coming back."

"What about me?" Jack said.

"I wouldn't come back unless you were with me."

Jack looked pleased. Harvey thought of the fishing trips ahead with his son. Harvey's father and grandfather remained estranged for most of their lives. It would be different for Harvey and Jack. He caught Felicia's eye. She knew what he was thinking. She always knew.

"I couldn't wait to cast off," Jack said. "John said I've got the hang of it."

"You're a natural, Jack. You did exceptionally well," Harvey said.

Felicia noted the pride in her husband's voice.

"Who's John?" enquired Anna, thinking that she, for one, wouldn't be rushing back to Doonmara. She couldn't get Wi-Fi in her bedroom and there were few people her age staying. One thing was for certain: there were no good looking boys. Still, she had to admit, there was a kind of haunting, romantic atmosphere about the castle. Come to think of it, she might take a selfie with the castle in the background.

"The gillie," Harvey and Jack replied in unison, startling Anna.

"Were there any salmon caught this morning?" Felicia asked a moment later.

"No," Jack said. "They're waiting for me."

"As if," Anna said, barely suppressing a snigger. "You'll be waiting!"

"There weren't too many fishermen about this morning but there was a shortage of beats," Harvey said, taking charge of the conversation before any more insults were fired. Like all teenagers, Anna and Jack had their moments.

"Why was that?" Felicia said.

"A group of French men here on a stag booked up several beats for the morning. They turned up two hours late and very hung over, and stayed fishing for less than an hour. The fishermen who couldn't get out on the river were seriously annoyed."

Lunch over, the family got up to leave. Harvey and Jack reconvened with John in the entrance hall. Harvey introduced the gillie to his wife and daughter.

"It looks like the weather has settled a bit," Felicia said looking out the window. "It's windy but at least it's stopped raining. I think we should go for a walk. What do you think, Anna? Are you up for it?"

"Yeah, whatever, Mum."

"Try not to sound too enthusiastic, Anna," her father said.

"You're not going to spy on us, are you, Mum?" Jack asked. He glared at his sister. "She'll put me off."

"Get over yourself, Jack," Anna said.

"No, of course not, darling," his mum replied, smoothing things over. "We'll see you boys after the fishing. Try not to empty the river. I believe stocks are low."

"I don't think the salmon population is in any immediate danger," Harvey said and waved them off.

John grinned. The Russells seemed like a nice family. He had enjoyed the chat with the father and son that morning.

"It's on with it so, lads," he told them.

"Have you any tips?" Jack said.

"Keep your fly in the water," the gillie said.

Harvey laughed. It was one of those days when you felt happy to be alive. Life was good. The trio collected their fishing tackle, and soon afterwards Harvey and Jack were putting their newly learned casting techniques into practise.

Felicia and Anna set off, anoraks on and umbrellas at hand, in case the weather turned unexpectedly.

"Mum, why don't we take a sneaky peak at Dad and Jack."

"Tempting as that sounds, Anna, I do think we should leave your brother in peace. Jack would have a fit."

"He's way too self-conscious."

"No matter, darling. And it doesn't help that you continually wind him up."

"Mum, everything winds Jack up."

They were strolling along the back avenue. A small fleet of classic cars drove by heading towards the castle. Two classic MGs were among them. Both cars had the roof tops down. The drivers were male and in their mid to late-twenties. One of the drivers hooted a horn. Felicia and Anna waved.

"They must be the stag party your father was talking about." Felicia noted that one of the passengers was drinking from a hip flask.

"Doonmara would be perfect for a wedding."

"You could have your wedding here," Felicia said. She smiled fondly at her daughter.

"That would be so romantic, Mum." Anna conjured up an image of herself in a wedding dress. The dress was spectacular – ivory lace, and figure hugging. A long veil, strewn with diamante and pearls, trailed behind her. She gave a little sigh. "It would be amazing. It's like a fairy tale here. I can't believe that dad's grandfather used to come here.

"He did and many times."

"Tell me about him again. I've half-forgotten."

"Your great grandfather was the local doctor and he was often invited to Doonmara to fish. Back then, the hotel was a private residence."

"When was that?"

"That would have been in the 1920s," her mother said.

"The people who lived here must have been very rich to afford a place like this."

"They were 'seriously wealthy' as your father would say. Doonmara belonged to an Indian Maharaja."

"A Maharaja! That's cool."

"In fact, this avenue was covered by marble chips that were raked over every day."

"Wow." Felicia smiled, as Anna wasn't easily impressed. "What else do you know about the Maharaja?"

"He came every summer. He would buy several cars, including a limousine or two, on each trip. Apparently, he gave them away as gifts when he left for India in the autumn. It was a big deal because very few people owned a car. There was a great deal of poverty in Connemara in those days. People didn't have much."

"It sounds like it was a tough life."

"If you were poor, it was. People had to endure a great deal of hardship. The Maharaja gave your great grandfather a present of a car one year."

"No way, Mum! Really?"

"Really!"

"Did he get a limo?"

"That I don't know. You'll have to ask your dad. The Maharaja often gave the staff fabulous presents. He was very extravagant. I believe one of the gillies got a pair of ruby cufflinks once."

"That's mad. What would he want with ruby cufflinks? I bet he'd have preferred cash."

Felicia gave a broad grin. Anna always hit the nail on the head.

"What made the Maharaja choose Doonmara, Mum? It's a long way from India?"

"He heard about Doonmara through its famous fisheries. The Maharaja was passionate about salmon fishing. Anyway, he came to Connemara one summer and he rented Doonmara. He fell in love with the place, and he bought the castle soon afterwards. He had several palaces but, by all accounts, he was happiest here."

"What was he like, Mum? Did he have loads of wives?"

"No. He never married. There was no Maharani."

"Was he gay?"

"I don't believe so."

"He probably had lots of concubines. Maybe he brought some of his harem with him."

"I don't think he brought a harem to Connemara, Anna. I imagine that wouldn't have gone down well with the locals, and particularly the clergy." Felicia laughed at the thought of it.

"I bet he took opium," Anna said. "A lot of the Maharajas did in the old days."

"Good gracious, where do you get your information?"

"History," her daughter said which made her mother wonder what on earth was being discussed in Anna's history class. In Felicia's day, it was all dates and battles. "Actually Mum, opium use was an accepted cultural practise in India back then. It was legit. You wouldn't get banged up for smoking it. It was one of India's most valuable exports."

Anna looked pleased with herself. She couldn't resist showing off what she had learned on the Discovery channel.

"You're a fountain of knowledge, darling," her mother said. "Anyway, well as that may be, let me assure you that the Maharaja wasn't an opium addict, and he certainly hadn't a harem with him in Doonmara. Besides, the local clergy wouldn't have allowed that kind of carry on. In those days, the Catholic church had a tight grip on the people."

"Dad's family were Protestants though. Did that matter then?"

"Indeed it did. That was crime enough, as far as the local clergy was concerned. They were very different times, Anna. It was a lot more conservative back then."

"Did the locals get on with the Maharaja?"

"They got on surprisingly well."

"I can see why he was popular, if he was giving fancy cars and jewellery as gifts."

"He also provided jobs in the area. Doonmara, and the estate as it was then, generated lots of employment. As a matter of fact, he built all of the fishing piers and huts along the river. The Maharaja was the biggest employer for miles around, and he looked after his workers well."

"He must have seemed very exotic to the locals."

"I imagine so. That said, the Maharaja was fairly Anglicised. He was educated in England and spent a lot of time there. He brought a big entourage with him each year and that must have raised a few eyebrows. And two of his nieces, who were princesses, were educated in a nearby convent."

Anna considered what her mother had said.

"But they weren't Catholic," she pointed out.

Felicia smiled again. Anna didn't miss much.

"No. Hindu, I believe. However, the nuns accepted them as boarders."

"I bet the Maharaja gave the nuns a big donation," Anna said. "I couldn't go to school here,

Mum. Its miles away from civilisation! The princesses must have been desperately lonely. It's not as if they could have Skyped home, or used Facebook. They didn't even have mobile phones in those days."

"Apparently, they made lots of friends and were very happy."

"That's weird. Still, I guess they had each other. What was his name, Mum? Or did everyone call him the Maharaja?"

"His full title was His Highness, the Maharaja Gai Singh of Kheata, but he was better known as Gai Singh."

"It's amazing to think that someone like him lived here in the middle of nowhere."

"Isn't it," her mother said, in complete agreement. "There used to be some old photographs of the Maharaja hanging up in the hotel. We can have a look at them later. I'd imagine they're still here."

Mother and daughter reached the castles gates.

"What time is it, Mum?"

"Time for a cup of tea I think." Felicia glanced at her watch. It was almost 2:30. "Let's head back."

Anna turned round. She looked at the castle with fresh eyes. "It's a pity dad never met his grandfather," she said. 'If he had, they might have come fishing here."

"You're right, and on both counts. But as your dad told us, there was a terrible family fall out. Your

grandfather never spoke to his own father afterwards. He left Connemara and he never came back."

"Not even for his father's funeral?"

"Not even for that."

"That's pretty extreme," Anna said. Her eyebrows knitted in confusion. "He must have hated
his father."

"Sometimes, there's a thin line between love
and hate," her mother remarked.

"What was the argument over?"

"Your dad never knew. His father refused to
talk about it."

"If I were dad, I'd be pretty desperate to know."

"That's because you're a nosy parker," said
Felicia, and they both laughed. "Your grandfather
was very troubled over what happened so your dad
never pressed him."

"Do you think it was anything to do with granddad's mother?"

"I don't think so. She died in childbirth.
Apparently, your great-grandfather was heartbroken. He never married again. She was the love of
his life."

"Like you and dad?"

"Like me and your father." That was true. She
loved the bones of Harvey, always had and always
would.

"Granddad didn't have a great time growing
up, that's for sure."

"To be honest, Anna, I know very little about his childhood. Neither does your father. It does all sound grim. But your dad told me that when your grandfather was a child he fished here with his father."

"And now dad is fishing here with Jack. Dad must be chuffed. That's good karma, Mum."

On their return, Felicia and her daughter parked themselves in the two empty seats beside the fireplace in reception. Felicia ordered drinks. Before long, Seán arrived armed with a complimentary plate of chocolate chip cookies and their order.

"They're insane, Mum," said Anna, and scoffed another biscuit.

"Save one for Jack. You know what he's like."

"Jack is always starving. He must have worms. It wouldn't surprise me at all."

Despite herself, Felicia laughed.

"What will we do now?" Anna said. "I'm bored."

"We could take a quick spin into Clifden? Have a look around the shops."

Anna brightened up.

"What about dad and the boy wonder?"

"We'll take a sneaky peak on our way out. I want a photo as a souvenir. You can bring some cookies for Jack."

"That should butter him up. He won't freak out when he sees me."

"I need to grab my bag and car keys. Do you need anything from the room?

Anna shook her head. The bedroom was a trek from reception. She was staying put. Felicia made her way to the bedroom. On the way, she passed the pretty chambermaid who had cleaned her bedroom. Something about her looked different, and Felicia threw her a second look.

The girl's honeyed blond hair fell in wavy cascades around her face. Earlier, her hair had been tied back in a severe pony tail. The young woman looked Slavic. Telltale signs were the high cheek bones and a square jaw. Felicia marvelled at her cheekbones. You could hang a coat hanger on them.

Blusher highlighted her bone structure and she had applied a heavy coat of bright pink lip gloss to her lips. Those small changes dramatically changed the chambermaid's look from merely pretty to beautiful. Tall and slender to boot, she could easily have been a model.

The chambermaid acknowledged Mrs Russell.

"Good afternoon," she said politely before knocking on a bedroom door. She was carrying an armful of white towels.

"Hello," Felicia said in passing. She reached her own room a few doors down. As Felicia turned the key in the door, she heard laughter. Glancing down the corridor, she saw the housemaid disappear into the room. She could have sworn she saw an arm pull the girl in. "*What's going on there?*" she wondered.

Felicia located her handbag. She could do with a bit of lippy herself and rooted in the bag for her makeup. Job done, she then ran a brush through her hair.

She looked out the window, hoping to catch sight of Harvey and Jack. Although, they were fishing on the other side of the river, she could see her husband and son clearly. It was a happy scene: father and son bonding over the fishing.

Unwilling to tear herself away, Felicia stayed put for a few moments, and observed Jack cast off. He really had got the hang of it. They were having a lovely time, all four of them. Felicia felt blessed. She never had the chance to record that precious memory.

CHAPTER FIVE

"For God's sake, Caroline! Will you put down that bloody mobile?"

Reluctantly, Caroline Cleary put her phone on the table. It was Friday, and she had met Ciara for an early lunch. The two friends were sitting in a cafe, close to Caroline's office base in Dublin.

"I hate to see you like this," Ciara said. "He's not worth it."

"I'm fine," she lied.

The truth was that Caroline was in over her head. Alex Hamilton had got under her skin. She had fallen for him, and now there was a further complication.

"He's never going to leave his wife. Surely you know that?"

Caroline didn't answer so Ciara tried again.

"You do know that, Caroline, don't you?"

"Yeah." She had picked up a sachet of sugar from the saucer beneath her cup and was turning it over in her hands. She didn't sound convincing.

Caroline had texted Alex twice the evening before, asking him to call her. He hadn't responded. It was unlike her to pester him like this but she needed to speak to him urgently. She had been constantly checking her phone since she had arrived, hence Ciara's fury and impatience. Ciara looked at her sceptically.

"Jesus, Caroline, why him? Why would you want to draw his baggage on yourself? It's not as if you've ever been short of admirers. You could have anyone."

But she only wanted him, Caroline reasoned. She had ended up a walking cliché.

As Ciara awaited a response, she assessed Caroline. Her old school pal looked awful. There were dark rings under Caroline's eyes; eyes that were red rimmed from crying.

"I didn't intentionally plan on falling for him," Caroline said. "That was the last thing on my mind. But he's the full package, Ciara. He's gorgeous."

"Gorgeous? Listen to yourself. You sound like a teenager. He's married for Christ's sake. And he has been for donkey's years. Get a grip, Caroline."

The sun was streaming through the window. It was catching in the steam of her freshly brewed coffee. Caroline took a mouthful as she searched for the right words.

"I met him on the rebound," she said. "Tom dumped me and I was feeling shitty about that. Alex was an ego booster. I thought it would be a little fun. My 'get over it' fling. I told you he's a dead ringer for George Clooney. If you saw him in the flesh, you'd be there yourself. Believe me."

"I'd have gone nowhere near him, no matter who the hell he looked like," Ciara replied briskly. "Besides, the 'get over Tom' plan didn't really work, did it?"

She deserved that, Caroline thought.

"At least I can see I didn't care about Tom that much," she said. "My pride got dented. That's all. I wasn't expecting him to break off the relationship like that. But he did me a favour. We weren't that compatible. It wouldn't have worked out in the long run."

"That's convenient. And it will, with Mr Lookalike, will it?"

Caroline winced. Ciara was cross but she was right.

"I'm a fool," Caroline said.

"It's obvious you're miserable. Why don't you walk away and save yourself the grief? Why are you being so self-destructive? This is so not you."

Caroline averted her gaze. Ciara's penetrating stare was unsettling. But Caroline was not quick enough.

"What is it, Caroline? Is there something else? There is, isn't there?"

Unsure of what to say, Caroline remained silent. Placing both her elbows on the small table, Caroline put her hands through her hair, drawing it back as she did.

"What is it?" Ciara reiterated.

Caroline lifted her head. She pulled her hair into a twist at the nape of her neck. She was playing for time. Ciara was missing a vital piece of the jigsaw. Caroline was only getting her head around the news herself. She hadn't told anyone yet.

"Come on, out with it, Caroline. You can't shock me."

Ciara was wrong about that.

"Do you want the good news or the bad news?" she said.

After a slight hesitation, her friend said, "The bad."

Caroline considered her words before replying.

"I had a pain in my side three weeks ago. It got worse over a few days and I went to see my doctor. He sent me for an ultrasound. They thought it might be kidney stones."

"And, was it?"

"No. They did a second test and that proved inconclusive. So they sent me to a specialist. I had to have an MRI of my abdomen and pelvis this week. They found something." Here, her voice faltered.

"What did they find?" she asked though a part of Ciara didn't want to know, not if it meant that something was wrong with Caroline.

"A tumour."

"Jesus!"Ciara drew her hand up to her mouth.

"They said it's about the size of a grapefruit. I've always hated grapefruit."

Ciara smiled in spite of herself.

"He wants to remove it to avoid the risk of rupture. I'm scared it might be malignant – that I have cancer."

Ciara absorbed the news.

"Caroline, I'm so sorry." She had been tough on her friend and now she felt guilty.

"Save the sympathy. I haven't died yet."

Caroline's black humour was one of many things that Ciara liked about her friend. That coupled with an enormous heart topped Caroline's list of attributes.

Caroline was putting on a brave front. Ciara clutched on to the only positive thing that Caroline had said.

"What's the good news? You said there was good news."

"The doctor said the tumour is more than likely benign."

"Then that's what you need to hang on to. When is the surgery? Did they give you a date?"

"Next Thursday."

"That's good news too. It's best they do it immediately just in case..." She left the sentence unfinished.

"Just in case I have cancer," Caroline said.

Ciara nodded. There was a moment's silence.

"I feel alive when I'm with Alex," Caroline said. "I'm able to put this out of my head. In some stupid way, it has helped me to cope. I know that makes no sense."

"No, it does," Ciara said gently. "But don't go thinking the worst. Remember what the doctor said." She gripped Caroline's hand and squeezed it. "Have you told Alex?"

"Not yet. I don't know whether I will. There's not much point. We don't have a future together. He doesn't love me. He's fond of me but that's all there is to it."

He didn't love her. Caroline had admitted it out loud. It was ridiculous how much it hurt. Ciara didn't contradict her.

"Caroline, you need to focus your energy on getting well. Don't put your energy into something that's going nowhere. He has a wife. I'm sorry to be brutal about it. I've your best interests at heart."

Caroline's mobile bleeped. She picked it up.

Let's meet Tuesday at 6 for a drink," the message read. "*We can talk then. Will text you with venue.*

"Alex?"

Caroline nodded.

"His ears must have been ringing," Ciara quipped.

"He's suggesting we meet on Tuesday," Caroline said

Alex sounded a bit off but she didn't share that reflection with Ciara. Alex usually sent flirtatious texts.

"Meet him by all means. Tell him if you want, but finish it, Caroline. You need to focus on you now."

Caroline said nothing.

"Why didn't you tell me sooner?"

Caroline didn't answer.

"I'm your best friend," Ciara said. "You shouldn't have gone through this on your own."

Caroline gave her an apologetic smile.

"Do your mum and dad know? Does Paul know?"

Paul was Caroline's younger brother. Caroline's two older brothers had emigrated to Australia during the recession. Caroline shook her head.

"I can't believe you didn't tell any of us. You must have been so worried."

Caroline looked completely crushed. Ciara realised she wasn't getting the whole story.

"Is it worse than you're letting on?" she asked.

Caroline nodded. The situation was far more precarious. Caroline's future was very uncertain. Seconds passed and then she broke down completely. Caroline hadn't been entirely truthful about her visit to the doctor. Ciara automatically got up from her chair. She gave her friend a warm hug.

Shortly after 11.30 on Friday morning, Alex Hamilton set off for Connemara. Alex had been in his office since 8:00 am with key members of his team, finalising details for the presentation that morning.

"That went according to plan. It's in the bag," Alex said afterwards, relieved to have secured a major contract for the company. "Well done everyone."

He was the managing director of Premium Foods. The company catered to the food industry, supplying ambient food products to the trade, mainly to hotels and restaurants. Business had improved considerably. Company targets for the year had been met and surpassed. Premium Foods had survived the blip.

As he drove, Alex had plenty of time to think. Depending on the traffic in Galway, it was a two and a half to three hour drive to Doonmara. He sent a text to Caroline, organising to meet with her the following Tuesday, intending to break off their affair then.

Alex and Caroline had a weekly rendezvous. Caroline worked in Limerick each Tuesday, staying overnight at the hotel where they had first met. As far as Alex was concerned, it was an arrangement that appeared to suit them both.

His message had been curt. That had been intentional on his part. He didn't want to be misleading, not when he intended on dumping Caroline at their next tryst. Unaware of the depth of her feelings, Alex didn't think Caroline would take the news too badly. He never made any false promises. He never gave Caroline cause to think that they might have a future. Right from the start, she knew that he was married.

He had kept things light. But as the months had gone by, he had grown fond of her. Caroline was a good-looking woman, very sexy, and with a terrific figure. She had other attractive qualities, which at first glance, were not as obvious. The latter became more apparent as the affair continued. Kind and good natured, she was a lovely person to be around.

Businesswise, Alex had been under a great deal of stress over the past few years. The recession had affected his line of work. The hotel and restaurant sector had been hit badly by the downturn. For a while, he thought the business might go under and his health suffered. He had been a very heavy smoker in his youth. With Laura's encouragement, he had managed to give them up for several years, only to resume smoking after Rachel died. Since then, he had been smoking too much, drinking too much, and working too hard.

"Your blood pressure is high and so is your cholesterol," his doctor had said. "You need to change your lifestyle or there will be repercussions, Alex. Serious repercussions," he had warned.

Alex had joined the gym, and had cut down on his drinking, and on his smoking. He had managed to get down to eight cigarettes a day. He had refused to take the statins prescribed to lower his cholesterol. He was dubious about the medication.

"You have heard lots of bad things about cigarettes too," the doctor chastised. "That doesn't seem to have had any effect on you, has it now? You defy all logic, Alex."

The post-coital cigarette with Caroline was the one that he enjoyed most. After a delicious bout of lovemaking, the two of them would lie on the bed and share a cigarette. Come to think of it, Caroline hadn't smoked the last few times they had met.

"Why not?" he'd asked the first time she had declined a puff from his cigarette.

"I'm trying to cut down. Alex. They're probably killing me."

"You don't know what you're missing," he teased, blowing a perfect circle in the air, and thinking that she would succumb to temptation.

He had to admit, he would miss Caroline. None of the affairs that he had over the years had mattered. Caroline had been the exception. Having made the decision to end the relationship, his load already felt lighter. However, breaking off his relationship with his mistress was the easy bit; ending his marriage was an altogether different story.

He would hold off until the weekend was over. This weekend was about Laura. She loved Doonmara. It would be cruel to orchestrate the breakup at the castle on her birthday weekend. Doonmara was a place where they had both found solace. He wanted their time there to remain untarnished.

Besides, he wanted to have finished his relationship with his mistress before he spoke to

Laura. Mistress! The word sounded archaic. He never thought he'd end up the type of man who kept mistresses. He had been in love with his wife. Once, she was everything to him. That was then. This was now. He loved Laura but he was no longer in love with her.

His wife would surely ask whether there was someone else. Alex wanted to say no. That was important to him because he wasn't leaving Laura for another woman. He was leaving in order to move on with his life. He was leaving because he was sick to death of living a double life. And Caroline was part of that double life. Yes, the decks would have to be cleared. Of course, he hoped that by doing so, that Laura would also move on, and start living again.

For much of the drive, his mind had been preoccupied but the beauty of the landscape had not gone unnoticed. Along the way, he had stopped at a garage and picked up lunch which, today, was a chicken sandwich and a bottle of water. Midway on his journey, when he had come to a particularly scenic spot, he pulled in off the road to eat his sandwich. It tasted like plastic. He wasn't fussed because he was dining well that evening. The food at Doonmara was always good. He took a swig of water to wash it down, before lighting a cigarette. He inhaled deeply.

A sheep wandered into the road. The car window was down and he could hear, amid the birdsong and the bleating of sheep, a small mechanical sound. Before long, on the opposite side of the road, a tractor same into view, moving slowly in his direction. Conveniently ducking into a nearby ditch, the sheep was well out of harm's way.

A lake that looked like glass stretched before him. The mountains hovered in the background, governing the landscape. Clouds were floating across the mountains and he watched their progress.

The landscape never failed to move him. He loved Connemara and he loved Doonmara. It would not be the place where everything fell apart for himself and Laura.

His thoughts drifted to the past. Remembering his initial encounter with Laura, he smiled. It had been on a plane, the summer he had finished his third year in college.

"I think you're sitting in my seat," he informed the young woman.

Lost in thought, she appeared not to have heard him. She continued to look straight ahead and ignored him entirely. Hair that was lank trailed down a face obscured from view.

"Excuse me," he said and this time, a little more loudly, attracting her attention. "You're sitting in my seat."

He flashed his boarding pass in her direction. She barely glanced at him.

"Sorry," she mumbled.

She got up to let him in, clearly annoyed at the bother. He had a better look at her then. She was a year or two younger than him and looked the worse for wear. Laura plonked herself down beside him, none too happy at having found herself in the middle seat. She didn't invite any conversation and he took heed. Any attempt of conversation was out of the question anyway, as she promptly fell asleep when the plane took off.

His fellow passenger awoke when the beverage and food trolley came round.

"Would you like anything?" the air hostess asked Alex.

"I'll have a coffee, please," he said.

"A coke, please," Laura said when it was her turn to be served.

As he lifted his coffee to take a sip, Laura stretched out her arm. She was searching for money in her bag to pay the air hostess. She hit his elbow and his coffee spilt. Some of the hot coffee splashed over the jumper she was wearing.

"For God's sake, would you be careful! You almost burned me," Laura said.

She glared at him, oblivious that it was her fault. She was too hung over to notice. Then that veil of hair descended. She was an annoying creature but she had beautiful green eyes. He'd give her that.

Although tempted, he didn't retaliate. A drop or two of the coffee had landed on her hand, and he was more concerned that he might have burnt her. She really was an awful cow. You'd swear he had spilt the coffee on purpose. It was her bloody fault anyway.

The air hostess gave them some paper towels to mop up the spill. She had overheard Laura's outburst. The young woman was a right little madam. The hostess was tempted to say something but held her tongue. She smiled sympathetically at Alex, infuriating Laura further.

Laura downed her coke quickly, appreciating the immediate sugar and caffeine hit. There was an ugly brown stain down the front of her cream jumper. It was too much of an effort to go to the toilet and splash some cold water on it. She had been partying at a club the night before, and she was dying from a hangover. She couldn't wait to get home, to crawl into bed, and sleep it off.

The two had gone their separate ways as soon as they had landed.

"Dad, hello," Alex had greeted his father at arrivals.

His dad gave him a hug. There was a man standing beside his father who looked vaguely familiar.

"Alex, do you remember Jim? Jim Cronin from next door?"

Alex greeted him. The Cronins had been their next-door neighbours until the family had moved when Alex was six or seven.

Alex, I hardly recognise you. I hear you were on the Heathrow flight. So was my daughter. She should be out in a minute."

And lo and behold the daughter arrived.

"There she is. Laura! Over here."

Jim Cronin waved to attract Laura's attention. Alex caught sight of her. It was the girl who had been sitting beside him on the plane. There must have been two hundred people on the plane and it had to be her. It had to be that moody cow.

"Hi Dad," Laura said, and wrapped her arms around her father. Then, she stood back. She looked confused at Alex's presence, until her father explained the connection.

"Laura, do you remember the Hamiltons. Our old neighbours?" Before she had the chance to reply he said, "Well, this is them. This is Frank Hamilton and his son. You and Alex were on the same flight."

Her father was delighted at the chance encounter. She thought he was going to keel over with excitement.

"You used to play together when you were little," he said. "Right old scallywags, the pair of you were."

"No we didn't," Alex countered. "We used to fight like cats and dogs."

Laura scowled.

Mr Hamilton chuckled and said, "Alex is right as far as I can recall."

Alex had been more interested in playing with her older brother, Peter. Laura constantly butted in. He remembered that she used to have pigtails. He used to pull those pigtails.

Even when she was little, she was annoying, he remembered. Annoying then, and bloody annoying now.

After some polite chit chat, they had left the airport and gone their separate ways. He didn't lay eyes on Laura again until two years later.

His thoughts shifted back to the present. The weather had eased up a little but the conditions looked promising for the fishing. He arrived a little earlier than expected. He drove over the cattle grids at the entrance before making his way up the drive.

He caught sight of Doonmara and, for the moment, his troubles left him completely. Any tiredness he might have felt from the drive lifted. He felt reinvigorated. It was the Doonmara magic. The castle and its beautiful surroundings always cast a spell over him.

Catching sight of Conor standing at the bridge, Alex slowed down. He stopped for a moment, to have a word.

"Any fish in there, Conor?"

"You'd better get a move on and check it out for yourself. The day's nearly gone."

Alex smiled. He enjoyed the repartee with Conor.

"There was a salmon caught this very hour," the gillie said.

"Where?"

"Up near the high bridge."

"Hopefully, there's one in there with my name on it. I'll go and get changed, and grab a quick cup of coffee. Let's say I meet you outside reception in fifteen minutes?"

"Righty oh then."

"What beat are we on?"

"Beat Two. If there's nothing stirring, we can try our luck up at the high bridge."

Alex drove off and found a parking space. Glancing through to the bar on his way to reception, he observed how packed it was.

As soon as she laid eyes on him, Maura perked up.

"Good afternoon, Mr Hamilton," she volunteered.

"Hello, Maura. How's everyone?

"We're all well, Mr Hamilton."

"Glad to hear it. The hotel is busy," he remarked.

"It was raining all morning so the bar is full of day trippers. People have been arriving for lunch non-stop. They'll all be gone within the hour, now that the weather has picked up."

"Looks like they're still coming," he noted, as a group walked past. "Maura, I can't seem to get hold of my wife and her car isn't here. Can someone let me into the room?"

"Certainly, Mr Hamilton. If you can bear with me and I'll organise that."

She disappeared. He looked around. A teenage girl stared at him strangely. He smiled back and her jaw dropped. Alex didn't burst her bubble.

Jane appeared in reception with Maura a few moments later. He greeted her affectionately.

"You're looking particularly well," he said.

"Thank you, Mr Hamilton," she replied, delighted with the flattery. She could feel the heat rise in her cheeks flushing them beet red.

Not half as well as you, she thought. Alex Hamilton looked fantastic. He'd obviously been working out. In Jane's estimation, a view held by all of the female staff, Alex grew more attractive as he got older.

The Russell girl looked star struck and Jane could imagine why. She thought George Clooney had arrived. The teenager had been attempting to put on a blue nylon jacket over a grey sweatshirt emblazoned with a tropical print. The appearance of a Hollywood movie star had stopped her in her tracks. Her arms remained caught half-way up both jacket sleeves.

Jane focused her attention back on her favourite guest and said "I'll let you into your room, Mr Hamilton."

"Thank you, Jane."

Key in hand, Jane escorted Alex to his suite. They had a nice chat as they navigated their way down the endless corridors and stair wells. Jane relished that brief interlude.

Fifteen minutes later, Alex Hamilton was standing outside the main entrance, enjoying a cigarette after an espresso. He leaned back and drew smoke down into his lungs. He had reached his cigarette quota for the day. Or was he over it? He'd have to start watching the fags again. He'd been slipping back into bad habits for the past few weeks.

Deep in conversation with his gillie, deliberating over which flies he might try out, it was the first time in months that Alex could say he was truly content. He was looking forward to a quiet afternoon fishing on the river. It was not to be.

CHAPTER SIX

Laura had been one of the last stragglers down to breakfast. It was ten o'clock, and Laura was dying for a coffee. She had slept restlessly. The window had rattled through the night, awakening her from time to time. When morning came, she pulled back the curtains, noticing as she did that the window was slightly ajar.

"You're in luck," Jane said, greeting her. "There's a table free by the window. Thank you for the books, Mrs Hamilton. The timing was perfect. I hadn't anything to read. I've been meaning to get into Galway but we've been very busy." Jane escorted Laura to her seat. "I'll bring you an Americano." Jane knew Laura's routine by now.

"Thanks Jane. I'm gasping for one."

Jane was back in a flash armed with Laura's coffee. Laura always had a coffee from the espresso machine. It just tasted better. She took a welcoming sip and immediately brightened up.

Pen in hand, Jane took Mrs Hamilton's breakfast order.

While she waited for poached eggs and bacon, Laura helped herself from the breakfast buffet. Fresh orange juice was followed by fruit salad and a slice of the delicious walnut brown bread. Laura went back for a second slice.

She scanned the newspaper she had picked up from reception on her way into breakfast. Bad news dominated the headlines day in day out, and today was no different.

Turning her attention to the river view, Laura put the paper aside. It was nearing eleven and she had finished her second coffee of the day. She was tempted to order a third.

"Can I get you anything else, Mrs Hamilton?" said Jane, who had reappeared as if from nowhere. "We're closing the breakfast buffet shortly."

"No thank you, Jane. That bread is dangerous."

Jane gave her a little smile.

"Any plans for this morning, Mrs Hamilton?"

"I think I'll mosey round Clifden."

Seeing Laura's empty cup, Jane said, "Can I get you another Americano?"

"No, I'm good," Laura said with restraint. She would hold off until later.

"Are you joining us for dinner this evening?" Jane asked.

"I certainly am. And my husband is too. He's arriving this afternoon."

Without realising it, she had made Jane's day. Mr Hamilton was a favourite with Jane, as he was with all of the female staff, without exception. Jane had fantasised about Alex, for he was always Alex in Jane's imagination, and never Mr Hamilton. Jane would have overstepped the mark with Alex Hamilton anytime. It was terribly sad what had happened to Laura Hamilton, but Jane thought that Laura was blessed to have a husband like him.

Laura returned to her bedroom to get her bag and coat. There was a handy side exit close to her room, which she took. She drove out the back entrance of the hotel and onto the Clifden road.

Half-an-hour later, she was strolling around the town, visiting a few art galleries. She lingered at one, a tiny gallery on the corner of the main street, where over the years she had bought a number of paintings.

Ursula, the gallery owner, greeted her warmly.

"Laura, it's nice to see you back in this part of the world again."

"I find it hard to stay away for long."

Ursula unpacked a picture. Every square inch of wall and floor space was awash with colour, mainly landscapes of Connemara. The region was renowned for its beauty, and popular with artists who tried to capture some of the magic on canvas. Two of the paintings that Laura had bought were of Connemara landscapes.

"What do you think?" Ursula asked." It's a new artist I'm showing. She's known for her beach scenes with children. She has a terrific brush stroke."

Laura studied the picture. Two small children, a girl and a boy, were running amuck on a beach. It threw her completely, even after all those years. Waves of panic began to engulf Laura.

"It's lovely, Ursula" she managed, before glancing at her watch and mumbling "Oh Lord, is that the time. I must be off."

Much to Ursula's astonishment, Laura dashed out of the gallery. It was a quarter to two. In an effort to gather herself together, Laura decided to have that cup of coffee now. Afterwards, she felt more composed.

She reprimanded herself. What a fool she was, so busy looking over her shoulder that she kept stumbling into the present. She wondered whether Alex was on schedule. He hadn't texted her or called all morning. That was odd. She opened her bag to search for her phone but it wasn't there.

"Damn," she said out loud. She must have left it behind in the bedroom. It was time to head back. Alex was due to arrive soon and it wouldn't do if she weren't there to greet him in person. Their relationship was strained enough as it was. She had to make an effort.

Registering on her arrival an ambulance parked outside the hotel entrance, Laura didn't give its presence much thought.

She took the short cut to her suite and found her mobile phone lying next to the bathroom sink. Laura checked her message minder. There were two texts, both from Alex, as well as a missed call. She went through to the lounge. It was only then she saw the note on the table.

It read:

2.30pm

Laura

Gone fishing. Arrived early but couldn't get hold of you on the mobile. I'm at Beat Two, directly across the river!

Al x

She looked out the window. It took her a few moments to comprehend the scene in front of her. A dead body, covered by a sheet, lay on the jetty. Two men stood guarding the body. One had his back to her, but she recognised the other. It was Conor. Two paramedics were walking down the path carrying a stretcher.

Laura screamed, just like she did when she saw Rachel lying dead that fateful afternoon at the seaside. It was a piercing screech. In that moment, she realised that she still loved her husband, despite everything. Only now, it was too late.

She had lost him. Regret flooded through her.

CHAPTER SEVEN

"A man has had a heart attack!" Seán said, panting. "Maura, call an ambulance."

Straightaway, Maura phoned the emergency services.

"An ambulance will be here in fifteen minutes," she told him.

The foyer was busy. She spoke in hushed tones so as not to cause alarm.

"I think he may be dead," Seán said.

"Who is it, Seán? Do you know?"

"It happened at Beat Two so it could be Mr Hamilton. Conor told me earlier that he and Mr Hamilton would be fishing there this afternoon."

"Mr Hamilton! No! I was only talking to him a while ago. I can't believe it."

"I'm not a hundred per cent sure, Maura."

"Do you know what happened?"

"I was in the restaurant when I noticed a bit of a commotion down at Beat Two. I opened the French windows and stepped out to see what was going on. Pawel must have spotted me, because the next thing, he came flying along the foot path, shouting my name.

"He yelled to me to call an ambulance. A man had fallen into the river after a massive heart attack. That's the gist of what he said. I came straight to reception."

"You never know the time, nor the place, Seán."

"You don't, do you."

"I hope it's not Mr Hamilton. Dear God, not Mr Hamilton. Mrs Hamilton has had enough tragedy in her life."

The phone rang. Maura answered it. "Doonmara Castle, one moment please," she said, her professionalism automatically coming into play "I'll take this call," she told Seán, "and then I'll alert Jane."

That was the protocol. James, the manager, had been out sick for the past few days and Jane was filling in for him.

Maura took the reservation but her mind drifted. She was thinking about Alex Hamilton. What a fine figure of a man he was. Surely it wasn't him. He looked healthy enough. He had looked particularly well today. Mind you, he was a smoker. Maura often saw Alex Hamilton sneak out the front door for a cigarette.

She was so preoccupied that she had to ask the caller to repeat their reservation dates. Meanwhile, Seán had taken off in the direction of Beat Two to see if he could be of any assistance. He was fond of Mr Hamilton. It would be a terrible shame if it were him.

Less than a half an hour before the tragedy had unfolded, Felicia Russell had signed for drinks on the docket Seán had presented.

Handbag and jacket in hand, she had returned from her bedroom, only to find Anna tremendously excited.

"You'll never guess what, Mum," Anna had said.

"What?" asked Felicia, playing along.

"You're not going to believe this, but George Clooney checked in. Can you believe it? George Clooney is staying here! Mum, he smiled at me! Wait until I tell my friends."

"George Clooney? No way! Are you sure, Anna? It seems unlikely."

Felicia was excited at the news herself. She had a bit of a thing for George, the old fox. He hadn't gone all Hollywood with plastic surgery and dyed hair. She liked his greying hair. It made him look distinguished.

"It was him! He looks a lot better in real life and way younger. I have to say, for an old guy, he really is good looking."

Felicia grinned. In Anna's eyes, Felicia and Harvey were prehistoric. In fact, anyone over thirty was ancient.

"My word," Felicia said. "George Clooney is staying in the same hotel. That's something. My own friends will be pretty impressed."

"I was surprised that he didn't have an entourage," Anna said, prattling on. "And he had no bodyguards."

"I suppose Connemara isn't really the sort of place where you'd bring bodyguards."

"Maybe he's travelling incognito."

"That could well be. Did he have a travelling companion?"

"I didn't see anyone with him. But he got the VIP treatment when he arrived. He didn't have to sign in like us ordinary mortals and the lady from the restaurant brought him to his room."

"Which lady is that?"

"She's rake thin with silver blond hair. She went bright red when he spoke to her."

"Oh, I know who you mean. I would have been lost for words if he had spoken to me," Felicia said.

"We can quiz her at dinner. I imagine he's staying in one of the river suites. They're near our rooms."

"I hope she gives us the low down. We might bump into him on the corridor."

"We might. Now, how about we set off for Clifden? Or, are you too star struck to go shopping?" she said.

"I'm good."

"And Anna, on second thoughts, I don't think we should disturb your father and Jack. I saw them fishing from the bedroom window and they seemed engrossed."

"Whatever."

Anna was too fixated on George Clooney to bother about Jack anymore. Besides, she had eaten Jack's cookies. Unable to resist the temptation, she had demolished the lot.

"We'll catch up with the boys later. I'll take a photograph then."

Felicia and Anna made their way to the car. Before she switched on the ignition, Felicia sent a text to Harvey, outlining her plans.

Maura was phoning for an ambulance as Felicia and Anna arrived in Clifden. They bumped into Laura Hamilton on the main street.

"Hello," Laura said. "How are the fishermen getting on?"

"Engrossed! Whether they will catch anything is another matter."

Laura laughed.

"My husband will be joining them on the river this afternoon," she said, "I'm heading back to the hotel to meet him. I'm running late so I had better go. Enjoy the shops. There are one or two nice art galleries here, too.

Anna crinkled up her face in disgust. There was no way that she was traipsing around art galleries.

Harvey Russell looked around, taking in his surroundings. It was a rare, blissful day, and one in which the castle gloried under clear skies. He fixed his eyes on the tree trunks across the river as they reached their branches up towards the sky. At that moment in time, the world did look exceeding lovely.

It was wonderful to be here, the four of them together. Jack had been sent to boarding school in Dublin like Anna. His son had completed his first year as a boarder. Harvey missed having Jack around. The house was quiet without the pair of them. In truth, it felt like the breakup of family life.

Unlike his sister, Jack had been homesick from day one. That had tugged at Harvey's heart strings. He didn't see enough of his children. Still, his embassy posting in Lisbon would come to an end in two years, and he had been promised a position in Dublin afterwards. It was time to come home. He had been working overseas for nearly half his life.

They would be reunited as a family then. Harvey would have more time to spend with his children. There would be plenty of time to be together. Time stretched before him.

The air was good in Connemara. He attempted to fill his lungs with air but it was hard to catch his breath. At that moment, Felicia sent a text but Harvey didn't hear his phone ping. It was switched to silent.

Jack cast off while his father watched.

"You really seem to be getting the hang of it," Harvey said. "You must take after your great grandfather. He was a great fisherman."

"What was the biggest salmon he caught?"

"I'm at a loss there."

John overheard the exchange and cut in. Earlier, Harvey had told the gillie that his grandfather had fished on the estate when Doonmara was the home of the Maharaja.

"Mr Russell, there's an old log book in the living room that might be of interest to you," he interjected. "Every salmon that was caught from the 1920s right up until 1940 is logged. The weight, and the date, and who caught what, are all recorded."

"That's very interesting, John. My grandfather will definitely be mentioned. He fished here frequently. Is that the room where they serve coffee after dinner?"

"That's it, first on your right as you exit the dining room. The log book is on the top shelf of the cabinet. It's a heavy leather-bound brown manual. You can't miss it."

"I'll check it out after dinner. Jack and I will be interested to take a look at it. Won't we, Jack?"

"I bet I'll find his name," his son said.

"I'm counting on it, Jack."

"As a matter of fact," John said, "Conor's grandfather used to work for the Maharaja. The old man is still alive."

"Conor?" quizzed Harvey.

"My counterpart. You met him earlier in the bar. His grandfather was a gillie here back in the 1920s."

"He must be very old now," said Jack.

"He's well into his nineties. But his mind is as clear as a bell. He has lots of stories about the old days."

"He might have met my great grandfather."

"It's well he might," the gillie said.

Harvey considered what Jack said. It was probably true. If that were the case, he would love to meet the old man. His own father was dead. Any opportunity of learning more about the family fall-out, and his past, was well and truly gone. What the hell had they fallen out over anyway? That question had plagued Harvey for years.

"At that age, I suppose he's hardly up to receiving visitors," he said.

"He's a bit poorly all right. He's in a nursing home and confined to a wheelchair these days."

John looked at his watch. It was ten past three. Conor would be on his way down shortly with Mr Hamilton.

"We're going to move across the river to Beat Five. We'll try our luck there," he said. Harvey nodded and began to reel his rod in. Jack followed suit.

"Would you like to go out fishing again tomorrow?" he said to Jack.

"Can we Dad?"

"We'll sneak in a few hours," Harvey promised.

"The room service in Doonmara is second to none," the occupant of Room 27 told his guest. He placed a lingering kiss on her left shoulder.

Lucy laughed. The beautiful Slovakian chambermaid stretched one leg out on the bed.

"What would your fiancée think about this, Jean-Pierre?" she said brazenly.

"What would yours?" he asked back.

She hit him playfully with a pillow. Jean-Pierre and Lucy had a bit of a history. This was not their first sexual encounter.

He had first met Lucy three years previously. He was twenty-four and single. Lucy was twenty, with a boyfriend back home. She had arrived to work in Doonmara at the start of the season.

Jean-Pierre had been coming to Doonmara since he was a young boy. His family had holidayed in Connemara most summers. At seventeen, he had spread his wings, and family holidays had taken a back seat. Alone with his parents in a remote part of Ireland was not his idea of a dream holiday.

But that year, it had been his mother's 50th birthday and she had wanted to celebrate the occasion with Jean-Pierre and his father in Connemara. Jean-Pierre had gone along with her wishes. This time he was old enough to appreciate the beauty of the place, something that escaped him in his teenage years. He had a high-pressure job in Paris, and the tranquillity and natural beauty of Connemara appealed to him.

He had spotted Lucy the day he arrived. She was another natural beauty. He'd chatted to Lucy whenever he bumped into her. He didn't speak Slovakian and she didn't speak French, but they both spoke English.

"Have you been working here for long?" he'd asked. He wondered whether she was single.

"I came to Ireland in April," she had replied.

"Do you have a boyfriend?"

"Yes. I have a boyfriend back home in Slovakia."

Boyfriend or not, there was no denying that there was an underlying chemistry between Lucy and himself.

Jean-Pierre had come back the following year. He was pleased to see that Lucy was still working at the hotel. Determined to get her into bed, he pursued her relentlessly. Eventually, she succumbed and they had a brief dalliance. It appeared that she had long forgotten the Slovakian boyfriend.

"Your English has improved," he'd commented.

"I took classes during the winter," she had replied. "And I've had lots of practise."

Her mobile bleeped and she ignored it. Lucy was always getting texts, usually from one admirer or another. How many men had she had been practising her English with?

Lucy didn't want the hotel management finding out about their romance.

"If they knew that I was sleeping with one of the guests, I might get into trouble."

"Its will be our secret," he told her, at the same time wondering why she had said that? Had she slept with one of the guests in the past?

"If they find out, they might charge you extra for the room," she'd said, and giggled.

"I'd pay," he had said, attempting to be gallant. "You'd be worth every cent."

He had to admit that the clandestine nature of their liaison added a little frisson to the summer romance, especially as they hadn't confined their romps to the bedroom. There had been an unforgettable encounter in a box room used to store guest room supplies for housekeeping.

Although he had a girlfriend in France at the time, it was not a serious relationship. Over the following months, that changed. His girlfriend, Marie, came from a top-drawer Parisian family and she was perfect wife material. In due course, he had proposed and Marie had accepted. Marie was right for all the wrong reasons.

His parents had invited them both to Connemara the following summer. Marie had been enchanted with the castle and the setting, so much so that they had decided to have the wedding in Doonmara. Or rather Marie had decided. Oblivious to their son's dalliance with the pretty chambermaid, his parents were delighted at his choice of bride and at her choice of venue. Jean-Pierre hadn't said a word about Lucy, and he never intended to. Why would he? Lucy was beautiful enough to make any woman feel insecure, he reasoned. Besides, he had slept with Lucy while he was in a relationship with Marie. He couldn't risk Marie finding out about that. That might scupper everything.

He had arrived to Doonmara with Marie in tow, only to find that Lucy had acquired a fiancée of her own.

"Congratulations," he'd said, relieved.

He had been afraid of any awkwardness between them with Marie present. But an entente cordiale had prevailed throughout his stay.

"Congratulations to you, too" Lucy had said.

"Who is the lucky man?"

"His name is Pawel. He started working in the hotel last summer. He's a waiter in the dining room."

"That was fast." He thought Lucy could have done a lot better for herself.

"It appears you didn't waste too much time yourself," she had replied briskly. "Did you tell your fiancée about me?"

"How could I tell her? You're far too pretty," he had said, appealing to her vanity. "You'd make any woman jealous."

He was a possessive man. Even though he was engaged, he didn't like to think of Lucy with another man, not when she was here in front of him, and looking so beautiful.

"Where is he from, this fiancé of yours?" he'd asked.

"He's Polish."

Time passed and Jean-Pierre had now come back to Doonmara for his stag weekend. Somewhere in the past twenty-four hours, he had had convinced himself that it was all right to indulge in a final fling in his few remaining weeks as a single man. Marie, his fiancée, would not have seen it this way.

He made a play for Lucy. Unhappy in her relationship, Lucy had responded to his advances. They had both thrown caution to the wind, winding up in bed that afternoon.

Jean-Pierre had retreated to the bathroom. He came out with a towel casually draped around his middle. He drew the curtains and light flooded the room. Lucy, confident of the way she looked, walked over to him, naked and unselfconscious. The windows ran the full length of the room. Anyone could see her from the grounds. She didn't care. After all, who would be looking in? The suites were to the back of the hotel.

Standing side by side, they studied the river scene outside.

"Beautiful," he remarked.

"You don't really see that, when you're cleaning up after others people's mess," she said.

"I was talking about you, chérie."

She laughed.

"They look like beginners," he said, pointing at the father and son fishing in the distance.

"They're no worse than you and your friends were this morning."

The fishing earlier that morning had been an unmitigated disaster. Jean-Pierre had been very hung over. The stag party had polished off three bottles off whiskey in the bar after dinner. They had stayed up drinking until the early hours.

Up until his stag weekend Jean-Pierre had never gone fishing in his life. He thought it might be a bit of fun for everybody, so it had been included in the stag itinerary.

"They're out with a gillie," Lucy said, catching sight of John, the third figure on the riverbank.

And that's when it happened. The father stumbled, before falling headfirst into the river. Lucy and her lover were both witnesses as the tragedy unfolded.

"I think the father is having a heart attack," Lucy said, startled.

They continued to watch as the gillie waded into the river. He tried to haul the father onto the riverbank. The young boy stood frozen to the spot. The gillie shouted to the boy, but he remained standing where he was.

The river was high and the water was fast flowing. For a moment, it looked as if the gillie would not be able to hold on to the boy's father. Again, the gillie shouted for help. This time the boy responded. However, the pair appeared to have great difficulty in lifting the man out of the river.

Suddenly, another man, dressed in a hotel uniform, appeared. He came running across the lawn and yelled across the river but Lucy didn't have time to register who he was. The man turned around unexpectedly, happening to look up as he did, at the window directly above him. It was Pawel, her fiancé.

Too late, Lucy ran for cover. Pawel had seen her in all her glory. It was not her finest moment.

CHAPTER EIGHT

Pawel had witnessed two unpleasant scenes and, to be honest, he didn't know which was worse. He had seen a fisherman fall into the river. This was followed moments later by the unwelcome apparition of his fiancée naked and wrapped around a semi-naked man, in one of the river suites. Despite his distress, Pawel had the presence of mind to go to the rescue of the fisherman. Clearly, John needed his help.

He ran as if his very life depended on it. As he ran, he attempted to obliterate the image of his fiancée with someone in an upstairs bedroom. It was a surreal picture. Why at that moment had he chosen to look up?

Pawel had been having a short cigarette break when he caught sight of the fisherman in difficulty across the river. The odd time, on his day off, he liked to fish. When he was a young boy, he had occasionally gone fishing with his dad.

Today, a father and son were fishing with John. He had been observing the trio. One minute the father was fishing, and the next he staggered, before falling into the river. The man fell with the full weight of his body. He made a big splash. It all happened fast.

It took the waiter several minutes to get to Beat Two. He ran down the side of the castle, up the avenue and over the bridge. He unlocked the gate, darted down the steps, and continued running along the river walk.

At the scene, the gillie and a young boy were struggling to retrieve the man from the river. The young boy was no more than twelve or thirteen so a third pair of hands made all the difference. Between them, they managed to hoist the body onto the jetty.

Pawel recognised the father and son. The family had dined in the restaurant the previous night. The gillie attempted to resuscitate the man but to no avail. After a while, he stopped. John shook his head at Pawel by way of telling him that the boy's father wasn't going to make it.

"Is he dead?" the young boy asked, in a sudden panic. "Please, don't let him die."

John remained silent.

"Dad, don't die," he begged, visibly distressed. Dripping wet, he knelt beside the outstretched figure. "Come back, Dad. You can't leave us." He tried again. "Please, Dad!"

When there was no response, he looked at John for direction. Tears streamed down the child's face.

"We'll get help here as fast as we can," John said.

Jack continued to plead with his dad. It was heart-breaking to watch. John was afraid the lad might become hysterical.

The gillie exchanged glances with the waiter.

"Pawel, we need to call an ambulance."John pulled his mobile phone out of his jacket pocket. The signal was weak and the battery was low. He had meant to recharge the battery the evening before but it had slipped his mind. "Shit," he mumbled, irritated. "I'll try emergency services but the coverage isn't the best down here."

He dialled emergency services and shook his head. "There's no signal. Pawel, can you get to reception as fast as you can. Get them to call an ambulance. Tell Maura a man has had a fatal heart attack."

Pawel set off. He looked towards the castle and caught sight of Seán standing outside the dining room French windows. He motioned to him but he was too far away. Pawel made off around the bend lightning fast, to a small grassy bank that was within shouting distance.

"Call an ambulance, Seán," he hollered.

Briefly, he relayed what had happened. Pawel ran back to Beat Two, thinking as he did, of the young boy. What a terrible shock the son had received. Imagine having your father fishing by your side one moment and the next, lying in front of you lifeless. Imagine having to pull him out of the river. Pawel couldn't comprehend it. He had never seen a dead body before.

The boy would never forget what had happened. Those images would remain with him, just like the image of Lucy, his Lucy with someone else, would remain with Pawel.

"All right, Pawel?" John asked a moment later, taking him aside. Pawel looked shook and he was very pale.

The waiter nodded.

"Do you think you could bring young Jack here back to the castle?"

Pawel nodded again.

"Take him to the morning room. There's a fire in there and the young lad will have a bit of privacy. You might get some towels to dry him down and see to it that he gets a hot drink.

"His mum and sister are staying in the hotel. They need to be aware of what's happened. They need to be found as soon as possible. I'll stay here till help comes."

Jack was still kneeling beside the body of his father. His breathing was sudden and short with shock. The boy began to shiver.

"Jack," the gillie said.

The boy didn't answer so the gillie tried again.

"Jack," he said, "you need to go back to the hotel with Pawel. He will find your mum and sister. They need you now." The gillie helped the boy to his feet.

Looking down at the body of his father Jack said, "I don't want my dad to be alone." The words were spoken between gulped breaths.

"He won't be, Jack. I'll stay here with your dad. We've called an ambulance and I'll stay with your father until the medics arrive. That's a promise."

"Is there any chance?" Jack said, timidly. Then, he broke down and sobbed. John put his arm around the boy. When Jack had managed to compose himself a little he said, "Is he really dead?" He found it hard to articulate the words.

"I'm sorry, but I'm afraid so," the gillie said. "Your dad has gone."

"He said we'd go fishing tomorrow." Jack gave a gasp of helplessness and disbelief. "Tomorrow will never come."

Jack was reluctant to leave his father but he didn't put up a fight. He was shell-shocked. Much to the gillie's relief, Seán arrived. Shortly afterwards, the porter and Pawel accompanied Jack to the castle. As they made their way back, they met Alex Hamilton and Conor.

"There's been an emergency at Beat Two," the porter said. "We need to get this young lad back to the hotel."

"What's happened?"

Seán stalled for a few moments and outlined what had taken place. Pawel and Jack continued their approach to the castle.

"You know, at first I thought it was you, Mr Hamilton," Seán said. "I got the heebee jeebees I can tell you. Conor told me you'd be fishing at Beat Two this afternoon."

"It seems you're stuck with me. You and Conor," Alex said, touched by the porter's words.

"I suppose we are," Seán said gently. "I'd better catch up with Pawel and the lad. And the rest of the family need to be found. They don't know yet."

"That's going to be tough on them. Very tough. Can we do anything to help?" Alex said.

"John is alone with the body. Maybe, you could go down to him?"

"We'll do that," Conor said, keen to offer his colleague support. "What a thing to happen on his watch." Conor was relieved that he hadn't been out fishing with the Russells.

"I need to get a towel for John," said Seán. "He's soaked through, so he is."

True to his word, John had remained on the boardwalk with Harvey Russell's body. It had been one hell of a day and a fishing lesson that he would never forget. He couldn't bear to think of the scene that waited at the castle once the wife and daughter found out. They would be inconsolable, especially the wife. He had seen how well the family had interacted earlier that day. They were a tight-knit bunch.

No, John certainly didn't want to be around when they told Mrs Russell. He'd rather remain with Mr Russell. Alex Hamilton and Conor arrived soon afterwards. John was glad of their company. It had been eerie standing alone on the boardwalk with a corpse at his feet.

"You did well to get him out of the river so fast," Alex said, looking at the dead body.

"To be honest, I don't know how we managed it. The boy is only a slip of a lad. We were in real difficulty until Pawel showed up. We would have never managed to pull Mr Russell out of the river without Pawel's help. The father's a big man and he weighed a ton."

"It must have been tricky. There's quite a pull in the river today."

"You can say that again. At one stage, I thought I wouldn't be able to hang on to him."

"As for the son," Conor said, "what a misfortune to happen. It's bad enough losing your dad, let alone to see him die in front of you like that. That's too much for any young fellow to cope with."

"The child became very distressed when I had a go at resuscitating the father," John said, visibly upset. The stress he had gone through was apparent. "Jesus, I'm rattled. I could do with a whiskey. A large one."

"I'm buying," Alex cut in. "You look as if you need a hot whiskey. You're soaked through, man."

"Oh no, Mother of God. That's all we need!" Conor exclaimed in disgust.

"What's up?"

"Look behind you?"

More than half a dozen people had arrived on the scene. Two, if not three of the onlookers, had their mobile phones out and were taking photographs."

"I don't believe this," Alex said. "Have they no respect?" Alex walked over to the small crowd. "Could we have a little privacy here," he said, immediately taking control of the situation. "It's completely inappropriate to be taking photographs. I'd ask you to have respect for the dead man and his family. This is not a side show. Please, could you all leave right now? The paramedics will be arriving any minute and you're blocking the path."

Alex held his ground, standing in the middle of the path and effectively blocking it, and any view of the dead body behind him. Those onlookers who had been taking photographs had the decency to look embarrassed. The crowd dispersed, making their way back to the castle in silence.

Alex turned round to face the two gillies.

"Can you credit that? What is it with people?" he said.

"There may be others," John said. "Look up at the castle."

Alex looked ahead. A few bedroom windows were open and a small crowd had gathered on the grassy slope in front of the restaurant.

"I'll deal with this if you like. I'll man the bridge gate until the paramedics arrive and Conor can stay with you. Seán is probably on his way back as I speak. I'll ask him to run back and fetch a sheet to cover the body."

Alex quickly made his way back, interceding with Seán at the gate. The porter was carrying a towel. Alex explained what had happened.

"Can you get a sheet to cover Mr Russell body?"

"I'm on it," Seán said, handing Alex the towel.

Quick as a flash, the porter turned on his heel, and began to run towards the hotel. Before long, Seán returned to the scene at Beat Two. He covered Harvey Russell's body carefully with a large sheet.

"You never know when your day will come," he said. "When your number's up, that's it, you're gone."

The men waited with Harvey Russell until the emergency crew arrived.

They had begun their browse around the shops when Felicia's phone rang. She looked at the number that came up. It was one Felicia didn't recognize.

"Hello," she answered.

"Is that Mrs Russell?" a voice asked.

"Yes, it is. Who is this?"

"Mrs Russell, this is Maura, the receptionist, at Doonmara Castle. We're trying to locate you."

"I'm in Clifden. Is there something wrong?"

"Can you hold one moment, Mrs Russell? Jane, the restaurant manager, would like to have a word with you."

Felicia held her breath. Something was definitely not right.

A moment later, Jane's voice came through on the line.

"Mrs Russell, this is Jane speaking. Mrs Russell, I'm afraid I have some bad news. Your husband has had an accident."

"What? Is it serious? Is he alright?" Felicia felt fear rise within her.

"I don't have the full facts but you need to get back straight away, Mrs Russell. I'll be waiting for you at reception."

"What's happened, Jane? Surely you know something?"

"I think your husband may have had a heart attack, Mrs Russell. We've called for an ambulance."

Jane wasn't going to give any more details over the phone, especially as Mrs Russell would be getting into a car to drive back to Doonmara.

"I'll get there as soon as I can," Felicia said. Waves of panic swept through her. "I'm leaving right now. What about my son? Can someone look after him until I get to you?"

"Your son is being looked after, Mrs Russell. One of the staff is with him. I'll meet you on arrival, Mrs Russell," Jane said and hung up.

"What is it, Mum? What's happened?" Anna said, aware something was amiss.

"It's your dad, Anna. We need to go back to the hotel immediately."

"Is dad okay, Mum?"

"I'm not sure, Anna. He seems to have had a bit of a turn," she said, playing down the incident. There was no point in alarming Anna when Felicia didn't know the full facts herself.

"What's happened to him?"

Felecia hesitated. "I think it's his heart, Anna."

"Oh, Mum. Dad's going to be all right, isn't he?"

"I'm sure he will be, darling," she said, hiding her distress. Felicia wasn't sure at all. Jane had been vague on the phone. The restaurant manager knew more than she was letting on. Felicia was scared. She could hear her heart pounding.

Afterwards, Felicia could never recall the journey back to Doonmara. Her mind went blank. She and Anna barely spoke in the car. Anna intuitively knew that her mother was having trouble focusing so she held her tongue. The drive was difficult enough without further distractions.

Felicia drove precariously. Somehow, they got to Doonmara in one piece. They drove past some sheep who were wandering about on the road. Felicia barely missed one, as it trespassed dangerously in front of the car. She swerved, narrowly avoiding the animal. It looked as panicked as Felicia.

"Stupid animal," Anna said.

Her mother looked shook.

"Please God, let dad be all right," Anna prayed silently, though she was not religious and rarely attended church.

She was unsure who or what God was, but she hoped he was listening. Anna made promises that she couldn't possibly keep. If God would only will that her father remained safe and well, she would never smoke again, and she would never tell another lie.

If Anna thought, that by giving up her vices, her father would remain out of harm's way, she was gravely mistaken.

Eventually they got to the hotel. Felicia drove through the gates and up the avenue.

"Look, Mum. There's the ambulance outside the entrance," Anna said, catching sight of the vehicle.

She didn't spot George Clooney sitting on a bench in the front garden. She didn't notice Jane, the silver blond from the restaurant, sitting beside him.

Prompted by Alex, Seán was manning a vacant car space near the front door.

"I'll move my car and Mrs Russell can park here," Alex had suggested to Jane. "Seán can keep the space free until she arrives with her daughter."

Seán signalled to Felicia to park in the empty slot. With a heavy heart, Jane made her way over. Felicia and Anna got out of the car lightning fast.

"Where is my husband? Can you take me to him?" Felicia asked. Her pulse was racing. She was desperate to see Harvey.

"Yes, of course I will. Why don't we go inside, Mrs Russell?"

"How bad is he?"

Something she read in Jane's eyes gave the game away. Felicia had a sinking feeling in her gut.

"If you could follow me, Mrs Russell," Jane said. "We can have a chat inside."

Jane wanted to bring the Russells somewhere private before she delivered the devastating news. Felicia stood her ground. She was going nowhere until she knew what was going on.

"Tell me what's happened," she said. Jane remained quiet. "Please tell me what's happened, Jane," Felicia insisted. A note of hysteria had crept into her voice.

"Mrs Russell," said Jane, relenting. "I have bad news. I'm afraid I have very bad news." She paused hoping that it would give Felicia time to prepare herself. The silence was deafening.

Anna was numb. She had an inkling of what Jane was going to say.

No God, No. Don't let Daddy be dead, she prayed.

"I'm so sorry to have to tell you this, but I'm afraid your husband has died, Mrs Russell. He appears to have had a massive heart attack."

Immediately, Anna started bawling. Overwhelmed at the news of Harvey's sudden death, Anna's distress eluded her mother. Felicia struggled to absorb the shocking news, the worst possible news. It was as though her world had ended and all the lights had gone out. Her legs almost gave way underneath her. Jane noticed her unsteadiness. For a moment, she was afraid that Mrs Russell might collapse.

"My husband can't be dead," Felicia said disbelievingly "He can't be. Harvey was perfectly well when I left him after lunch. That was only two hours ago. Are you sure it's my husband?" she asked, as if Jane had somehow got her wires crossed; as if it were someone else's husband and someone else's father.

"It's definitely Mr Russell," Jane said. "I'm so sorry."

It was as if someone had punched Felicia hard in the stomach. She needed to see Harvey. She needed to be with him. She wanted to cradle him in her arms one last time.

"Can you take me to him?" she said, dazed.

"The emergency personnel are with your husband now, Mrs Russell. They are down at Beat Two. They will be bringing Mr Russell up shortly. Your husband was fishing on the river when it happened." Jane hesitated. "He had a heart attack," she said, "and then he fell into the river."

It was too much for Felicia.

"Oh my God! This can't be happening. It can't be." Felicia swayed again. Her anguish was tangible. This time, Jane put her arm around her.

"The gillie and one of the staff, along with your son, managed to pull Mr Russell out of the river," Jane said.

Felicia looked at her uncomprehendingly. She found it impossible to piece the facts together. At the mention of Jack, she somehow managed to refocus.

"Oh God. Poor Jack. Where is my son?" she said. "Where is Jack?"

"Your son is inside. He's in the morning room. I'll take you to him directly."

Paralysed, Felicia stood where she was.

"Mrs Russell, let's go inside now. Your son is waiting for you." Jane led Felicia in by the arm. Anna followed behind them.

Alex Hamilton watched from the bench. The mother looked completely distraught. He wished he could do something to help but it would be too intrusive to intervene at that moment.

Harvey Russell was only a couple of years older than himself and that shook Alex. Replaying his doctor's warnings about his health, Alex took a final pull from his cigarette before stamping the butt into the grass. This time, he would give them up for good. He resolved to get his cholesterol checked again. He would take those bloody statins if need be.

"You never know what fate has mapped out for you," he had said to Jane earlier. At the time, they were waiting for the dead man's family to arrive. He was studying the ambulance parked outside the hotel entrance door.

"No, you don't," she replied. "We're probably better off not knowing. Well, the bad stuff at any rate."

"You're right," he said, thinking of the day when he, Rachel and Laura had set out on what was to be their last family excursion; a trip to the seaside that turned into a trip to hell.

Alex had a flashbulb memory, a snapshot of the emergency crew lifting Rachel's small body into the ambulance. He saw his child's dead body on a stretcher inside the vehicle, a vivid memory burned into his brain. He felt the pain of Rachel's death all over again, as raw now, in that moment, as it had been seven years previously. Hers had been a death out of time, a death of the future he expected.

With time had come an acceptance of sorts. Some days Alex accepted Rachel's death, and on others, he struggled. In moments, such as these, he utterly failed.

Jane tuned in to how he was feeling and with empathy said, "I know you suffered a great loss, Mr Hamilton. I'm sorry."

"Thank you, Jane," he said quietly. "When your child dies, your life shatters. You never get over the death of your child. It goes against the grain of things."

"It does," she agreed. "My baby brother died from the whooping cough. I think of him, even now, a lifetime later. My mother was never the same after his death. He was the only boy you see. There were three of us girls and he was her youngest. My mother was shattered."

"What was his name?"

"Rory. Mind you, we always called him baby Rory. Even to this day."

"Our daughter was called Rachel."

"Rachel is a lovely name, Mr Hamilton."

"Thank you." After a moment, he said, "Jane, speaking of names and on a lighter note, isn't it about time you called me, Alex."

"Very well then, Alex," she said simply, and smiled at him.

CHAPTER NINE

Laura saw two paramedics arrive on the scene from the window in her suite. They were carrying a stretcher. She remembered seeing an ambulance parked out front.

Once again, death had arrived at her door. She hadn't been with Alex, just like she wasn't with Rachel when the accident happened. She wrenched herself from the scene played out across the river bank. Alex needed her now.

She exited the suite like a bat out of hell. All those wasted years. If only she could turn back time.

As she passed the hotel front door, she heard someone call her name.

"Laura," a voice called. "Laura," the voice shouted louder.

Incredulous, she turned.

"Over here, Laura," Alex beckoned.

Her husband was in the garden, standing in front of the blue hydrangeas, and very much alive. She had been given a second chance. Laura ran to him.

She collapsed into his arms. Alex held her close, stunned at the intimacy of the moment. He hadn't held Laura for an age. He inhaled the smell of her freshly washed hair. He had always loved the smell of Laura's fruity shampoos.

"I thought I'd lost you," she blurted out. "Forgive me, Alex."

"Forgive you for what?" he murmured.

She released him reluctantly and took a step back to look at him.

"Let's sit down, Laura," he said, taking stock. "You've had quite a shock. I can see that."

They sat on the bench. Much to his surprise, she gripped his hand tightly.

"Forgive me for being so wrapped up in my own loss that I forgot about you, forgot about us," she began. "This may sound crazy, but up until a few moments ago, I thought you had died. I saw the note in the suite and I looked out the window expecting to see you fishing at Beat Two. There was a body on the boardwalk, Alex. A dead body with a sheet draped over it."

"And you thought it was me? You thought that I was dead?"

"Yes. And in that moment, I realised that I still loved you and that I had ruined everything between us. Only now it was too late. I'd lost you too, Alex, like I had lost Rachel."

"It's all right," he said, more than a little startled. "I'm here."

She burst into tears.

"There, there, it's okay," he said soothingly, and put his arm around her shoulders. She found comfort in the gesture. "You must have got some fright, Laura."

She wiped away her tears with a tissue she had pulled from her jumper sleeve. She collected herself.

"Actually, I'm a bit shaken myself. I saw the body," he said.

"Did you? That must have been difficult."

"Awful."

She bit her lip.

"Am I too late, Alex?"

He didn't reply immediately. This was an unexpected turn of events, one that Alex Hamilton, in all of his wildest dreams, hadn't foreseen.

"I'd like to be honest with you, Laura," he began ominously. He took his arm from her shoulders and sat up.

"Have I already lost you?" Laura interjected, dreading his response.

Looking straight ahead, Alex said, "It's not that I don't love you, Laura. I never stopped loving you. But you shut me out. I felt useless. And somewhere along the line, I stopped being the man I once was. Now, I'm someone I hardly recognise."

"Don't say that, Alex", she said, and dabbed at her eyes with a tissue. "You're the same man."

"No, Laura. I don't believe that I am," he said. "I know you blame me for Rachel's death. I blame myself. I've never stopped blaming myself. I can't bring Rachel back."

"What happened was an accident," she said.

He turned towards her.

"Even so, you blame me, Laura."

She shook her head.

"I find that hard to believe," he said. "It would never have happened, if Rachel had been with you. That's what you think. That's what I think. I blame myself. If you could forgive me for what happened, Laura. If you could, then that would be something."

"Of course, I forgive you." For a few seconds she was silent. "I just couldn't forgive myself for what happened," she said and looked up at him. I felt like such a bad mother. I had failed Rachel. One minute our life was perfect, and the next, it was a catastrophe. Just like that," she said clicking her fingers in the air. "We were happy. So damn happy.

Then she was taken from us and there was nothing left."

"There was," he said. "You had me. You had us."

"I lost sight of that," she said, blinking away fresh tears. "After Rachel died, I withdrew into my own little world. I spiralled downwards into a black hole. It felt like I had died too."

"What about me? I was heartbroken too."

"I couldn't cope with my own pain, let alone cope with us, or your grief. I had nothing left for anyone else. I had to focus on Rachel. For the first two or three years, I was angry all the time. I was permanently exhausted. Sometimes, I think that mental exhaustion is worse than any physical pain that you could have."

"You may be right," he sighed.

She took a deep breath before continuing. This was her last chance to save her marriage. It was now or never.

"I wanted to die because if I was dead, then the pain would go away," she said. Her eyes, still wet with tears, held his. "I thought about dying a lot. There were so many times when I felt that I could not go on. I wanted to curl up and die.

"One day when I was driving, I saw an articulated truck stopped ahead on the road. Its warning lights were flashing. I thought about crashing into it, ending it all, there and then. I picked up speed and began to drive really fast."

A floodgate had opened. Laura had his full attention.

"What was going through your mind?" he asked.

"I was thinking I can be with her now. I can be with Rachel and the pain can end."

"What stopped you?"

"In a split second, I knew I couldn't do it. Not like that. Not take my own life."

For a moment, Alex closed his eyes as he contemplated what might have happened had Laura killed herself.

"You'd have left me on my own," he said, reproachful. "I'd have had to deal with your death too."

"I had convinced myself you'd be better off without me. I wasn't able to see beyond my own pain and torment."

He looked at her gravely. What she had divulged cut through to his very core.

"Then came the bargaining," she said. "When I think back on it, I realise that I must have been mad."

"What would you bargain about?"

"I used to make deals with God. I'd promise, that if he would let Rachel walk through the door, I'd never ask any questions about where she had been. I'd sit at the kitchen table and I'd wait for her to come through the door. This was two years after Rachel had died."

"If only it were that simple," he said, and gave a weak smile.

"I couldn't bear to have anyone touch me. I didn't know how to feel. I didn't want Rachel to think that I would be happy without her. I thought that she would be very unhappy if she saw me happy. It got to where I wanted to exist, but not to feel. But I do love you, Alex. I never stopped loving you. I know that now."

"Do you? Do you really love me? We haven't been together for years."

She looked at him, puzzled for a moment, before she understood what he was implying.

"You're equating love with sex. I think men do that. Women are hard-wired differently. But I want to be with you now, Alex."

Another tear escaped from those green eyes and gently, ever so gently, he wiped it from her cheek.

"It's not as straightforward as that, Laura. Surely you can see that," he said. "We haven't had a physical relationship since Rachel died. I've done things I never thought I'd do."

"I turned a blind eye."

"Why? Why would you do that, Laura?"

She faltered for a moment, unsure how to reply.

"It let me off the hook for rejecting you the way I did," she said eventually. "I thought that you wouldn't bother me then. For sex, I mean. There was nothing left inside of me to give to you."

"I suppose that's honest." He sounded sad and weary. She had confirmed what he had long suspected.

"I felt such a failure as a wife. You were still young and I couldn't give you any more children. That had something to do with it."

"Now that is mad!"

"I was in a bad place."

"And so was I," he said. "I wanted to help you. It's hard to cope when you see the person you love in pain, yet you can't do anything. I couldn't save you. I became exhausted trying.

"You needed to feel needed."

"Perhaps I did. I can recall the absolute kindness of people, but I also felt as though the skin had been peeled off my whole body. I had no one. When I'd meet someone, whether it was one of the family, or a neighbour, or a work colleague, they would all, without fail, ask how you were. No one asked how I was doing."

He was right. Everyone had been concerned for her. It had all been about her, the mother.

"As time went on, I felt that you were not my wife anymore. You had become Rachel's mother, not Alex's wife. That's how people defined you. I had lost my wife. And you were full of anger. I was afraid to say or do anything. I dreaded coming home every day. I couldn't stand being in the house with you."

She flinched.

"It has been easier the last few years, hasn't it?"

"It has. But this isn't a real marriage, Laura. We're civil. We're friends. That's it. We both deserve more than that."

"That can change. I will change."

He looked uncertain.

"I've been unfaithful," he said. "Do you think we can ignore that?"

"I don't have all the answers, Alex. Can we forget all the hurt and the bad stuff for a couple of hours? For today?"

He squeezed her hand but he remained silent. She motioned to the shrubbery behind her.

"When we first came here all those years ago, this hydrangea was pink. Then the colour changed. Hydrangeas change to this blue colour when the soil gets acidic."

"I never knew that," he said.

"It's not impossible to turn this blue hydrangea back into a pink colour. It's not easy, but it's not impossible, either."

"Meaning?"

"Maybe we could be the same again."

"That's a lot to ask, Laura."

"It's a tall order, but we can be the same again. I know we can."

"Laura, I've just seen a man, around the same age as myself, die. He died suddenly and without any warning. It's brought home to me how transient life is. We have to grab the moment, because honestly, Laura, neither of knows how long we've got left."

He briefly outlined what had happened earlier.

"God Alex, I know who you're talking about. His name is Harvey Russell. I met his wife in Clifden earlier. I asked how her husband and son were getting on with the fishing. I told her you would be joining them on the river. Can you credit that?"

"Goodness. That is a bit close to the bone. Had you met the husband?"

"Yes. He was at reception last night when I was checking in. We got chatting. And they were sitting at the table next to me at dinner last night. They are a lovely family. They seemed happy."

"Like we were?" he said.

"Like we were. They reminded me of us, Alex; of you, me, and Rachel. This is my wake-up call. I've been living in limbo ever since Rachel died."

He took his time before he spoke.

"The blue is a striking colour," he told her. He looked deep into her eyes. He could never resist those eyes. "It's a strong colour. There's nothing wrong with the blue. Some might say that it's a far nicer colour. Perhaps we won't be able to get back to where we were, Laura, but we can endeavour to be somewhere better, and stronger."

"Thank you," she whispered. Her relief was palpable.

"Mind you, pink was Rachel's favourite colour," he said, and flashed a grin.

Everything had to be pink in Rachel's little world.

"Let's aim for a blue pink." Laura said.

He draped his arm around Laura's shoulder. For one day, he would like to forget their troubles. That's what he was thinking.

Laura moved in closer beside him, the armour of grief she wore shorn. They sat on the bench under the blue hydrangea until the paramedics came up from the river.

Felicia swept her son into her arms and hugged him for what seemed an eternity.

Eventually she let go, reluctant to disengage herself from Jack, as if afraid that she might lose him too.

The family had gathered in the morning room. Seán lit a fire and Jane hovered in the background.

Then John arrived. The gillie had relayed the play of events to the ambulance crew. When he could be of no further assistance, he had made his way back to the hotel with Alex and Conor.

"The paramedics are attending to your husband," he told Felicia. She was a shadow of the woman he had seen at lunch time. He read the pain in her face. Her eyes were dark pools of sadness with no life and her face was pinched white and dazed.

"If they had got here sooner, could my husband have been saved?" she asked quietly.

"I'm afraid not, Mrs Russell." Looking in the direction of Jack, he said," I'm afraid your son got an awful shock."

"Oh, Jack," Felicia said. She hugged her son again. Then she said to him, "I'm sorry you were on your own, pet. I wish I had been with you and dad. It must have been so frightening."

"I wasn't on my own, Mum," he said. "John was with me. He tried to save dad. He did his best but it was no use, Mum. We couldn't bring dad back. If we had pulled dad from the river quicker..." Here, he broke off for a moment, clearly troubled, before saying, "Maybe then, we could have saved him."

Felicia was at a loss for words. John read the confusion in her face. He endeavoured to shed light on what had happened.

"I did my best, Mrs Russell, but I'm afraid it was too late. Your husband had a fatal heart attack. He stumbled and then he fell into the water, head on. I'll warrant he was dead before he hit the water. We lifted him out as fast as we could. I attempted to resuscitate him. It was of no use. He was gone."

Jack found comfort in John's analysis. Jack had been torturing himself with questions that, until that moment, had remained unanswered.

If they had pulled his father out of the river sooner, could his father have been saved? Those extra minutes trying to drag his father from the river could have meant the difference between life and death. Would he ever know when exactly his father died? Was it before or after he hit the water? Now, Jack looked relieved.

Felicia sat on the couch between her two children, tears streaming down her cheeks, one hand gripping Jack's tightly. Where once there were four, now they were only three, Jane observed. The family huddled close together. They were in shock. Yet, Felicia had the presence of mind to acknowledge her gratitude to the gillie.

"Thank you, John. I owe you a huge debt," she said.

"You owe me nothing, Mrs Russell. I'm sorry that your husband couldn't be saved."

"You did your best, John. Thank you for taking care of my son. It was a blessing that you were there. You and Pawel."

She looked around, searching the room to thank the waiter.

"Pawel will be back in a short while, Mrs Russell," said Jane.

On Jane's orders, Pawel had been dispatched for tea.

"A hot cup of sweet tea will do them all good," she had told the waiter discreetly. "It's good for a shock. You could probably do with one yourself," she added, noticing for the first time how shook Pawel looked. "Take your time, Pawel. Have a cup of tea down in the kitchen while you're waiting. Put plenty of sugar in it," she advised.

Felicia was forlorn – completely desolate. Her husband was gone forever. If only she had taken that photograph. She could have said goodbye to him. She could have been with Harvey before he died. She could have kissed him one last time. She was going to regret that for the rest of her life.

She had told Harvey that it would be a day to remember. Had she really said that? Her composure broke and she began to cry – heart-wrenching sobs that alarmed Jack and Anna. Jane wondered ought she call a doctor. Mrs Russell might need a sedative. Next, Anna flung her arms around her mother, and then she too started to bawl. With that, Felicia found strength and courage. Though her heart was breaking, Felicia managed to stop her own tears. If she didn't pull herself together, her children would become more distressed. She would have to hold it together. She couldn't give up.

She said to her daughter: "There, there my love. Hush, darling, hush." She stroked the hair on top of her head. The movement seemed to soothe Anna.

Felicia was thinking: *Why did you leave me? Come back to me, Harvey. Don't leave your children without a father. Don't leave us.*

She started in surprise at a discreet knock on the door. Jane went to open the door.

"We have the body up from the river bank," one of the ambulance men said. "The deceased is in the ambulance."

"His wife wants to see him," Jane said. "Can you come in for a moment?"

Jane swung the door open and the paramedic entered the room. The room fell silent.

"Mrs Russell," Jane said. "Your husband is in the ambulance."

Felicia stood up but her legs were wobbly.

"I'd like to say goodbye to my husband," she said.

"If you'd like to come with me, I'll take you to him," the medic said.

Anna got up to go.

"Can you stay with Jack?" Felicia asked.

It was best not to bring Anna. Felicia didn't know how bad Harvey would look.

Felicia accompanied the paramedic to the ambulance, walking slowly, and braving herself to face the body of her dead husband. A few dozen footsteps, that's all it was, and a further descent into a nightmarish hell.

The medic opened the ambulance door and Felicia went inside. She would never forget the sight that awaited her. Felicia was relieved that Anna hadn't accompanied her.

Harvey was a greyish blue colour. Already, rigor mortis had set in and his muscles had stiffened. It was Harvey, yet at the same time, it wasn't.

The lifeless body, inches before her very eyes, couldn't be her husband. It couldn't be. Harvey was always full of life and bravado. None of this seemed real. None of it made any sense.

She sat on the ambulance bed, edging herself closer to her husband. She clasped his hand. She tried to grasp onto a life force that was no longer there. There was no sign of life whatsoever. It hit home to her then, he was dead.

He was still her Harvey. She wanted to hold him in her arms but there was little room to manoeuvre in the ambulance. She pressed her head against his chest and lay there for a moment. Then, she caressed his forehead. Finally, she kissed him. She kissed him with infinite tenderness, but his lips were cold.

"Good bye, my love," she whispered.

Turning to the paramedic, she signalled that she was ready to leave.

"Anna", she said on her return, finding strength out of nowhere, "your father doesn't look great. I'd prefer if your last memory of him wasn't this. Dad will look a whole better, darling, when they fix him up a little. It might be for the best, sweetheart, if you said goodbye later. I think your father would prefer that too."

"Do you think so?" Anna said, overwhelmed. She paused momentarily and considered what her mother said. "Okay, Mum," she said. "Dad always liked to look his best. Didn't he, Mum?" Her voice was low and trusting.

That pulled at Felicia's heartstrings. Anna was like a little girl again. All of her teenage bluster had dissipated.

"We can visit your father in the funeral home," Felicia said. "The three of us can say our final goodbyes together."

Having confirmed that Anna was agreeable, Felicia told the paramedics to leave. She stood on the drive, accompanied by Jane, as the ambulance drove off. Harvey was being taken to a hospital in Galway.

Felicia was torn. She wanted to accompany her husband in the ambulance. It seemed like an act of betrayal to let Harvey make the journey without her. She should be with him but her children needed her now. The dead would remain dead. The living would have to be taken care of. Her place was with Anna and Jack.

An autopsy would have to be performed. She couldn't bear to think of Harvey being cut up. Before Felicia could dwell on an autopsy any further, Pawel re-entered the room, carrying an enormous tray. He set the tray on the table and then, he and Seán busied themselves, preparing tea for everyone.

"Mrs Hamilton, why don't you sit down," Jane suggested. "I'll bring you a cup of tea. There you go," she said, placing the cup and saucer in front of Felicia.

"Thank you," Felicia said, hiding her despair. Why was it people always thought that tea in a crisis worked? She wished it were as simple as that. Her husband was dead. What bloody good would tea do?

She reminded herself that the restaurant manager was only trying to help. Felicia didn't want to appear rude so she took a sip. Jane had put a spoon or two of sugar in it. Surprisingly, the sugary tea had an immediate soothing affect. Her mouth had been very dry.

"I don't ever take sugar in my tea," she said, "but it tastes comforting."

"They say hot sugary tea is good when you've had a shock," Jane said. She would be unable to offer any solace to Mrs Russell. Neither could Seán, or Pawel, for that matter.

The staff didn't know what to do so they did what they do best and attended to their guests. Seán busied himself stoking the fire while Pawel buttered Jack a hot scone. After he had put a dollop of strawberry jam on top, he handed it to the boy. When everyone had been served tea and the fire had been attended to, Pawel and Seán left the room. Only Jane and John remained with the family.

The gillie quickly downed his tea and had a refill. He had managed to towel himself down but his clothes remained damp.

"You need to out of those wet clothes, John," Jane said.

"You're right. I'll do that," he said, relieved to escape the room.

He got up to go.

"Thank you, John, for everything," Felicia said. She got up and shook the gillie's hand.

"Thanks," said Jack.

John nodded to Jack in acknowledgement.

"If I can do anything at all for you, Mrs Russell, let me know," he said. "Reception will know where to find me."

He left the room.

"Can I do anything, Mrs Russell? Can I contact anyone for you?" Jane offered.

"I think I can manage, Jane. I have my phone and Anna has an iPad. I have to make some calls and I'll need to contact the hospital later."

"If you have trouble contacting anyone, you're more than welcome to use the phone in the office. And if you would like us to contact anyone on your behalf, we could do that."

"Thank you, Jane. It's not going to be straightforward because we don't live in Ireland. But my husband is Irish and we have relatives here. My husband's father is dead, but my mother-in-law is living in Dublin. We had planned on staying with a cousin of my husband's after our stay at Doonmara. I'll get in touch with him first. I'm hoping he can break the news in person to my mother-in-law. She's elderly. I don't want to phone her with this kind of news."

"We will do everything we can to assist you, Mrs Russell."

"I appreciate that. I'll make some calls and I'll let you know our plans. We'll stay here tonight anyway."

Jane was relieved to hear that. Mrs Russell was in no state to be behind the wheel of a car.

"You can let Maura know if you need me. I'll be on duty for the rest of the evening," she said.

It was actually Jane's night off, but she didn't tell Mrs Russell that. There had been an emergency and Jane had no intention of shirking her responsibilities. She had a duty of care to the Russell family.

"Thank you, Jane. All of the staff have been so kind."

"You're welcome, Mrs Russell. And on behalf of everyone at Doonmara, can I offer you our heartfelt condolences. I'll leave you now but you know where I am, if you need me."

Jane went outside for some air. It had been a difficult afternoon. No amount of hotel training could prepare you for that kind of tragedy. No wonder poor Pawel had looked distraught. He hadn't been working in the business for long. And he was young. He may have never seen a dead body before. She had better check on him.

CHAPTER TEN

"She looks so alone," Alex said.

Felicia reminded Laura of how she had felt when Rachel died. She didn't voice that thought. She had not been alone that day, the day Rachel had died. Alex had been at her side. If they had any chance of rebuilding their marriage, she needed to remember that.

The ambulance drove away. It was heartbreaking to watch. Felicia went back inside.

"I wonder is there anything we could do to help?" Laura said.

"I could offer to drive her into Galway. She may need to go to the hospital. I'll have a word with Jane."

"That's a good idea," she said. "We can offer our sympathies later."

"How about some tea?" he asked.

"How about a chilled glass of white wine?" she suggested.

"Now, you're talking," he replied. "Good woman!" The expression didn't grate on her this time. For once, she heard it as a term of endearment. He got up to go. "I'll order from the bar. Or would you prefer to sit inside? "

It was nippy, but she was afraid that she might break the spell between them if they left the garden.

"It is getting chilly. We'd better go inside," she said, reluctantly.

"Here's an idea," he said, as if reading her thoughts. Alex didn't want to break the intimacy they had established either. "Let's order a bottle of wine and have it sent to the room. I've always loved the view from that room."

"Let's do that," she said, and they went back inside.

Conor was sitting on a bar stool, sinking a pint of Guinness.

"Can I get you another one of those?" Alex asked.

"You can."

"Awful business, isn't it?"

"I won't forget this afternoon in a hurry."

"Nor will I." Alex caught the barman's attention. "Can I have another pint for Conor, and can you send a bottle of white wine to my room," he instructed.

"Certainly, Mr Hamilton. What would you like?"

"A bottle of the Sauvignon Blanc. Can you make sure it's well chilled?"

"I'll put one in an ice bucket and have it sent up straight away, sir."

"I'm waiting for John," Conor said. "He's with the family."

"Where are they?" Alex asked.

"They're gathered in the morning room. They're having a cup of tea as I speak. I'm sure he'd fancy something stronger. I would if I were in his shoes."

"I bet he would. Which reminds me: I promised the man a drink. One more thing," he told the bartender who was placing a pint in front of Conor. "When John comes in, will you offer him a whiskey or whatever he wants on my behalf? And make it a large one. You can charge it to my room."

"Certainly, sir," he said, noting how well Mr Hamilton looked after the staff.

"I managed to get hold of a pair of pants for his nibs," Conor continued. He lived nearby, and he had gone home to fetch a change of clothes for his colleague. "Whether they'll fit him is another matter. He's a bit thinner than me, mind."

That was a bit of an understatement and Alex smiled. John was like a rake. He certainly didn't have Conor's beer gut.

"Better too big than too small," he countered.

"Especially when it comes to catching a salmon," the gillie said.

Alex smiled.

"Conor, I'll catch up with you later."

"Righty oh then. Thanks for the drink," he said, and raised his glass.

A short while later, Alex Hamilton and his wife retreated to their suite. They sat on the couch and held hands, captivated by the river view.

A few doors away, Jean-Pierre sat in his room. He too was looking out at the river. Lucy had long fled the scene. Clearly distressed at having been discovered by her fiancé naked in the bedroom of one of the guests, she had dressed in a hurry and scuttled.

Thereafter, Jean-Pierre had taken up residence on the couch, bearing witness to the increased activity at Beat Two.

The body had been dragged out of the river. The French man had watched as the gillie attempted to resuscitate the man. He had seen Lucy's fiancé, Pawel, accompanying the young boy back to the castle. Two other men had joined the gillie and a little later, a sheet had been placed over the dead man. Seán, that nosy porter, had been busy going to and fro. Finally, the paramedics had arrived and removed the body.

At present, all was quiet on the river. The setting was magnificent. It was hard to believe that only an hour or two previously a death had occurred.

Jean-Pierre was in a quandary. A number of problems faced him. Would Lucy's fiancé approach him? What would happen if he did?

He and Marie had planned on having their wedding at the castle. That would not be feasible now, not when he had bedded a staff member whose fiancé had caught them in the act, a staff member whom Marie had met.

There was another and more immediate dilemma to face. Marie's brother had accompanied him on the stag weekend. What if he got wind of what had happened? What then?

Jean-Pierre had risked his whole future for a quick shag with the chambermaid. Would he get away with it? It was too much to hope for. The French man was more than a little angry with himself, but only briefly.

It was entirely the waiter's fault, he concluded. Why the hell had he looked up at Jean-Pierre's bedroom window anyway? To think, some insignificant waiter could ruin everything for Marie and himself. Jean-Pierre had been unlucky to have been caught with Lucy. Very unlucky.

His mobile phone rang.

"Olivier," he said, sounding relieved.

"Where have you been hiding?" his best friend asked.

"I'm in my room. Where are you guys?"

"I'm on my way back to the hotel and the rest of the boys are in Clifden."

"Can you come to my room when you get here? I need to speak to you urgently, Olivier."

"What's up, Jean-Pierre? You sound worried."

"I think your duties as best man may have been added to."

"What do you mean?"

"I'll explain when I see you. You're not going to believe the mess I've gotten myself into."

"Why don't we meet in the bar, Jean-Pierre?"

"I can't go down to the bar. I'll explain when I see you." For all Jean-Pierre knew, Pawel could be on duty. He had seen the waiter in there that very lunchtime. "I'm in big trouble, my friend."

"Not for the first time," Olivier said, intrigued.

"This takes precedence over everything else!"

"I'm driving up the avenue as we speak. I'll see you in a few moments," Olivier said, before hanging up.

Jean-Pierre remembered the bottle of whiskey he had bought in the duty free. He went to find it now. There were two clean glasses on top of the drinks cabinet and he set them on the table beside the whiskey.

Before long Olivier arrived.

"What's up?" he asked, curious. Jean-Pierre poured them both a generous measure of whiskey.

"Her name is Lucy," Jean-Pierre said. Olivier grinned. "Remember, the Slovakian chambermaid I told you about."

Olivier knew all about Jean-Pierre's previous dalliance with Lucy. Jean-Pierre couldn't resist boasting about his prowess, not when Olivier had commented on how good-looking Lucy was.

"La jeune fille avec les grands seins? I remember her," he said, raising his hands in the air, palms open, as if scooping both her breasts.

Jean-Pierre responded by way of a mirthless laugh.

"She does have great breasts," he confirmed a moment later.

"What have you done?"

Jean-Pierre outlined the circumstances of the tryst.

"Merde!" Oliver said, looking suitably shocked. "You are in trouble." Olivier empathised with his friend. It was a nice fantasy – beautiful girl like Lucy, dressed in a maid's uniform, coming to your room.

Would he have succumbed to the same temptation? Who knew? He had been infatuated, once. But he had never been in love. Not really, he told himself. And he never had a fiancée.

Besides, he owed no loyalty to Marie. Not after the way Marie had treated Olivier. He may have been willing to forgive Marie, but to forget was another matter entirely. He had been infatuated with her. That's all there was to it.

So he said, "I can't say that I blame you. Lucy's a sexy girl."

"She is something. But that's neither here nor there. What am I going to do?"

Olivier considered the options.

"You need to talk to Lucy," he advised. "She must know if her boyfriend intends to take this further. Once you know, you can decide what to do next."

"You're right. I'll do that now."

"I think we should stay away from the hotel tonight. I'll tell the boys there's been a change of game plan. I'll suggest that we meet them in Clifden and have dinner there. I can say there's been a death and that the hotel is a bit gloomy."

"*Parfait!* Good thinking, Olivier. I knew there was a good reason why I chose you as my best man."

"I think this goes above the call of my duties, *mon ami.*"

"I owe you, Olivier."

"It's not over yet, Jean-Pierre. Was she worth it?"

Jean-Pierre's ego took hold. He liked to be the top dog among his peers, especially Olivier.

"She had her moments," he said.

"You're only sorry you got caught," Olivier said. Clearly, Jean-Pierre had little, if any, remorse. "I hate to state the obvious, but there will be trouble if Leon finds out."

"Don't go there, Olivier!"

Leon, Marie's brother, would be angry, and what about her father? Jean-Pierre didn't wish to make an enemy of Henri Leclair. His fiancée's father was a highly influential man in the banking community.

Lucy was sexy and beautiful. She was a very pleasant girl. There was no doubt about that. But she cleaned rooms for a living. She was going nowhere on the social stratosphere, whereas Marie, she was another matter entirely. Though not as voluptuous as Lucy, his fiancée had her attractions, one of them being that she came from a top-drawer Parisian family. She would be a valuable ally in Jean-Pierre's ascent to the top. And no matter what it took or, who he hurt along the way, Jean-Pierre intended getting there.

"I'll phone Lucy and see if I can sort this mess out," he said. He picked up his mobile and hit Lucy's name on the contact list.

She answered immediately.

"Chérie, how are you?" he asked. "I've been worried about you." He was a smooth operator. His voice portrayed a concern he certainly didn't feel. Jean-Pierre listened as Lucy took the reins of the conversation.

"C'est bon." Jean-Pierre looked relieved which made Olivier wonder if his friend was off the hook entirely. "At least, that's something," Jean-Pierre said. "We won't be in the dining room tonight, Lucy. I'll stay away from the hotel for the rest of the day."

"Where are you now?" Lucy enquired.

"I'm in my room. I haven't left the suite. I thought it best to stay out of sight." He had been lying low in his room all afternoon and not out of concern for Lucy. The champagne and late night drinking had caught up with Jean-Pierre, and he had a kip on the couch. He had slept without any bother at all. "I need to ask you one last thing, Lucy. Are you sure your fiancé is not going to do anything stupid? Is he planning on confronting me?

"Pawel won't make a move on you," she said. Unlike Jean-Pierre, Pawel and Lucy had jobs to worry about.

Jean-Pierre didn't care to ask why not. Any reason was good enough for the French man if it meant he could avoid an altercation with Pawel.

"That's something," Jean-Pierre said, reassured. "It's all very unfortunate. Maybe Pawel will forgive you in time."

Lucy knew there was no hope of that. She had been well and truly rumbled. Her fiancé was a proud man and he had standards. Where had her standards gone? She hadn't been raised to behave like this. She had let herself down badly and for something that meant nothing. Jean-Pierre had no genuine feelings for her. Nor had she for him. What had she been thinking?

Teary voiced, she said, "I'd better go now. I'm on duty in a few minutes."

She hung up, wondering as she did how she could have hurt Pawel like this. She had seen his crestfallen face. He had been gutted. He had always behaved decently towards her. Besotted, Pawel had put Lucy on a pedestal.

Lucy had toppled off that pedestal. Now, the young Slovakian woman felt genuine remorse for her actions. Unlike Jean-Pierre, her partner in crime, Lucy wasn't merely sorry she had been caught.

She had already apologised to her fiancé in person.

"I'm so sorry, Pawel. I really am," she said ashamed. She read disgust in his eyes. Or was it hurt? He could scarcely bare to look at her.

By contrast, Jean-Pierre hadn't a guilty thought in the world.

"Looks like I've had a lucky escape," he told Olivier.

The phone call over, Jean-Pierre poured them both a second generous measure of whiskey.

"It's been an eventful weekend," he concluded.

"Would you forgive her if you were her fiancé?" Olivier asked thinking as he did that his friend was a lucky bastard, a lucky bastard who always got the girl.

"Are you crazy? I'd never forgive Marie if she did that to me."

Jean-Pierre didn't care about double standards. Why would he? He didn't have any standards to begin with.

"Tchin – tchin."

"Tchin – tchin," repeated Olivier, clinking Jean-Pierre's glass.

"Seán, can you bring this order to Room 27?" asked Maura.

"That will be for the French man," he said.

"You're on the money."

Seán headed straight to the kitchen where he collected a tray. Jean-Pierre had requested a pot of coffee and a patisserie. Two complimentary cookies had been added to the order.

The porter didn't much care for Jean-Pierre, whom he had known since the Frenchman's early teenage years. It appeared that the spoilt teenager had turned into an arrogant young man.

"Room service," Seán said, knocking on the door.

Jean-Pierre, dressed only in a hotel bathrobe, let the porter in.

"Good afternoon, Jean-Pierre. I have your coffee. I'll put it on the table near the window."

Jean-Pierre mumbled something incoherent.

Seán walked through and placed the tray on the table. He noted an empty ice bucket on the table. The bottle had been removed but the bucket was half-full with water. The ice had long melted.

The room was in a mess. It was an enormous bedroom. Jean-Pierre had been upgraded to one of the suites. Management had thoughtfully supplied a complimentary bottle of champagne and a bowl of fruit.

Jean-Pierre was being well looked after because he was having his wedding at Doonmara. The hotel had been booked out for the wedding. It was to be a big splash. A very big affair, with no expense spared, according to Maura.

Passing the bathroom on his left, Seán saw two towels strewn across the tub. More surprising, however, was the unmade bed. The sheets had been kicked back. Both sides of the huge canopy bed had been used.

Two empty champagne glasses and a bottle of champagne were on a bedside table. That confirmed Seán's suspicions. That bed had seen some action. Jean-Pierre had been entertaining someone in the room. One thing was for sure, it wasn't his charming fiancée. Seán had met Marie when she stayed at Doonmara. In his opinion, she was wasted on the Frenchman. She was a classy bird.

Jean-Pierre was in no mood for conversation and Seán didn't delay.

"I'll take this with me and allow you some space," he said, picking up the ice bucket.

No sooner had the porter got back to reception when another room service order came through from the bar.

"You're being kept on your toes this afternoon, Seán," said Maura. "Can you collect a bar order for the Hamiltons?"

"I'm getting enough exercise walking up and down these corridors, so I am. It doesn't seem to be having any effect," he said, patting his tummy lightly.

Maura laughed.

"It's amazing the things that you see," he added mischievously.

"Oh, go on. Tell me more. What did you discover?"

Maura loved a bit of hotel gossip and Seán seemed to have access to everyone's secrets. Staff referred to him as the grapevine.

"Monsieur Jean-Pierre had company in that big bed of his."

"You're joking? Was there someone with him when you went up?"

"Not when I arrived. I'd swear he had some poor unfortunate young one up there earlier. One look at the bed and I knew that. Mind you, the empty champagne bottle and the glasses beside the bed were a bit of a giveaway too. I don't know how he managed it, Maura, so I don't. I served him in the bar at lunch and he didn't have anyone with him then."

"He's been a busy boy," said Maura.

There had been a lingering stale smell in the bedroom. The room reeked of sex. Seán didn't divulge that piece of information to the hotel receptionist. He didn't want to be saying that sort of thing to Maura. That sort of talk was a bit too crude for her ears.

"He has some cheek, I can tell you. I pity that poor fiancée of his. To think they're getting married here in two months' time."

"I can't say that I envy the girl," the receptionist said. "She doesn't know what she's let herself in for, Seán. He's nasty piece of work. A real brat."

"Always was, Maura. Always was. Now," he said and looking down at the order, "I'd better collect this from the bar and bring it up to the Hamiltons."

"Off you go, twinkle toes."

"At least there'll be no high jinks in that room," he said with a parting word.

Off the porter went to the River Suite, probably the nicest room in the hotel, and the Hamilton's first choice, if it were available. It was the only suite to feature a separate sitting room. The other suites, while impressively large, didn't share the same layout.

It was unusual for Mr and Mrs Hamilton to be ordering a bottle of wine in the room at this time of day. More often than not, Mrs Hamilton ordered a pot of tea. She liked to have tea in the afternoon, and she often had it in her suite, alone. And Mr Hamilton was a fine man, an amicable man, unlike that French pup. They were poles apart.

"Come in, Seán," said Mr Hamilton, letting the porter inside.

"Shall I open this for you, sir?" he asked momentarily.

"Would you please?"

Alex rejoined his wife on the couch. They held hands. Seán had never seen an intimate gesture between the couple before.

"That was a tragic affair this afternoon, Seán. How are the Russell family?"

"They're still in shock if you ask me. It was a terrible business altogether. I'm not the better of it yet myself."

"Neither am I," Alex Hamilton confessed.

Seán withdrew the cork from the bottle.

"Shall I pour you a glass?" he asked.

"You can."

Seán poured the wine. He placed a glass in front of Laura. He placed a second glass in front of Alex Hamilton.

"Will you be trying your hand at a spot of fishing tomorrow, Mr Hamilton?"

"No. I think I had better spend some time with my wife. We have a birthday to celebrate, Seán. It was Mrs Hamilton's birthday yesterday."

Laura smiled. When she smiled, her face lit up. It was one of the first things that Alex had noticed about her.

"Belated Happy Birthday, Mrs Hamilton."

"Thank you, Seán. Mind you, I'm too old to look forward to birthdays any more. At my age, you want them to go away."

"Wait till you get to my age!" the porter said, and they all laughed.

"Mr Hamilton has my permission to go fishing tomorrow. I'll give him some time off for good behaviour, Seán."

"I'm spending the day with you, love."

"Alex, I want you to go. Why don't you fish in the morning? If you're back by lunch, we'll still have most of the day together."

"If you insist," he said good-naturedly. "I did offer not to go. Seán is my witness. You heard me, Seán."

"I'll back you up there, sir. Now, is there anything else I can get you?"

"No thank you, Seán. We have everything we need."

They did, didn't they, he thought. The Hamilton's were quite loved up this afternoon. He had noticed the way Laura looked at Alex. There was a softness about Mrs Hamilton today. She looked happier than he had seen her in a long time, all things considered.

Seán made his way back to reception, passing the French man's room as he did. Who had Jean-Pierre smuggled up to the room?

A thought occurred to Seán. There had been two large towels strewn across the bath but he had also seen two bath towels neatly folded on the couch. Someone had brought extra towels to the room when they weren't needed. He remembered passing Lucy on the corridor earlier that afternoon. Her arms had been stacked with towels. He had taken notice because she looked different to her usual self – sort of done up. Her hair was out of its usual ponytail and she had make up on. She looked very pretty, although he preferred the natural look himself.

"You're looking well today," he had told her.

Lucy had been making her way to Jean-Pierre's room. Seán was certain of it. He had the answer to his riddle. Come to think of it, didn't he see the pair of them having a bit of a snog a couple of summers back? He hadn't said a word to anyone, other than to tease the chambermaid. Management didn't approve of that sort of carry on between the guests and staff, and Seán hadn't wanted to get the lass into any trouble. She was only a slip of a girl, and she was far away from home. Besides, she was a gorgeous young thing. She was entitled to have a bit of fun. She worked hard enough.

Seán had a soft spot for Lucy. He was concerned for her now. What was she doing letting herself be messed about by that little pup? And why was she messing poor old Pawel about? He was a nice lad.

Seán was privy to the fact that Lucy and Pawel hadn't been getting on recently. They had been quarrelling a lot. Lucy had come to the porter in tears on more than one occasion. Sometimes, Seán felt he was a bit of a father figure to Lucy. He was correct in that assumption.

"Now dry your eyes," he had said gently. "I don't like to see you upset, Lucy. What's up lass?"

"Pawel and I are always fighting. It's getting me down," she'd confided.

"What's it about this time, Lucy?"

"Pawel wants to go back to Poland and I see our future here. I don't want to live in Poland. We have a better life in Ireland. It's not as if my family are living in Poland."

"That's a big problem all right," he'd said.

"Pawel wants us to go on our holidays to Poland. I want to go home."

"Can't you do both?" Seán had suggested.

She shook her head.

"We're not within easy commuting distance. Not for a short holiday. Besides, we went to visit his parents at Christmas. I don't really get on with his parents, especially his mother. His mother would prefer if Pawel had found a Polish girlfriend. It's complicated."

"It all sounds very tricky. It can't be easy for you, Lucy."

Obviously, they hadn't resolved their differences. Still, that didn't explain Lucy's behaviour today. That was a bit below the belt on Pawel. Seán certainly didn't condone Lucy's carry on.

CHAPTER ELEVEN

Yearned. That was the word. Laura yearned for her husband. It was late and they were in bed. She snuggled in beside Alex, one arm wrapped around him, relishing his nearness.

They hadn't made love. Not tonight. Not for the past seven years. How many nights was that? She tried to work out the exact number but her brain was addled.

That evening neither of them wanted to force the intimacy, better it progressed at its own pace. Yet for him, it was more than that. She was aware that he was hesitant. Maybe he had someone else in his life right now. Alex had drifted off to sleep, but Laura was lying in bed wide awake. He moved and she lifted her arm.

She wondered what time it was. Laura was thirsty. She had forgotten to bring a glass of water to her bedside. There was a bottle of water, two in fact, in the sitting room. As quietly as she could, she got up and tiptoed from the room.

After she had poured herself a glass of water, she sat into the armchair, with both legs curled up underneath her. There was a full moon that night. It dressed the river in soft focus, allowing for a barely-there shimmer. The trees had taken on a blackish hue and they grouped themselves differently. From her armchair vantage, Laura could see the boardwalk at Beat Two. Though beautiful, the forest and river had a kind of menacing air at night. It was as if everything that was familiar to her had taken on another character under the cover of darkness.

Revisiting her past, she recalled the first time that she had met Alex and smiled as she remembered the drama on the plane. The morning in question, she'd had a spectacular hangover, and he had spilt his coffee over her.

She could have sworn that the air hostess had given her a dirty look. And why was the air hostess looking at Alex sympathetically? Laura was the one who got burned. Well, nearly burned. It was only a drop or two of coffee, but it was scalding. The whole cup could have spilled on her. It was just her luck to be sitting beside a total eejit.

Laura had been so hung over that she had scarcely registered his good looks. Then, when she had seen Alex in the arrivals hall chatting with her father, she had groaned audibly. She was astonished to discover that the eejit in question was none other than Alex Hamilton

Fancy that. It was Alex Hamilton, all grown up. She remembered him as a little boy, that exasperating little boy who lived next door. She had recognised his father immediately. Mr Hamilton didn't appear to have aged much. She had always liked Mr Hamilton and his wife.

Laura had been working for the summer in London. She was nineteen. Summer over, she was returning to Dublin for the start of her second year at university. Her pals in London had given her a send-off the night before. She had been in bad shape when she boarded the flight.

Time passed and then, much to her annoyance, her father had invited the entire Hamilton family to her twenty-first birthday party without her permission.

"What did you go and do that for, Dad?" she had said crossly when she'd heard.

Laura was having a big party at home. Her parents had invited some of their friends and family along to celebrate the occasion.

"What have you got against the Hamiltons, Laura? I've been meeting up with Frank regularly since we bumped into each other that time at the airport. Alex is almost the same age as you. Besides, he used to be a great friend of your brothers."

Yeah, when they were five!"

"For Pete's sake, there's only the three of them. There must be at least ninety people coming to the house. What difference are the Hamiltons going to make?"

They were setting up a marquee in the back garden. Her parents were going all out. Realising that she sounded ungrateful, Laura back peddled.

"I'm sorry, Dad. Don't mind me," she had said, changing her tune fast. "Of course, it doesn't matter if they come. Mr and Mrs Hamilton are nice. It's their son who is so God damn annoying!"

"You won't even notice he's there, Laura."

But she did notice him, and so did every other girl in the room when Alex made his entrance. Even at a young age, Alex Hamilton made quite an impression.

"Who's that?" her friend Claudia had asked

"That's Alex Hamilton, our old next door neighbour," Laura had said, registering for the first time how attractive, how annoyingly attractive, he was.

"That's the 'eejit' that you were giving out about? Are you out of your head or what? If ever there was a ten, he's it."

Laura and Claudia marked all of the boys they encountered out of ten. Laura was gobsmacked.

How had she not noticed that he was so good-looking?

"I have to admit I was really hung-over when I met him," she had said by way of an explanation.

"Or blind. Every girl here has given him the once over. Yikes! He's heading in our direction. Laura, I'm telling you now, I'm more than happy to take him off your hands."

Alex made his way towards Laura and Claudia, with his parents in tow.

"Laura, Happy Birthday," he'd said.

"Thanks, Alex. And thanks for coming."

He looked surprised. Clearly, he hadn't forgotten their last encounter either.

"Hello. It's so nice to see you," she'd said, greeting his parents effusively.

Laura was trying to make a good impression. Much later, and to the envy of all her friends, he had asked her to dance. Claudia had made a play for him. Much to Laura's relief, he wasn't biting.

"Great party," he'd said.

"Thanks. I was a bit of a drama queen the last time we met. Sorry about that. I was hungover."

"No harm done. Forget it," he had said, admiring her green eyes for the second time. They were the colour of the sea.

She smiled. Her smile lit up her face.

"You have a great smile. Not that I got the chance to see it before," he'd said. His manner was deadpan, giving nothing away.

"You mean it's better than my sulky look," she had ventured playfully. Unabashed, she gave him a large scowl.

"Anything beats that look, believe me!" he said, grinning. "You nearly crushed me with that."

They both laughed. And that's how it had started. There on the dance floor, in a marquee in her back garden, at her twenty-first birthday party. She had fallen in love with the boy next door.

A thud of some sort had woken him. Alex turned to his side. Laura wasn't there. She must be in the bathroom.

For a moment, he didn't remember the events of the day, but then it all came flooding back. His memory jolted, he considered how his personal circumstances had changed within the past twenty-four hours. It had been a day out of the ordinary.

However, so many questions remained unanswered. Would they be able to rekindle their relationship? It would be a mammoth task, of that, he had no doubt. Laura had simplified everything when she had spoken earlier. As they sat in the garden underneath the blue hydrangea, she had made it sound easy. It was not that simple. After all of these years, would they be able to pick up the pieces again? Would he? His mind began to work overtime as he considered the dilemma he faced.

He had been having an affair with another woman for several months. Of course, he had decided to finish with Caroline. But he had also been planning on leaving Laura. It wasn't right to resume a physical relationship with Laura just because he intended leaving Caroline. There was nothing honourable about that.

Besides, would Laura really want to make love to him if she knew he had been sleeping with another woman for the past six months? He doubted it. No matter how much Laura blamed herself for the state of their marriage, he didn't think she could handle a revelation of that kind. Laura was only human. For that matter, would he even be capable of making love to his wife again? Did he desire her? This was, after all, the woman who had rejected him for years? He wasn't in love with her anymore. It was a conundrum.

He had been moved that afternoon, almost overwhelmed. Laura had finally reached out to him and he had taken the life-line. That afternoon, he and Laura had experienced real closeness again.

They had drunk their wine and talked easily, establishing an effortless camaraderie. Once, they had enjoyed a deep bond. That had been missing from their relationship for a long time. It was coming back. Or, so it had felt, the past couple of hours. She said she loved him. Could it be that he was still in love with her?

After a glass or two of wine, they had dressed and went down to dinner, popping into the hotel bar on their way, to confirm the fishing.

"I thought we might find you here," Alex had said, addressing Conor. The gillie was in his usual spot, propping up the bar with John. "Are we good to go tomorrow?" Alex had asked.

"Right as rain," Conor piped. "Evening, Mrs Hamilton."

His eyes dilated like ink on blotting paper.

"Thanks for the drink earlier, Alex," John had said. "It was good of you."

"You're welcome. How are you?" he'd enquired. "Have your recovered from your ordeal this afternoon?"

"A few of these have helped," John had said, picking up his glass.

"I'll bet. How are the Russell family?"

"Still in shock, if you ask me. There's a family member arriving tomorrow morning so at least Mrs Russell won't be on her own. She'll be down later with the children for a bite to eat. Jane has a table set up for them inside."

"That's where we're headed ourselves," Laura had said.

"We'll leave you both in peace," Alex had said. "I'll see you tomorrow morning about 9.30, Conor."

"Righty oh then, Alex."

The gillie was on time whatever he drank. Alex joked that he had a hollow leg.

"Another round for the two lads here," he'd told the bartender discreetly on the way out. "You can charge it to my room."

Alex spotted the Russells as soon as the family entered the dining room. They arrived as Alex and Laura were having their starters cleared.

"They've just come in," he had told Laura. "They're two tables behind you."

"We'll offer our condolences, but let's wait until we're leaving."

"It's a wonder they came down at all."

"She doesn't want to be here," Laura had said. "She's thinking of her children and that it might do them good to come downstairs for a while."

On their way out, Laura and Alex had stopped at the table.

"We wanted to offer our sympathy," Laura had told the family.

"Thank you," said Felicia. "It's been an awful shock."

Her omelette remained untouched. Alex thought that she seemed a little disorientated.

"Of course it has," Laura said. "To lose your husband so suddenly and in such dreadful circumstances is unimaginable. I'm so sorry for your loss."

"We both are," said Alex.

Felicia glanced in his direction.

"This is my husband, Alex," Laura had said, introducing Alex.

"I heard you were fishing on the river this afternoon," Felicia had replied, her voice tinged with sadness.

"I was on my way down to Beat Two, when it happened," he said. "We disbanded the fishing after that. If there's anything we could do to help, anything at all, we'd be glad to."

"Thank you," said Felicia. "That's very kind of you."

Alex and Laura didn't want to encroach on the family further, not when they were so obviously grief stricken. They had retired to their suite and gone to bed.

"Good night, love," Alex had said, before kissing Laura gently on the lips. He hadn't taken things further. That would be too pressurising. In some ways, it was daunting. It would be like making love to his wife for the first time. What would happen if it didn't go well? What would happen if she was unresponsive or worse still, if he messed up? He couldn't bear to dwell on that.

Alex was now fully awake. Fifteen minutes must have elapsed since he had woken. Laura hadn't come back. She was hardly in the bathroom.

He doubted whether he'd be able to get back to sleep. Maybe Laura was having the same difficulty. Could she be tossing everything around in her head?

Alex got up and made his way to the sitting room. His wife was standing beside the window.

"Laura?" he called out and she turned round.

"Hi. Can't you sleep either?" she said.

"I heard a noise and I woke up. Then, I couldn't get back to sleep again."

"Oh, I'm sorry. That was me. Something startled me, and I dropped the bottle of water on the table."

Laura hadn't put a light on. She stood there bathed in moonlight. Her night dress clung to her body.

"What startled you?" he asked.

"If I tell you, you'll laugh. You'll think I've lost the plot altogether."

"Try me," he pressed, thinking that in the dimness Laura looked like a young girl again.

"I was sitting on the armchair and looking out the window when some movement out there caught my attention."

"Where?"

"Over at Beat Two. For a moment, I thought I saw a figure out there on the boardwalk.

"Animal or human? Or, was it something else altogether?" he asked, bemused.

"I'm serious Alex. As a matter of fact, it looked like a woman. And come to think of it, there was something ethereal about her. She was dressed in a long white gown and she was standing on the edge of the boardwalk. I went to the window to have a closer look. In my haste, I knocked over the bottle. When I looked again she was gone."

"Maybe it was a trick of your imagination."

"I don't think so. I'm sure of what I saw. I'll tell you something, Alex, it felt real. For a moment, I wondered if it was Felicia Russell."

"In her nightdress? Hardly! Not in the middle of the night, at any rate, unless some primeval force had taken hold of her. But I doubt it."

"You're probably right," Laura said. "It's a little creepy at night. The forest I mean. I'd never venture down that river path at night. I'd be scared out of my wits. But I saw something or, should I say, someone. I know I did."

She gave an involuntary shiver. There was something very vulnerable about her. Alex had to admit that it was a vulnerability that he found alluring. He walked towards her. She really did look like the

Laura of old; the Laura he had first met, all those years ago.

She stood before him. Her neckline was low and her breasts were straining against the flimsy material, which clung visibly to her thighs too. He was aware of her on a physical level in a way he hadn't been for years. At first, he didn't realise the effect she was having on him. Almost without thinking, he caressed her face and as he did, he pulled a stray strand of hair back. It was an intimate gesture and one that ignited his fervour.

Out of nowhere, came an irresistible urge to kiss his wife. Alex pulled Laura toward him and kissed her, gently at first, but more passionately as the kiss progressed. He wanted her. She could feel his erection and it ignited her own physical response. She kissed him back as fiercely as she could. She touched him and he wanted to explode. With enormous effort, he pulled away.

"What is it, Alex?"

"I can't do this, Laura," he said with regret. "There's something that I need to tell you before we take this any further."

"Shhh," she said, placing a finger on his lips to quieten him. "It doesn't matter, Alex."

She reached out and drew him close to her. She lifted her head and kissed him again. She kissed him tenderly this time. He couldn't resist her.

"Let's take this into the bedroom," he said.

Before he knew it, they were both naked. She had whisked her night dress off and he had pulled down his pyjamas, kicking the bottoms off impatiently. They kissed again and fell onto the bed.

"Come here," he said gently as he lay on his back. Obediently, she straddled him. All thoughts of Caroline and of the other women who had been in his life over the past few years vanished. He was with Laura now. Laura was the only one he was thinking of.

He had been nervous about making love to his wife, but when it came to that, all his worries and anxieties dissipated. He could feel her moistness and that excited him more. He turned her over until he was on top, taking her with a passion that surprised them both.

"Laura," he cried out. "Oh God, Laura."

She climaxed seconds later underneath him. He could feel her body shudder. When it was over he held her, binding her close, both of them loathe to part.

He ran his finger along her collarbone and said, "I've missed you. How I've missed you."

"I never thought I'd feel this way again," she said and faltered.

For the next few minutes, she cried, letting go as she did, of a deep-rooted pain. Alex could feel his own tears, and he let them fall. The last time he cried had been when the pallbearers had lowered Rachel's coffin into the grave.

Down the corridor, and only a few rooms away, Felicia Russell lay wide awake in her bed. She too had been weeping. Her anguish had only begun.

Felicia had been grateful for the solitude of her bedroom. It gave her a chance to grieve openly. She didn't have to pretend.

Dinner had been an ordeal. The dining room was the last place she wanted to be, and she had felt exposed. Felicia wasn't up to facing anyone but her children needed to be fed, and they had been cooped up in her bedroom long enough. She had sat at the table looking at the spot where Harvey had died. What were his last thoughts? Had he any inkling he was going to die? He would have wanted her beside him. Was he frightened? That's when the silent screaming began in her head.

When her children had eventually gone to bed, she had retreated to her room. She remembered banging her forehead repeatedly on the bathroom door, raging against the unfairness of it all, before sliding into a heap on the bathroom floor, pitifully weeping. She lay there on cold tiles, tightly coiled like a spring. She cried until she was spent, consumed by grief and breath-robbing sobs.

And when there were no tears left to shed, she got up and lay on her bed, perfectly still. She stared at the empty pillow beside her. Only twenty-four hours earlier, she and Harvey had slept together in this bed. His head had lain on the pillow. A future had awaited them. A lifetime of memories remained to be built and shared, and stored with the ones that had preceded them. That future had been stolen from her. Harvey had been taken from her, suddenly and without warning. She was desolate, a broken woman.

She never had the chance to tell him how much she loved him, to tell him what happiness he had brought to her life. There was no chance to say goodbye. He couldn't be dead.

But Harvey was dead. He was gone forever. The thought of facing a life without Harvey devastated her. She loved Harvey. There had only ever been Harvey. Felicia didn't want to go on but she had no choice. Her children needed her now more than ever. Anna and Jack were her priority. Her poor, beautiful children had lost their father. To lose a parent at such a young age was an enormous blow.

The day Harvey died had been split into two: the before and the after. The before had been joyous and full of promise. The after would account for the saddest hours of her life.

Reliving her time with her husband earlier that day, she remembered Harvey's parting kiss on this very bed before he headed down to breakfast with Jack. She replayed lunch with the children in the bar. She hadn't kissed Harvey goodbye after lunch. Felicia regretted that.

She and Anna hadn't gone down to the river to see Harvey and Jack fishing. That was a bigger regret, and one that ate away at her now.

She had watched Harvey and Jack from the bedroom window. They had been so absorbed with the fishing that Felicia hadn't wanted to intrude. Who knows, if she had gone down, she might have stayed awhile. Felicia could have been with Harvey when he died. Was he in pain? Was he distressed? Her mind raced through these scenarios, torturing her. She could find no peace. She would never get over this.

The suddenness of Harvey's demise was overwhelming. Her mind and body were still struggling to absorb the shock of his death. That morning she had kissed Harvey. He was brimming full of life and eagerly anticipating the day ahead. That afternoon, as he lay in the ambulance, she had kissed her husband good bye forever.

That evening Harvey was on a mortuary slab in a hospital. Tomorrow morning an autopsy would be performed.

She would have given anything to hear his voice again. Already, she missed his presence dreadfully, the touch of his hand, his very nearness. She had anticipated that they would grow old together. They would have faced the milestones together: their children's birthdays, graduations, weddings, and even the birth of their grandchildren. Now, she would face these landmarks on her own.

She thought of the grandchildren she might have one day. They would never know their grandfather. Harvey would have enjoyed having grandchildren. He was a wonderful father. He would have made a wonderful grandparent.

In one afternoon, all those dreams had been shattered. They had been quashed in an instant. Their future together had fizzled out as quickly as a tablet dissolves in water. It was too cruel.

There was a history of heart disease in Harvey's family. She hadn't lost sight of that. She considered it now. Harvey's own father had died of a heart attack. But dear Lord, Harvey was only forty-nine. With that, Felicia began to weep again. It was dawn before she cried herself to sleep.

While she slept, she dreamed. She and Harvey were in some foreign place; the sky was very blue and Felicia could feel the heat on her skin. It seemed to be somewhere exotic because they entered a bazaar. There were people everywhere and there was a strange aroma. She couldn't quite make out what it was. Harvey was laughing. He was wearing a Panama hat and it suited him. Suddenly, they were running down a narrow alleyway, but from what or whom, Felicia didn't know. Next thing, they were sitting in a cafe and drinking espressos. Harvey was leaning over to kiss her. As he did, she woke up with a start. His lips had been cold, like they had been when she had kissed Harvey goodbye in the ambulance.

She awakened only to remember that Harvey was now dead. His death hit her all over again.

How could he be dead? He was here with her yesterday in this very bed, alive and well. This couldn't be happening. It couldn't be.

Felicia tried desperately to return to her dreams and to Harvey. The dream had seemed very real. She could feel Harvey's presence. She could see him and hear his voice. She had felt his lips on her mouth. Try as she did, she was unable to get back to sleep. She was unable to return to the Harvey of her dreams.

Checking her watch, she saw that it was already eight am. She would have to get up. There were certain practicalities to be dealt with. Harvey's first cousin, Richard, would be arriving soon. She wanted to huddle under the duvet and stay there. Her children needed her and so, with effort, she got out of bed. It took more effort than she thought.

She dressed but she was numb. Harvey was gone. He was gone forever. Harvey was dead and she was a widow.

She was stunned at her sudden bereavement. The anger would come later.

CHAPTER TWELVE

"Has James arrived?" Jane asked Maura. James was the general manager of the hotel. The breakfast rush was over and it was almost 10.30.

"He phoned earlier to say he wouldn't be in until this afternoon," Maura answered, throwing her eyes up to heaven. "Honestly, Jane, you'd swear he owned the place the way he carries on. He's got a handy number if ever there was one."

Maura was not alone in her opinion. Pretty much all of the staff, including Jane, felt the same way.

"The way that fellow saunters in and out of here, beggars belief. He doesn't do a stroke of work, if you ask me."

Jane smiled. Maura wasn't far off the mark.

"You have to pick up all the slack," Maura said. "It's not fair."

"Me and everybody else, and especially David," Jane said. "I mean, look at the poor man. I don't know how he manages to run the bar some days."

Popular with hotel guests, day trippers and fishermen, the bar was a big money spinner for the hotel. As well as lunch and dinner, a late breakfast was served.

"It's mayhem in there," Maura said. "David's rushed off his feet all day long, particularly this month, and that new fellow he has with him is still wet behind the ears."

"The restaurant is busy enough, but we're well staffed."

"I've yet to see James help out in the bar. God knows, he's in there often enough having a drink with the guests."

The general manager was affable enough, to the customers at any rate.

"It's beneath his lordship," Jane said. She trusted Maura. The receptionist had been working at the hotel for over a decade. She wouldn't be repeating what Jane said to the rest of the staff. "The Russells are in the dining room," she continued. "Mrs Russell looked as if she hadn't slept a wink. A relative of Mr Russell has joined them."

"I know the gentleman. He asked for directions to the dining room. He mentioned that he was meeting Mrs Russell."

"At least Mrs Russell has a family member with her," Jane said.

What's happening, or do you know?"

"They've carrying out an autopsy this morning to determine the cause of death. It's tricky as the family don't live in Ireland. Can you imagine something like this happening when you're on holiday?"

"It's beyond belief," Maura said. "They can't even grieve properly. They're in a hotel. It must be a nightmare for Mrs Russell."

"It's so invasive," Jane said. "How she sat through dinner last night I don't know. And she got those children down for breakfast in one piece. It must be very hard to do normal when your world has fallen apart."

"She has a quiet dignity about her, Jane. I'd be pumped up on Valium. With all that's happened, you'd think Lord Muck would have made the effort to come in."

Jane giggled.

"You'll call him that one day to his face, Maura."

"I won't. I need the job, Jane. I can only imagine what he said when you spoke to him yesterday."

"Hmm."

"Go on. Tell me. Put me out of my misery. "

"Let's say James was more concerned about getting a dead body out of the place than anything else. He thought it would be bad for business."

"Why doesn't that surprise me? He's all heart, is our James."

"He was concerned, but not concerned enough to make a guest appearance," Jane said dryly.

"You stayed on and it was your night off. You had to pick up the pieces. Again!" Maura emphasised the word. "It's amazing the way a polished accent and the right background can get you ahead in this country."

"You've a very smart manner with the guests, Maura," Jane teased.

"That's my reception manner. I can be very polished when needs be!"

"You're a pro," Jane said.

"I've had years of practise. Have you nearly finished inside?"

"We're expecting a couple of late comers to straddle in. I've seen a few pass since I've been here. I'd better go back inside and check that the orders are in."

"Here's a few more," said Maura. "The French crew has arrived."

Jane looked around. Jean-Pierre and his cronies were heading into breakfast.

"I'd better get back. I'll see you later."

Jane returned to the dining room. She arrived in time to seat Jean-Pierre and his companions at a table.

"Would you like tea or coffee?" she enquired after she had dispatched menus.

She quickly took the drinks order and gave it to Pawel.

"For table six, Pawel," she said, handing him the order.

The waiter had a face like thunder. Pawel had most definitely crawled out of the wrong side of the bed this morning. His manner was surly which was unlike him. Something was amiss.

"For heaven's sake Pawel, would you put a smile on," Jane told him crossly. "You'll put the customers right off their breakfast. You'd turn milk sour."

Jane surveyed the room. About a half a dozen tables remained occupied. Neither of the Hamiltons had made it down to breakfast. On the odd occasion, Mr Hamilton breakfasted alone, usually if he had an early start for fishing. Mrs Hamilton would appear later. She was not an early riser. In all the years that they had stayed at Doonmara, this was the first time that the Hamiltons hadn't appeared at breakfast.

Jane returned to Jean-Pierre's table to take the breakfast order. When the order went through to the kitchen, she went to check on the Russell family.

"Can I get anybody anything?" she asked.

The children looked at Jane vacantly. Felicia sat with her hands clasped.

"I'll have another coffee, please," Felicia said. Her voice was a murmur and her eyes were puffy. She looked wretched. *She's here and she's not here,* Jane thought.

"And so will I," said Harvey's cousin.

Jane returned quickly with two coffees. By then, Mrs Russell had pulled herself together. She thanked Jane for the coffee and introduced the guest at the table.

"This is my husband's cousin, Roger," Felicia said. "He would like to have a word with John later, if he could."

"I'm afraid John won't be in today," Jane informed them.

John had been shaken after the events of the previous afternoon. He had asked to change his days. Jane didn't tell Mrs Russell that.

Instead she said, "He's not on the roster until tomorrow."

"Maybe we could get a phone number for him if that was possible," Roger said. "I wanted to thank him personally," he explained.

"I can organise that, sir. I'll leave his number at reception for you. Is there anything else I can help you with?" Jane asked Felicia.

"We won't be able to see my husband until later this afternoon," Felicia said, choosing her words carefully. "We'll stay in the hotel this morning, Jane. There's a lot to be done."

Jane nodded her head sympathetically. She wondered what the funeral arrangements were.

"The funeral is in Dublin," Felicia said, answering her unasked question. "My husband's body will be moved to Dublin once they have completed the autopsy this morning. That's where he is from and the children are at school there, but we've been living in Lisbon for a couple of years. My husband has a diplomatic posting in Lisbon. I'm not Irish so the logistics of it all are a bit complicated."

"I can imagine," said Jane, thinking that Seán hadn't got the Lisbon connection wrong after all. "Where are you from?"she enquired politely.

"I'm from Sussex. All of my family will have to travel over."

"If we can do anything to help, let me know," Jane told her. "Don't worry about checking out this morning. You can hold the rooms until whatever time needs be, Mrs Russell."

"You're very kind. Thank you for that. The children might prefer to stay in their rooms this morning. We have a lot of phone calls to make."

Felicia hadn't contacted anyone at the embassy yet. She was going to let Roger make that phone call. She thought of the upheaval in their lives that would surely follow. They would have to move house. Move country. She would have to take the children out of boarding school because she wouldn't be able to afford the fees now. How was she going to afford to pay for anything, for that matter?

Had Harvey a large life insurance policy? They had never discussed it. She thought he had something. Would she be entitled to any financial assistance from the embassy? What would Harvey's pension entitlements cover now that he was dead?

She would have to go back to work, more than likely. Good God, she hadn't worked for fifteen years. Why had she taken their lives for granted? Why? She felt the panic rise again. She was petrified of what the future might entail.

There was the sound of crockery clattering loudly on the floor. Felicia looked up, startled. Jane turned round. Jean-Pierre was standing up, wiping what looked like the remnants of scrambled eggs off his pants. Pawel was shuffling on his feet.

"If you'll excuse me, Mrs Russell," Jane said, and headed in the direction of the Frenchman.

"Are you all right, Jean-Pierre?" she said.

The old staff referred to Jean-Pierre by his Christian name, even Jane. After all, she had known him since he was a child.

"It was entirely my fault," Jean-Pierre said graciously, and much to the restaurant manager's surprise. Jean-Pierre was being very good humoured. It was unlike the Frenchman. His up and coming nuptials must have mellowed him. "I didn't see the waiter arrive with my breakfast. I stood up as he was putting my plate down."

Jean-Pierre's entire breakfast had been dropped on him. The French man was fastidious about his appearance. His immaculately pressed white shirt looked like a war zone. A broken plate, along with remnants of a full Irish were scattered on the wooden floor, and bits of scrambled egg and tomato had hit the table. Jane could have sworn that she saw Pawel smirk. He escaped to the kitchen before she could have a word with him.

"We'll get this tidied up immediately, Jean-Pierre. Shall I move you all to another table? It looks as if the table cloth hasn't escaped," she said light-heartedly.

"We're fine here, Jane. But I'd better go and change."

"Very well. I'll put through another breakfast order for you."

"Actually, I've gone off the idea of a full Irish breakfast," he said. "Can I have another coffee and some more toast please? I'll back be in a few moments," he told the others.

Jean-Pierre made a humiliating exit from the dining room. Pawel had toppled the plate on purpose. Jean-Pierre hadn't reacted and his friends would be wondering why. They had all seen what had happened. He hoped Olivier wouldn't breathe a word.

Jean-Pierre hadn't rebuked the waiter. He knew that he was lucky to have got off so lightly, especially with Marie's brother in attendance. It was a small price to pay. He hoped that Pawel hadn't any more surprises planned.

Laura Hamilton got out of the bath and towelled herself down. She had been luxuriating in the tub for over twenty minutes, and reminiscing. She could scarcely believe that she and Alex had made love, and not just once.

Every nerve in her body had tingled. Her emotions had been pared right back. The sex that had followed was liberating and elemental.

"Is this what you want?" he'd demanded.

"Yes," she had whimpered.

"How much?" he'd teased, knowing he was in control and enjoying the moment.

"I really want it." Her voice was low.

"You want me to fuck you, don't you?"

She couldn't get enough of him. She threw her legs around his waist trying to bind him even closer. He paused. She thought that he was going to stop altogether. He didn't resume, even though she was thrusting herself at him wildly. She thought he didn't want her anymore. It was unbearable.

"Don't stop," she had begged. "I want you to fuck me." To her immediate relief, he began again, slowly at first, driving her mad with desire.

She had said things that she thought she would never say, or had ever said before, not once in all of their married life. She would have been willing to let him violate her in any way, as long as he didn't stop.

He had increased the tempo. Unable to hold back the tide, she climaxed. As she did, she shook uncontrollably.

Alex hadn't stopped. He rolled over until she lay on top of him. He had taken his time. He sucked and bit at her nipples until the pain was almost exquisite. Then he'd pushed her buttocks up and down against his body, faster and faster, to accommodate his own rhythm. He thrust away until he was ready to orgasm himself. When he was, he had flipped her over and entered her roughly again from behind, and pushing furiously this time, harder than before.

He called out her name before he imploded inside her. Then, he collapsed beside Laura on the bed. She had felt the warmth of him seeping down her thigh.

He had cradled her in his arms afterwards. She had burst into tears. She had cried for several minutes.

"Hush now," he had said in a gentle voice. "It's all right, love."

"I don't know what came over me," she'd said, moved.

It had been an incredible start to the day. Laura could still feel his arms around her, holding her tightly. It felt familiar but new.

"I'll cancel the fishing," he'd said.

"No, go, Al. I insist. But why don't we phone down and order some breakfast in the room."

"There's an idea." He had dialled room service and ordered breakfast. Then he turned to her and said "Laura, I'm lost for words. That was something else."

"For me too," she'd said.

A tear escaped, and then, another.

"Come here," he had said, and Laura slid into his arms. He stroked her head gently. "Tears, again?"

"These are happy tears," she had replied. "It's as if I'm emotionally stripped."

He could empathise with her. An emotional dam had burst for both of them. An element of hope surged within him. What if they could overcome the past?

All the years of frustration, sadness and hurt had been obliterated in their lovemaking. It had felt like a baptism of fire. The passion she had for him, shocked him, as it had shocked Laura. She had been calling the shots and controlling the way their life had run for so long. That morning, Alex felt he was in command of his life again.

Slowly, it was becoming clear that Laura did love him. It wasn't simply words to that effect. If he had been in any doubt, then this morning had shown him otherwise. Last night had been wonderful in its own way, but he had thought it might be a once off. This morning changed everything. It renewed his confidence in himself as Laura's husband and lover.

A day previously, he wouldn't have thought any of this was achievable. They hadn't been intimate for many years and Alex had believed they would never get past that. It had seemed an impossible task. Somehow, they had.

She asked, "And you. How are you feeling?"

"Never better," he said, and turning her face upwards, he kissed her gently on the lips.

"I will never forget this morning," she said. "I couldn't get enough of you."

"I wanted you so much, too."

"I feel raw, but centred, calmer."

"It was wonderful," he said and smiled fondly at her. "To be honest, I wasn't sure if we'd be able to resume a sexual relationship. I couldn't get my head around it. It's been so long, Laura."

He had reached for her and she had taken the lifeline. Finally, after all those years of loss, grief and loneliness, they had made love, and it had been magical.

Laura wanted him. He was in no doubt about that. She needed him and that felt good. In fact, it felt bloody marvellous.

"I'm a little punch drunk," she said, and he chuckled appreciatively.

Content, they both lay side by side for a while, savouring the moment. Before long, Seán arrived with their breakfast. Laura and Alex sat on the couch, dressed in the towelling robes that the hotel supplied, and ate their breakfast.

"This is a first," said Alex. "I'm enjoying this."

"Me too." She looked at him tenderly. "I can't believe you're not gagging for a cigarette," she said good-naturedly.

"I could murder a cigarette right now," he admitted.

"I could do with one myself!"

His grin broadened.

"I'm going to try and cut down."

She threw her eyes up to heaven.

"Seriously, Laura. I mean it. Seeing that man die yesterday has knocked a bit of sense into me."

"Good." She remained unconvinced.

"So, tell me. Do you really think you saw someone last night?"

"Ah, my white lady! Yes, I'm sure of what I saw."

"How could you tell that she was dressed in white? There may have been a full moon last night, but the light wasn't that good."

"I can't answer that but I do know that she was dressed in white. She gave me goose bumps."

"I can only imagine."

"I wonder why she appeared."

"I guess you'll never have the answer to that question either," he said. "If she makes an appearance on the river this morning, I'll let you know."

"Very funny." She smiled sarcastically.

"I had better grab a quick shower before I go," he said as he got up off the couch.

The time was ten past nine but Alex made no move to leave the room. He looked lovingly in her direction. Her heart melted because it had been years since her husband had looked at her like that.

The next moment he said, "We have a lot of years to make up for. The fishing can wait a while. I'll phone down and reschedule Conor."

A fantasy was already playing in his head. Something she had said earlier had sparked it off. Laura understood. No further words were necessary. She got up, as eager as he was, and she went straight to the bedroom. He phoned reception.

By the time he had taken off his robe, she was lying naked on the bed, with her legs spread. She was already moist and it was a real turn on. He buried his head in that moistness, and he began to do what she said she had wanted earlier. She groaned with pleasure and it excited him enormously. He had a sense of control he hadn't experienced in years and it was intoxicating.

She begged him to enter her. He held off until he thought she would go crazy. Her body was putty in his hands. Neither of them was in any doubt about who was in charge. Laura may have got her 'mojo' back but it was Alex who was handling the reins. That morning, he experienced the best sex of his life.

After it was over, he got up and showered. As Laura lay in bed, nagging thoughts crept into her head. She couldn't bear the thought of losing him again to someone else. She would never share Alex with anyone again.

Up until then, Laura hadn't a possessive bone in her body. Not when it came to Alex. This morning, that changed. Remorseful that she had driven Alex away, Laura promised herself that she was going to make it up to him, starting from today.

The barriers had been shunted aside on that bed. The transition from a sexless relationship into what had transpired this morning astounded her. Today, she had lots of possibilities. Yesterday morning, she had nothing.

Alex had intended to leave her. He had told her that. What a difference a day makes!

Later, Laura had picked up a newspaper from reception, intending to read it in the sitting room.

"Can I order an Americano?" she asked Maura. "I'll be sitting in the lounge."

Laura wasn't alone. Felicia Russell's son, Jack, was examining books from the cabinet.

"Hello," Laura said.

"Hi," he responded shyly. He was obviously looking for something and having difficulty.

"Are you looking for anything in particular? Can I be of help?" she asked.

"I'm looking for the hotel fishing log. The gillie was talking to my dad about it."

"Oh, I know the log you're referring to. My husband had it out once or twice. Look, there it is on the top shelf."

She stood on her tiptoes and pulled the logbook down from the shelf. She handed it to the boy.

"My great grandfather's name is in there somewhere," he explained. "He used to fish here with the Maharaja."

"Did he really? How exciting. That was back in the 1920s. That was when the Maharaja lived here. Shall I help you look for him?"

"Would you? I think my mum would like to see it. It might cheer her up a little."

"I'd love to," Laura said, hoping that it would cheer this little fellow up too. "Let's sit over there beside the fire. We'll find his records together. What was your great grandfather's Christian name, do you know?"

"His name was Fred."

They poured over the records, starting in 1920 and working their way forward from that date.

"Gosh, there seems to have been loads of salmon caught in those days," Jack said.

"I've heard that supplies were a lot more plentiful then," Laura said.

"They were big too. Here's one weighing twenty-two pounds!"

"That's a bit of a whopper all right," she said, before turning the page.

"There he is! There's his name, right there," Jack said excitedly, pointing to an entry half-way down the page.

"You're right, Jack. Here it is. *'Dr Fred Russell. One salmon, weight twelve pounds,'*" he read aloud. "The date is July 2nd, 1928. And see, there's the Maharaja's entry right beside it."

"Wow! My dad would have loved to have seen this."

"I'm sure he would have. I think that he would be very happy that you got to see it."

"Do you think so?"

"I'm certain of it."

He looked pleased. Laura turned the page.

"There's another entry, and another," the boy said in wonderment.

"Your great grandfather was a very good fisherman," she noted. "My husband has been fishing here for the past two years and he's only managed to catch one fish."

Jack giggled. Laura was delighted to hear him laugh.

"Jack, here's another entry with the name Russell. But it's a Nancy Ann. See here."

Jack leaned forward to have a closer look.

"Was she a relative of yours?" Laura asked.

"I've never heard of her before."

"Here's another listing for her. Your great grandfather's name is there too, just underneath. They both caught a salmon on the same day. They must be related. Maybe it was your great grandmother?"

"I don't think so. Dad would have said. My great grandmother died in childbirth, but that's all I know."

All through the summers of 1927, 1928 and 1929, the names of Fred and Nancy Ann Russell made a regular appearance on the log entries.

"Her name stands out, doesn't it?" she said. "Not too many women are listed here."

"Yeah, it does. I wonder who she was."

"It would be nice to find out. Anyway, Jack, we'll leave the page open here and you can show it to your mum and to your sister."

A moment or two passed and then he said hesitantly, "Can I ask you something?"

"Of course you can."

She smiled sympathetically. He wavered.

"Fire away," she said.

"You know when someone dies."

"Yes," she said encouragingly.

"How long does the pain last?"

"Do you mean for the person left behind?"

He nodded. That was the moment that Laura realised her own pain had lifted. The loss of Rachel no longer weighed her down. Laura considered her reply carefully. She needed to put this in context. Jack was only a young boy.

His loss was very different to hers. She had lost a child. That was the worst loss that could be inflicted on anyone. Yet, to lose a parent this young was a loss of huge magnitude.

Laura didn't want to frighten the child so she said, "You will feel different emotions, Jack. You will feel sad, and then you might feel angry. After a while, you will find that you can accept that your dad has passed away. The intensity of your feelings will lessen over time."

"But how long does it take?" he pressed. "How long will I feel like this?"

"It's different for everyone, Jack. You will feel a whole lot better in a few months. You will feel sad about your dad but you won't be feeling like you do today. That's for sure. What you are experiencing now is huge loss. And that grief is a bit overwhelming, isn't it?

He nodded his head.

"Your mind and body got a dreadful shock yesterday. It takes time for a person to absorb that kind of shock to the system. Does that make any sense?"

"I know what you mean. I'm still trying to take it all in."

"You could be in shock today as well. You will have some bad days ahead. There will be days when you feel sad, and the grief hits you hard. Days like your dad's birthday," she said.

"Or, like Christmas day or my birthday?"

She nodded.

"That's common. Grief is sometimes triggered by reminders such as anniversaries or places. It's an emotion that sends a vague alert to help you to remember, rather than to forget. Even so, what most people do is attempt to forget and to get over it, which is quite contrary to the purpose of that emotion. Rather than try to forget, you should attempt to remember."

"I'm not sure I understand," he said.

"You can remember what you learned from your dad and remember what you enjoyed doing together. And you can cry if you feel like crying. You will miss your dad on those days and for the first year or two especially. After that, it gets a little easier."

If only it had been that simple for me, she thought.

"Did someone you love ever die?" he asked.

She took a deep breath. She rarely spoke about Rachel to people who hadn't known the child. Today, it didn't seem as painful.

"My little girl died."

He looked at her thoughtfully

"What age was she?"

"My daughter died a week before her fifth birthday. Her name was Rachel."

"Gosh. I suppose I'm lucky in one way. I had my dad until I was nearly fourteen. He helped to form my character. My dad helped me to see things in a certain way. If I had been only five, I might not have been able to remember him."

"I think you might be right about that," she said, touched by his words.

"Do you still miss her?"

"I miss Rachel every day. But you know, when someone you love dies, they don't disappear altogether."

"What do you mean?"

"Their memory stays with you. It's like you carry part of them with you and that's comforting."

"I feel that way about my dad already."

"You'll always feel your dad's presence."

"I was afraid that I would forget my dad."

"You won't. I can promise you that."

"I'd like to come back here one day. He loved it here. He said so."

"Did he?"

"Yes, right before he died. He talked about how beautiful it was. He said that it was a magical day."

"Many people die in awful circumstances, Jack. Your dad died somewhere that he thought was very special. He was doing something he loved and he was with you. He died quickly and in no pain. I know that won't bring him back but it is something. We all wish for that for ourselves and for the people we love."

"I didn't see it like that before. How did Rachel die?"

She hesitated briefly before saying, "It was an accident, Jack. My daughter's death was an accident. It was very sudden. It was nobody's fault."

"That's sad. She was only little," he said with feeling.

Laura had all the answers for Jack. She'd had none for herself when Rachel had died. There was an irony to it.

"Thank you," he told Laura. "It's been helpful talking to you."

"Hello," someone said, interrupting their conversation.

Laura looked over her shoulder. Felicia was standing inside the door. Laura wondered how much of the conversation she had overheard.

"Mum, you've got to see this. Look what we've found," Jack said.

Felicia joined her son on the couch. Laura immediately moved to allow her to sit between them.

"What is it, Jack? What am I looking at?"

"Dad's grandfather. His name is here. It shows the number of fish he caught and how much they weighed."

"You clever boy! Let's have a look."

Jack placed his forefinger under an entry.

"Yes, I see his name. That's amazing. Your dad would have been so pleased."

"*'Dr Fred Russell,'* Jack read out proudly. "*One salmon, weight 10 lbs. July 15th, 1929.'*"

"Isn't that something," his mother said. Her voice wobbled. She started to cry and he looked at her with concern. "I'm sorry, Jack. I'll be fine in a moment. It's just that this would have meant so much to your father."

"Look at this, Mum," he said and turned the page back. "A Nancy Ann Russell is listed alongside my great grandfather's name."

Felicia looked at the entry, puzzled.

"It isn't your great grandmother. Her name was Bride. That I remember. I wonder who Nancy Ann was?"

"Nancy Ann's name appears a lot," Laura said.

"Your dad would have known, I suspect" Felicia said, thinking that she would never have the opportunity of asking Harvey this and a thousand other questions. It made her very sad.

"Do you think Roger might know?" Jack said.

"Let's ask him anyway. We might be in luck."

"I'm going to ask him now," Jack said, jumping up. Off he went to find Roger.

"Is your husband's family from around these parts?" Laura said.

"They are. My husband's grandfather lived a couple of miles from here. But there was a bit of a family fall out back in the day. Harvey wasn't told too much about his grandfather. Any discussion about the old man was off limits as far as my husband's father was concerned.

"I know a little about him. He was the local doctor. I believe he was a frequent visitor to Doonmara. He used to fish here when the Maharaja was in residence."

"How interesting," Laura said. "They must have been extraordinary times for Doonmara. I've heard that the Maharaja lived in rather splendid opulence."

"Apparently he did. It must have been fascinating to witness. There must be some great stories. We came here once before, you know. Harvey and I.

"So your husband said."

"Oh, it was years ago, right after we first married. We fell in love with the place and promised each other that we would return some day. We even traced the old family home where Harvey's father grew up."

"And this was your return visit?"

"Yes. The years flew by and our good intentions to return went with them. You know how it is. This summer, we said we'd finally do it. As a matter of fact, today we intended to bring the children to see the house where their grandfather was born. We were going to try and find the graveyard where their great grandfather was buried. Instead, I'm bringing my husband home to Dublin in a coffin. I'll be burying my husband the day after tomorrow."

"It's a cruel twist of fate," Laura said. "My heart goes out to you." Laura only knew too well that Felicia wouldn't get back to 'normal' for a very long time. Grief was a long haul business and offered no tidy conclusions. However, loss was intrinsic to life.

Felicia bit her lip. Her hands were clasped, and her fingers interwoven.

"Your son told me something that might be of some comfort," Laura continued.

"What did he say?"

"Right before he died, your husband commented on how much he was enjoying the fishing. He told Jack it was a magical day in a beautiful setting."

"I didn't know Harvey said that."

"So your son told me. And I said that your husband had died instantly, with someone he loved, doing something he was enjoying, and in a place he found very special."

"That doesn't bring him back. Nothing or no one can bring him back and my heart is broken. But what you're saying is consoling. Thank you. And thank you for talking to my son."

CHAPTER THIRTEEN

John had asked for the roster to be changed. Jane had been accommodating but that was typical of Jane. James Mansfield was a different kettle of fish altogether.

"He's a bit plastic," John had said to Conor." The man's not genuine at all."

"You're on the money there," Conor said. "Mind you, Mansfield's a good fisherman. I'll say that for him."

"I'll give him that," agreed John grudgingly.

"And he's good with the punters. He rubs them up the right way."

"That's a skill, is it? Sure any old fool could do that."

Unaccustomed to having a Saturday free, John was at a loose end. Weekends were the busiest days of the week at Doonmara. Seldom had he Saturday off.

"Why don't you visit your mother," his wife, Nora, had suggested.

Nora had her own routine on a Saturday morning. It was her morning for her yoga class. She looked forward to the class and she wasn't about to change her plans.

"I might do that," he said. "I haven't popped over in a while. I'm due a visit."

A little after eleven, John got into his car and made the journey to the nursing home. It took him almost an hour to get there.

"How is she?" he had asked the nurse earlier that morning. He had phoned in advance to tell them that he was coming.

"She's comfortable. There's little change."

"Okey-dokey. I'll be out this morning to visit her."

"Oh, there is one thing. Your mother has started singing to herself,"

"That's a surprise! She was never one for singing."

"There you are then. She's very fond of one particular tune."

"Which one?"

"It must be an old song because none of us are familiar with it."

When John arrived, he went straight to his mother's bedroom. He kissed her hello. She looked at him with no recognition. Five years previously, she had been diagnosed with Alzheimer's.

He sat with her for a while, holding her hand. She was dressed, and she sat in a chair alongside him. His mother looked frail. Once she had been a plump woman. These days, she didn't weigh much at all.

"Susan and Mary are getting on well," he said. "Susan has gone to America for the summer. Her exam results came and she's passed everything with flying colours."

His mother didn't comprehend but this was how he went about his visits. John would chat away, telling his mother the family news, updating her on how both granddaughters were. It was the only way that he could cope with his mother's Alzheimer's.

Previously, his mother had doted on her granddaughters. She had been a strong, dependable figure in the girls' lives. John had struggled with her diagnosis in the early years. Really struggled.

On his way out, John passed the day room. He spotted Conor's grandfather, sitting upright and having a cup of tea. He went over to say hello.

"Good day to you, John," Tom Price said, recognising the gillie immediately. "How are things up at the castle?" he enquired. He retained a keen interest in the goings on at Doonmara.

"We had a bit of a tragedy down at Beat Two yesterday," John said and outlined what happened.

"That's dreadful altogether," Tom said.

"The chap's name was Russell. Apparently, his grandfather used to fish at Doonmara with the Maharaja."

"That's a long way back, begorrah." His voice, though audible, was not loud.

"That's right," John said, straining to hear him. "He was the local doctor, I believe."

The old man was thinking carefully about what he had heard. He was going over the past, retracing the years.

"I remember him now," he said eventually. "Dr Russell. Fred Russell. He was a decent man." He spoke slowly and in a measured way.

John marvelled that the old man could remember Dr Russell. It had been such a long time ago, and he must have met hundreds of fishermen during his days at Doonmara.

"I have to hand it to you, Mr Price. You've got one hell of a memory. You put me to shame!"

The difference between the old man and his mother hit him hard. Once you'd lost your memory, you'd lost everything.

The old man smiled at him before saying, "He's the kind of fellow you'd remember, especially after what he went through."

"Oh, is there a story there?"

"Indeed there is. Not many people knew. It was never spoken about."

That made John all the more curious.

"Go on, tell me. I'm all ears," he said, pulling his chair nearer to the old man.

"As I recall events," Tom Price began, when he was unceremoniously interrupted by a nursing aid.

"The doctor will see you now, Tom," she said. "I'm afraid you'll have to come back another day," she told John. "It's time for us to go."

"I'll do that," he said, reluctant to leave. He didn't get to hear what had happened to Dr Fred but it certainly aroused his interest.

"Did your mother sing?" the nurse asked him on his way out.

"No, not today," he replied.

"How was she?" his wife asked later that day.

"She's started to sing."

"Really?"

"Some old song, the nurse said. They don't know what tune it is. My mum can't feed herself and she's incontinent. She doesn't know me, or indeed, any of us for that matter. Somehow it's comforting to hear that she is singing. It made me happy to hear that. I think it might comfort her too, in some small way."

"Come here to me you," his wife said. She opened her arms and gave her husband a hug. "It must be tough visiting your mother. It takes a lot out of you. I should have gone with you this morning."

"Stop there, Nora. You're great with mam and you always have been. As it is, you visit her more than I do."

"Be that as it may, I know it's hard for you."

"There's sadness in my heart but you have to get on with life."

"Tell you what, John. Why don't we splash out and go out for a bite to eat? You could do with a little pampering today."

"You're on." he said. "I hope it never happens to me. The Alzheimer's I mean."

"Or to any of us," Nora said.

"If I started to lose my marbles, I'd want to shoot myself. I wouldn't want to end out my days like my mother"

"Don't be fretting, John. There's no point in worrying about something that hasn't happened. Besides you'd probably forget to shoot yourself."

He laughed.

"You know what?" he said. "You're a tonic, so you are."

Alex Hamilton was enjoying a late lunch with his wife in Roundstone. The picturesque harbour village was a couple of miles drive from Doonmara and a popular spot with tourists.

"How's the new rod?" Laura asked. Her hair was pushed off her face by a pair of sunglasses perched on top of her head. She wore the gold locket around her neck and gold hoop earrings.

"It's much better than the one I had. It was great to get the chance to try it out."

"What do you fancy?"

"Seeing as how I didn't catch anything, I'll have a fresh salmon sandwich," he said, scanning the menu.

"You caught me and make no mistake about that," she joked. "Anyway, there's always, tomorrow. The fishing season ends soon. You might as well get one last bit of fishing in before we head back."

The season ended the last day of September. They would hardly get back up to Connemara before then, she thought.

"Yet again, I'm sorely tempted," he said.

"And I'm tempted by the fresh mussels!"

Their waitress returned with two glasses of white wine and they gave her their order. Laura took up the thread of the conversation.

"You've given me this afternoon, and you didn't get the chance to go out yesterday."

"Ah, but this is a special weekend for us. I don't want it to be all about me."

"We can compromise. Let's do what we're doing now. Why don't you go out tomorrow morning and I can have you all to myself for the rest of the day."

"You drive an easy bargain, Mrs Hamilton."

"It's no hardship. I'm happy to go for a walk and read the Sunday papers. We can head back late."

Laura was apprehensive about going home. Would their life retreat to what it was? Could one weekend change everything? She needed to concentrate on the present and to live in the moment. For the remainder of the day, she would box the past into a corner of her mind.

"What if we stay another night," he suggested. "What do you think?"

"Are you sure?" she said sounding pleased. "Can you swing it at work?"

"There have to be some perks to being the boss," he said. "Besides, I let you down on Thursday. I missed your birthday. This is my way of making it up to you. Let's stay tomorrow night. We can head back first thing on Monday."

"Let's," she said, delighted with the change of plan.

They had managed to grab a window table and were rewarded with a view of the harbour and mountains. The setting was spectacular. While they waited for lunch, Laura told Alex of her earlier encounter with Jack – how she had helped the boy to find the entries in the fishing log.

"I'm sure it meant a lot to him," he said.

"I think it did. He was pretty low in himself. He wanted to know had someone I loved ever died. He asked how long it would take to get over losing someone."

"What did you tell him?"

She hesitated. She wanted to keep a lid firmly on that box. Their new-found harmony was fragile.

A waitress arrived with their food. It gave Laura a moment to consider her reply. She would have to be honest with her husband, even if it meant opening that box, revisiting the past. He deserved that.

"I told him about Rachel. I said that I miss her every day. I told him that when someone dies you don't lose them altogether. You carry their memory with you. Then he asked me how she died."

Alex looked at her expectantly.

"I told him it was an accident," she said. "I meant it, Alex. Rachel's death was an accident. I don't blame you. It could have happened as easily had she been with me that day."

"Do you really mean that?"

"If I'm honest, I didn't believe that when it happened. Not initially. In the aftermath, I told myself it never would have happened if I had been there.

Even now, I find that hard to admit. I should never have blamed you."

"I blame myself, Laura. I was her dad. I should have been able to protect her."

"Alex, I felt like I had failed her as a mother."

"I felt like I failed to protect you too, Laura," he said, and paused for a moment. "I failed to protect my family. You see that was how I saw my role. I failed at being a husband as well as a father."

"Oh, Alex. Don't say that. You were a wonderful dad to Rachel. And you were always a great husband."

He looked at her directly. He was about to say differently.

"You are a great husband," she said, meeting his eyes. "You're not going to get me to change my mind, so don't even go there."

She read the torment in his eyes. She correctly read the guilt.

"Alex, you spoke a moment ago of how you had failed as a husband because you couldn't protect me. You said that was your role."

"Yes," he agreed. "That's how it was for me."

"I meant what I said yesterday," she said. "I felt like I had failed you as a wife. You were only thirty-eight when Rachel died. You were still relatively young and I couldn't give you another child. There was no hope of that," she said, referring to her last failed pregnancy.

Laura had a miscarriage before Rachel was born, followed by two ectopic pregnancies after Rachel. There was no chance of her having a natural pregnancy. One of her fallopian tube had been removed, and the other was badly damaged.

"You loved being a father. You'd have loved more children. I thought that I had failed, not only as a mother, but as your wife. That's part of the reason I couldn't respond to you, or reach out to you. I felt bad that I couldn't give you another child."

"You pleaded with me once to go off and have a baby with someone else," he said. "Do you remember what I told you?"

"You said that you only wanted to have a child with me."

"I meant it, Laura."

"I believe you. I went a bit loopy. I said that to you yesterday. I couldn't handle my own pain; let alone yours. I couldn't reach out to you, or to anyone. I was crippled."

"You scared me, Laura," he said. "I wanted to help you but I couldn't. I couldn't protect you. Sometimes, I think that the past is like a noose around our necks."

"I can't argue with that. I want to move on from all of the bad stuff that happened between us. We've both suffered enough."

"Do you think it's as easy as that, Laura?"

"I don't know. That's what scaring me right now because I don't want to lose you again. When I was talking to Jack, I realised that the pain of losing Rachel, that mind-numbing grief, had gone. It had lifted. That's huge. I don't want to oversimplify things, Alex, but what happened yesterday has been a catharsis."

"Maybe you're right," he said, and considered her words. "Maybe yesterday was a catharsis. Last night and especially this morning, makes me believe that we stand a chance. I definitely felt that we recaptured something. I don't want to lose that either."

"It reminded me of what it was like when we first got together. You know, that initial mad attraction, where we couldn't keep our hands of each other."

"I remember," he said, grinning from ear to ear. "We had nowhere to go. Our folks never left the house."

"God, yes. They were always at home. I tried to sneak you into my room one night. Do you remember?

"How could I forget? We were barely in the door when your father went to use the bathroom. I was so terrified he'd find me that I dashed down the stairs and legged it."

She laughed.

"You had a silver Honda," she said.

"We spent a lot of time in that car!"

This time they laughed together.

"It was a great car. I was very fond of that car," he said.

"Me, too. I want to make a toast. To the present, and to us," she said as she picked up her glass of wine.

"To us. To the here and now," he said, and clinked glasses. "Let's dig in. I'm famished."

"You can't be," she replied, and her manner was flirty.

He was tickled pink. It was years since they had shared a sexual innuendo.

"This is nice," he said, and smiled back at his wife.

Then he tucked into his food. Laura Hamilton ate her mussels with relish, but there was little doubt that her appetite for life had been whetted too.

Later that afternoon, they returned to Doonmara. The Russell family were saying goodbye to Jane when Alex and Laura walked into reception.

Felicia was smartly dressed, as were the children. Her make up was carefully applied and she had styled her hair.

That struck a chord with Laura. She had been exactly the same with Rachel. On the day of Rachel's funeral, Laura had arranged for someone to come to the house to do her hair and make-up. Laura wanted to have the funeral perfect for Rachel, and that had meant every tiny aspect, down to Laura's hair and makeup.

Alex had been aghast.

"Why are you worried about your hair and makeup? Our daughter is dead. It's Rachel's funeral, not a party."

"I want to be right for Rachel," she had said. "I want to look my best for her today. I want everything to be perfect for Rachel." She saw the understanding in his eyes.

"Forgive me," he'd said, ashamed. "I'm an idiot. I'm sorry, love."

Afterwards, she could never recall having her hair and makeup done. She barely remembered the funeral and burial.

One day, some two months after the funeral, Laura was in the village store with her mother. She saw Mary, one of her neighbours, in the queue at the till, and went out of her way to avoid contact with her.

"She never came to Rachel's funeral," Laura had admonished, casting dagger eyes at her neighbour.

"What do you mean, Laura?" her mother had said. "Mary was there. She shook your hand. She was at the funeral with all of her family. They came back to the house afterwards."

Laura had no recollection of Mary having been at Rachel's funeral.

Just then, Felicia caught sight of Laura and made her way over.

"Laura, I'm glad to have caught you before we left. I want to thank you for your chat with Jack. It seems to have helped him a lot."

"I'm glad. Tell me, how is your daughter coping?"

"Not too well. She disappeared this morning. I found her sitting in the dining room. She was looking out the window at the spot where her father died. She was in a bad state and that set me off again. She was very close to her father. Both the children were."

"The poor pet."

"Jack showed her the fishing log. She seemed a bit brighter when she saw her great grandfather's entry. It would have meant a lot to her father you see, and Anna knew that."

Turning her attention to Alex she said, "My daughter thought you were George Clooney."

"It happens sometimes," Alex said, and smiled.

"You bear more than a passing resemblance. It must happen all of the time."

"Yes, it does," Laura confirmed.

"Anyway, Anna thought you were the improved, younger version."

"Not as many grey hairs as George," Laura said.

Felicia was trying hard to make conversation on a lighter note. Laura admired her courage. She knew what an effort that must have taken.

"Are you going to see your husband now?" Laura asked gently.

"Yes. We're heading into Galway to say good-bye. We've all made an effort to look our best. Harvey took care of his appearance. He was always well turned out. 'Dapper' as my mother often says." Felicia's eyes welled up again and her mascara began to dribble.

"You look lovely. You all look well."

"Are you all right to drive?" Alex asked. "It would be no bother at all to drive you."

"I'll be fine," Felicia said. She dabbed at her tears with a tissue. "Roger will be driving in front of us. Roger is Harvey's cousin. He arrived this morning. Thank you for the offer. It's very kind of you." She looked at the tissue which was streaked with black mascara. "I must look like a witch."

"There's a little mascara here," said Laura, and placing a finger on her own checks to pinpoint where Felicia's mascara had dribbled.

Felicia wiped the clump away.

"I'm sorry that we met in such tragic circumstances," Laura said. For a brief spate of time, Laura had been in Felicia's shoes. Laura had thought her husband was dead: lying dead underneath the sheet on the boardwalk.

And her life, like Felicia's, went into freefall. Laura would never forget the turmoil she had experienced yesterday. Was it only yesterday?

"It looks like you have two wonderful children there," Alex said. He looked in the direction of both children, who were standing with their father's cousin.

"They are. They'll keep me going I expect. We'd better leave. Thank you both again for your kindness."

Alex and Laura bid the children farewell. They watched the Russell family leave with Richard.

Turning to Alex, Laura said, "That so easily could have been me. I got a second chance."

"We both did," he said.

Placing his arm around her shoulders, Mr and Mrs Hamilton headed in the direction of their suite.

Seán was standing inside the doorway, waiting to say his own goodbyes to the family. He was surprised at the get up of Felicia Russell. You'd swear she was going to a party. She was dressed immaculately and her face was done. To look at her, you'd never think her husband had died a day previously.

He clocked the Hamilton's. They had been coming to Doonmara for several years, but he had never seen either Mr or Mrs Hamilton look as happy as they did that weekend. Mrs Hamilton was positively glowing. He had a hunch that things might have been lively in the bedroom department before he arrived with the breakfast tray. Good for them.

Richard escorted Felicia to her car.

"Careful how you drive," he said as he shut the car door.

Felicia attempted to collect her thoughts. She felt like she was living in the back of her head, watching what was going on, as if the rest of her was on autopilot: a sudden, yanking separation of self. She took a deep breath.

A few moments later both cars drove off. Richard was glad to be leaving Doonmara. He never wanted to step a foot inside the castle grounds again. Jack had asked him about Nancy Ann and Richard had feigned ignorance. It was sad enough that Harvey had died at Doonmara. He didn't need to hear about another family tragedy at that castle. Neither did Anna or Felicia.

The last time Richard had heard Nancy Ann's name had been many years previously. His grandmother had spoken about Nancy Ann, only once, and only then, on her death bed. Nancy Ann had been airbrushed from the Russell family history. It was best she remained so.

CHAPTER FOURTEEN

"Jesus, I'm into one!" Alex said. "Conor, get the net."

For the next twenty minutes Alex played the fish.

"Keep the tension on the line," Conor roared. "Don't let the line go slack. Don't lose it. Hold steady there," he said encouragingly. "Easy does it. Careful now."

"He wants to go!" Alex said, clearly agitated.

"Let him off, Alex. Give him line."

Alex adjusted the tension on the reel. This process was repeated for some time. Alex brought the fish in, and then let him off, each time adjusting the tension on the reel, until the fish tired out.

"Quick, get the net under him, Conor."

"I'm trying to for God's sake. Don't let him go mind," the gillie warned.

"Conor, hurry up!" Alex shouted, afraid the fish would escape. His heart was racing. He was tremendously excited.

"Will you stop shouting at me," the gillie argued.

A moment or two later, and to the great relief of both men, Conor finally netted the fish. It was Sunday morning and Alex Hamilton had landed a salmon, his second ever.

"It's a fine spring salmon," Conor told his comrade-in-arms. Any tension had dissipated. Admiring the silver salmon, he said, "We can weigh it inside. I'd say it's just shy of nine pounds."

There was a fishing scale in the bar. The fisherman frequently brought in their catch to have it weighed.

"The drought has ended," Alex said, chuffed.

"Either that or your new fishing rod has paid off handsomely."

"This rod is well and truly christened. My wife will be delighted. It was my Christmas present. Conor, this calls for a celebratory drink." Alex looked at his watch. "It's a quarter-past-one. What do you think?"

"I think it must. It's thirsty work!" As far as Conor was concerned, anytime was a good time for a drink.

Alex packed up his fishing tackle and the two men made their way back to the castle. Alex carried the salmon proudly in his net.

"Eight pounds, 13 ounces," Alex said, looking at the scales in the bar.

"What did I tell you?"

"You weren't far off the mark, Conor."

"Correct. I've done this before, you know."

The bar was packed. News of Alex's catch went round fast, and several fishermen came over. One by one they congratulated him. A few shook his hand.

"What beat were you on?" they wanted to know. "Were you on the far side, or the near side?" What fly did you catch him on? Was it a Badger? What size of a fish is he?

Alex had the foresight to have reserved a table for lunch. Laura was meeting him in the bar but he had arrived early. He took a photograph of the salmon on his mobile and sent it to his wife along with a message saying where he was.

She appeared a few moments later.

"That was quick," he said, beaming from ear to ear.

"I was in the morning room. Well done, Alex," she said, catching sight of the salmon. "Very impressive! That's a beauty you've caught."

"Not bad. Not bad at all."

"Looks like you're doubly blessed." She gave Alex a sparkling smile.

Conor who overheard, looked confused. Alex smiled back at his wife. She was flirting with him again and he was enjoying it wholeheartedly.

"What weight is it?" she asked.

"Almost nine pounds," said Conor.

"That's bigger than your first salmon, Alex."

"Yes. The first was only seven pounds."

"Correct," Conor confirmed.

"I'll ask David to hold the salmon in one of the kitchen fridges. We can bring it home."

"You'll be having fresh wild salmon tomorrow night then," the gillie said. "You've probably forgotten what wild salmon tastes like."

"Cheeky!" Alex said. "Conor and I have ordered a celebratory pint of Guinness. Mind you with that kind of insubordination, I might cancel his pint!"

Conor chortled.

"What will you have, love?"

"Since it's a special occasion, I'm going to have a glass of Prosecco."

Laura wasn't a Guinness drinker. She found it too bitter.

"Good idea."

The bar attendant arrived armed with two pints of Guinness. Alex ordered a drink for Laura.

The bar man hovered.

"Excuse me. What did you say?" he asked hesitantly.

"A glass of *Prosecco,* please." Alex said.

The young bar man remained puzzled.

"It's a sparkling white wine," Laura added helpfully.

"Ah, yes," he said.

When her *Prosecco* arrived, Laura made a toast.

"Congratulations," she said and the trio clinked glasses. Laura took a sip of her drink. "Gosh, this is good."

Conor's tongue began to loosen. He loved to hold court in the bar, especially over a pint of the black stuff.

"See that fellow over there," he said, his tone conspiratorial, nodding in the direction of a seventy-something man at a neighbouring table.

"That's Dr Murphy. He's retired and lives in Oughterard. He comes out to fish here every weekend. Quite a character I'll have you know."

"He looks harmless enough," Laura said, taking in the bespectacled fisherman.

"He can be ruthless when he wants to be. He's very competitive when it comes to the fishing, mind. As you might know, we have a fish out in Doonmara on September 30th every year. It's the last day of the fishing season. Whoever lands the biggest salmon on the day is awarded a prize, and whoever lands the biggest catch of the season gets a special prize. It's a fairly big deal. Dr Murphy here had a bit of a game plan going last year."

He paused for dramatic effect and took a mouthful of Guinness.

"What happened?" Alex said agog. "I'm all ears."

"Last year, he brought in a very large salmon. It was the biggest catch of the day. Only, it had been defrosted. We could tell because the fish's eyes were glassy. That was a bit of a giveaway."

"You're joking," Alex said, miffed.

"I'm deadly serious. I wouldn't joke about such matters, Alex."

Laura hooted with laughter.

"Laura, you don't realise how serious these guys take their fishing. That sort of stuff wouldn't go down well," her husband said. "Am I right, Conor?"

"Right as rain, Alex. That's not all. There's more."

"More? I wouldn't have wanted him as my doctor if that's what he's like!" Laura said.

"And no one would blame you, Mrs Hamilton. Another year, didn't our doctor friend here bring in a photograph on his mobile phone of a fish he purported to have caught that morning. It was a black salmon, not a fresh fish, so it was being released back into the river. We have a catch and release policy for those salmon," he clarified for Laura's benefit. "The black salmon are old salmon, and they don't taste good at all, Mrs Hamilton, unless you smoke them. And then, only the larger ones are suitable for smoking.

"There was something not right about the photograph. One of the lads had it blown up on his lap top and the next day, we took a closer look at the picture. The sky was blue and there were masses of buttercups in the background. We knew that it couldn't possibly have been caught on the day in question. The day of the fish out was drizzly with grey skies and there wasn't a buttercup to be seen. It was the wrong month for buttercups. The salmon in the picture was a fish your man had caught months previously."

"That's hilarious," Laura said, amused. She glanced in Dr Murphy's direction again. He looked as if butter wouldn't melt in his mouth.

"Another year, he put lead in the salmon so that it would weigh more. He's imaginative! I'll give him that."

Alex sniggered.

"I'd nearly drive up next month to see what he's planned," he said.

"Oh, he knows we're on to him now," Conor said. "If he pulls anything this time, there will be war. Outright war! We'll be keeping a close watch on his antics."

Alex ordered another round of drinks for the three of them.

"I wouldn't usually go for a second glass this time of day, but this *Prosecco* is really good," Laura said.

David arrived shortly with two bowls of seafood chowder, a bowl of carrot soup and a ham sandwich. He placed the two bowels of chowder in front of the Hamiltons.

"I'm going the full hog," Conor said, eyeing up his order.

"You've earned it, "Alex said.

"It's about time this fellow did a bit of work," David said as he served Conor.

There was a bit of a rumpus and Alex looked behind him. Collectively, the French men had got up to go.

"Speaking of antics, it looks like the stag party is off," he said.

"They checked out earlier," David said. "Mind you, they'll be back soon. The groom is getting married here in two months' time. The hotel has been booked out for the entire weekend. It's going to be a big do. All the guests will be coming from France."

"That will be a costly affair," Laura said.

"Not for the groom," David informed then. "His new father-in-law is picking up the tab. For everything! And it will be the best of everything. I can vouch for that. The finest wines and champagne have been ordered."

"Speaking of which, this *Prosecco* is excellent, David. I must get the name of it before we leave."

"That's no bother, Mrs Hamilton."

After a high-spirited lunch, Conor stood up to go.

"*I will arise and go now, and go to Innisfree.* Blah, blah, blah," he joked.

Alex and Laura laughed and Conor made his exit with aplomb.

"He's an old dote," Laura said with affection.

"I'm pretty fond of him myself," her husband said.

The rest of the day passed quickly. Alex and Laura decided to have a pre-dinner drink in the bar.

"Could we have two glasses of *Prosecco* please, David?" Alex said.

Moments later David appeared with their order.

"They're on the house" he said.

"No! Are you sure?" Alex said.

David nodded.

"That's very kind of you. Thank you."

"I have the name of the bottle for you," David told Laura. "I'll get it."

He swiftly returned and plonked the bottle down on the table with a flourish.

"Oh my God!" Laura exclaimed. "It's a vintage *Dom Perignon.*

"No wonder you thought it tasted fabulous," her husband said.

"It turns out that the new lad didn't know what *Prosecco* was, let alone a vintage *Dom Perignon*. He can't read any English which is a bit of a problem."

"So I see! Where is he from?" Laura asked. "I can't make out the accent."

"Lithuania."

"David, we insist on paying," Alex said.

"I wouldn't hear of it. It wasn't your fault, Mr Hamilton."

"Only if you're sure then."

"Absolutely, Mr Hamilton."

"This is such a treat," Laura added. "Thank you very much."

"Not at all," David said. "You might as well finish the bottle. It's uncorked and I can't justify wasting it." With that, he topped up their glasses.

"Only in Doonmara," Laura said when he had left.

"Only in Doonmara," Alex concurred. "That's what I love about the place, all of the idiosyncrasies, as well as the people you meet, from all walks of life. I hope this place never changes."

"There is one thing I might change," Laura said.

"James?"

"James!

"Mind you, he's hardly here as it is," he said. "Let's head in to the restaurant, shall we?"

⊰⊱

Lucy Sukova dried her eyes. She had phoned in sick on Saturday morning.

"I have a stomach bug," Lucy lied to the housekeeper.

"Mind yourself, Lucy," her supervisor said, sounding concerned. "Don't come back until you're fully better." She hadn't been too pleased because the hotel was booked to capacity and they needed Lucy.

Nonetheless, the housekeeper had meant every word. The girl rarely missed a day and she was a good worker. Lucy's supervisor took account of that track record now.

It was touching midday. Lucy had no one to confide in. At times like this, she missed her family most. She considered her predicament. She couldn't face Pawel at work and she didn't want to risk the chance of running into Jean-Pierre. That's why she had phoned in sick. She thought it best to steer clear of the hotel for a day or two.

What was the word her fellow Irish workers used? It came to her a few moments later. She had taken a 'sickie'.

She had seen Pawel, first in the aftermath of the tragedy, and later that night at their apartment. He had arrived in from work a little after eleven.

"I'm moving out," he announced brusquely. Then he packed a few bits and pieces. "I'll come by for the rest of my stuff tomorrow or Monday."

"Where will you go?" she enquired nervously. She looked down at her nails. She had chewed every single one off.

"That's none of your business," he replied, even more bad-tempered.

Immediately, she recoiled. She was surprised at how angry his tone was because Pawel was a mild-mannered man.

Earlier, when she had run into him briefly in the hotel, he had held back. He had seemed hurt more than anything else.

"Please, don't make a fuss," she had begged. "I need this job. My family are dependent on me."

He was an immigrant too. He understood. It wasn't easy to pick up a job in Connemara mid-August. The season was half-over.

He was not a vindictive man and he had said, "I don't intend to." Besides, he didn't want the other staff to know that he'd been made a fool of. That would be humiliating. Pawel had his pride. "I'll see you later back at the flat," he had told Lucy. "We'll talk then. But it's over between us."

She had been waiting anxiously for his arrival all evening, wondering if there was anything she could do or say to salvage their relationship.

Now, with immeasurable sadness and very quietly, he said: "Why Lucy?" He was standing at their bedroom door. He had packed a carry all. "Just tell me why? "Wasn't I good enough for you?"

"You are. You're a good man, Pawel. I don't deserve you."

Lucy had been practising her little speech all evening. She planned on telling her fiancé that she had made a huge mistake. She would tell him how much she loved him and how sorry she was. It would never happen again. When it came to it, Lucy said nothing. She was ashamed.

"You haven't answered my question."

"I don't know, Pawel, I don't know why I did it. I'm not ready to settle down. I don't know what I want."

He reflected on their relationship. It was true they hadn't been getting on recently, but that was more a case of rubbing each other up the wrong way and not agreeing on things.

"We've been arguing a lot recently but I thought you loved me," he said. "I know I love you. Loved you," he said, correcting himself. "I thought we were happy."

"I do love you, Pawel. But I don't want to move to Poland. I didn't want to go on holiday there in September. You put a lot of pressure on me."

"That's no excuse to do what you did," he said, his voice raised. "And with that weasel! How could I ever trust you again?"

"I'm sorry, Pawel," she said, realising that their relationship was beyond repair. "I never meant to hurt you."

"But you did. I thought the world of you, Lucy," he said, sad and disillusioned. "How could you cheat on me with someone like him? That man is here on his stag. I heard he's getting married in the hotel. What kind of lowlife does that to the girl he is going to marry in a few weeks?"

There was silence for a few moments, an unbearable silence that unnerved her. She searched for excuses.

"He's a regular guest. We had a thing going one summer."

"You never said anything. When was that?"

"Two years ago. It was before you came to the hotel."

"What else don't I know about you, Lucy? How many other guests were you screwing?" he said unkindly.

I don't deserve that, thought Lucy.

"Here," she said, handing Pawel the diamond engagement ring he had presented her with. "This belongs to you."

It was a small diamond and all Pawel could afford on his wages. Even so, Lucy loved her engagement ring.

"We'll keep this between ourselves," he said, pocketing the ring.

"There will be a lot of questions," she pointed out.

"It's in your own interest not to say anything."

If word got out, other staff members would be horrified at her treatment of Pawel. She could lose her job. She might not get a reference.

"I won't be saying anything," she told him. "I promise."

He gave a weak laugh.

"A promise from you means nothing, Lucy. You broke all your promises to me just like that. Everything we had, you threw away without a second thought."

He looked at her with disgust. Lucy crumpled and folded like an accordion. There was nothing left to say. Pawel picked up his bag. He slammed the door on his way out.

CHAPTER FIFTEEN

Caroline was sitting in a quiet alcove when Alex arrived. It was a bar they frequented from time to time.

Alex took a seat opposite Caroline. His greeting had been impersonal. They avoided any displays of affection in public.

"Am I late?" he said, noticing that the glass in front of her was half empty.

"I was a little early."

"That's all right, then. I'm going to get myself a drink. Can I get you one?"

She shook her head. Alex went up to the bar and ordered a gin and tonic. When his drink arrived, he took a quick sip to brace himself.

"How was your weekend?" she asked

"Very good on the fishing front," he said, trying to keep things light. He intended to lead into the conversation gently. "Believe it or not, I caught a salmon"

They chit-chatted for a few moments. Though Alex was his usual charming self, she noticed that he was gulping down his gin and tonic.

"That's not like you," he said, looking at her glass – not her usual tipple.

Caroline favoured a glass of red wine after work, usually a glass of Merlot.

"I didn't eat much at lunch. A glass of wine would have gone straight to my head."

"Very sensible," he teased.

She sensed that he was nervous, though he was trying his best to hide it.

"You're not coming down with anything, are you?" he asked, for she was desperately pale.

"I'm okay."

"You work too hard, Caroline. You look tired."

He was right on both counts. A washed-out version of herself had stared back at Caroline in the mirror earlier. The war paint wasn't working today. She had wanted to look well for him.

"When people say tired, especially a man, they mean something entirely different. It isn't a compliment," she said, half-jokingly. "Do I look that bad?"

"Don't mind me," he said quickly, trying to make amends. "You're a beautiful woman, Caroline. How could you ever look bad?"

"I look like shit and you're backpedalling" she said. "But I'll accept the flattery, Alex." She hesitated briefly. "Look, there's something I want to talk to you about," she began, attempting to steer the conversation in another direction.

"I thought as much," he said cutting in. "I got the gist of that from your texts. Before you say anything, there's something I need to say first."

Caroline was going to say that she loved him. She was going to present him with some kind of ultimatum. That's what he suspected and why he took control of the exchange.

He didn't want her to feel that she had made a fool of herself, not when he was about to break off their relationship. It was better to get in there first. He would save Caroline her dignity.

"Go ahead," she said, thinking how well he looked after his weekend in Connemara. He had it all. No wonder she was mad about him.

"Caroline," he said. "I've enjoyed the last few months. It's been terrific. You're terrific. You're kind, warm and open-minded. I was in a bad place and you brought a little sunshine into my life. I mean that. Truly."

For a brief moment, she thought that Alex was about to commit to her in some way.

Was there was a chance that this man, with whom she had fallen hopelessly in love, would be by her side in the dark months ahead? Could Alex be about to say he was leaving his wife? What if he were free? Everything was wrong in her life, but that could all change, if Alex was by her side.

"And if I wasn't married," he continued, "then perhaps you and I would have a real chance. But I am married, Caroline, and that's the fact of the matter."

Like that, her hopes were cruelly dashed. She knew he was going to finish with her there and then.

"We can't carry on like this," he said, confirming her fears. "It isn't fair to you or to my wife. I think it's time to draw a line under our relationship."

She threw back the rest of her drink but said nothing. An uncomfortable silence followed.

Eventually he said, "You're very quiet."

"What's there to say?" she replied, wringing her hands helplessly.

"Caroline, I'm sorry if I've hurt you. But you must have known that this would happen, if not to-day, then one day. I never made any promises. You knew about my wife from the beginning. I thought this was only a bit of fun for both of us."

She was a reasonable woman so she said, "It was in the beginning. Over time, things changed. You're not just 'my bit of fun' Alex. Along the way,

I developed real feelings for you. It's not as if we had a one-night stand. This has been going on for months. It's been wonderful, all of it, and not just the sex. It was for me, at any rate."

Listening carefully to what she had to say, he concluded his gut instinct had been right. Caroline had been about to look for a commitment of sorts. She sounded vulnerable and hurt, and he regretted having caused her pain. He thought he should acknowledge her feelings.

"I've been very clumsy with my choice of words and I'm sorry. I can be an insensitive idiot sometimes. A lot of the time, actually," he said, and gave her a little smile. "I grew fond of you too, Caroline. I don't deny that. I enjoyed being with you. But we don't have a future together. Were you hoping that we could take our relationship further? Is that what you wanted to talk to me about?"

"No, not really," she said. She tried to smile back but failed.

The truth was that Caroline had been going to tell him her own news. This changed everything. Alex no longer wanted her in his life.

"Oh. What was it then?" he asked, surprised that he had been wrong-footed.

"Nothing important," she said, thinking that Ciara had been right. Caroline needed to focus on herself and getting through her own ordeal. She had an uphill battle on her hands. She would walk away from this relationship today and leave it behind her, where it needed to be. "There is one thing I'm curious about," she added. "Why did you suddenly decide to finish with me? This day last week, everything was hunky-dory. You've done quite a U-turn, Alex. Overnight, you've developed a conscience."

He shifted uncomfortably in his chair.

"You're right," he said, holding his hands up. "I'll be honest with you, Caroline. At some point last week, I decided I couldn't continue like this. I couldn't go on leading a double life. I decided to end our relationship and to end my marriage. That's the truth."

"I didn't see that coming," she said, floored by his response. Caroline was taken aback that he intended to leave his wife too. "So it's goodbye, Caroline and goodbye, Laura."

"No."

"No?"

"I'm staying with Laura. We're going to give our marriage another shot."

That little arrow wounded Caroline deeply.

"Why the change of heart?" she couldn't resist asking. She struggled to keep the bitterness out of her voice.

"It's hard to explain but something happened over the weekend that changed everything."

Although she was interested to know what that something was, there was only one thing Caroline wanted to know.

"Do you still love your wife?" she asked.

"I've always loved her."

"So why me? Why all the others?"

"The others?" he said.

"Alex, I'm aware there have been lots of other women. I'm not stupid!"

Her words stung. He shifted uneasily in his chair again.

"If you loved your wife, why did you cheat on her all along? I don't get it," she said, more than a little frustrated.

He downed his gin and tonic fast.

"I need another one of these," he said." How about you? A glass of Merlot?"

She could do with one. *Better not, she thought.*

Instead she said, "No. I'll have another sparkling water."

She watched him retreat to the bar and considered what he had told her. He was going back to his life. Laura and he must have had some kind of reconciliation. The three of them are going to live happily ever after: Alex, Laura and their little daughter. They were going to play happy families.

She had seen a photo of the child but Alex had never spoken to Caroline about his daughter. She didn't know the child's name. Caroline had known that his wife was called Laura. Alex had let her name drop once, by mistake. Now, she thought back to a conversation she had with Ciara.

"Does he have any children?" Ciara asked, not long after the affair commenced.

"He has a little girl. She's the image of him."

"How do you know that?" Ciara said.

"I saw a picture of her, of both of them, his daughter and his wife."

"He showed you photographs? The nerve of him! Has he no scruples at all?"

"It wasn't like that, Ciara. I'm ashamed to admit this but I sneaked a look through his wallet once. I found a family photo."

"How did you manage that?" Ciara said, appalled at her friend's behaviour.

"He was in the shower. I couldn't help myself," she said. "Oh, I knew he had a wife. His wedding ring was a bit of a giveaway."

Ciara threw her friend a questioning look.

"He said he was married but further discussion about his family situation was strictly off limits. I grew curious. I wanted to see what I was up against."

"You're quite the detective," Ciara said. She was seeing a whole new side of Caroline. "And what was she like? The wife, I mean."

"She was slim. Pretty. She has light brown-hair. She's older than me. I don't know by how much. It was an old photograph."

Caroline thought about that picture now. It had been taken several years previously because Alex looked older now.

The child was about to blow out the candles on her birthday cake. Caroline was unable to decipher the name on the cake. The little girl's mum was standing behind her proudly. The wife looked like a nice person. She had a lovely smile. And Alex looked happy. He looked happier than Caroline had ever seen him.

Caroline had felt her place in his affections undermined radically. She'd turned the photo over but there was no inscription.

She didn't relate any of this to her friend. She had been crushed when she had seen the picture. It made her feel seedy. Caroline felt like she had gate crashed in on the birthday party and in on his life.

Caroline switched back to the present and considered what she had just been told. Alex hadn't used his daughter as an excuse. He was staying in this marriage because he loved his wife. That's what he had said. There was no mention of the little girl. He hadn't said that he was staying with Laura for the sake of the family. It would have hurt less if he had. Caroline wouldn't be taking his rejection so personally now. As things stood, Laura had won all on her own.

She wanted to burst his bubble. She wanted to wound him back. She needed to calm down. By the time he had returned with their drinks, Caroline felt more in control.

Alex delayed at the bar for a few extra moments in an attempt to diffuse the situation, and to consider his next move. He owed Caroline an explanation. She was a good person.

"Here you are," he said, handing her a sparkling water. He returned to his seat, his own glass still in hand.

"You asked a valid question, Caroline. Why would I keep cheating on my wife if I still loved her?"

She cocked an eyebrow, interested to hear his explanation.

"It's complicated, Caroline. Let me begin by saying, Laura and I got married, and we were very happy. And then, Rachel our daughter was born and our lives seemed doubly blessed. We had our own little family. Rachel really was the most adorable child and our life was pretty damn perfect. But then Rachel died."

Caroline put her hand to her mouth, completely taken aback. Alex stalled for a moment. He swirled the ice round in his drink, absently. Then he gave an account of what happened.

"Neither her mother or I recovered afterwards," he said finally. "Our lives were never the same again. We couldn't get back to where we were."

"Alex, I had no idea. No idea at all," Caroline said, shocked at his disclosure.

"Why would you? I never said anything."

"I'm sorry, Alex. What you must have gone through. It must have been horrific."

"It was. It drove us apart in the end."

She considered what he had said.

"Could you find no comfort in each other?" she asked "You had loved each other so much."

"I'm afraid not," he said. "I felt that Laura blamed me for Rachel's death. My daughter was with me when it happened. It was an accident. A stupid accident and it happened when Rachel was with me. I blamed myself and I thought my wife blamed me too.

"Now, I think it was more that Laura was in such pain, that she shut everything and everybody out, including me. We stayed together, and in all but name, the marriage was over. The physical side of things ended when Rachel died and I found that hard to deal with. I was weak and I was lonely. And that's when I began to stray."

"Does she know?"

"I confessed the first time. I wanted us to get help. I thought it might save our relationship. Laura wouldn't agree to any kind of therapy. After a while, I was unfaithful again and the pattern continued. I think my wife knew all along but she turned a blind eye. I'm not proud of any of this, Caroline."

His discomfort was obvious and she said, "I can see that." A moment later she asked him, "When did your daughter die?"

"Seven years ago. Rachel was dead seven years in June."

No wonder he sought solace elsewhere, she thought.

"And something happened in Connemara that changed everything?"

"Yes," he said and related the events of the weekend.

"She thought you had died?" Laura said.

"It took that for my wife to realise that she still loved me."

"I should, but I don't begrudge you your happy ending," she said. "You've been through the mill. I can imagine what the pain must be to lose your child."

"Can you?" he said, unconvinced. After all, she had no children.

"I think I can," she said, but didn't expand further.

"I hope you find someone," he said. "I hope you have a family of your own one day. You're young. You've got time on your side."

Had she?

"I don't mind admitting that I fell for you," she said, taking stock. "I wanted to make this something more that it was. Now I can see, it was what it was."

"And what was that?" he asked with another winning smile.

"Like you said. An affair. No strings attached."

"It was good why it lasted, Caroline," he told her. His voice had softened.

"Good doesn't come close, Alex."

"Why did you come after me, anyway?" he said, puzzled. "You knew I was married. I hate to say this, but you did make a play for me."

"Yes I did, didn't I?" she said, remembering that time in the Jacuzzi when she first encountered Alex. She had eventually noticed his wedding ring, but by then it was too late. She had been attracted to him immediately.

"It was a case of classic rebound really. My ego got dented after my last relationship went south. This was meant to be, as you called it, a little fun. I should never have gone after a married man. I should have known better."

"You deserve someone better than me, Caroline. I hope you find that someone. You deserve to be happy."

She believed she had found that someone, only it was Alex.

"And so do you," she said, and meant it. "I think it's time for us to part ways."

"I suppose you're right."

"We won't be bumping into each other," she said, and put her jacket on. "There's little chance of that."

"How so?" he asked.

"Oh, they're changing my territory soon. I won't be working in Limerick much longer."

Caroline stood up ready to go.

"That will make things easier for both of us," he said.

He rose to his feet, and stood awkwardly. There would be no farewell embrace. They could be spotted. Caroline looked sad and defeated. At the last minute, he relented.

"Come here," he said, throwing caution to the wind.

She stepped a little closer. He hugged her.

"Goodbye," she said, drawing strength from the warm lingering embrace, before walking away.

He watched her leave, enormously relieved that the affair was over. No matter how fond he had been of Caroline, she had been his dirty secret. There was no getting away from that.

Now that he and Laura were home, Alex hoped that their relationship would continue to thrive.

Reality had kicked in the moment they had left Doonmara. He hoped that they could erase the last couple of years. It was a lot to hope for but he would give it his best shot.

A cousin of Laura's sat in the bar. Wrapped up in his own thoughts, Alex didn't notice her. She was watching his every move. Alex drained his glass before making his own exit.

He could murder for a cigarette. But he had promised Laura that he was giving them up. It was a promise that he intended to keep. He inhaled the night air, hoping a few deep breaths would alleviate the tension.

A wave of guilt hit him as he remembered the intimacy he had enjoyed with Laura only the day before. It had stirred powerful emotions within him. He felt dreadful about his infidelity with Caroline. It made him feel grubby. He was thrown after their encounter, unnerved after the events of the weekend.

Laura was at home waiting for him, and here he was, meeting his mistress, and breaking off a clandestine affair which his wife knew nothing about. Laura wasn't aware that he had been involved with another woman for over six months.

Out of the blue, his thoughts turned to Rachel and to the pages of memory, and of times spent with his daughter. To one in particular: Rachel sitting at the kitchen table in Cratloe and having her tea.

"What are they, Rach?" he asked, pointing to her plate.

"'Shish shinkers'," she replied.

He always asked the same question. He got a kick out of the way his daughter would pronounce fish fingers.

Rachel – wilful, imaginative and hilarious, who bounded into his arms when he came home from work, with a range of faces to rival a comedian. She had been dazzling. He had revelled in her chuckle and glorious little grin, and the unselfconscious way her fingers had curled against his. The thought made him flinch. Too ashamed to go home and face Laura, Alex decided to get hammered.

CHAPTER SIXTEEN

The short walk back to the hotel had helped to clear her head. Caroline went directly to her room. The relationship was over, and she was miserable.

She flopped, exhausted, onto the bed, kicking off her shoes. She stared up at the ceiling, thinking about the conversation in the bar.

"I hope you have a family of your own one day," Alex had said. "You're young enough. You've got time on your side."

Those words played on Caroline's mind. She might not have time on her side but she might have a child. The baby's father would play no part in their lives. That much she knew, because Caroline Cleary was pregnant and Alex was the father.

He remained blissfully unaware. He's already lost one child, she reasoned, and there was every possibility that he would lose this child. She had sacrificed her own happiness for his. She was wrong to have taken Alex from Laura, and Caroline accepted that. She was paying the price but it was a hefty price to pay.

Placing her hands on her stomach, she whispered to her unborn child, "It's just you and me."

After a while, she lay on her side and curled up into a ball. She was exhausted and before long she fell asleep. When she awoke it was touching nine pm. She had been asleep for more than an hour.

She had promised to phone Ciara to tell her friend how things had panned out with Alex. Ciara must have been waiting for her call, because she answered immediately.

"How are you?" Ciara asked concerned. "How did it go?"

Caroline related the events of the evening.

"I'm glad he was honest with you," Ciara said when she heard about Alex's domestic situation. "That's something. After hearing what you've said, it's hard not to feel sorry for him. I never thought I'd hear myself say that. He's not the cad I thought he was. At least he had the decency to come clean."

"That's true."

"So he broke off the relationship before you had the chance to say anything."

"Yes," she said. "He dumped me before I had the chance to dump him."

From her friend's tone of voice, Ciara guessed Caroline hadn't intended to stick to the plan they had hatched at lunch.

"You were going to tell him you were ill," she said. "You were going to tell him about the baby. Weren't you?"

"I was, right up the last minute. I told you I'd finish the relationship and say nothing, but over the weekend I had a change of heart."

"Are you glad you didn't?"

"It's for the best."

"I'm relieved. You need to focus on getting well, Caroline."

"You're right. My only concern from now on is the baby and getting through this."

"Promise me?"

"I promise. By the way, I told my boss yesterday."

"About the baby or your operation?"

"Both."

She said that the company would support me in any way they could."

"That was nice of her. At least you won't be travelling up and down to Limerick every week. That would have made things harder. It would be a constant reminder of Alex."

"You're right. She offered to cut my journeys while I'm still able to work. I won't have to do any overnights."

"She seems to have been very understanding. I thought she was a bitch."

"When it came down to it, she was really decent. I saw a different side to her. I feel bad for all the awful things I said."

"You're not the first person to bad mouth your boss. I do it all the time."

"Even so."

"How are you feeling now?"

"I'm pretty tired. I left Dublin at six this morning. I fell asleep when I got back to the hotel. I only woke up a little while ago."

"That's hardly surprising," her friend said gently. "You're sick and you're pregnant. And today, has been an emotional rollercoaster."

"It's been a long day for sure. Anyway, that's about it," Caroline said, wrapping up the conversation.

"I'll collect you on Thursday. I should be with you by ten."

"I'm glad you're coming with me. Thanks, Ciara. Thanks for everything."

With that, Caroline hung up. Reluctantly, she hoisted herself off the bed and went into the bathroom. She ought to eat something. Besides, she wasn't ready for her beauty sleep yet. She certainly needed it, and catching her reflection in the bath-room mirror, she grimaced.

She ordered a sandwich and a pot of tea from room service. While she was waiting, she switched on her laptop and reread a file she had saved. Caroline had been doing her own medical re-search on the internet.

Room service interrupted her and she answered the door. Her mind was bamboozled with the in-formation she had read. Her laptop remained open on the table.

Pouring herself a cup of tea, she took a sip before tackling the chicken salad sandwich. Questions plagued her. What if the tumour was malignant? What if she couldn't continue with the pregnancy? What if they couldn't save her or the baby? What if she died and the baby lived? Who would raise her child?

The internet was a powerful tool. You could re-search everything. However, she was beginning to think there was too much information you could tap into. You could worry when perhaps there was no need. She was already envisaging the worst-case scenario. She would know soon enough.

She switched off the computer, and decided that she would wait until Thursday.

Thursday came. Caroline was about to be wheeled down for surgery.

"Wish me luck," she said.

"Good luck. It will be over before you know it," Ciara told her. "I'll be rooting for you. You're going to be fine."

Ciara was wrong.

Caroline recalled what the surgeon had said when she had met him. She had put a lot of faith in what he had told her, and so had Ciara.

"More than likely, the mass is benign," he had said. "It might be a fibromyalgia hyperplasia or a hepatic adenoma, both of which are benign. It's best to remove the mass as soon as possible. You're at risk of rupture and you're pregnant. I'm scheduling you in for surgery the week after next."

Although he had been very matter of fact at the time, his tone had been soothing. He seemed confident with his prognosis.

He was wrong.

The operation went ahead. When she woke up after surgery, the surgeon spoke to her in the same soothing voice, but the news had been alarming. The words came at her like arrows. *Aggressive. Malignant. Cancer.*

"Caroline, I'm afraid it doesn't look good," he continued. "It wasn't any of the things that we suspected. What you have is a form of ovarian cancer. The tumour is very large."

Her first thoughts were to her unborn child.

"What about my baby?" she said. "What do we do about the baby?"

"We'll know more in a day or so," he said. "I'll be able to give you a definite prognosis then."

After the surgery, they checked the foetal heart rate regularly. Caroline became increasingly anxious. "Stop torturing me," she said to the nurse. "What if I don't hear a heartbeat? What if my surgery has endangered my baby?"

She hadn't been able to eat anything that day or the next. She finally managed to eat something on Saturday morning. Her surgeon came to see her again.

"You will be able to continue the pregnancy," he said.

"Thank God," she said relieved.

"But you will need to start treatment. You'll need chemotherapy."

"How can I have chemotherapy? I'm pregnant."

"The research on mothers who underwent chemotherapy treatment while pregnant notes prematurity as a possible side effect, but overall the babies were unharmed," he said. "If you don't have treatment and wait until after the birth, there's a strong possibility that you won't survive, Caroline.

Your cancer is severe. To save your own life, and the life of your unborn baby, you will need to start treatment immediately."

That gave Caroline hope. *I have something to fight for,* she thought. *I have my baby. I will fight this.*

"The type of tumour you have is fairly aggressive," he explained, "but it does respond well to chemotherapy. What I'm suggesting is four rounds of treatment."

"When do I start?" she asked.

"You'll start Monday week."

"So soon?" she said, thinking the gap between diagnosis and treatment was very short.

"The sooner you start, the sooner your treatment is over," he said. "You'll be admitted to the hospital every three weeks for five days of treatment. You'll come in on a Monday and go home on Friday. The chemotherapy therapeutic agents that we are giving you are safe to use with the pregnancy. The risks are very minimal.

"In between treatments, you have to come in for a day of bleomycin each Monday. That's one of the drugs that you will be given. We've set up an appointment with an oncologist for you early next week. Your oncologist will explain everything in depth."

Ciara had been a brick throughout. Thankfully, Ciara had persuaded Caroline to tell her family before she had undergone surgery. But they hadn't known about the baby. Caroline had broken the news to them about the baby after the operation. There had been an emotional scene in the hospital when her parents came to visit. They were completely shocked.

Caroline was released from hospital on Tuesday. Ciara collected her.

"How are you today?" Ciara asked.

"I'm trying to stay calm and positive. The worst thing about all of this is worrying about the baby. I want to have enough fight in me to beat this but I'm scared something might happen to the baby. I'm so happy that I can have this baby, Ciara. I'm not worried about me."

In hindsight, Caroline realized she'd had some of the symptoms of ovarian cancer. She was always bloated. She would eat something and feel full right away, which was unlike her. She had lost weight without dieting. She had felt tired, but attributed the fatigue to a new job that came with its own stresses.

Caroline had been diagnosed with ovarian cancer when she was fourteen weeks pregnant. Her own chances of survival now hung in the balance. The next couple of months would be harrowing. She was under no illusion about that. Caroline didn't want to die. She wasn't ready to die. She was determined to fight the cancer with everything she had because she had everything to live for.

At the end of August, she began a regimen which consisted of four rounds of three different types of chemotherapy. The treatment was due to finish before her due date in January.

⊷ ⊶

Caroline had her hair cut short the day before her first round of chemotherapy. It now fell to the nape of her neck.

Over the years, she had developed an easy rapport with her stylist. Yesterday, there had been little conversation as Caroline had her hair cut. Locks of long blond hair littered the salon floor. The stylist seemed as uneasy as Caroline who sat with her eyes turned away from the mirror.

Eventually, Caroline would lose all her hair. Alex had always admired her long blond hair. There was nothing glamorous about cancer. She wondered if her nose hair would fall out. She didn't care if she lost her hair and her eyebrows, or if her lashes fell out. She would cope with anything, as long as she didn't lose this baby. This could be her only chance to have a child.

"How do you like my new hair style?" she asked Ciara. She pouted coquettishly.

Ciara laughed. It was Caroline's third day of chemotherapy.

"And here was I thinking that the chemo had started to work very fast," Ciara said.

"At least I still have hair," she said, patting her head. "Not for much longer it seems. The doctor said it will start to fall out in the next four to six weeks."

"You look fine," her friend reassured her. "And it's great you got a private room for your chemo stays. Now tell me. How are you?"

"I'm a bit shattered. I wasn't sure what to expect. They've given me Bleomycin, Etoposide and Cisplatin."

"So that's what you've been hooked up to. That sounds like a pretty powerful cocktail. How's it been so far?"

"Not like any cocktail you've ever downed. It was kind of weird the first day. They gave me the Bleomycin and my first thought was: Is it doing any good? Do I feel it working? Of course, I didn't! I'm full of drugs. My body doesn't know what's hit it. Before the chemo, they pump me up with steroids, Benadryl and antibiotics. That's what affects me the most. All that stuff makes me feel woozy and dizzy. I get double vision for a little while. But they have to do it. That's the drill and there's no escaping it."

"Have you had any nausea yet?

"There's that to look forward to! I was given anti-nausea tablets to take earlier. One of the nurses said I won't feel anything until tomorrow, but another nurse said it won't hit me until I go home. The nurses have been great. All of the medical team have been so kind, and they're very mindful of the baby."

Two more days passed. Her stomach was a bit off, and she suffered heart burn. She developed mouth ulcers. She had to rinse her mouth our four times a day with peroxide to ward them off.

"It doesn't help with the nausea," she told Ciara.

Overall, Caroline was feeling it was tolerable. She walked around the ward for exercise and got to know people. It helped to pass the day. Visitors had broken the tedium of her hospital stay. The family had made a rota. Each day, a family member had been in to sit and chat with Caroline in the hospital, and the emotionally truthful catch ups had been the best of all silver linings. The kindness of the people around her, from those she loved to those she hardly knew, pushed her forwards like a warm wind. She loved and felt loved in a way that she never had before.

Friday arrived. She had her pre-meds and then her chemo. Her father arrived to collect her soon afterwards. Caroline was going to stay with her parents until the chemotherapy was over.

Caroline was pleased to leave hospital. She'd be able to have a shower when she got home. She hadn't been allowed to shower during her treatment. And the hospital food had been awful.

From time to time, Ciara had brought in a little treat; a scone perhaps, or a cold plate. That had brightened Caroline's day no end. Caroline was looking forward to some of her mother's home cooking. Her mother had promised to make a lasagne, a favourite.

She hadn't slept well in the hospital, only a couple of hours each night. She would lie awake in bed, thinking of the baby. She knew the sex of the baby now. She was going to have a baby girl, a daughter. Imagine that.

The second round of treatment began.

"I'm not sure what's ahead of me this time," she told Ciara. It was day two. "I didn't suffer many side effects after the first round. I had one day of dehydration but other than that I was fine. I did well. And I'm back to normal after the operation, as far as my energy levels are concerned."

"That's all good," Ciara said. "By the way, you've started to show."

Caroline patted her bump proudly.

"A little," she agreed. She ran her hands through her hair and a clump of hair fell out. "Look at that," she said, "my hair is falling out. I keep finding it all over my pillow and in the bed. It's like sleeping with a hairy dog that is shedding! I wake up in the middle of the night and there's hair in my mouth. The nurse is going to cut it later."

The following day Ciara arrived to find her friend partially bald. Caroline looked very pale and haggard. She was unrecognisable from her former self: the beautiful, blond, sex siren.

"I have a little present for you," Ciara said, blinking back the tears. She handed Caroline a brightly packaged gift.

Caroline opened the package. It was a bright red woolly hat.

"This will keep my head warm," she said and put it on her head immediately. "You might have to get one for my brother. He's shaved off his head as a gesture of support."

"Oh, that was a nice of him," Ciara said. "Maybe I should do the same."

"Don't you dare," Caroline said. "Mind you, I feel a lot more comfortable with my hair cut off. It's not falling out all over the place and I'm sleeping better. Everyone says you just know when you have to shave your head. And guess what – they were right. I should have shaved it off before now. But my hair had been long since I was ten years old. It took a long while for me to reach that point."

The second round of chemo hit her harder. She needed minding. Caroline was very grateful for her mother's care. She was ill for an additional three days this time.

The third round hit Caroline harder still.

"I feel more tired with each round of treatment," she told Ciara. "This round really hit me. And I'm nauseous at night and picky about food."

The Monday after her third round of treatment, Ciara drove her to the hospital. Caroline looked dreadful. The dark circles under her eyes were very prominent.

"Moving around is harder and I'm out of breath," Caroline explained. "I'm wrecked, Ciara. I really didn't want to come here today. I felt like going nowhere. They're giving me some fluid with potassium and a five-day anti-nausea before the Bleomycin. The nurse said that the potassium will give me more energy."

Her hair had almost completely fallen out except for one little patch at the front.

"I don't know myself anymore," she joked. "I look like someone else and it's not an improvement. And it's not just the hair on your head that goes. It goes everywhere, and I mean everywhere. I feel sexless. I put some make up on today because I felt it was the only way to differentiate from being a boy."

"You might need to add some earrings," Ciara said.

Caroline smiled.

"I'm feeling very pregnant and very bald. Seriously, Ciara, it's all kind of bizarre. It's like I'm living in a twilight zone. That's the only way to describe it. I hope I never have to go through this again. I feel so unlike myself. There are days when I actually feel dead. It's ironic that a drug designed to stop you dying makes you feel as if you have."

"You're nearly there," Ciara said. "You've only one more round to go. Focus on that."

"It can't go fast enough. I feel crap today, because I'm emotional. But the baby is doing well and I'm thrilled about that. I keep telling myself that I will get through this."

Finally, it was time for the fourth and final round of treatment. Caroline had lost her final tuft of hair. She was now completely bald. The week went by. Friday came and Ciara collected her friend.

"I'm relieved to have it finally over," Caroline confided. She had cried when the intravenous drip machine had bleeped it final bleep, tears of pain and relief that came from somewhere deep inside of her. "Believe it or not, there's something oddly life-affirming about getting to the end. There is a warped sense of achievement in that. And I'm relieved I'll be getting my hair back. My head has been cold this winter! But I'm scared too."

"Why so?" Ciara asked.

"In a way, the chemotherapy is a lifeline. It's killing all the bad stuff. Now, that the chemo is over, I'm wondering will the cancer be all gone. I won't know if I'm cancer free until after I have the baby. They will do all the tests then."

"You have to stay positive," Ciara said. "How is the baby?"

"The baby is growing as it should be. The doctor said that I should go to full term so I don't have to take any steroids to help the baby's lungs mature. And I don't have to have an amniocentesis at 36 weeks. I was thankful to hear that. I wasn't excited about either."

The nurses came in to say goodbye. Caroline gave them a big box of handmade chocolates by way of a thank you.

"They've all been incredible," Caroline told Ciara, "except when they come at you with a four-inch needle!"

Caroline packed her belongings and they left the hospital. The chemotherapy was finally over. She hadn't thought of Alex Hamilton too much these past few weeks. The chemotherapy and pregnancy dominated her thoughts. Fighting the battle of her life had taken priority.

Only Ciara knew about Alex. No one ever mentioned his name. Her mother quizzed her once or twice about the identity of the baby's father. Caroline had given her short shrift.

Ciara thought they should celebrate but Caroline hadn't the energy to do much. Still, there was a family celebration of sorts. A few family friends called over to the house that night to wish her well. Her brother had bought balloons and a cake.

Caroline felt like she had so many hurdles ahead. She had to get her blood counts up as well as give birth. And even though she had been assured the baby was healthy, she held a fear about her baby's health.

Caroline was a fighter and so was her baby. Though underweight and a little premature, the baby survived. Una arrived on January15th, a cold and frosty morning, via caesarean section. The baby weighed five pounds and four ounces.

Ciara saw Caroline and the baby soon afterwards. She had been waiting with Caroline's parents in the hospital. The two friends gave each other a huge, long hug and began crying, stopping to look at the baby, and then continued to hug again.

"I was pacing back and forth down that corridor like an anxious father," Ciara said. "I couldn't contain myself. I was that nervous and excited."

"She's tiny and she's mighty," Caroline said. "When the doctor handed her to me, it was a huge relief to see that she had even more hair than I do. No one knows what her exposure to the chemo really was, but her mop of black hair seemed like proof that she was protected, somehow."

"This little baby was somebody who needed to come into this world," Ciara said. "We're going to expect great things from you," she told Una.

Caroline made a silent promise to herself to never not be grateful again. Because life, what a gift it was.

She christened the child in April.

PART TWO

CHAPTER SEVENTEEN

April 2012

Laura reached the castle, the tranquil quiet broken only by occasional birdsong. Her thoughts returned to the present moment and to the ring she had found. The solitaire sparkled on her left hand. It positively dwarfed her engagement ring.

"Mrs Hamilton," she heard a familiar voice call. She was steps away from the hotel entrance.

"Conor, hello," she said warmly, turning around.

"I was wondering if you're all right, Mrs Hamilton. Unless my eyes were deceiving me, I thought I saw you standing in the river a little while back."

His wizened, weather-beaten face was curious. Too many beers, over too many years in the hotel bar, had made that face distinctly jowly.

"I wasn't fishing without a licence, Conor," she deadpanned.

The gillie laughed.

"I'm glad to hear that, Mrs Hamilton. You gave me quite a shock, I can tell you. I couldn't believe my eyes!"

"It wasn't a salmon I was after," Laura said by way of explanation. "It was altogether a different kind of catch."

Conor was puzzled. Laura flashed the diamond ring before his eyes.

"Believe it or not, I found this little dazzler on the riverbed."

"Well, I'll be damned," he said, puzzlement turning to bewilderment. "That will be a first. Is it the real deal?"

"There's no doubt about that," Laura said as she handed over the ring.

The gillie examined it carefully between heavily nicotine-stained fingers.

"I'm absolutely gobsmacked," was all he could muster.

"It took me by surprise too."

"I'll bet it did! It's the biggest catch I've ever come across," he said, his brown eyes twinkling. "It's bigger than anything that husband of yours has caught. He'll be impressed and rightly so."

"He's in for a surprise."

"Correct. That he is. He's on the missing list today, I believe."

"Alex had a meeting in Galway that he couldn't get out of. Or so he told me. He's due back this evening."

"He might have been telling the truth, Mrs Hamilton," he said. "He's fond of the place, I've noticed."

"We both are, Conor."

"He's not going to believe that you found this ring at Beat Two."

"I can scarcely believe it myself. I wonder how long it was lying there. I wonder who it belonged to," she said.

"It's yours now, Mrs Hamilton. I'm here thirty-five years and believe you me; no one has ever come looking for a diamond ring. A diamond that size, I'd remember!"

"It's an amazing piece of jewellery. Have a look at the inscription."

"I'll put my glasses on, Mrs Hamilton. The old eye sight is not the best for reading anymore. I'm getting on a bit."

Laura gave a little titter.

Conor took his spectacle case out of a jacket pocket and put his glasses on. He took a closer look at the inscription on the ring band.

"Suri? Is that what I'm reading, Mrs Hamilton?"

"Yes. That's what I thought too."

"I've never heard of anyone with that name."

"Me neither," Laura said.

"It sounds foreign if you ask me." He looked at the inscription again, and took his time. "I can't fully read the date, not the day or the month anyway. I can make out a 9 and a 2. It could be 1920 something."

"Well done, Conor! I couldn't make out the date at all. I think you're right because the setting looks Art Deco."

He looked absently at her.

"You have me there, Mrs Hamilton," he said.

"Art Deco was the period style used in jewellery design in the 1920s," she explained.

"Ah. Right. Okay. I'm with you now. That will date back to the Maharaja's time, Mrs Hamilton. He was living here then. My grandfather and indeed, his father before him, were gillies here back in the day."

"So Alex told me. That's remarkable, Conor. Your grandfather must have had some interesting tales to tell from his time working here."

"Indeed, he did! Suri could be Indian, you know. It sounds Indian."

"You could be right," she said, and smiled at him.

He smiled back, noting as he did how well Mrs Hamilton looked. The woman seemed happier, more engaged with life.

Her hair was longer and the style was flattering. She had started wearing makeup and it suited her. Usually, Conor never spotted these kinds of things although you couldn't help but see a difference in Laura Hamilton. There was something very attractive about her these days. There was more of a spark between her and Alex too.

He was not the only one to have noticed. Several of the staff had remarked on it.

"Those two are canoodling like a pair of youngsters," Seán told Conor the last time the Hamiltons stayed.

And Maura had remarked to Jane: "Mrs Hamilton is looking awfully well these days. Do you know what? I think she looks younger now than she did when she first started coming to Doonmara."

Noticing the transformation herself, Jane agreed.

"She does, doesn't she?" she said. "And why wouldn't she, Maura? After all, she's married to George Clooney."

"Ah, the lovely George! Mr Hamilton doesn't look too bad himself."

"When has Alex ever looked bad?" Jane said.

"Oh, I forgot, it's Alex now and not Mr Hamilton," Maura teased.

"Only to the privileged few," Jane said and giggled.

Alex Hamilton remained Jane's favourite customer. She was more fond of him now, since that
day in the garden, when they had shared secrets
and sat comfortably together, beside the blue
hydrangea.

Mr and Mrs Hamilton were definitely more
touchy-feeling with each other. Alex often had his
arm draped around his wife when they entered the
restaurant. On occasion, Jane would see him reach
for her hand when they sat at the table. There was
an intimacy about their relationship that had been
absent before.

And there was lightness; easiness had crept in.
Yes, Jane could see that. Alex would sometimes
tease Laura when Jane was taking their order.

"For a change, my wife is having the scallops,
Jane."

Jane would laugh, because year in, year out,
and without fail, Laura would order the scallops
whenever they were on the dinner menu.

Or it might be: "We're back, Jane. Hold back on
the walnut bread. There'll be a rush on the walnut
bread the next few days. Mark my words."

It was always said kind-heartedly. His love and
devotion to Laura was plain to see.

"Don't take any notice of my husband, Jane,"
Laura would retort. She pretended to be annoyed but she clearly enjoyed the repartee. "I've

never seen you refuse a slice of walnut bread, Alex!"

These days, she looked like a woman in love. That struck Jane. She was happy for them both. Jane was not a betting woman but if she was, she would bet that something had been recaptured for Alex and Laura. Something had been missing from the relationship and whatever that was; it was back, and with a vengeance.

A little after six, there was a knock on Laura's bedroom door. It was Lucy.

"Would you like the bed turned down, Mrs Hamilton?" the chambermaid enquired politely.

"Yes, thank you. Come in," Laura said, opening the door a little wider to allow Lucy to pass.

"How are you?" she asked as Lucy went about her business.

Laura was fond of the girl. She had been sorry to hear that the engagement between Pawel and Lucy had been broken off. Laura wondered what had happened.

"I'm well, Mrs Hamilton."

"You'll never guess what I found this afternoon?" Laura said, and showed the chambermaid the ring.

"Where did you find that?" Lucy said, astonished.

"In the river, of all places! Here, have a closer peep."

Lucy took the ring.

"It's stunning, Mrs Hamilton. The diamond is huge. Is it real?"

Laura nodded.

"Try it on."

Lucy hesitated.

"Seriously, try it on. Go on."

Lucy slipped the ring on to her engagement finger.

"Wow. It's beautiful." She twirled her hand approvingly. "The last time I had a ring on this finger I was engaged," she said. "But it was nothing like this. I've never seen a diamond this big. You are a lucky woman, Mrs Hamilton."

Am I? Laura thought. One thing was true. Her fortune had changed over the past year.

"I was sorry to hear that you and Pawel broke up," Laura said. "I hope you've been able to put it behind you."

"Pawel has left and it's a lot easier now that he has gone. Actually," she said, and looked bashful, "I've met someone."

"Oh, Lucy, I'm delighted to hear that. Tell me all about him."

"He's an Irish fellow. He works in a hotel nearby. I'd never go out with someone working in the same hotel again. Never again!" she said with vehemence.

It wasn't easy for Lucy working with Pawel after the couple had parted ways. It was equally as hard for her fiancé, Laura reasoned.

"I can understand that. Is he nice, this new man of yours?"

"He's a cutie. I like Irish men. I'd never go out with a Polish or a Slovakian boyfriend again. Never!"

"Why ever not?" she asked, curious.

"They're all ego. It's all about them. They don't listen to you and to what you might want. And they're too possessive. Irish men are different. This fellow is anyway. He's lovely, Mrs Hamilton."

French men too, were off Lucy's list. She wouldn't be telling Mrs Hamilton that. Such an admission might lead to too many uncomfortable questions. Lucy wouldn't be revealing anything about her liaison with a certain French man, especially as that French man was now married.

The wedding had gone ahead. Lucy's engagement had ended in tatters, while Jean-Pierre and Marie had enjoyed their dream wedding in Doonmara and in the process Lucy had broken Pawel's heart with her treachery.

Normally a happy go lucky sort of guy, Laura had seen a change in Pawel after the break up. He had tried to put a brave face on, but frequently he had looked despondent.

"Are you still planning to go home?" Laura asked the chambermaid.

"Not anymore," Lucy said and shaking her head. "I like it here. I like the life. And my sister has come over. She's working in Clifden."

"That's wonderful. You must be delighted to have your sister living here. And you really like this guy, don't you?" Laura said, thinking that Lucy appeared very content.

"Yah, I really do."

"There might be another engagement ring on that finger before not too long," Laura said.

Lucy chuckled and said, "Not like this one! I'm in no rush, Mrs Hamilton. I rushed into things before and look what happened."

There was another knock on the door.

"Laura, it's me love," Alex said loudly.

Instantly, Lucy saw Mrs Hamilton perk up. Laura went to open the door. She gave her husband a warm embrace.

"I missed you," she said. "It's not the same here without you."

"I left as soon as I could. The meeting went on longer than I expected."

"Is there anything else you need, Mrs Hamilton?" Lucy said, interrupting. "Would you like some more water?"

"We could do with two more bottles of the still, Lucy. Thank you."

"I'll go and get them, Mrs Hamilton. Good evening, Mr Hamilton," Lucy greeted Alex. Lucy hoped she'd be as happily married one day. "Mrs Hamilton, I better not forget to give you this," she said, grinning. She returned the ring to Laura before vacating the suite.

Laura slipped the ring on. Turning to her husband, who couldn't take his eyes off her hand, she said, "Do you like my new purchase?"

By way of response, he whistled his approval.

"You're kidding," he said, for he knew immediately that the diamond was real. "That's way out of our league!"

"It's more of an acquisition than a purchase, Alex. But I believe it's mine."

"Seriously?"

She related what had happened earlier.

"That's some catch, Laura."

"Conor said exactly the same thing."

"God only knows the size of the salmon you'd catch if you took up a fishing rod."

"There's an inscription on the band, Alex. I can make out the name *Suri*. Conor was able to decipher part of the date. It's 1920 something. Here, have a look yourself." Laura took the ring off her finger. She handed it to her husband.

"This is a serious piece of jewellery," he said, examining the ring. "How does a ring like this end up at the bottom of a riverbed in Connemara? There must be a story behind it. The mind boggles."

"Conor says that it dates back to the Maharaja's time. That would make sense, don't you think? Perhaps there is some link to him or to someone in his family. He was famously wealthy by all accounts, and he lived a very opulent lifestyle."

"You could be right. That seems more than likely. I remember hearing about the Maharaja giving ruby cufflinks to Conor's great grandfather."

"That was extravagant, by normal standards, anyway."

"This is an engagement ring, isn't it?"

"With that inscription, I'd say so."

"It's an improvement on the one you have. I was penniless at the time."

"You're ring will always be precious to me," Laura said. "However, that doesn't mean that I'm not thrilled to bits with this!" she said, and laughed.

She laughed a lot these days, he thought.

"I have to admit that even I think it's magnificent. And as you know, I don't ever wear diamonds!"

"They're not really your thing," she said. "But in all seriousness, Alex, whoever owned this must have been heartbroken to have lost it. Though how you could lose a piece of jewellery like this is beyond me."

"It's a mystery. It will be interesting to have it valued."

"What's the law, Alex? Am I allowed to keep this or what?"

"I imagine you'll have to hand it into the guards. They will probably hold the ring in safe keeping and then, if no one claims it, the ring is yours to keep. Of course, I could be wrong. It could be a case of finders, keepers. Why don't you phone your brother? He'll know where the law stands in relation to this."

Laura's brother, Peter, was a solicitor.

"I had thought of Peter," she said. "Anyway, let's have a glass of wine. I got room service to bring up a bottle. It's chilling in a bucket on the table."

"Good woman. I like the way you're thinking."

Just then, Lucy knocked on the door, Alex opened it and retrieved two bottles of water from the chambermaid. He followed Laura through to the lounge area and sat on the couch. She poured him a glass of white wine and then poured one for herself.

"Cheers," she toasted as she raised her glass.

"To us," he said.

"To us."

They clinked glasses. He took a sip of his wine.

"Mmm. That's nice." He looked at her and said, "We've come a long way, you and I."

"It's been quite a journey. But we got there, Alex. I'm happy again. I never thought I'd be able to say that."

"And you make me happy, Laura, and on occasion, very happy indeed."

She laughed again. She knew what he was referring to.

"The intimacy we've shared over the past few months has been special," he said, continuing the conversation. "It's been wonderful, Laura." He took her hand and kissed it. "Really wonderful," he repeated.

"It has been," she agreed, "I feel very passionate about you, Mr Hamilton. All the time, it appears. It must be all those years of self-denial."

She could joke about it now. Everything had fallen into place. That had not always been the case; not in the early days after their reunion that fateful August weekend.

Laura had left Doonmara on a bit of a high, full of optimism and so had her husband. The following morning, Alex appeared quiet in himself. Overnight, his mood had changed entirely. Laura feared a setback. Were they back to where they were?

Unknown to Laura, Alex was fretting about his rendezvous with Caroline. Though Alex intended to finish the relationship with his mistress, he was feeling horribly guilty about meeting Caroline. He was full of remorse about the affair.

"What time will you be home tonight?" Laura had asked before he'd left for work that morning. She was planning a special dinner. She'd cook the salmon he had caught.

"I'm not sure, Laura. I'll text you later," he had said, in a tone that didn't encourage further discussion.

He had texted her later to say that he wouldn't be home for dinner. The text was vague. She didn't know his whereabouts or what time Alex would be home. The salmon went into the deep freeze.

Doonmara had been heaven. After all of these years, she and Alex had reconnected, and against all the odds. She had thought her marriage was back on track. They had been happy the day before. It had been a perfect day.

She had tried to phone Alex later that evening but his phone had been switched off. That made Laura suspicious. Then, shortly after 10pm, Alex had rolled in, looking the worse for wear. He had arrived home in a taxi. It was obvious that he had a few drinks on board which explained his mode of transport.

Her heart had sunk into her shoes. Where had he been? Who was he with? Laura had held her tongue and kept at bay those bothersome questions that she would have liked answers to.

Instead she'd said, "Have you eaten? Would you like me to fix you something?"

"No, I'm good," he had told her. "I had something earlier. It's been a long day and I think I'll hit the sack."

He didn't want to talk and Laura didn't push it. She didn't want to start any kind of confrontation, not when they had only just called a truce. It was unclear territory too, because for years Alex had come and gone as he pleased.

She reviewed his habits. Tuesdays? Alex usually went to the gym on a Tuesday. He was open about that. Had that been a cover story all along or was she being paranoid? Alex had said nothing about going to the gym this evening.

Then she remembered the Tuesday night, three or four in fact, when he had been away on business. There was a definite pattern of behaviour on Tuesdays.

"I'll be up later. I'm going to watch something on the telly," Laura had said, and left it at that.

She was uneasy. What she had suspected in Doonmara and what he had tried to tell her was true then. There was someone else. Had he ended it this evening? Or was it still going on? Laura wasn't sure.

Alex had gone to bed. Laura had remained sitting on the couch in front of the television. She had turned the sound down when Alex had come in and it remained mute.

Laura had taken stock. She could look back, or she could look forward. This was her last chance of happiness and Laura Hamilton was going to take it. It was time to start living again. They had wasted enough years. She had been given a life line that weekend.

For a short while, Laura had thought Alex was dead and she had been devastated. It had taken that for Laura to realise that she loved her husband. Laura was transformed after the weekend. She was no longer fading into oblivion. She would fight for her husband. Laura could forgive and forget his infidelities because she was partially to blame.

She had considered her options. If there was someone else, and if that was who Alex was with tonight, he may have ended it. What had happened between them in Doonmara gave Laura hope for optimism. What had taken place between them had been real. She was certain of it.

If there was someone else and if the affair was now over, Laura could live with that. She didn't want a full confession. What good would come of that? Confessions were overrated, in her opinion.

His would be anyway, because it would upset Laura enormously to hear the details. It would make her feel insecure about her husband. Laura wasn't completely secure about the place she had in his affections. Not yet. That would take time.

What if Alex needed to tell her? What if he wanted to tell her everything in order to clear his conscience? What then? Affairs or not, Alex was a principled man. That she knew. Maybe, the strain of leading a double life was getting to him. After all, he had tried to tell her about his infidelities in Doonmara.

"There's something I need to tell you, before we take this any further." That's what he had said that night. She had told him it didn't matter. She had hushed him up. And that afternoon, sitting underneath the blue hydrangea, he had admitted there had been other women.

Once, she hadn't cared. She cared now. She had cared too when he sat beside her on the bench. That afternoon, she hadn't wanted to hear what he was telling her. She had thought that Alex was dead, and that she had lost him forever. She wanted to forget all of their difficulties. She wanted to block out the present. Just for one day.

The weekend had given them both a second chance. Could they pull through? Could they move on, and without any professional help?

Laura was against therapy. She had revisited Rachel's death enough. They both had. Neither of them needed to work through all of the sadness and the pain again. It would be like putting a magnifying glass on their anguish and loss. Therapy was exhausting sometimes.

And Laura didn't want to hear about any liaisons her husband might have had. She accepted what had taken place and that there were other women. She wanted to put that into the past and to draw a line underneath it. Laura could understand why it had happened and she had forgiven Alex in her own head. After all, hadn't he come to her the first time he had strayed?

"I'm sorry, Laura. I feel terrible about what I have done," he had said repentant.

At the time, Alex had suggested counselling. He had been willing to take ownership of his actions. He had been honest with her. That would have been the right time to consider counselling, not now.

Back then, she had buried her head in the sand. If she were honest, she'd have to admit that she gave Alex the green light to go ahead with his little dalliances. He had been discreet. He had always been discreet.

Now, she had finally chosen to move on with her life. She had spent too many years living in the past, and drowning in a sea of sadness. There and then, she decided that she would trust Alex to do the right thing. He was a good man.

That was her gut instinct and she went with it. There would be no more to it. She would give him time. Hadn't he been more than patient with her?

Her expectations needed to be realistic. Everything couldn't change overnight. Not everything. It would take time and patience to get their lives back on an even keel, no matter how fantastic the sex had been in Connemara. She smiled at that thought. It had been fantastic. Amazing. Thrilling. There was no reason for Alex to stray again.

When Alex awoke the next morning, she greeted him chirpily.

"Good morning, sleepy head," she said. "Speaking of which, how is that head of yours?"

"Rotten," he acknowledged. "I'm sorry about last night, Laura. I had a few too many. It's not like me."

"Noted. How about some caffeine?"

"I think it's more a case of some vitamin C and a couple of pain killers first," he said.

"I'll see what we have."

As she was leaving the room he said, "Laura, thanks. Thanks for not getting on my case."

Alex heard her bustling around downstairs. He presumed that she had tried to phone him. Yet, she had said nothing about his phone being switched off. There had been no boundaries between them for so long. That would have to change. Their day to day lives would have to change. He would work at it. At least his relationship with Caroline was over. Laura and he were truly starting afresh.

A few moments later, Laura came back.

"Thanks," he said gratefully as he took a glass of water from her and swallowed the two Solpadine she handed him. She had a glass of orange juice in her other hand and she placed it on his bedside table.

"I'll see you downstairs in a while," she said.

He looked rough but Laura said nothing. Alex came down a little later and they had breakfast together. Laura had gotten over the first stumbling block.

She trusted that same gut instinct even when her brother confronted her a few weeks later about Alex.

"Laura, I hate to break this to you, but I think Alex is seeing someone. Elsie, saw him with someone recently and it looked very cosy. Too cosy. I've been hearing rumours about Alex. I've had my suspicions for a long time."

She said nothing.

"It was about a month ago. A Tuesday evening, Elsie said. "She saw him with some woman in a pub in Limerick."

On hearing that, Laura was relieved. It had been that Tuesday, the night after they had returned from Doonmara. Alex had been at home every Tuesday after that first week. Her husband hadn't seen the woman again.

Laura said, rather firmly, "I'm sure Elsie was mistaken, Peter. He was having a drink with someone, and that's all there was to it. We're good and everything's fine."

"Oh wake up, Laura," her brother said, sounding aggravated. He had witnessed at first hand the disintegration of his sister's marriage after his niece had died. "Everything's not fine and it hasn't been for years. Have you no self-respect, Laura? Don't you care that your husband is out screwing around? It's probably not the first time either. Not from what I've heard."

That hit home.

"You're right in one respect, Peter," Laura hit back. "Things haven't been good for years. But we've turned a corner. I've turned a corner. Whatever Alex has done, I pushed him. I'm not going to explain any further because it's between me and my husband. But I will say this. If Alex has been with someone else, it was because he got nothing from me. No love, no understanding and no affection. It must have been like I was punishing him for Rachel's death because I took it out on him.

"It was like that since the day Rachel died. I was so wrapped up in my own loss that I forgot about my husband. And believe you me, he tried. He tried so hard, Peter. Cut him a little slack. I'm not a victim."

"Okay, sis," her brother said, admonished. "I'm backing off."

He was surprised at her outburst. He hadn't seen her that fiery for a long time. He shifted his weight to his other foot.

"Good. And Peter, one more thing. Don't dream of mentioning what Elsie said to Alex. Stay out of it."

"Like I said Laura, I'm backing off. I'm going to leave now."

"Fine."

As he was leaving, her brother asked with concern, "Have you really turned a corner?"

"We both have."

"Then, I'm glad. I mean that, Laura."

"It's easy to judge when you're standing on the side-lines, Peter. Behind closed doors, you never know what's going on between two people. When two people's lives are turned upside down like ours were, it is never an easy path."

"Point taken. I'm sorry about what I said about you having no self-respect. I should never have said that. I worry about you. That's all. I know how tough it was for you losing Rachel. But we lost a bit of you too when she died."

That got to Laura.

"Come here to me," she said, drawing her brother towards her.

Peter hugged his sister, holding her tight.

"I miss her too," he said, thinking there was a determination and a sparkle about his sister today that he'd not seen in many years. The light had been switched on behind eyes that had appeared dead for a long time.

"You were a great uncle and a great godfather," she told him.

Her brother said goodbye and took his leave. He phoned his mother later that evening.

"I called over to see Laura today, Mum."

"Oh, how is she? How did you think she looked?" his mother asked, concerned. She was worried about her only daughter and had been, ever since the day Rachel had died.

"She's back, Mum. We have Laura back. She's back to her old self," Peter said.

His mother began to cry.

CHAPTER EIGHTEEN

Gradually, over the coming months and with a little effort, everything in their day to day lives shifted into place.

Laura had been working in the Civil Service for seventeen years. Incapable of working when Rachel died, Laura had taken a career break for two years. She could barely function. After that, and for the following three years, she had gone back to work on a part-time basis, before resuming her position full-time.

Laura worked in the Revenue Department. She liked her job well enough. She needed something to get out of bed for each morning. However, Laura wanted a new challenge.

"I'd like to do a Masters, Alex," she said after Christmas. "I've been researching it a bit. The Business Management Programme in UL sounds interesting. I'd have to start September next."

"You should go for it," he said, delighted.

Laura's appetite for life was back, and it was affirming.

"It's a full-time programme. I'd have to apply for a sabbatical from work. What do you think? Can we afford for me to give up work for a while?"

"Of course, we can."

"I'd feel bad about becoming a kept woman," she said.

"Don't be silly, love. Business hasn't been this good for a long time. We're not back to the tiger days but the company is doing well, very well. If you went ahead with this, I'd be thrilled for you."

"I'll get in touch with the course tutor and put my name in the hat."

"Do that. Anyway, there are other ways you can earn your keep," he said, pulling her down on the bed, and unbuttoning her top. "Any number of ways and starting from now."

He buried his head in her neck and kissed her gently there. She felt her body opening up and pulled at his trousers.

"Wait," he said softly, and pulled her hand away. "All good things come to those who wait."

He kissed her on the mouth, slowly caressing her body, taking his time. He liked the way she was impatient for him. It continued to thrill him because she had rejected him for so long. Alex never tired of her. He could never tire of Laura.

He had wondered if her desire for him might wane after the first flush. The months had passed and that hadn't happened. Their sex life was gratifying. That was an understatement. Their sex life was great. It was an unexpected joy which bonded them completely.

March was their wedding anniversary. Alex took Laura out to dinner on the day in question and had a floral bouquet delivered to the house. Flowers had arrived on Valentine's Day too. Prior to their weekend away in Connemara, Alex hadn't sent his wife flowers in years. They had exchanged anniversary cards this year. They hadn't done that for several years.

"I think we're going to be okay," he said, hesitantly. He looked at her expectantly. They were sitting in the restaurant. They had finished their starters.

"Me too," she said.

"There's no one else," he said, as he held her gaze. "And there never will be."

Laura believed her husband. Whoever she was and whatever she had meant to him, the other woman was long gone. Laura had been right to trust her gut.

"You mean the world to me, Laura."

"Connemara changed everything," she said.

"It did," he agreed. "I should tell you something. When I drove up to Doonmara that weekend, I had come to a decision." He paused for a moment. "I was planning to leave you," he continued. "Not that weekend, but in the coming weeks."

"For someone else?" she said with a sharp intake of breath. They were sailing close to the wind here.

"I wasn't leaving you for someone else. That wasn't it at all. I was leaving for us. I hated myself and I couldn't continue my life the way it was. I had reached the point where I couldn't stay. I thought if I left, that it might force you to move on with life. It was the only conceivable way I could see you moving on. I thought Rachel's death had destroyed us."

Laura considered what he said. Neither of them spoke for a few moments. The waitress arrived to clear their plates. She returned and refilled their glasses. When she had left, Alex resumed the conversation.

"I can assure you, Laura that if I had left I would have been very much on my own. That's the truth. There was someone else but I had already decided to end that relationship."

Laura took a leap of faith.

"When did you end it?" she asked nervously.

"The day after we came back. I had arranged to meet with her with the intention of finishing things before I ever set foot inside the hotel."

"I knew there was someone else. You tried to tell me that Friday night."

"Yes, I did."

She sipped some wine then cradled the glass in both hands. He was telling her the truth but that didn't stop her from hating the other woman. How long had it gone on? Did Laura want to know?

"I believe you, Alex," she said, deciding that she didn't want to know. "It's hard to hear, because I can't bear the thought of you being with someone else. But it's in the past."

"I love you. I've always loved you. You're the love of my life, Laura."

"I love you, Alex, with all of my heart. I just forgot that for a while. And I very nearly lost you in the process. It's ironic. I thought you had died and that I had lost you. It seems that I was on the verge of losing you anyway."

"We both nearly lost each other, Laura. We've come so far. We're happy. Look what we would have lost."

"I know. I hoped that we could pick up the pieces but I would never have guessed that I could feel this alive or be this happy. It took thinking that you were dead, for me to finally wake up."

"We found each other again, Laura. I was crushed after Rachel died. And I saw at first- hand how Rachel's death destroyed you. I tried my best to be there for you, but I couldn't reach you, no matter how hard I tried. As the months turned into years, it was hard not to take your rejection personally. Instead of Rachel's death bringing us closer together, her death drove us apart. But we've found our way back."

He smiled.

"Why are you smiling?"

"It's our anniversary and I meant to be romantic tonight. I was planning on going all out. I've made a balls of it. I should have held off on this conversation for another night."

She smiled back at him.

"I don't think we would be having this conversation if we hadn't got to such a good place. I never wanted a full confession, Alex. I was thinking the worst but you've filled in the gaps. Knowing that you were going to end things with this woman before Connemara happened makes it easier. I can let her ghost rest. I can smile, because I'm going to make you stick to your plan. We haven't even got to the main course. Go on, impress we with your romantic strategy."

"Game on," he said

The rest of the night went according to plan and their conversation took on a lighter tone. After they had shared a desert, he presented her with a present, gift-wrapped.

"Oh, Alex," she said. "What is it?"

"Open it," he said encouragingly.

She carefully unwrapped the small package to reveal a midnight blue jewellery box. She prised open the lid.

"They're beautiful," she said, looking at the emerald earrings. "That must have cost a small fortune!"

The earrings had been expensive. Not that Alex cared. The money was irrelevant.

"I love them," she told him, her voice joyful. She couldn't remember the last time that her husband had bought her jewellery and even then, nothing as nice as this. "Game set and match, Alex. Your game plan worked."

She took off the earrings she was wearing and tried the new ones on.

"They suit you," he said, pleased, eyeing his purchase from across the table. "They pick up the green in your eyes. By the way, have I told you that you look beautiful tonight?"

"Thank you." she said, delighted that her appearance had not gone unnoticed.

Laura had gone to a little effort. She had her hair done and the dress was new. Laura was wearing a royal blue chiffon dress. One he hadn't seen on her before. The colour suited her. Her gold locket glistened against the bare skin on her low neckline. She really did look beautiful.

"New dress?" he asked.

"Yes,"

"I like it."

"It likes you back. I feel bad. I have nothing for you."

"We can work on that," he said mischievously.

"Tell you what, if you play your cards right, I might consider giving you a special present later."

The waitress appeared out of nowhere to clear their desert plates.

"Would you like tea or coffee?" she asked.

"No, thank you," he said, before Laura could even consider. "Can you get me the bill, please?"

"In a rush, are we?" Laura teased as soon as the waitress was gone.

"I'm at your mercy."

Laura slowly wiped her mouth with the napkin, before folding it and putting it on the table.

"I like the sound of that," she said provocatively "I'm going to keep you at my mercy, all night if needs be. Meanwhile, you can anticipate what may or what may not happen when we get home. Actually, I might have a peppermint tea before we go, Alex."

Laura was toying with him. She wanted to leave as much as he did.

A moment or two passed. He shifted in his seat. He was mad for her.

"I can't wait a second longer," he said.

Neither could she. However, she was enjoying this scenario so instead she said, "Really? Tell you what, I'll skip the tea. Let's order a night cap instead."

He looked disappointed.

"All right," he said, deflated but taking the bait.

"Alex, don't you know that all good things come to he who waits," she taunted.

The shoe was on the other foot now and she was enjoying herself. She had him right where she wanted him.

She burst out laughing.

"I'm only teasing," she said. "Let's get out of here fast."

Alex paid the bill promptly. They were home in ten minutes flat. Normally, he was in control in the bedroom but on this night, Laura Hamilton took control and Alex relished every moment.

Much had changed in those short months. Laura felt invigorated. Reborn. It spilled into all corners of her life. She painted the house and she redecorated their bedroom – her *boudoir*, as Alex christened it.

These days they entertained. She invited family and friends to the house on a regular basis. Before,

Laura seldom had anyone over. The house had come alive again.

Before, Alex used to dread coming home. He'd sit in his car, psyching himself up to walk through the front door. He dreaded facing the wife he had who was only half-alive. The beautiful girl that he had married who had been so full of life and joy had long gone.

Now, he looked forward to coming home. Invariably, when he turned the key, he's get the whiff of something aromatic coming from the kitchen. Laura would greet him in the kitchen with a welcoming smile. Laura, the old Laura, had come back. She had turned their house into a home again.

He could see the effort she had made. He was making an effort too, on the big things and on the little things.

Cutting down on his office hours, Alex began to prioritise his wife over work. They would go for a walk together several evenings a week in the woods nearby. Alex had instigated that routine.

He bought her a new coffee machine, one that had a grinder attached. He's go out of his way to find nice coffee to buy. Every Sunday morning, he'd grind the beans and make Laura an Americano. He'd place it beside her on the bedside table.

"Good morning, Mrs Hamilton," he'd say as he sat on the bed. He'd lean down and place a butterfly kiss on her forehead or, if she was awake at this point, on her lips. "I'm going to get the papers. Do we need anything? Would you like me to get you a croissant?"

These were small gestures, and ones she appreciated. He was making an effort. He was a lousy cook. Nevertheless, he began to cook a meal for her every once in a while.

He was far more attentive, particularly when they were out and in company. Women monopolised Alex and he had let them. Why not? Around Alex, they were like bees to honey. He had been lonely and for years it was the only attention he got. He hoped it might make Laura jealous. She hadn't taken a blind bit of notice. Laura had been in her own little world at the time.

That was then. Now, he was always sure to give his wife his full attention. He gave her no reason to worry about his affections. He had eyes only for Laura. Before long, Laura felt secure in her place as his wife, as his friend, and as his lover.

Early one morning, as March drew to a close, Laura phoned her mother.

"I have a favour to ask, Mum," she said. "I was wondering if you could help me sort some of Rachel's things. It's not something that I want to do on my own. It would be great if you were here."

Sarah was happy to oblige. Rachel's bedroom had become a shrine to the little girl. Nothing had changed in the room since the day Rachel had died. Her granddaughter's clothes remained in the wardrobe, dresses pristine. Rachel's cuddly toys still lined the pillows of her bed.

"Of course, I'll come over and help you," she said. "We can tackle it together. When were you thinking of?"

"Today, Mum. I know it's very short notice but if you could come over today, I'd really appreciate it. I'm feeling brave today. If I leave it until another day, I might put it off altogether."

Her mother had a hair appointment but she didn't tell Laura that.

Instead, she said, "I'll be over in an hour. I've nothing on today. It's no trouble at all."

"Thanks, Mum. I'll see you then. I'll pop down to SuperValu and see if they will give me some boxes. I don't want to be putting Rachel's things in refuse sacs."

That wouldn't do at all. Nothing about Rachel was disposable. Not her clothes. Not her shoes. Not her toys. Not her books. There was something unseemly about putting the child's belongings in bin bags.

As soon as the call had ended, Sarah phoned her hairdresser to cancel her appointment. Her hair could wait another day. Sorting out Rachel's room shouldn't be held off a moment longer.

Sarah had seen Laura blossom over the past year. As Peter put it, they had got Laura back. This year would mark Rachel's eighth anniversary. Laura had stopped living the day Rachel had died. After all of these years, Laura had chosen to start living again.

⊷ ⊶

"Mum, you and Dad need to come to the Regional straight away," Peter had said over the phone. "Rachel has had an accident and they've taken her into A&E. Call me when you get to the hospital and I'll meet you at the door."

Peter wouldn't elaborate further. Rachel was already dead. Thinking of his mother, and how alarmed she would be at the news, Peter tried to get hold of his father first. Tom hadn't answered his mobile.

"How is Rachel? Is it bad?" Sarah had asked her son. They were standing outside the hospital.

"It's not good, Mum."

Sarah thought that it must be very serious indeed. It didn't occur to her that Rachel was dead.

"Rachel's going to be all right though? Isn't she?"

317

He shook his head. His parents looked at him in bewilderment.

"You need to prepare yourselves," their son had said. "I'm afraid I have the worst possible news."

One look at her son's face confirmed the worst. Sarah had known then that her granddaughter was dead. Sarah waited for him to say the words because it couldn't possibly be true.

"Rachel is dead. She's gone," he said, before breaking down himself.

He brought his parents into a room where Laura, Alex, and members of the medical team were gathered. Sarah attempted to hug her daughter. Laura froze. Laura had already been told that Rachel was dead but she hadn't processed what the doctor had said.

"I'm very sorry," the doctor repeated now. "Your daughter is dead. I'm so sorry to have to break this news to you. We tried to resuscitate her but she was dead on arrival."

Although Laura was in shock, this time his words hit home. Laura had jumped out of her chair and run into the adjoining room where her daughter was lying on a makeshift bed, hooked up to a web of tubes and monitors. Laura had pulled every tube out of Rachel's body. She'd had to be restrained by staff. Sarah worried that Laura was acting like a crazy woman.

The doctor had then told the family that they were going to transfer Rachel somewhere more private. While they waited, Laura had picked up her mobile. Sarah had watched as Laura had begun to phone everyone she knew.

"It's Laura. Rachel's dead," she'd said. And with that, Laura hung up. She rang all her friends and relatives with the same message. Eventually, Alex managed to get the phone off her. Later, Laura had told her mother that she had no memory of phoning anyone.

She remembered pulling the tubes out of Rachel.

"I thought they might be hurting her, Mum," she had said by way of an explanation. "Rachel wouldn't want strangers looking at her like that. Not with tubes stuck into her body. Rachel wouldn't have liked it."

Laura revealed something else.

"Deep down, I think I knew that Rachel had died in the ambulance," she'd said. "On some level, I was aware of it, but I was in shock.

"I could see the looks the paramedics gave one another. I could see the way Alex was looking at them in disbelief. I thought if no one said the words, 'she's dead', that somehow, she was going to make it and that Rachel was still alive and fooling everyone. The only way I could cope was by being in denial.

"When the doctor said 'your daughter's dead', I knew it had to be true. And then I died too."

A little later, they had access to Rachel. Both set of grandparents followed Laura and Alex into the private room.

"Get out," Laura had screamed at all of them.

Alex had gently ushered the family from the room. Laura had got into the bed with Rachel, hugging the little girl close. She wouldn't allow anyone into the room for the next hour or two, not even her husband. Alex was in pieces but he put Laura's grief before his own.

The family had stood outside in the corridor, helpless and confused. A guard waited with them. Rachel's death was sudden and unexpected and the police had been notified immediately. The guard was under orders to remain with the body until an autopsy had been performed.

"Get out," Laura had screamed at the guard when he attempted to enter the room. He was a young policeman, not long on the force and totally unprepared for the scene he encountered at the hospital. He had tried again a little later.

"Get out," she had roared.

Unable to answer, the guard left. He stood outside the door with the family.

"He's not long out of Templemore," Sarah had said to her husband.

The young guard looked uncomfortable. He had never seen the dead body of a child before. His face was ashen and drawn in a look of pain. They didn't prepare you for this kind of thing at the Garda College in Templemore.

"Thank you for being so understanding," Jim had told him.

"It's terrible what happened. Just terrible," the policeman had said. "I'm sorry for your loss."

Sarah had wanted to hold her grandchild in her arms but Laura wouldn't let any of them near Rachel. Alex had forced his way into the room and in due course, Laura had allowed him to hold the child.

"It was like a primal force took hold of me," Laura had said to her mother years later. "I couldn't let any of you near Rachel in the hospital. Some kind of superhuman maternal instinct kicked in and took over. I should have let you hold her, Mum. I regret that now. I'm sorry. You were always so good to Rachel and she loved you."

Sarah had picked up Rachel every day, Monday to Friday, after playschool and minded her granddaughter until Laura collected the child on her way home from work. Sarah was part of the fabric of Rachel's life. Grandmother and granddaughter were close.

"I loved her with all of my heart, Laura. Rachel was a great joy to me and to your father."

"I don't know what came over me in the hospital," Laura had said. "I was like an angry lioness minding her cub. I thought I was protecting her from everything and everyone. I can't explain it, Mum."

Things had got worse as the night proceeded. Laura became frantic when she was informed that an autopsy had to be carried out.

"No one's going to cut open my daughter. Do you hear me?" Laura had screamed at the doctor. "No one is going to touch a single hair on my child's head."

She was given something to drink and before long, Laura was visibly calmer.

"They must have put a sedative in her drink," Jim had told Sarah.

"I could do with one myself," his wife had replied.

Once the tranquillizer had kicked in, the doctor returned to the room.

"The pathologist will carry out an autopsy first thing tomorrow morning," he had informed them, with compassion. Much to his relief, Laura had remained quiet.

"What will happen to my daughter in the meantime? Will she remain here?" Alex had enquired.

"We'll move her to the hospital morgue," the doctor had said.

On hearing this, Laura became agitated once more.

"You can't do that," she'd told the doctor. Turning to her husband, Laura then said, "We can't let them put her in the morgue, Alex. We can't have our little girl lying on a slab, alone. Tell him," she had pleaded.

Laura wanted to spend as much time with Rachel as she could before the child was taken away for the funeral and burial. A night in the morgue, followed by an autopsy the next day, meant Laura would be parted from her child for much of that time. Every effort was made to accommodate Laura.

The pathologist came to the hospital that night and performed an autopsy on Rachel. He wrote a report that Laura could never bring herself to read. It remained unread in a drawer at her home in Cratloe.

The undertaker had been marvellous too. Overnight, Alex, Laura and Sarah had waited in the hospital chapel until the autopsy was over. Laura sat there in a fog of disbelief and sedation. When it was over, the undertaker came to find them.

"They've finished the autopsy," he'd said.

It was touching five-thirty am. He had waited through the night.

"We're going to take Rachel to our Chapel of Rest and prepare her. Then we will bring your daughter home," the undertaker had said, sensitive to their needs. "We will be with you as soon as we can."

In the small hours of the morning, Jim had driven Sarah to Laura and Alex's house. They retrieved the outfit that Laura wanted Rachel to wear. Then, Sarah had returned to the hospital to sit with Alex and Laura.

Sarah had handed the items of clothing to the undertaker. Next, she phoned her husband.

"The autopsy's over. They're taking Rachel to the funeral home," she had said. "Can you collect us?"

"I'm leaving now," he'd said.

Jim was at the house in Cratloe, along with son Peter and daughter in law, Alex's parents, and a bunch of neighbours. Everyone had been working through the night preparing the house.

At the time of Rachel's death, the house had been upside down. Laura and Alex were having some interior design work done. The dining room and lounge were being painted and the curtains changed. On the day Rachel died, the walls had been prepped and the furniture moved into the centre of both rooms. The place was in a mess.

When Rachel came home later that morning, it was to a newly painted house. Overnight, the dining room and lounge had been painted and new curtains had been hung. The house had been cleaned from top to bottom. Everyone had pitched in.

People helped in the only way they could. What could you do for a couple whose only child had died in such a cruel accident?

"You did a fantastic job," Sarah had told her husband.

"It was a relief to be busy," he'd said. "It was a relief not to have time to think."

When Rachel arrived home, Laura remained as fiercely protective. The coffin stayed closed. Laura had been insistent.

"I don't want an open coffin," she had said. "Rachel wouldn't like people staring at her like that. Don't you know how shy she can be, Mum?"

Who am I to argue with that kind of logic? Sarah had thought.

When Sarah had tried to enter Rachel's room, she found the bedroom locked. It remained locked until the day after the funeral.

"I don't want anyone rooting around," Laura had said. "Rachel wouldn't like it. She wouldn't want anyone going through her things."

Rachel was waked at home. Over the coming days, Laura had refused to talk about Rachel. She didn't share stories. She didn't recall any precious memories. Later, Sarah had realised why.

"She didn't want to share Rachel with any of us. She refused to share a single memory. I think she wanted her all to herself."

"Why?" Jim had asked Sarah. "Why would she do that?"

"Because that's all Laura had left of Rachel," Sarah had said. "She didn't want to give that away. It was precious little as it was."

The coffin had remained closed in the lounge. When the undertakers came to the house to remove the coffin to the church, it was opened for the final time.

"We'll let you say goodbye in private," the undertaker had said before exiting the room.

Laura went to kiss Rachel. Next, Alex had kissed his daughter. Sarah badly wanted to kiss her grandchild goodbye but she remained motionless. Sarah was afraid Laura would lose it altogether if she approached her granddaughter.

Finding courage, she'd said, "Can I kiss Rachel goodbye, Laura?"

There was a short silence and then, much to Sarah's relief, Laura had turned to her mother and said, "Yes. You can all kiss Rachel goodbye."

Sarah then walked the few steps to the small coffin. She kissed her grandchild gently on the forehead, as if not to wake her. To this day, she could remember how Rachel's brow had felt. It was like marble.

There were a select few in the room with Laura and Alex, just both sets of grandparents. In turn, each grandparent had kissed Rachel goodbye. Sarah was grateful that Laura had allowed each of them to say their own personal farewell to little Rachel.

Peter and his wife had waited outside in the hall. Peter hadn't been allowed in and it had felt like a rebuff. He had wanted to say a final good bye to his goddaughter. It wasn't a deliberate snub. Laura was in too much pain to notice anyone else's suffering. She had nothing left for anyone else. All her focus was on Rachel.

Sarah stared at her beloved grandchild dead in the coffin. Rachel looked asleep. She looked as if she might wake up any moment. She was dressed in a pretty pink dress; the one Laura had bought Rachel for her fifth birthday. The birthday Rachel never lived to see.

Now against all the odds, Laura, their Laura, was almost back to her old self. Sarah accepted that Laura would never be the same again. Not exactly the same. That would be impossible.

Helping her daughter to clear out Rachel's room would be another step in the right direction. As soon as she could, Sarah got into her car and drove to Laura's house.

There were plenty of tears that morning as they packed away Rachel's things. There was the sound of laughter too.

"My word, she did love pink," Sarah said.

"Yes, she did," Laura said and laughed. "In all its variations!"

Laura studied the little pile of clothes that were neatly folded on the bed. She had kept a few things back.

"I have her christening outfit put away," she told Sarah. "And I'm going to keep one little dress. Maybe this one." She lifted up a red velvet dress.

"She wore it on Christmas day," Sarah said. She remembered the day vividly. The entire family had spent the day together, unaware of the awful tragedy that loomed ahead. "Rachel looked so sweet in that dress."

"And maybe this tee shirt," Laura said, holding up a pink tee shirt that had diamanté scattered across the front. "She called the diamanté 'sparklies'. Remember, Mum?"

Sarah smiled and said, "She did, bless her. She'd get very excited over 'sparklies'."

"I'll keep a few of her favourite cuddly toys too."

"Keep whatever you need, sweetheart."

The dresses, shorts, tee shirts, jumpers – they all looked diminutive, and Sarah fought back the tears. She had forgotten how tiny Rachel was.

Sometimes, Sarah would call her granddaughter Thumbelina. When she did, Rachel would plague her grandmother until she relented and told Rachel the story of Thumbelina.

Laura kept a pair of shoes too. She showed them to her mum.

"Pink?"

"Naturally," Laura said. "Would you like a keepsake, Mum?"

Sarah pointed at a pair of shoes on the bed. They were patent black. They looked impossibly small. Rachel had worn them on Christmas day with the red dress.

"Can I take these?" she asked, picking one shoe up.

Laura nodded and pressed the remaining shoe into her mother's hands.

They stored everything carefully into boxes. One large box contained nothing but dolls and doll paraphernalia. There were seven boxes in all. It wasn't much to show for a life.

Together, they dismantled Rachel's doll's house. The pieces proved too big to place in a box, as did Rachel's pram for her dolls.

"Maybe Kitty could have them, Mum? She might play with the doll's house. What do you think?"

Kitty was Laura's niece and Peter's youngest child.

"It would be a nice memento," Sarah said. "Kitty will be delighted. And Peter. " Their task complete, Sarah asked, "What will you do with all of this?"

"I'd like to take everything into St Vincent de Paul. I phoned the shop earlier. I asked them if they could they give Rachel's things to a family in need. I don't want her things sold in a charity shop. It seems impersonal."

"That's a great idea," Sarah said encouragingly.

"Do you think we could head in there today, Mum? If I we don't, I might lose the courage to go. I might start pulling everything out of these boxes."

"Yes, of course, we can. We can go this afternoon. We can have a sandwich and a coffee first."

After a quick snack, they loaded up Laura's car and Sarah accompanied her daughter to the St Vincent de Paul shop.

"Thank you for today, Mum," Laura said as she was saying her goodbyes later that afternoon.

"Not at all, pet." Sarah said, pleased that she was able to be there for her daughter.

"I couldn't have done it without you."

Sarah looked fondly at her only daughter.

"I feel we have you back," she told Laura. You don't know how happy that makes me. Your father and I worry so much about you." Sarah hesitated, unsure of whether she should say what was on her mind.

"What is it, Mum?" Laura asked.

"When Rachel died, my heart was doubly broken, Laura. I lost the two of you that day. You and Rachel. You were my daughter. My little girl. I wanted to help you but you wouldn't let me in. I lost my granddaughter and I lost you."

Laura leant over to hug her mother.

"Now, I have you back," her mother said.

Laura took stock.

"I suppose I am back, Mum. That said, a part of me died that day. A part of me died with Rachel and I know that will never come back. Alex says there's ninety per cent of me back. I guess there will always be that ten per cent that's missing."

"That's enough for me, Laura. More than enough."

"Oh, Mum, I wish I had let you hold Rachel the night she died. I regret that now. I think that I wanted every memory of Rachel to be mine."

"I had worked that one out, pet."

"At the time, I was thinking, this is my child. This is my space and my time with Rachel. I didn't want to share any bit of Rachel with anyone. I didn't want to share any of the time that she had left with me. That included you, Mum, and even Alex.

"That's part of the reason I didn't want the coffin opened. I thought I was protecting Rachel too. She was my child and I was protecting her. That's what I remember telling myself. I wanted people to remember Rachel alive. I didn't want their final memory to be of Rachel laid-out in a coffin."

⊷ ⊶

When Alex came home, Laura showed him Rachel's room. She had phoned him earlier that morning to inform him of her plans.

"Remember I said I was going to try and pluck up the courage to pack up Rachel's things?" she had said. They had had a conversation a few weeks back. "That I thought I'd be able to? That it was time?"

"Yes," he'd said. "I remember."

She drew a sharp intake of breath.

"I'm going to tackle her room this morning, Alex."

His wife had sounded determined.

"I was afraid to say it earlier in case I chickened out."

"Would you like me to help? I can come home now," he'd offered.

"No, it's okay. Mum is coming over."

In a way, Alex had been relieved not to be coming home to pack up Rachel's things. He was a strong man. But he was afraid that he might have crumbled in front of Laura as they went about packing up Rachel's belongings. The last thing Laura needed was him being upset.

"If you're sure, Laura," he'd said.

"I am. I'll be fine. I promise."

Sometimes, Alex would steal into Rachel's room. He would open her wardrobe, touching her dresses with care. Or, he would sit on Rachel's bed and hold her favourite cuddly toy. She had been an adorable child, a little girl but always his baby.

In the early days after Rachel had died, Alex would open her wardrobe and push his face against her clothes, inhaling her scent in the darkness. For a long time they smelt of her. In those first few months, he got used to the way grief rushed towards him and then retreated, but on the day he discovered that Rachel's clothes no longer smelled like her, it felt like losing his baby all over again.

"Laura," he had said, and hesitated.

"What? What is it? Would you prefer to be with me while I'm at it?"

"No. That's not it, love. I was wondering. Can you keep her teddy?"

His voice had nearly cracked. Alex could see Rachel lying on the bed, arms around that teddy, as he read her a goodnight story. He'd steeled himself before continuing the conversation.

"And Laura, maybe that doll Bessie," he'd said. "It was Rachel's favourite, even though it seemed to me that she bashed that doll to bits!"

"How could I ever forget, Bessie," Laura had said, and smiled as she remembered Bessie trailing behind Rachel.

Alex was right. Poor Bessie had been bashed around.

"I think Rachel thought Bessie was a real baby half of the time," he'd said. "I caught her trying to force feed that doll one day. She could have been up for doll abuse."

Laura had laughed.

"I'll hold on to Bessie. And I'll keep a few of Rachel's favourite things, Al."

All day, he had worried about Laura. When Alex had arrived home, he was more than a little anxious.

"It can't have been easy," he said.

"It wasn't as bad as I thought it would be. I was ready. It was time. And mum was terrific. She was a great help."

"I'm glad your mother was with you. It's nice that Rachel's things will go to another little girl. It's fitting."

"I'm happy about that. Rachel had some lovely bits and pieces."

"You kept the doll's house?" he said, surveying the room.

"I thought that we might give it to Kitty."

"Well thought of. I think that Peter will appreciate the gesture."

Alex sat with Laura on the bed. He had the teddy in his hands.

"I was thinking," Laura began, "that we might turn Rachel's bedroom into an office for us both. Otherwise, it will remain an empty room. A sad room."

"That's a good plan, love. It's kind of always been off limits because it was Rachel's room. I can't see us using it as another guest room. It wouldn't sit right."

Over the coming weeks, Laura went about making the room into an office. She put a few family photographs in the room. There was one, of the three of them, with Santa. The child smiled shyly at the camera. Laura remembered that her daughter had been a little overawed by the presence of Santa Claus that day. Rachel was clutching a present from Santa. It was the last Christmas they had spent together as a family.

And there was a photograph of Rachel with Alex and Laura on her christening day. Laura had the infant scooped up in her arms. Alex had his arm around his wife and child. He looked proud.

"We look so young," he observed.

"We were," Laura said. "And clueless about parenting. I was scared stiff bringing Rachel home from the hospital."

"You were amazing, Laura. You were a great mum from day one. I remember being so nervous when I first held Rachel. She was incredibly small. Such tiny hands and feet. I was afraid I'd crush her or let her drop."

Laura was happy working in Rachel's room and so was Alex. He felt Rachel's presence strongly. That was comforting. It was another step forward for both of them.

Little did he know that Caroline had given birth to his baby three months previously?

Una spent the first two weeks of her life in hospital. She had developed breathing difficulties and initially, she had to be kept in an incubator. Caroline was worried about any possible side effects on the baby from the chemotherapy.

"I'll probably be checking for side effects for the rest of her life," she told Ciara.

Eventually, the day came to go home. Caroline had brought the baby home from hospital, and she set about making a new life for them both. It was just her and Una.

There would be ramifications if Alex ever discovered Caroline's secret. It would destroy his marriage and devastate his wife. It would impinge on Una, turning her life upside down. It would also turn Caroline's life upside down.

There was a possibility the child would be adversely affected. Caroline couldn't afford to take that chance. Her little daughter was too precious. Una had suffered a difficult enough start in life as it was.

Caroline could get sick again. That was a possibility. Each time she suffered a slight ailment, Caroline worried that the cancer had come back. If it did, what would happen to the child? She would have no mother or father.

Caroline put those niggling worries to the back of her mind. She had been given the all clear. Two days after she had given birth to Una the doctor had told Caroline that she was cancer free. She wasn't going to get sick again. That wasn't going to happen.

CHAPTER NINETEEN

"Show Jane your present," Alex said.

Laura lifted her right hand.

"I thought it was time I upgraded Laura's engagement ring," he said.

"What a magnificent ring! I've never seen anything like it," Jane said.

"My husband is teasing you," Laura said, and explained her find. "Besides, it's on the wrong hand. See." She held her left hand up. By comparison, her engagement ring looked very small.

"I thought you must be millionaires," Jane said. "Or that you had won the lottery!"

Alex threw his head back and laughed.

"Neither, I'm afraid."

"I'm here twenty-six years," Jane said, and "no one has ever reported losing a ring like that. Obviously, I'd remember. I wouldn't be surprised if it was in the river since before my time."

"Conor said much the same," Laura said. "The ring dates back to the Maharaja's time, so who knows."

"The Maharaja would have been able to afford a ring like this," Jane said. "The diamond is spectacular. What's it worth? Have you any idea?"

"Not one iota, Jane," Alex said.

"You should have it valued."

"To be honest, we aren't sure what to do," Laura said.

"It's finders, keepers, if you ask me," Jane said.

Before long, the talk moved to dinner. Jane handed them both menus.

"You're out of luck, Laura. No scallops on the menu tonight," Alex said, scanning the dinner menu.

"I've had my fair share of luck, today Alex. I can live without the scallops!"

After dinner, they went through to the lounge. A couple, seated in front of the fire, got up to go. Alex and Laura quickly redeemed their places.

Before long, Seán arrived bearing a tray.

"One peppermint tea for Mrs Hamilton," he said, carefully placing the tea in front of Laura, "and one espresso for you, sir." Seán knew the drill by now. "I'll leave the petit fours with Mrs Hamilton," he added and positioned a small plate in front of Laura.

"Good thinking, Seán," she said, eying up a miniature macaroon. She devoured it immediately. "They're as light as air. Have one, Alex," she offered. "They're pistachio."

"Delicious," he confirmed.

Seán was hovering around pretending to stoke the fire.

Eventually the porter said, "I hear you had a bit of luck today, Mrs Hamilton. Word has it that you found a bit of treasure, so you did."

"News travels fast around here," Alex said.

Usually Seán was the broadcaster. Not today. Three different people had told Seán about the diamond that Mrs Hamilton had found – first Conor, then Lucy, and now Jane. For once, Seán was not first in the know and he was a little put out.

"Lucy mentioned something about a ring," he said.

Laura showed him her find.

"She was very excited at trying it on."

"You can try it on if you like, Seán," Alex said. "My wife wouldn't mind. Would you, Laura?"

"You're grand. That won't be necessary," Seán said, and the three of them laughed. "It's a fine ring all the same. A very fine ring if I may say so."

"To tell you the truth Sean, I can't believe that I found it. By the way, I hear Lucy has got herself a new boyfriend."

"That's right, Mrs Hamilton. He's a local man. He seems like a nice lad. After that business with Pawel, it's good to see Lucy happy again. She's only a young lass and she's far away from home."

"That's true. I believe her sister has come over."

"Indeed she has. The sister's working in Clifden, so she is."

"What happened to Pawel?" Laura enquired.

"He handed in his notice and went back home, Mrs Hamilton. Pawel always intended to go back to Poland. That was part of the problem, you see. Once they got engaged, Pawel piled on the pressure to go home. Lucy didn't want to leave her job here. Sure, it would have meant starting all over again in a new country."

"I guess she did that when she came here," Laura said.

"There you have it, Mrs Hamilton; my sentiments entirely. If Lucy was ever going to leave Ireland, it was to go back home to her own country. She didn't get on particularly well with Pawel's family either. Do you think he would listen to her? He ignored her completely, so he did. I'm afraid it was all about Pawel and what he wanted from life."

"Lucy indicated as much," Laura said, remembering what the chambermaid had told her earlier. "They got engaged quickly, didn't they?

"Too quickly, Mrs Hamilton. They had barely known each other a wet weekend when he put a ring on her finger. If you ask me, Lucy never thought it through. When Pawel insisted they move to Poland, she panicked. I was fond of Pawel but he was a bit bossy with Lucy. She can be a bit of a handful at times but underneath it all, she's a good girl."

The porter's affection for Lucy was plain to see.

"I liked Pawel," Laura said. "I hope it all works out for him and that he meets someone else someday."

"He will. He's young. He has plenty of time," Alex said.

"That he has," Seán agreed. "They miss him in the restaurant. He was a very good waiter."

As they were checking out the following day, James suddenly appeared.

"Good afternoon, Mr and Mrs Hamilton," the manager said brightly. He was a short, burly man with a broad face. Since their last stay, he had grown a beard. Alex didn't think it did the manager any favours. "I hope you enjoyed your stay with us."

"Thoroughly," Alex said, "as always".

"A little birdie told me that you found a diamond ring," the manager said, looking directly at Laura.

"I did as a matter of fact."

"I'm dying with curiosity. Can I see it?"

Alex looked at him sceptically. James hadn't come near them for the entire weekend, but now here he was. No doubt, he was wondering if the hotel had a possible claim.

Alex was correct in his assessment. He had the measure of the man. That was exactly what the hotel manager was thinking.

Laura was wearing the ring. She showed it to James.

The manager assumed Seán had been exaggerating when he described the ring that Mrs Hamilton had found. Seán was prone to that. On this occasion, James had wronged Seán. In fact, the hotel porter might have even underplayed the size and value of the diamond altogether.

"That's very impressive," the manager told Laura. He rubbed his hands in glee. "If you don't mind me asking, where exactly did you find this, Mrs Hamilton?"

James already knew the answer to that particular question, but it would lead very nicely into what he intended to tell the Hamiltons next. He had thought this through.

He wanted an admission from Mrs Hamilton that the ring had been found in the river. The river ran through Doonmara grounds and the hotel owned fishing rights to the river. Now that James had seen the ring for himself, he would be seeking legal advice as to what claim the hotel might have. This wasn't some worthless bauble. On the contrary, the ring could be worth thousands.

If James could lay claim to the ring for the hotel, he would be in line for a nice little reward for his efforts. It could go towards the new set of wheels he had set his heart on. He had the owner of the hotel wrapped around his finger. Any reward would be coming James' way.

"He can talk the talk," as Maura had often observed. "Walking the walk is another matter entirely."

The owner was based in Amsterdam and luckily for James, the Dutchman was out of the picture for most of the year. James took credit for everything. As long as the hotel made a healthy turnover, it all went swimmingly for James. There were no awkward questions asked.

He could feel that new Jeep within reach.

"Could I have a word with you both in private?" he asked a moment later. Things could get messy here. The manager didn't want a scene – not in front of other guests or staff. James wasn't sure how the couple would react to what he was about to say.

"Certainly," Alex said. The trio moved away from the reception desk and out of earshot.

"I hate to point this out," James said, lying through his teeth, "but technically the ring was found on Doonmara property. Surely you both must be aware of that?" He sounded patronising. "I think you may well find out that the ring remains the property of the hotel."

"We'll be taking advice on this, James," Alex said. "We won't be breaking any laws."

"I'd be happy to see this ring return to its rightful owner," Laura said. "By that, I mean the person who owned it."

"That's not likely, Mrs Hamilton. Not if it dates back to the 1920s," the manager said, a bit too sharply for Alex's liking.

"James, you know where we are and how to get in touch," Alex said. "We had better hit the road. We have a long journey ahead of us. For the moment, the ring is staying with us."

James looked perplexed.

"Don't look worried, James," said Alex. "We're hardly going to flee the country. Laura and I are not fugitives. You must have our address on file. We're coming here long enough. I'm sure you'll be able to track us down if need be."

James decided to take a different tack.

"I think you've misjudged me, Mr Hamilton. I don't mean to offend either of you in any way," he said, backtracking. "If I caused any offence, I apologise."

He paused for a moment to gauge their response. Alex wasn't buying a word of the apology. James was fighting a losing battle with the Hamiltons but he was a stubborn man.

"Nonetheless," he persisted, "I do think the ring should remain in my keeping until this is sorted out. As hotel manager, I have an obligation to do the right thing here." His tone remained accusatory

"Have no fear, James," Alex said, distain creeping into his voice. "My wife and I will do the right thing."

"I wouldn't keep anything that didn't belong to me," Laura said indignantly.

"No, of course not," James said in an effort to appease Mrs Hamilton. The Hamiltons were proving awkward. Bloody hell. James was surprised at Laura Hamilton. He hadn't realised she had such spirit.

"We'll hang on to the ring in the meantime," Alex said firmly, leaving no room for further discussion. "Like I said, James, you know where we are. I'm confident we can clear the matter up quickly."

You can bet your sweet life on that, thought James. He'd be phoning the hotel solicitor as soon as this pair was off the premises.

"Very well. I'll be in touch," he said stiffly. "If you'll excuse me, I had better go and attend to my other duties. I hope you have a safe journey home, Mr and Mrs Hamilton. We hope to see you back at Doonmara before long." Back with that ring, he hoped.

"Thank you, James," Alex said, playing along. "We'll be back soon enough."

"What did you make of that?" Laura asked, once they were seated in the car.

"I suppose he has a point. But that fellow rubs me up the wrong way."

"He was furious."

"He was hot and bothered all right! It was comical."

"He's so blinking obvious," she said.

"That he is. He's only looking out for himself. He's thinking what he could get out of this."

"That crossed my mind too. I wouldn't mind leaving the ring at the hotel, but not in his keeping. I don't trust James."

"Me neither. We'd never seen the ring again. You can take my word on that, Laura. We'll talk this over with Peter. We'll get the necessary advice and sort this out one way or another. In the meantime, enjoy wearing your ring while you can."

"I might as well. I may not have it on my finger for much longer. Apart from the send-off, it was a lovely break, Al. Thank you."

"I enjoyed it too. Who knows? If the ring belongs to you, if you sell it and make a fortune, then we could be back here all of the time."

"Whereby, Doonmara would benefit too! Then, everyone would be happy!"

"Not James," Alex said.

"No, not James."

They both laughed. They drove past the hotel gates. The cattle grids rattled as the car wheels rolled over them.

"Not bad, eh?"

"It's a beauty, Laura. Tell me again how you came across this. You were sketchy on the phone."

You could definitely see a family resemblance, more so, as they grew older. Peter had the same green eyes and heavy eyebrows. They shared the same colouring. There the resemblance ended, for while Laura had remained slim, Peter was overweight.

They were sitting at the kitchen table in his sister's house. Alex had made tea for everyone. Taking her time, Laura outlined what had happened. Intermittently, Peter stopped his sister for clarification. In his opinion, the devil was in the detail.

"That's amazing," Peter said when he had heard the story. "What a find!"

"Peter, would you like a refill?" Alex asked as he held up the tea pot. "I'm making a fresh pot."

"Yes. Thanks, Alex."

Alex pottered around as he went about the business of making a fresh brew.

"Legally, do you know where we stand?" Laura asked her brother.

"Since your phone call, I've had the chance to do a little research."

"And?"

"It's complicated. There are several factors involved here."

Laura looked deflated.

"Tell me," she said.

"I'll top you both up first. Tea?" Alex asked Laura.

"Yes, please," she said, proffering her mug.

Alex gave them all a top up and when they had settled, Peter continued.

"Bear with the legal jargon. It's important you understand the legalities."

"Don't worry. I won't be tuning out," Laura said good-humouredly.

"I'll hold you to that, sis. I'm going to read you something that I've downloaded in relation to the law on this."

With that, Peter pulled a page of foolscap paper from a folder he had placed on the kitchen table.

"You mean you didn't know?" his sister mocked.

"Like I said, Laura, it's complicated, and it's not my specialism. I had to do my own bit of research."

Peter removed a soft leather glasses case from his inside jacket pocket. Once he put his reading glasses on, he leaned forward and began to read out loud from the page before him. His belly strained against the buttons of his blue-striped shirt.

"'*Lost, mislaid, and abandoned property,*" he read, "*are categories of the common law of property which deals with personal property which has left the possession of its rightful owner without having directly entered the possession of another person.*

"*The rights of a finder of such property are determined in part by the status in which it is found.*' I'm going to skip the next bit guys," he said. "It's a bit of a minefield. Right up till this bit here," he said scanning the page. "'*The general rule attached to the three types of property,*" he continued, "*may be summarized as: A finder of property acquires no rights in mislaid property, is entitled to possession of lost property against everyone except the true owner, and is entitled to keep abandoned property.*'"

"That's interesting," Alex said. "I take it that Laura's ring falls into the lost property bracket?"

"Yes, it does," Peter confirmed before taking off his glasses, placing them and the sheet of paper that he had been reading from on the table.

"Legally, property is generally deemed to have been lost if it is found in a place where the true owner likely did not intend to set it down, and where it is not likely to be found by the true owner. Since Laura found the ring in the river, no one is going to argue against that."

"Even James might have a difficulty," Laura said.

She had informed her brother of the hotel manager's reaction.

"He certainly would," her brother agreed. "In a nutshell, the finder of a lost item can claim the right to possess the item against any person except the true owner or any previous possessors. However, there's one stipulation."

"Which is?" Laura asked.

"You have to turn the property, in this case the ring that you found, over to the guards.

If the true owner does not arrive to claim the property within a certain period time, then it is returned to the finder as their own."

"And that's it" she said. "It's as clear cut as that?"

"When was the law ever clear cut, Laura? I told you it was complicated. We're in murky waters here. Exceptions may be applied to the rule that the first finder of lost property has a superior claim or right over any other person except the previous owner," he said. "For example, a trespasser's claim to lost property, which he finds while trespassing, is generally inferior to the claim of the respective landowner."

"I wasn't trespassing," Laura said. "That pathway is open to the general public as well as to hotel guests.

"I know that. It may be a ploy that James will try to use though. I'm making sure that you are both aware of everything. Listen to this."

He put his glasses on again and began reading.

"'*As a corollary to this exception a landowner has superior claim over a find made within the non-public areas of his property, so if a customer finds lost property in the public area of a store, the customer has superior claim to the lost property over that of the store-owner, but if the customer finds the lost property in the non-public area of that store, such as an area marked 'Employees Only', the store-owner will have superior claim, as the customer was trespassing when he found it.'*"

"So the bottom line is what?" Laura asked.

"The hotel doesn't have a superior claim. I found out that they don't even own the fishing rights to the river. Not solely."

"Is that so?" said Alex, somewhat surprised. "I never knew that. I assumed they did."

"Apparently not. What's more, they definitely don't own ring finding rights. You're on terra firma. You have superior rights. In my opinion, there's no doubt about that."

"That's a relief. How should we proceed from here?" Laura asked.

"My advice is to get the ring independently valued. After that, hand it in to the police station in Clifden. That's the nearest police station to Doonmara. It's best that you hand it in locally. That's standard practise."

"That's what we'll do," Laura said. "How long does the ring remain in police property?"

"In Ireland, it's a year and one day rule that applies."

"I see. Thanks for your help, Peter. We appreciate it," his sister said.

"Yes, thanks, Peter. We owe you one," Alex said.

"That's no problem, guys. You can thank Wikipedia!" Peter said light-heartedly

"It's good to know where we stand legally," Laura said.

"There may well be a bit of publicity around this," Peter warned them. "You may have some lost causes coming out of the woodwork to stake a claim on that ring. One thing is certain. That ring on your hand is valuable."

"I wonder what it is worth," Alex said. "Would you care to hazard a guess?"

"I'd estimate anywhere between twenty and thirty thousand euros," Peter said.

"Are you serious?" Laura asked.

"I'm no authority on diamonds. It's not as if I've had a lot of expertise in this area but it wouldn't surprise me at all. Anyway, I'll leave you guys to it. It's time I got home."

Laura stood at her hall door, waving him off. She waited until the car had exited her driveway.

"I think our luck has changed," she said to Alex later.

"I think our luck changed a while back," he said.

That same day, Caroline's daughter was baptised in a church in Dublin.

CHAPTER TWENTY

O n the day of the christening, Caroline thought about the father of her child. She was not alone. Many of the assembled guests wondered who the baby's father was and where he was.

Despite the absence of Alex, the day had been a happy one, a celebration of Una's birth, and an occasion for Caroline to celebrate her recovery from the cancer that had plagued her body. There was nothing like having your life threatened to make you feel alive, and grateful for that life. Time and time again, she found herself humbled by the wonder of the smallest things: the warmth of the sun on her face, Una sleeping in her arms, the smell of a flower.

Although her financial circumstances were strained, Caroline pushed the boat out. She invited friends and family. She had asked her boss as well. Caroline was taking a year out from work to look after her baby daughter. Once again, her employer had been nothing but supportive. Once again, Caroline reminded herself, she had been too quick to judge the woman.

Caroline's hair was growing back fast and the light in her eyes, happily framed by lashes and brows, was returning. To the outside eye, she was becoming 'Caroline' again.

It was a very special day and an opportunity to thank everyone who had supported Caroline throughout her illness and pregnancy. Chief among them was her friend Ciara.

Caroline didn't know how she would have managed without Ciara's support, advice and never-ending good humour. She had thanked Ciara in the only way she could. She had asked her friend to become Una's godmother.

Ciara had shared the highs and the lows, the good things that had come from Caroline's experiences as well as the bad, and the stuff that Caroline still had trouble wrapping her head around. They had laughed and cried together.

"There was nothing that I ever said that you batted an eyelash at," Caroline told her. Nothing her friend had said ever rubbed her the wrong way. Well, almost nothing. Ciara wanted Caroline to tell Alex about Una. Nonetheless, Ciara had respected her friend's decision.

Later that night, as Caroline lay in bed unable to sleep, she thought about the past. Una was now three months old. Caroline had only known Alex for six months. The brevity of their relationship hit home.

Initially, they had met only once a week. By the third month, it was twice a week. Beyond that, they had spent the occasional night together, whenever Alex could manage to get away, which wasn't often.

Their relationship had been short lived in the scheme of things. It was no time at all, a drop in the ocean. She had carried her daughter for longer than she had been with Alex.

Alex Hamilton. Had she really loved him? For a moment, she tried to convince herself that it had only been an infatuation; a passion that had run its course.

She was lying to herself. Deep down Caroline knew that she had loved the man. Whatever had happened, there was no use in denying it. Rightly or wrongly, she had fallen in love with Alex Hamilton.

Alex would never know the joy of knowing Una. She had pity for Alex. Truly she did. She remembered with feeling what he had told her the day they had broken up. He had explained what had happened to Rachel.

"It was my fault, Caroline. I blame myself." He could see Rachel running in and out of the water, hear her hooting with laughter. He remembered her little hands wrapped around his neck as he had walked into the sea.

"Why? What happened, Alex?" she had asked gently.

"Rachel and I were on the beach the day that she died. We were in Kilkee. It was blisteringly hot and Laura had gone to the shops to get some drinks. I took my eyes off Rachel. For a few short moments, I took my eyes off her. A neighbour of ours had come over to say hello, and when I turned around, Rachel was gone.

"I spotted her almost immediately. She had run over to the rocks near us. Some children were playing there. I made my way over and called out her name. Rachel turned to me and she was smiling. I remember that clearly. But then she slipped on the rocks and fell."

For a moment, he stalled. She waited for him to continue.

"Those rocks can be slippery," he had said, by way of explanation.

It didn't explain why God had chosen to punish him so cruelly.

"As she fell, Rachel banged her head," he'd said, "And that was that. Within the hour, Rachel was dead and our lives were destroyed. An ambulance came but my daughter was dead by the time we reached the hospital. She was in my care. It was my fault."

⇥ ⇤

"Is that Mrs Hamilton?" a man asked.

"Yes, this is Laura Hamilton speaking."

"Mrs Hamilton, my name is George Wren. I'm phoning from Broadway Antique Jewellers. You came in earlier this week to have a ring valued. You dealt with Linda."

"That's right. Thanks for getting back to me. Have you made any progress?" she asked.

Because the ring wasn't insured, Peter had advised Laura not to leave it with the jewellers. It had been examined thoroughly and a photograph had been taken.

"I didn't see the ring myself, Mrs Hamilton. I was wondering, could you possibly come in again today? I'd like to examine the ring personally, so that I can confirm our findings."

"I could be with you about two."

"Very well, then. I look forward to seeing you and your ring then."

Arriving at her appointment five minutes ahead of schedule, Laura was eager to hear what George Wren had to say. He sounded pleasant.

He shook her hand across the counter.

"It's nice to meet you, Mrs Hamilton," he said. "It's not every day that someone comes in with something this special."

She smiled.

"I'm aware that Linda has examined your ring, but I'd like to have a look at it if I may. No disrespect to my colleague, but this is more up my alley."

"A second opinion is always wise," Laura said.

She took the ring off her finger and handed it to him. A jeweller's loupe and a lint free cloth lay on the counter. Taking his time, he appraised the ring. While she waited, Laura appraised the jeweller. In his early sixties, George Wren had grey hair and steely blue eyes. Smartly dressed in his dark navy suit, he wore a pale blue shirt and a pink tie with small navy polka dots. At his wrists, a pair of gold cufflinks peeked out from either jacket sleeve.

After several minutes, the jeweller turned his attention to Laura.

"Mrs Hamilton, I'd like to clean the ring before I examine the diamond," he said. "That will remove any surface dirt that might distract from a proper assessment."

"You do what you have to do," she said.

"Please, take a seat, Mrs Hamilton. This may take some time." He came out from the shop counter and pulled a chair towards her.

Laura sat down gladly. She laid her handbag on the floor and began to unwrap the burgundy cashmere scarf tied round her neck.

After the cleaning, George Wren showed Laura the ring. Immediately, she noticed a difference.

"The sparkle would almost blind you," she said, clearly pleased. "I can make out the date now."

She reflected on the date for a moment: August 8th, 1929.

"That's as good a starting point as any," the jeweller said, interrupting her thought process. "What we look at, in order to estimate a value, Mrs Hamilton, are the cut, colour, carat, and clarity of the stone."

"Which is the most important?" she asked.

"In my opinion, the cut is the most important factor. Sparkle and brilliance are determined by the cutting, because it is the cutting that affects the way the light travels through the stone, how much it is reflected back to the eye, and how much 'leaks' out at the back. A stone that is cut too thin will have a lot of light leakage. It won't sparkle much and will look lifeless. A well-cut diamond, such as the one I have in front of me, will have lots of sparkle, and lots of liveliness."

"I assume the cut affects the price," she said.

"Put it like this, Mrs Hamilton. A poorly cut diamond should sell for half the cost of an exceptionally cut diamond."

"What about the clarity?"

"Don't let anyone convince you that a high clarity grade is necessary to have a brilliant, sparkling diamond, or that cut refers to shape for that matter. You'll make a big mistake. Clarity is often mistakenly believed to be the factor that affects the amount of sparkle and brilliance. This is not true. Clarity refers to the presence of microscopic features that formed within the diamond as it crystallized. If readily visible to the eye without magnification, poor clarity will greatly reduce value, but otherwise, clarity has minimal impact on beauty or desirability.

"I see. What about the colour and carat?" she asked. "How do they determine the value?"

"In brief, the top colour grades are much more expensive than the lower grades. D, E and F, for example, are all colourless. Diamonds are not all colourless, but it's the colourless diamonds, sometimes called white diamonds, that all other shades are judged against. By the way, setting the stone in white gold or, in platinum, like your ring, can make it appear whiter. As far as the carat goes, there are a hundred points to a carat. The cost of a diamond increases significantly when it reaches the full carat mark, and for each carat thereafter. And while the round, brilliant cut diamond is considered to be the cut that exhibits the most brilliance, it normally looks smaller than diamonds cut in other shapes. An oval, pear shape or marquise will look larger than the round.

"How interesting," Laura said. "Until today, my knowledge of diamonds was pretty limited."

"I hope I haven't overloaded you with information," he said.

"I find it fascinating," she replied truthfully.

"Good. I was afraid I might be boring you."

"On the contrary."

"Now then, back to the stone in front of us. This is an old, and what is known in the trade as a European cut diamond. The modern round brilliant cut wasn't commercially popular until the late 1930s, early 1940s. But I have to point out one thing. Obviously, I'm not viewing the diamond unmounted and the centre diamond should be examined from all angles. Perhaps you can have the setting removed and have that done further down the line."

"I'll definitely do that," she said. "Is it a safe process?"

"It's a simple process, but that doesn't mean that it's gentle to the metalwork. It's risky. The chances are about fifty-fifty whether the tip of the prong will crack and break off. If the ring is platinum like your ring, the chances of cracking are lower, maybe forty per cent. However, it is fairly easy to re-build prong tips, especially with a laser welder, so it's not usually a huge concern. But it's not cheap."

"This is proving to be a real education," she said.

George Wren was pleased. He had her full attention. She could have sworn she saw a twinkle in those blue grey eyes.

"First, I'm going to inspect the diamond by the naked eye to see if I can spot any major defects," he said.

"Would the magnifier not show that up?" she asked, curious.

"That's a good question. Actually, it's important to inspect the diamond by eye first. If you do this after viewing with magnification, your eyes will only see what they expect to see."

He took a good look. Then he got up. He walked the diamond away from the shop's army of bright lights to a window to see how it sparkled there by comparison.

"Now, I'm going to use my loupe," he said on return." It will show up any flaws."

With one hand, the jeweller brought the loupe right up to his eye, holding the ring in the other, and positioning the diamond about one inch away until the entire diamond was in clear view. All the while, he kept his head up as if her were talking to someone, so that he wouldn't block out the light from hitting the diamond.

"I can't view the diamond's underbelly", he said, "and to be completely accurate I'd need to have the stone unmounted to determine the colour. Many diamonds appear white when looked at face up. You need to place the diamond face down on a white background and look through the slanting sides going up to its point, which we refer to as the 'cone' of the diamond."

He checked on Laura. She remained engrossed.

"Then," he continued, "you can notice how saturated the colour is at the thickest points. That's the only way to judge a diamond's true colour."

"If that's the case, I assume you can't accurately determine the colour and the clarity of my ring?"

"I can make a good estimated guess, Mrs Hamilton" he said, and smiled. "It's a very special stone. What's more, the ring is signed and numbered."

"What does that mean?" she asked.

"The ring band is stamped inside with the maker's mark. See here," he said, showing her.

She looked at the band and drew a sharp intake of breath. She was flabbergasted.

"Cartier!" she exclaimed. "How did I miss that?"

"You weren't looking for it," he said. "Besides, it wasn't easy to spot until we cleaned the band properly. Cartier is a particularly 'hot' name in the auction world. This is a gorgeous diamond, weighing about 4.70 carats or thereabouts. I'd say that the baguette diamonds add another half-carat, and the centre diamond may well be a D colour.

"That means it's colourless," she said.

"That's correct," he said. Mrs Hamilton had been paying attention. "What we have here may well be a flawless diamond. We would need to view it unmounted in order to confirm that it's flawless internally.

"This all sounds very promising," she said.

He looked amused.

"That must be the understatement of the year, Mrs Hamilton. This is a rare and ravishing piece of jewellery. I think, and it's a conservative estimation, that we can put a figure of seventy thousand euros on your find."

"What did you say?" she asked, certain she hadn't heard correctly.

"Seventy thousand euros."

"Seventy thousand euros," she repeated.

"At least," he said.

A look of disbelief was written all over Laura's face.

"This is hard to take in, Mr Wren. It feels like I've just won the lottery. The ring is worth seventy thousand euros?" she said, sounding sceptical.

"That's correct. As I said, Mrs Hamilton, that is a conservative estimation. It could be worth up to ninety, and even one hundred thousand euros. Cartier pieces can vary a lot depending on the provenance and quality of the diamond."

"I hardly know what to say. I knew the ring was valuable but I had no idea that it was worth this kind of money."

He handed Laura the ring.

"How a ring like this ended up in the river beggars belief," she said, mesmerised. "Surely, it must have been a prized possession?"

"Who knows what happened?" he said. "You may never know, Mrs Hamilton."

"Perhaps not," Laura said as she slipped the ring back on her finger. "Now that I know the true value, I'll be afraid to wear it. Thank you for your help. What do I owe you?"

"There's no charge, Mrs Hamilton."

"For your time, surely?"

"You don't owe me anything. It was my pleasure. I'm over forty years in the business and I've never had the opportunity of assessing a piece as rare or as precious as the one you brought in today."

"That's very nice of you," she said. "It's been a real learning curve."

The jeweller had enjoyed talking to her. People were usually interested in one thing, and that was the price. Not Mrs Hamilton. He could tell that her interest had been genuine.

The door gave a little rattle as Laura Hamilton exited the premises. She's a fortunate woman he thought. Unless the ring was reclaimed, the lovely lady in the navy rain coat had left the shop one hundred thousand euros richer. He wondered how it would all play out.

As soon as she left the jewellers, Laura reached for her mobile and rang Alex.

"How did you get on?" he asked.

"I hope you're sitting down because you're not going to believe this."

He could hear the excitement in her voice.

It's a Cartier ring worth anything from seventy up to one hundred thousand euros."

"You're joking, Laura," he said, equally incredulous. "That much? Really?"

"I had pretty much the same reaction. And no, I'm not joking. George Wren, the man I was telling you about earlier, was definite about the value. He said that seventy thousand euros was a conservative estimate. He was very helpful, Alex. And informative."

"Laura, you're walking around with 100,000 euros on your finger," he said. "That ring isn't even insured!"

"Don't frighten me, Alex. I'm terrified I'll be mugged."

"This calls for a celebratory dinner. I could leave the office in about an hour and bunk off. What if we meet for a drink and have an early bird somewhere?"

"That sounds like a plan."

"Where would you like to go?"

She suggested a small restaurant on the riverside, one they both liked.

"Okay, then. I'll meet you in the pub next door about five."

Until the appointed time, Laura decided to have a browse around. Off she set with a bounce in her step. Within minutes, she exited the shop. She was too excited to be meandering around, wandering in and out of shops.

She arrived at the pub at five on the button. Minutes later, Alex walked through the door. He ordered a round of drinks.

"I can't believe that you found a Cartier ring worth one hundred thousand euros," he said. He took a sip of his sparkling water. "I should have ordered something stronger, to get over the shock."

"You're not alone. I'm in a state of shock myself."

"To your good fortune," he said, clinking glasses.

"To our good fortune," she corrected him. "Mind you, we're not exactly quids in yet. Someone may step forward and claim the ring."

"That might happen. We'll have to wait this one out. I think you should hand the ring into the Garda station in Clifden in the next day or so."

"When I do, that may well be the last time I see this ring. I hate parting with it. Not because I've found out what's it worth, but because of how I came across it, and where I found it."

"I understand how you feel," he said. "Who knows what will happen? The owner is dead, that's for sure, Laura. It could belong to a daughter, or even to a granddaughter."

"A year and a day. That's what Peter said."

"It will be a long year. Tell you what, let's drive up on to Clifden on Saturday morning and get this business done. "

"Ok. Let's do that."

"Enjoy wearing it while you still can," he said, taking her right hand to study the ring. "The diamond has cleaned up well. There's a huge difference in the sparkle."

"The guards in Clifden are in for a bit of a surprise. I'm sure the lost property box has seen nothing like this before!"

They finished their drinks and moved on to the restaurant.

⇒+⇐

The duty officer got up from his chair and drew himself up to his full height. He was over six feet tall and Laura was surprised. From a sitting position, she would never have guessed that the man was that tall.

"What have we here?" the guard said astonished.

The town was quiet that Saturday morning for it was early in the season and little was stirring. That is until this couple walked through the station door.

Laura and Alex had left the house shortly before nine. They stopped along the way for a coffee, breaking up the journey in Oughterard. They arrived in Clifden at midday and found their way to the local Garda station.

Laura showed the officer the ring and explained how it came to be in her possession. She told him what their solicitor had advised.

"You've had a bit of a journey but it wasn't a wasted trip. Your solicitor was right," the guard confirmed.

He typed their details into the computer and Laura filled in a form. The guard gave her a receipt and then he took the ring.

"April, 22nd next year. That's when we'll be see-ing you next," he said. "It falls on a Sunday."

"Perhaps you won't be seeing us. Someone could come forward," Laura said.

"We'd want proof, if they did. We'd need prop-er verification,

He looked up at them approvingly.

"You're very honest, the pair of you," he said. "It's not everyone who would hand up a piece of jewellery like this. Some people would have pock-eted that ring and said nothing."

They left the station. They heard nothing un-til six months later. Laura came home one day in October, to find a message on the house phone, to contact the station in Clifden. Someone must have come forward.

CHAPTER TWENTY-ONE

"It's been a difficult year," Felicia said.

"I can only imagine," Richard replied. The pain that came across her face was impossible to miss. He was sitting opposite Felicia in the living room.

"I find it hard to believe that Harvey's anniversary is tomorrow," she said. "It's crept up on me."

"It's crept up on all of us, Felicia. Tell me, how are you?" he said, thinking as he asked how tired she looked. There were lines around her eyes that hadn't been there before. Felicia had lost weight too. It made her face appear angular and drawn. Her hair was lustreless and the roots were grey.

"I'm coping as best I can. It's tough. This week has been very tough."

"It must bring back a lot of memories."

"Yes, good and bad. I find myself constantly reliving what happened that day." She moved her fingers in a small circular pattern on the silk cushion beside her. "It was such a shock," she said. "I'll never forget how Harvey looked in the ambulance. I'm glad the children didn't see their father like that. Even now, I keep seeing his face. But I try to remember all the good stuff."

"You must have wonderful memories, Felicia."

"They won't bring him back but they help."

"He was a wonderful father," Richard said.

"And a great husband. I miss Harvey. I miss him every day. I'm lonely without him. I'm still grieving but I try to hide it as best I can from the children. I don't like them seeing me sad all the time. And I'm afraid of anything happening to them. I've become overprotective of them both."

"That's natural. I miss Harvey too, Felicia. I was very fond of him."

"You and Harvey were great pals. He appreciated your friendship."

He heard the loss in her voice.

"How are the children?" he said, probing gently

"A little bit quiet in themselves over the last few days, especially Jack."

"That's understandable. It was tough on Jack. He was there when Harvey died."

"Don't remind me. I hate to think what Jack must have gone through that afternoon."

"It was a very traumatic experience. What was that gillie's name?"

"John," she said quickly. Laura hadn't forgotten the gillie's name. She never would.

She remained quiet for a moment, lost in thought.

"Are you worried about Jack?" he asked.

"Oh Richard, I worry about both of them all of the time. They've lost their father at a young age; at an age when they need both parents. They're not coping too badly. They miss their dad dreadfully, but Harvey's death has brought Jack and Anna closer together. It's forged a deeper bond between them. Before, they were always in each other's hair; not so much, these days. Anna has almost taken on an adult role with Jack. I don't know where she gets her strength from. She's very caring with him, and with me."

"That's nice to hear," he said, although privately he thought that Anna put too much pressure on herself trying to be the perfect daughter and sister. She seemed weighed down with responsibility for someone so young. He hoped she wouldn't go off the rails one day. "So Jack is coping" he continued. "What happened didn't leave any kind of damaging effect?"

"Not that I can see. The nightmares haven't come back. Though I must say, Jack was tremendously relieved that the autopsy confirmed his dad was dead before he hit the water. The nightmares stopped after that. He was reassured that he had done the best he could that afternoon"

"That was a heavy weight to carry."

"Yes. Mind you, sometimes it can be hard to tell grief from normal teenage behaviour. As it is, they tend to become withdrawn, stay in their room and sleep a lot!"

"Don't I know," he said.

"He'll be here soon. He's due in the door any minute," she said as she checked her watch. It was touching seven o'clock. "Will you join us for a bite to eat? You're more than welcome." She smiled at Richard. It was her first smile of the evening.

"I'd love to but I had better not. Alice is expecting me home for dinner. I dropped by on the way home from work on the off chance that I would catch you. I'll stay until Jack arrives. Is Anna around?"

"She's holed up in her room. She doesn't know you're here. If she did, she'd have come down immediately. You're very much flavour of the month in our house, Richard. I'll go and call her. That is if I can get her off her phone. I bought her a new iPhone and she's never off it."

"My three are the same, Felicia. They live life through social media but they don't have time to be social.

"They don't live real lives. At least I know where she is. There is that."

"But do you know who she's on line with? Anyone could be looking at her Facebook pictures and details."

"That's enough, Richard. You're scaring me," she said.

Felicia got up and walked to the door.

"Anna," she called. "Richard is here."

There was no response. She looked at Richard and shrugged her shoulders, as if to say, see what I mean.

"Anna," she called out and a little more loudly this time. "Anna"

A bedroom door opened.

"What?" Anna shouted down the stairs.

"Richard's dropped by to see us. Come down and say hello."

They heard her light football on the stairs. She burst into the room seconds later.

"Hi, Richard," she said, and gave him a hug. Then she sat down beside him on the couch.

Anna considered Richard an honorary uncle. He had always been a part of their lives because Richard and her dad had been close. Anna appreciated Richard all the more because of that relationship. She was deeply attached to him.

Richard had come to Doonmara in their hour of need. Richard had delivered the eulogy at her father's funeral service.

Her father's cousin visited the family regularly. More often than not, the kids, as he referred to Felicia and Harvey's offspring, were at home when Richard called.

Anna loved to hear Richard talk about her dad. Richard would tell her what they got up to as young boys and later on as young men. It brought her dad back for a few short moments. She hid her sadness. Inside, she was devastated at her father's death, a loss that could not be fixed or forgotten.

Jack arrived a few minutes later. Richard received an equally warm welcome.

"My goodness, you've shot up overnight," he told Jack. "Let me have a look at you," he said, appraising him.

"I'm as tall as you," Jack said.

"Richard, maybe you're shrinking!" Anna teased.

Felicia observed the interaction between Richard and her children. Harvey's cousin had become something of a father figure to both her children. Felicia knew that Richard would always look out for Anna and Jack.

"I called by because it's your dad's anniversary tomorrow," Richard said.

"Tomorrow is going to be very strange," Anna remarked.

"For me too," Jack said.

"I'm dreading it," Anna said.

"It's a sad day that we're remembering," their mother said. "But we have to remember the person who was your dad. We have to bear in mind all the wonderful memories that we shared as a family – not just his death."

Everyone was quiet for a moment. They were remembering Harvey: the father and the friend, and the husband.

"Will we ever go back to Doonmara, Mum?" Jack asked out of the blue.

Felicia had asked herself the same question many times over the past week. It seemed her children had been thinking along the same lines.

"Someday, Jack, but not anytime in the near future. It's too soon. I would find it too sad. Would you like to go back, Jack?" she asked carefully.

"Not yet, Mum. I would like to one day. I'd like to visit Beat Two where Dad died."

"And you, Anna? What about you?"

"I don't think I could bear it, Mum. I wouldn't be up to it."

Anna spoke in a low voice. Tears had welled up in her eyes.

"I can understand that, Anna. That's how I feel myself. I want to share something with you both, and with you too, Richard."

"What, Mum?" Jack said already curious.

The three of them looked at Felicia expectantly.

"I had an email from Laura this morning. Do you remember Laura? She helped you to find your great grandfather's name in the fishing log, Jack."

"I remember her."

"I thought that her husband was George Clooney when I first saw him," Anna said.

"You had me believing it too," her mother said and Anna giggled.

"He did look the spitting image of George Clooney," Richard said. "I remember thinking he looks like someone I know. Only I couldn't think of whom!"

"What did she say in her email, Mum? And how did she find you? It's not as if you're on Facebook or anything."

"I presume she asked the hotel," Felicia said. She guessed correctly. "She was asking after you both. I'd like to read the email to you. Stay put and I'll go and get my laptop."

She was back in the room a few moments later.

"Bear with me, guys. I'm not as fast as you two," she said. Her words fell on deaf ears. Anna and Jack looked on impatiently as Felicia scrolled through her messages.

"Ah, here it is," she said.

"Dear Felicia

I met you last summer at Doonmara Castle under heartbreaking circumstances. I spent some time with your beautiful, brave son the morning after his dad died."

Felicia paused. Her audience was captivated. She looked at Jack before continuing.

"I am emailing to say that you, Jack and Anna have been in my thoughts over the past few days. I know this week marks the first anniversary of your husband's passing. I have been in Doonmara two or three times this year. I always think of you all, particularly on my walks around the lake. Once, I even saw a salmon jump where your husband, Harvey, died. Somehow that seemed fitting. I hope that the treasured memories you must have, help you through your grief.

Please remember me to your children.

Warm Regards
Laura Hamilton"

Felicia looked up from her laptop.

"Wasn't that nice of her?" she said to no one in particular.

"Dad would have liked that," Jack said. "The bit about the salmon jumping in the spot where he died."

"He would," Richard agreed. "What a lovely email. She's a thoughtful person."

"Yes, she is. I'm touched that she remembered Harvey's anniversary."

"Mum, do you know what?" said Jack.

"What?" she said encouragingly.

"One day, I'm going back to Doonmara and I'm going fishing. And I'm going to catch a salmon."

"Your father would be happy to hear that, even if you didn't catch a salmon."

"I'll catch one," he said, determined.

"Will you email her back, Mum?" Anna asked.

"Oh yes. I intend to," her mother replied.

Richard got up to go.

"I'd better go home before there's a divorce," he said.

"Say hello to Alice from us all, and to the girls."

Richard had three grown up daughters.

"I will," he said. "You'll see them tomorrow anyway. We're planning on calling over after you visit the grave. I'm wondering if it isn't a bit of an invasion."

"You must all come," she said. "You're a big part of our family. Besides, your girls will really cheer up my two. We'll be glad of the company. Harvey's mum will be here too."

"It will be nice to see Betty," he said.

"What's for dinner, Mum?" asked Jack cutting in. "I'm starving."

"Just for a change," Anna said.

"It's *Carbonara*," Felicia said.

"Oh, good," said Jack. "I love *Carbonara*."

"So do I," Richard said. "I'm missing out!"

Richard bid Anna and Jack goodbye. Felicia walked him to the door.

"They both look well," he observed.

"They're growing up fast, Richard. This past year, the two of them have grown up in different ways. Jack in inches. Look at the height of him. And Anna has matured beyond belief. She grew up overnight when her dad died."

"I can see that. Harvey would be proud of both of them. And of you. You're doing a great job with those two."

"I do wonder sometimes. It's tough on them both without a dad."

He leant towards her to kiss her on the cheek. Felicia stood at the door, and waved him off. She went to the kitchen, directly afterwards. She switched on the kettle to boil the water for the pasta.

I can't believe you're already gone a year," she said quietly to her husband. She often spoke to Harvey. Usually, she communicated silent thoughts. Harvey was constantly on her mind.

She missed Harvey. Oh, how she missed him. She wondered whether she would ever get over the loneliness. She was only forty-five. It wasn't old. To think that all the years stretched before her without Harvey. She missed everything about him. Now that he was gone, she realised what a source of happiness her marriage had brought. He had made her very happy. She hoped that she had done the same for him.

In the space of a year, there had been monumental changes in her life, and in the lives of her children. She had uprooted herself and her children from Lisbon, and rented a house in a leafy suburb in Dublin. Thankfully, the life policy that Harvey had taken out was more than adequate. She didn't face any immediate financial difficulties and there was enough money to provide for the education of her children. Down the road, she intended to look for employment. There was no hurry.

Anna and Jack had remained in the same schools but they were now day pupils as opposed to boarders.

"It will be a lot less expensive," Felicia had explained to Richard. "The fees are astronomical. I'd prefer to put the money towards their college education. More importantly, I think the two of them need to be at home with me now, Jack especially. With Harvey gone, there's a huge vacuum in all of our lives. We need each other."

Her son regretted that he had been sent to boarding school. He had spoken to Felicia about it.

"If I hadn't gone, I could have been with dad more. I'd have spent the final year of his life with him, Mum. That really bothers me. I think about it a lot."

It broke Felicia's heart to hear her son say that. There was no denying, Jack had missed out. And yet, by the same token, she had been glad to have that final year with Harvey on her own. They'd had more time for each other. They had done more as a couple. They had made love more often in that final year of Harvey's life.

"I feel very different from everyone else in my class," Jack said quietly. "I'm the only one whose father is dead."

"Are all of the mums and dads together?" she asked, aware that Jack was conscious of how his friends saw him.

"No. But that's not the same. Everyone's dad is alive except mine."

Whenever the opportunity presented itself, Harvey had taken his son along to rugby internationals. Felicia had no interest in the game. Harvey had been passionate about the sport.

Jack was now on the rugby team at school. His father would have loved that. Jack went to training twice a week and he played a match every Sunday morning. Felicia attended every game that he

played and could be heard yelling from the side-
lines on a Sunday morning. She had become Jack's
biggest supporter.

She drained the spaghetti in a colander and
finished the sauce. She had set the table while the
pasta was cooking.

Once or twice, in the weeks after Harvey had
died, she found herself setting a place for her husband at the table. She'd had moments like that
when she had forgotten Harvey had died. Once,
she had picked up the phone to call him; she had
looked out for him in a crowded room; she had
found herself listening out for his car to come
home. Sometimes she felt her beloved husband
with her, appearing at once-shared moments such
as an evening drink. His presence had felt like a
warm breeze wafting nearby. She was firmly convinced that death was not the end. Felicia saw it as
the passage to another life, and not as an abrupt
end of life.

The pasta was ready. Felicia plated up and
called her son and daughter down to dinner.

CHAPTER TWENTY-TWO

"That's when I saw my great grandfather's name," Jack said solemnly. "His name appeared lots of times."

"How extraordinary," his grandmother replied. "You must have been chuffed. Your father would have been delighted."

Her grandson's grave expression evaporated. It was the confirmation that Jack hoped for.

"And your granddad too," she added.

Pleased, Jack gave his grandmother a wide grin.

"Your grandfather used to say that his father was a good fisherman. Your dad didn't know much about his grandfather, but he knew that."

Felicia stuck her head around the door and asked "How are you two getting on? I hope Jack is looking after you, Betty?"

"I'm being well looked after. We're having a nice chat, aren't we Jack?"

Her grandson nodded. He seemed happy. Betty had an affable manner. Felicia was very fond of Betty, as were her grandchildren.

"Jack told me about the email you received," her mother-in-law said. "That led to a discussion about the morning he and that woman spent trawling through the pages of the fishing log."

They were not long back from visiting Harvey's grave. Richard and his family were not due for a while yet. Anna was in her bedroom.

"The family fallout is a bit of a mystery," Felicia said.

"Yes. It is," Betty agreed.

"I'd love to know what happened," Jack said.

Turning to her grandson, Betty said, "I haven't any clues, I'm afraid,"

His face filled with disappointment.

"There was another Russell mentioned in the fishing log. Wasn't there, Mum?"

"Yes, there was. Tell your gran about that, Jack. I'll be back in a jiffy with tea, Betty" Felicia said, and returned to the kitchen.

"Now Jack, tell me about this other person," his grandmother said. "I'm interested. What was their first name – do you remember?"

"I do. It stood out actually. "

"How do you mean?" she asked.

"It was a woman's name and there weren't too many. Her name was Nancy Ann."

"Nancy Ann," Betty said, so quietly it went almost unheard. For a moment the old lady was lost in the past. She sat very still.

"Yes, that was her name. She fished with my great grandfather. I saw their names together in the log. And sometimes, their names appeared separately." His grandmother didn't respond. "Gran," he said sharply, transporting her back to the present.

"Forgive me, Jack. What was it you said?" she said, as if lost in a mysterious deafness.

Her grandson repeated what he had said. This time she heard every word.

"Have you any idea who she was, Gran?"The old lady said nothing further. With some impatience, he asked "Who was she, Gran? Do you know?"

"I do know, actually. Let's wait till your mum returns before I tell you what I know. Your mum will want to hear this too," Betty said.

Many years had passed since Betty had heard the name Nancy Ann. A few moments later, Felicia came in with tea and a plate of Madeira cake. Anna joined them.

"Gran knows who Nancy Ann is," Jack informed them excitedly before reaching for a slice of cake.

"Who is this mystery woman then?" Felicia asked, once Betty had a cup of tea in hand.

"Yes, who is she? We're dying to know," Anna said.

"Let me start by telling you this. Before your dad was born, your grandfather and I were discussing names for the baby. In those days, you didn't know what the sex of the baby was until they arrived. He said that if we had a baby girl that he would like to call her Nancy Ann. He was very keen on the name."

"Is that it?" said Jack, in a voice that indicated he was hoping for more.

Betty shook her head.

"I have to say that I wasn't at all keen on the name myself," she continued. "I thought it was a dreadful name. I asked him why he liked the name so much."

"And what did he say?" Jack asked.

"That was it, you see. He wouldn't tell me why. However, he was adamant that if we had a baby girl that she would be christened Nancy Ann. Anyway, your father was born and I said to your grandfather, 'We don't have a Nancy Ann'. I remember it clearly because your grandfather was holding your father at the time. It was the first time he held him. I can still picture him holding this tiny baby in his arms. He looked proud and happy." Betty paused.

"I'm sorry. My throat's a little dry," she said.

"Take your time, Betty" Felicia said.

Jack could have murdered his mother.

"Have a sip of your tea," Felicia ordered. Betty did as she was told. She continued her story, much to Jack's relief.

"'No, we don't,'" your grandfather said to me. "'But we have a beautiful son.' I could tell he was overcome with emotion. 'Why the name Nancy Ann,' I asked him? 'Why won't you tell me?'

"He was standing by the window with your dad in his arms, looking at the baby all of the while. 'Nancy Ann, was my father's sister,' he eventually said. 'She was like a mother to me. My aunt lived with us. She died when I was eleven and it was like I had lost my mother all over again. I've never forgotten her.'

"That came as a shock because he had never mentioned Nancy Ann before. 'What happened to her?' I asked? 'How did she die?'"

"What did he say?" Jack said.

"'She should never have died,' he said. He wouldn't elaborate further. He said it stirred up too many painful memories. Your grandfather was a closed book, Jack. He was very reserved. He found it difficult to show his feelings. I put that down to the fact that he had lost his mother early in life."

"I wish I could remember him," Jack said.

"You and Anna had a special place in his heart. He loved being a grandfather," his grandmother said.

"I remember him," Anna said. "Gran, was Dad close to grandad?"

"They were very close. Your grandad changed after your father was born. He became a lot less reserved. He was affectionate with your father, especially when he was a small child. He simply adored your father. He found it hard to be strict with him. I think your grandfather was deeply affected by his aunt's death and by the death of his own mother. He felt the loss of his aunt more because he had never known his mother."

"I can understand that," Anna said.

"I think we all can," her mother said. "Your father played a huge part in all our lives. Each of us was affected by his death enormously."

Jack agreed. His mother was right about that.

"Your grandfather was determined that he would be a good father, even though he came to it late in life. He was a lot older than me."

"What age was he when dad was born?" Jack asked.

"Old enough," Betty said. She didn't like to dwell too much on such matters.

"Do you think the fall out between Harvey's father and grandfather was in some way related to his aunt's death?" Felicia said.

"I don't know for certain. That may well be. Whatever it was, your grandad felt bitter about his father."

"At least we know who the woman in the fishing log was," Anna said, pragmatic to the last. "That's something, isn't it Jack?"

"We've solved that mystery!" he said.

"Nancy Ann and your great grandad must have had a good relationship," Felicia said. "Nancy Ann moved in with her brother, and she reared her nephew. It's not every sister who would do that. She must have sacrificed her own happiness a little."

"I agree," Harvey's mother said. "She must have been a special person."

"Harvey planned on visiting his grandfather's grave when we went to Doonmara," Felicia told Betty.

"He mentioned it to me. He asked me if I knew where he was buried but I had no idea. There is one more thing I should tell you."

"What?" Jack said.

"I may have a photograph of Nancy Ann."

"What? Gran, why didn't you tell us that before?"

"Before what, Jack?" asked his mother.

"Before she told us the whole story."

"You're very impatient, Jack," his mother said.

"He's interested, Felicia. That's all," Betty said.

"So there might actually be a photograph of Nancy Ann?" Felicia said

"Is there one, Gran?" Jack said.

"I think there is. After your grandfather died, I had to go through his personal effects. I found an old black and white photograph in an envelope along with his birth certificate. It was in a desk drawer in his study. As far as I could make out, the photograph was of your grandfather when he was a small child. He's standing beside a young woman who is sitting in a chair. The woman in the photograph must be Nancy Ann."

"That's insane," Anna said. "Did you find any other old photos, Gran?" she asked.

"That was the only one I came across. There were no photographs of your great grandfather or of the house where your grandfather grew up. Not a single one. I think that when your grandfather left Connemara, he wanted to leave the past behind him."

"But he never forgot Nancy Ann. He brought a photograph of Nancy Ann."

"He did. And yet, he never showed it to me, not once, in all of our married years together." A single tear escaped Betty. "The pain of losing Nancy Ann went too deep for your grandad," she said, and dabbed her eyes. "It was like she was ripped from his life, and he never fully got over her loss."

＊

Felicia glanced over the email she had composed.

Dear Laura

Thank you for your lovely message and kind words. I remember you so well and how kind you were to us, and especially to Jack, last August. My children have remained brave and have been doing really well.

I have discovered that I have a lot more inner strength than I ever imagined. I have found a lot of comfort with family and friends.

We are now back living in Ireland. We are renting a house in Dublin. But I haven't gone back to Connemara yet. Someday perhaps... But I think of the place every day and the thought of salmon leaping up is beautiful and fitting indeed.

Thank you again
Felicia

She hit the send button and the message disappeared from her screen. Just then, Anna walked into the room.

"Mum."

Felicia looked up from the screen.

"I think you need a makeover."

"A makeover?" Felicia repeated.

"Yes," Anna said in a tone that suggested she meant business. "Your hair is rubbish and you haven't bought anything new for ages."

Felicia said nothing. Anna tried again.

"You always looked your best when dad was alive, Mum. He wouldn't want you to let yourself go."

At this rebuke, Felicia looked flummoxed. She quickly composed herself.

"What did you have in mind?" she said.

"You need to do something about your hair, Mum. That's a no brainer. And we should go shopping in Dundrum."

Dundrum was a vast shopping centre in South County Dublin and a Mecca for Anna.

"All right then," her mother agreed.

The truth was that Felicia didn't care how she looked these days. But what Anna said had struck a chord. Felicia had always made an effort to look nice for her husband. Harvey wouldn't want her to let herself go. Anna was right about that.

CHAPTER TWENTY-THREE

June 2013

"The flowers look like yellow lanterns," he said, observing the laburnums.

"How the landscape changes with the seasons," she remarked. "This is my favourite time of year."

Laura and Alex were staying in Doonmara for the June Bank Holiday weekend. Taking advantage of the fine morning, they had taken a stroll after breakfast. Pink and red rhododendrons dotted the long and winding avenue. They walked past fragrant white rose bushes interspersed amongst a selection of glorious trees, including an enormous giant monkey tree which stamped its presence.

"I can smell honeysuckle," said Laura. On cue around the bend, she eyed a large honeysuckle plant. Laura picked two or three of the flowers and rubbed them in her hands. She inhaled their perfume and said, "I think spending two days here is like spending a week somewhere else."

Alex looked at her tenderly.

"Do you remember I told you that the hotel had begun a Tree Register Book?" she said. Laura had seen the book on a table on her way into the bar one evening. Curious, she had flicked through the pages, and read the entries.

"I remember."

"What if we planted a tree for Rachel's anniversary? What do you think?"

"That's a great idea," he said, pleased. "I don't know why I didn't think of it myself."

Laura always dreaded the anniversary. This year, she and Alex would face the day as a real couple, two people united in their loss. On previous anniversaries, Laura would block out the events of that fateful day in Kilkee. She would read a book and keep herself busy. They met up with no one on Rachel's anniversary.

Laura and Alex visited the cemetery separately. Up until recently, they had rarely visited their daughter's grave together.

"That's not uncommon with parents who have lost a child," Laura had once explained to her mother. "We can barely deal with ourselves at the graveside, let alone with each other's pain."

On the anniversary, and generally in the afternoon, Laura would walk to the cemetery alone and place a bunch of flowers on Rachel's grave.

"I'm like a robot. I just go through the motions," she had told her mother.

It would be different this year.

Laura's thoughts returned to the tree planting

"I read the entries," she said to Alex. "Some people planted trees in memory of loved ones who had died, and others to celebrate engagements and birthdays. There are trees planted for all sorts of reasons.

"What trees are planted?" Alex said.

"Beech, mainly. Oak trees were planted as well."

"I like the idea of an oak tree," he said.

"Me too. So?" She left the sentence unfinished.

"So, let's do it."

Passing the lake on their left, they arrived at the gate lodge. Along the riverside, the trees were heavy with greenery.

"The trees look as if they are going to tumble into the river. And you can see the reflection of the pink rhododendrons on this side," Laura said, looking at the water, "and of the red rhododendrons on the other."

"I find it vaguely hallucinogenic," Alex said. "It's a perfect mirror image. The water is like glass."

"What a lovely house," she said, admiring the gate house. "It could be ours someday. I could sell my ring," she said, in jest. She placed her right hand in front of her and studied the ring. "I can't believe it's mine. I'm still getting used to the idea."

"It's legally yours. You had better believe it."

"Much to the chagrin of James."

"There's always going to be one killjoy," he said.

They had collected the ring in April. The story of how she had come to find the ring had featured in one of the national newspapers along with a prominent picture of the castle overlooking a stretch of the river.

Once James was aware that the hotel had no legal entitlement, he had given their story to the paper to drum up publicity for the hotel. Laura had been contacted by the newspaper. On advice from the police, she didn't give much away about her find, and she had refused to pose for a photograph.

The article appeared and caught the public's imagination. Because of the ensuing publicity, the police had warned Laura that it was likely that a few individuals would come forward to claim ownership. The first claim was on the day after the story's publication. Laura had received a phone message from the police in Clifden telling her about the claim and to expect more.

None of the claimants succeeded with their assertions. Not one person who came forward was able to describe the ring in significant detail. James hadn't seen the inscription or the date and if any of the staff knew, they hadn't told him. Those details hadn't appeared in the article.

On April 22nd, Laura and Alex had driven to Clifden Police Station and collected the ring from lost property.

"It's now with its rightful owner," the policeman said. It was the same officer that they had dealt with previously.

She slipped the ring on her finger.

"I'd forgotten how beautiful it is," she said, thrilled.

The same paper had contacted her again and this time she agreed to be photographed wearing the ring. The ensuing publicity provided a boost for the hotel.

"Once, people came here to catch a salmon," Conor had said. "Now, its metal detectors they're using instead of fishing rods.

The hotel owner had been delighted with the publicity coup. He congratulated James. The manager had been falling over the Hamiltons since their return visit this weekend.

"I preferred it when he ignored us," Alex said.

"Me too. All this palsy-walsy nonsense is cringeworthy," Laura said.

"He wasn't so friendly the day he tried to stake a claim on your ring."

Laura grimaced.

"He certainly wasn't," she agreed. "Mind you, I don't blame him for trying to generate business for the hotel. It's the first time that I've seen him use his initiative."

"Jane told me that business has been through the roof since your picture appeared in the paper. I'm surprised the guests aren't hounding you for a photograph."

They continued their walk in a comfortable silence. As they neared the hotel Laura said, "I don't suppose we'll ever find out who owned this ring."

"It had to have been bought by the Maharaja. Or else, it belonged to someone in his entourage. That seems the logical explanation. Someone went to a great deal of extravagance."

Later that afternoon, accompanied by a gardener, Laura and Alex planted an oak tree in memory of their daughter. They chose a spot along the river walk, close to the bridge.

"In memory of our beloved daughter, Rachel," Laura wrote in the *Tree Register Book*. She recorded the type of tree that had been planted and the date. Afterwards, they decided to have a drink in the bar.

"To our darling girl," Alex said, and lifted his Guinness.

"To Rachel," Laura said, clinking glasses.

There was a moment's silence. Laura remembered Rachel circling her arms around her in a warm embrace. Alex was reliving the circumstances in which Rachel had died.

Laura looked at her husband. In the way that many couples can guess each other's thoughts, she knew what Alex was thinking.

"Don't torture yourself." she said.

"You know me too well," he said sadly. "It started out as a happy day. If only I could turn back time, Laura." He shook his head.

"You can't and neither can I. We can hold onto the precious memories we have. We had five wonderful years with Rachel."

"That we did."

"I used to feel isolated in the early years," she said. "I thought that no one could ever feel the pain and loss that I did, as if it happened to no one else but me. I kept thinking, why me? What did I do? Did I ever hurt someone? Was I ever cruel? Why would God punish me like this?

He gripped her hand tightly.

"I'd make myself walk around other graveyards, not just the cemetery where Rachel is buried, and look at the headstones. I'd read about other children who died, and I saw that I was not alone. It helped, Al."

"I supposed it helped to reassess her death," he said. "Something similar happened to me. I remember watching a documentary about Madeleine McCann. I thought about the agony that her parents went through and still face today. That helped me to reassess Rachel's death a little. Rachel's safe and we know where she is. She never experienced any harm or pain, or heartache. I don't have to worry about that. She's waiting for me."

"For me, too," Laura said softly.

Conor came into the bar. He saluted Laura and Alex.

"Will you join us for a drink, Conor?" Alex asked.

"I don't mind if I do."

Alex ordered a pint of Guinness for the gillie.

"Are there any salmon out there?" said Alex.

"Nada. We need rain and lots of it. There's nothing stirring. The river is low. We haven't recorded a salmon all week. I checked the gauge."

"It's hardly worth my while going out tomorrow."

"Correct. You might catch a trout, Alex. I can give you some flies."

"I'm not here for the trout!" Alex said.

The conversation turned to general chit chat.

"I had an email a while back from Felicia," Laura said.

Conor's face drew a blank.

"You have me there, Mrs Hamilton," he said.

"Her husband died while he was fishing with his son."

"Ah, Mrs Russell! I'm with you now. How is she?"

"I imagine she's finding it difficult. Her children are doing well."

"Do you think she might come back?" he asked, interested.

"She said they might return some day, but not for a while."

"I suppose it's too soon."

"That's more or less what she implied," Laura told him. "She said that she thinks of the place every day."

"Her husband's grandfather used to fish here back in the day of the Maharaja. Did you know that?"

"Her son told me. As a matter of fact, I helped him to look up his great grandfather's name in the fishing log."

"Did you find it?"

"We found several entries. The name Nancy Ann Russell also appeared but Mrs Russell had no idea who that was. Apparently, there was some sort of family fall out. Harvey Russell's father left Connemara when he was a young man and he never returned. He never spoke to his father again.

"My grandfather remembers the family. He was a gillie here then."

"That's going back a bit. He must be very old."

"Would you believe that he's ninety-eight and still going strong! He was only a young lad during the Maharajas' time but his father, that's my great grand-father, was head gillie when Gai Singh resided."

"Do you know what caused the family rift?"

"I do."

Laura edged closer to the gillie.

"I'm all ears, Conor. I can tell you it was a mystery to the Russells."

"No way, Mrs Hamilton! I assumed they knew. I expect John did too. Mind you, it's a heartbreaking story. It's not the kind of thing you'd be bringing up in conversation."

"That might explain it then," she said. "Please, put me out of my misery, Conor. Tell me what happened."

Conor took a sip from his pint of Guinness. Laura and Alex sat beside him, intrigued.

"I only found out because my grandfather brought it up," Conor said. "He's in a nursing home now, but there's nothing wrong with the old man's memory. To cut a long story short, John's mother is in the same nursing home.

"John met my granddad when he visited his mother. It was the weekend Mr Russell died. He mentioned what had happened up at the castle, and he told my grandfather about Harvey Russell's connection to Doonmara. My granddad brought it up on my next visit. He told me the story. As it happened, his own father knew Dr Russell well."

He paused for dramatic effect. Laura and Alex were following his every word.

"There was much speculation in the village at the time, of course, but only a handful of people knew," Conor said. His voice had become low and conspiratorial.

"The village?" Laura said

"Roundstone. The doctor and his family lived outside Roundstone. Fred was his name. Dr Fred Russell."

Conor glanced around the common room. There were seven or eight elderly people sitting in chairs. A few, like his grandfather, were in wheelchairs. Most of them looked dead to the world. He found the nursing home a depressing place, no matter that his grandfather was well looked after, and appeared happy enough. Conor's secret fear was that he'd end up in one of these places himself.

He preferred to sit with his grandfather in his bedroom. That had the semblance of normality.

Then, it was just his grandfather and himself. The old man was in full charge of his faculties. Sadly, that couldn't be said for the majority of the elderly people sitting around him today. He disliked the big communal room. It forced him to face his own mortality. There was nothing fun about being old.

His grandfather had brought up the Russell name. The death of Harvey Russell had occurred two weeks previously.

"I saw John last week," the old man had begun. "He mentioned the commotion up at the castle."

Conor looked puzzled. His grandfather tried again.

"He told me about the death of that Russell chap."

"Ah, yes. I'm with you now, Grandad. It was a sad day, all right."

"I remember the grandfather, Dr Russell. A real gent, so he was. The doctor didn't have it easy, mind you. The son went away after what happened and Dr Russell never heard from him again."

"After what happened?" Conor had asked, now curious. The old man had caught his attention. "Tell me."

"It was a heartbreaking story," his grandfather had said after a moment's deliberation. "The doctor had only the one child, and the mother had died in childbirth. After she died, his sister, Nancy

Ann, came to live with him. She reared that boy and she was only a lass herself. She was devoted to the pair of them.

"It can't have been easy for her. She was rearing someone else's child and looking after her brother, when she should have been married herself and rearing her own children. She was a real beauty too. She stood out with her long red hair."

The old man stopped and reminisced. In his mind's eye, he recalled Nancy Ann walking through the main street in Roundstone. Her red hair was secured in a bun and she had milky white skin. He remembered that because her complexion was different to his mother and sisters. His mother's face was weather beaten. And Nancy Ann had beautiful emerald green eyes. They were a rarity.

The old man cleared his throat. Conor fetched a glass of water and handed it to his grandfather.

"Here, take a sip," he'd instructed.

"Thank you. Now where was I?" his grandfather had said.

"You were telling me about Nancy Ann."

"Ah, yes, the lovely Nancy Ann. She was a real looker in her day and she was a great fisherwoman. Dr Fred taught his sister how to fish and she took to it. In time, she became far better at the fishing than he ever was. A natural, my father used to say."

"Did she fish at Doonmara?" Conor had asked.

"Yes, the doctor would bring her along. My father said that the Maharaja took a real shine to her. Mind you, he liked western women. He was quite Anglicised. He had been educated in Britain.

"Quite the roving eye, he had too, begorrah. I saw that for myself. He never married but he always had a nurse with him, if you get my meaning. He had a lot of nurses." He gave his grandson a wink. "Do you know that I am the last surviving employee of Gai Singh?" he added.

Conor's grandfather had told him that many times before but he humoured the old man and said, "Is that so? That's remarkable, Grandad."

"There you go. He was a good man, the Maharaja. I remember hearing of his death with sadness and disbelief. You'd meet people on the road crying their eyes out. The locals would set off fireworks along the train route to welcome him when he arrived. Did you know that? Did I ever tell you that?"

He had but Conor had said, "Imagine that."

"He would descend at the old railway station in Doonmara and a caravan of limousines and cars would follow him."

"He was well-loved in these parts, Grandad."

"That's the truth. He did so much for the area. There was real poverty here then. Nobody had anything to speak of."

"They were tough times, Grandad. But tell me what happened to Dr Fred and Nancy Ann?" he'd said, steering the conversation back to the Russells.

"Ah yes, the lovely lady herself. Well, Nancy Ann took to fishing with the Maharaja.

He was passionate about the fishing. He would fish all day and all night on occasion, if the mood so took him. He was older than Nancy Ann but a bond developed between the pair of them."

"They had the fishing in common, I suppose," Conor had said.

"True enough. That they did. The Maharaja entertained at the castle. A lot of British guests and important people from Dublin were invited to stay. There were parties and dinners when he was in residence and the good doctor and his sister were always on the guest list.

"In those days, this place was quiet enough. It was bleak in the winter, let me tell you. The Maharaja brought life to the place. There were always comings and goings up at the castle. I expect the Maharaja opened up a whole new world for Nancy Ann. She never had the chance to experience much of life before that. She was still in her teens when she came to live with her brother, and she spent the next eleven years of her life devoted to him and her nephew."

"The child must have been very attached to her," Conor said.

"The child adored her. With all this social intercourse, Nancy Ann came into her own. In time, it became obvious that she and the Maharaja had fallen for each other, in spite of the age difference."

"How much older was he?"

"About fifteen years. But he was a very charismatic figure and he was a handsome fellow in his own right. You've seen the pictures up in the castle."

"I have. What else do you know about Nancy Ann? What was she like?"

"My father said that she was very unworldly. I think that was another reason why the Maharaja fell for her. She was very good humoured too. She had a good sense of fun about her. She was different to the upper class British ladies who used to come here."

"She sounds like a lovely lady," Conor had said, stating the obvious.

"Indeed she was. Nancy Ann had an easy way about her. She loved a smoke," he'd divulged and he gave a little chuckle. "She would smoke in secret with the Maharaja in the fishing huts. She was afraid to smoke in front of her brother."

"What? You're joking."

"Their father had been a rector in Dublin, and it seemed to me that Dr Russell was a devout man and a conservative one. He could be quite the authoritarian. He wouldn't have approved of his sister smoking."

Conor had looked at him fondly and said, "I seem to remember you telling me that my great grandmother smoked."

"You're not wrong there. My mother would sometimes smoke a pipe. She used to light it at the kitchen fire with a piece of paper. Back in my day, no woman was ever seen smoking in public."

"Things have certainly changed since then," Conor had mused.

"It's a different world you live in, my boy."

"What happened next? I mean, with the big romance" asked Conor, captivated.

"For her birthday, the Maharaja threw a huge luncheon party for Nancy Ann. It was a lavish affair, held in the grounds, and no expense was spared. Sometime that day, or so my father believed, the Maharaja spoke to the doctor and asked his permission for Nancy Ann's hand in marriage. That was how it was done in those days.

"I remember the party. It was very grand. The place was alight. There were pony traps coming up the avenue, and all the ladies and gentleman were in their finery. There were foods served that we had never heard of, let alone seen. It was a sight for sore eyes."

"Tell me, Grandad, how did your father know that the Maharaja spoke to the doctor?"

"A cousin of my father's was the laundry woman at the Russell's. She worked in the household one

413

or two days a week. She got the gist of what was going on. A lot was heard from behind closed doors."

"What did the doctor say to Gai Singh? Was he pleased?"

"It came as a surprise to the doctor. He wasn't one bit happy about a relationship, let alone a marriage. A lot of that was racial, I expect, because in those days, a non-white man marrying a white woman could provoke a lot of hostile reaction. A stern line was taken on mixed-race matches. That was the case with the doctor, never mind the Maharaja's enormous wealth, and no matter how friendly he and the doctor had become. Like I said, the doctor was a conservative man."

"Talking about double standards," Conor had remarked. "Dr Russell sounds like a bigot. He had no trouble accepting a car from Gai Singh."

"He was a man of his times," said the old man. "To be honest, he was a good man. A great doctor too. A humane sort."

"Not when it came to his family, it seems. What happened then?"

"The doctor forbade the marriage. Apparently, he left the party early. He insisted that Nancy Ann go with him but she refused to leave. The Maharaja was returning to India a few weeks later. He planned to leave with Nancy Ann. After the doctor's reaction to the relationship, the Maharaja had second thoughts about her accompanying him. He thought that Dr Russell would eventually come round. All that was needed was patience to win him over.

"Nancy Ann was very angry with her brother. Her nephew was eleven and heading to boarding school in England that September. She had given up her youth and while she had been happy to do that, this was her time and her chance, perhaps her only chance, for personal happiness.

"Think of the freedom and the opportunities that this would have offered Nancy Ann. You see, in those days, an unmarried woman of her age was quite the spinster. And here was her brother, denying her this chance of happiness. He threatened to disown her. He told her that she would never see her nephew again were she to marry the Maharaja. He threatened to cut all ties with his sister if she went ahead with the marriage."

"Jesus, that was pretty extreme," Conor had said.

"To cut a long story short, the Maharaja left without her. Nancy Ann was heartbroken. The months passed. My father said that she wasted away. The Maharaja promised to come back later in the autumn. He didn't. In mid-December, Nancy Ann took a boat out into the upper lake, down past the lower bridge where the water is at its deepest." He paused for a moment before saying, "And that was that. She took her own life."

"She committed suicide?" Conor had said, shocked.

His grandfather nodded.

"I remember the search for her. It took days to recover the body. There were rumours that she might have been with child. She was wearing a long white gown; the gown she wore for her birthday luncheon. They said that the Maharaja had it made especially for her in London."

"And Dr Fred? What happened to him?"

"The doctor was beside himself. He never forgave himself and the son was inconsolable. The little fellow came home from boarding school at Christmas to find his beloved aunt dead. Dr Fred managed to hide her suicide from the child for several years but eventually the truth came out. When it did, the son left. He never spoke to his father again."

"What happened to the Maharaja?"

"It appears the Maharaja had repeatedly written to Nancy Ann. The doctor never passed on the correspondence. The Maharaja hadn't been able to return in the autumn because of ill health. Nancy Ann never knew. She thought Gai Singh had deserted her."

"Do you think that she was pregnant?"

"My father's cousin was certain of it. She claimed to have overheard an argument between the brother and sister. She heard something about a baby and the shame of it all. She said the doctor ordered his sister to leave the house. But that's only hearsay. Who knows?

"I will say this. If Nancy Ann found herself in that situation, then she must have felt isolated, for there was no greater shame in this country, in those days, than to be unmarried and pregnant. It would have been an impossible situation. She would have been cast out of society. No other family member lived near the village. With Gai Singh out of the picture, she must have had no one to turn to."

"She should have had her brother," Conor had cut in. "It was a pity he didn't show some of the humanity you spoke of to his sister, especially since she did so much for him and his son. For someone so pious, he certainly didn't behave in a Christian manner."

"You're right there, my boy. But let me tell you, if an unmarried woman became pregnant back then, she was shunted out of society. Nobody wanted to know. It was the worst thing that could happen to a lass."

"What happened next?"

"The Maharaja returned in the spring to visit her grave."

"Do you think that Gai Singh loved her? He was a ladies' man from what you said."

"That's true. The women were very fond of him and he was never short of admirers. He was a very charming man. But the Maharaja loved Nancy Ann, make no mistake about that. There was something very special about Nancy Ann. You should have seen her, Conor. My own father used to say that there was sadness about the man after Nancy Ann died. He knew the man well. I only started working at the castle a few years later."

"And the Maharaja never married?"

"I'd say that was as close as he'd ever come."

"And the nurses you spoke about. Did any more arrive at Doonmara?"

"Oh, after Nancy Ann, there were no more 'nurses'. Not to my knowledge anyway. After that, every year, on the occasion of Nancy Ann's birthday, until the Maharaja died, a dozen red roses were placed on her grave. There were not too many bouquets of roses left on graves round here, let me tell you."

"I'd imagine not. Where is she buried, Granddad?

"She's buried in the Protestant cemetery in Roundstone. So there you have it: the story of the Russell family. Put that in your pipe and smoke it."

"That's some tale, Grandad. And very well told, if I may say so."

"You may. The Maharaja didn't last too long afterwards. He was dead eight years later. Folk around here said that he died from a broken heart. The place was sold after his death."

"Did many people know what happened?"

"Not too many. Not about Nancy Ann's suicide anyway. That was made to look like a tragic accident. There were rumours of a dalliance, that's all. Hardly anyone knew he had proposed."

The old man looked tired. He suddenly looked his years.

"I tired you out, Grandad."

"You're grand. But I am tired. I think I'll take a short nap."

Conor bid the old man goodbye and went on his way.

CHAPTER TWENTY-FOUR

Ciara had read the article in the newspaper. She had seen Laura's photograph. Laura Hamilton was a good-looking woman, and her smile was warm and friendly.

Ciara debated whether she should tell Caroline or not. Caroline wasn't looking her best. The last few years had taken their toll. By contrast, Laura Hamilton looked a million dollars. What good would it do for her friend to see Laura Hamilton's photograph and read about her wonderful luck.

Ciara couldn't believe the size of the diamond. The article said that the ring was almost five carats and that it was a rare Cartier piece. It must be worth a fortune. No wonder Laura Hamilton looked happy.

Meanwhile, poor old Caroline was struggling to make ends meet. Her friend had returned to work but part-time until Una was a little older. With the cost of childcare, Caroline's take home pay was minimal. Childcare cost was astronomical in Dublin, more so if you were a one parent family. You had no one to share the burden with. Ciara had tried to persuade Caroline to tell Alex about Una. She thought he should contribute towards the child's care. But Caroline was adamant that Una remain her secret.

Yet, here were the Hamiltons lapping it up in five-star luxury hotels. There was Laura Hamilton right before her very eyes wearing a ring that cost a lot of money. Ciara was angry at the unfairness of it. She thought back to the day she had seen Caroline in hospital, shuffling around corridors in a dressing gown, thin despite being pregnant, and pale, bald and browless.

Felicia had seen Laura's picture in the newspaper and read the accompanying article. Initially, Felicia had been taken aback that the ring had been found at Beat Two. Felicia had only memories of heartbreak at Beat Two. Yet, it was where Laura had found good fortune.

A few days later, she had felt less emotional and emailed Laura to congratulate her on her find. Laura had replied back, thanking Felicia for her good wishes and enquiring as to how they were getting on.

That afternoon, Laura had composed a second email to Felicia, detailing what had happened to cause the rift in the Russell family. Now, Laura hit the send command and watched as the email disappeared from view.

"Job done," she said, more to herself than to Alex. Laura sat at the kitchen table, her second mug of tea cooling. She paused to think for a moment before saying, "Nancy Ann threw herself into the upper lake. Where is that exactly, Alex?"

Alex finished his slice of lemon cake and rose to his feet. He put his plate and mug into the dishwater, and then he straightened up.

"The upper lake extends from the mouth of Doonmara river, known as the canal to Sná Beg," he said. "That's the narrow part of the lake. I'm sure you've often heard me talk about Sná Beg."

"I know where you mean. It's a good spot for spring salmon."

"Precisely," he said. "Nancy Ann must have taken a boat out, up near the old house on the lake. There's a slipway there."

"We pass it on the lake walk. There are often one or two boats on the slipway. What a sad ending to have. She must have felt very alone. It must have seemed like such a hopeless situation. In those days, women were being sent to the Magdalene laundries."

"Even as far back as then?"

"God, yes."

"She was Protestant. Would that have made a difference?"

"I don't think so. Think of the times she lived in, Alex. There was a Protestant home in Dublin. It was called Bethany house. As far as I can recall, it was opened in the early 1920s. I remember reading about it once. The archbishop, who opened it, described it as a 'door of hope for fallen women'. The phrase stuck with me."

"That says everything I need to know about the place," Alex said. "Poor old Nancy Ann."

"Indeed! One moment, she had a glittering future and the next, it was snatched away. If only the Maharaja had come back like he promised. If he had, their story could have had such a different ending."

"Communication must have been a nightmare in those days," he said. "Most communication was done by letter or telegram. I don't know if they'd have had access to a phone then. Were phones widely in use in the 1920s?"

"Search me," Laura said. "If she was pregnant, I'd imagine Nancy Ann had no options. If she wasn't, she may have thought that Gai Singh had given up on her, and that he wasn't willing to fight for her hand in marriage. The whole racial divide was pretty strong in those days. I Googled it earlier, out of interest."

"It was," Alex said. "Nancy Ann's brother refused to even consider a relationship, and he was a friend of Gai Singh. Tell me, what did Google have to say?"

"More or less what Conor indicated. Inter-racial marriages were severely frowned on."

"Even if you were a rich Maharaja? I thought that might make people a bit colour blind."

"You're half-right," she said. "If it was more a case of class trumping race, they were. But there was an interesting point made in an article that I read."

"Which was?"

"If the men involved in these marriages were upper class, then they were often Anglicised."

"As in the case of Gai Singh?"

"Precisely. There were in fact a number of middle class women who married Indian Maharajas and other royalty from Britain's Empire throughout the early 20th century. There was a Hindu temple in Woking which played host to several mixed-race marriages during the period. My guess is that Nancy Ann would have had to convert to Hinduism in order to marry the Maharaja."

"That wouldn't have gone down well in the family. Her father was a rector. And I imagine Connemara was more provincial than most places. Doonmara is full of secrets."

"And ghosts."

"Ghosts?" he echoed, confused.

"I saw a lady dressed in white at Beat Two on the night that Harvey Russell died."

"And was she, by any chance, flinging her jewellery into the river?"

"Very droll."

"Maybe it was Nancy Ann," he said.

Exacerbated, Laura threw her eyes up to heaven.

"I saw what I saw, Alex. Anyway, the ring didn't belong to Nancy Ann. It's not her name that's engraved on it. Besides, the engagement never went ahead."

"I was only joking."

"Isn't it eerie how Harvey Russell, the son of Nancy Ann's beloved nephew, died on the river bank. Or even, perhaps, as he fell into the river."

"There's a sense of poetic justice that Doonmara was Harvey Russell's finally resting place," he said.

"Sheer serendipity," she acknowledged.

"Laura, I'm going to ask you something very important?"

Curious, she looked straight at him.

"What's for dinner?" he asked.

She had brought flowers, fresias, and carried them inside a cone of patterned paper as she walked to Betty's front door. Felicia had called round to her mother-in-law's house earlier that day to tell her the story in person. Felicia suspected that Betty might become emotional, and she was right.

"Forgive me for babbling like this," Betty said. "Dirk must have been destroyed by his aunt's suicide. It explains everything. And to think my son died at Doonmara as well."

"That struck me forcibly," Felicia said.

"Did you tell the children?" Betty asked.

"Not yet. I wanted to tell you first."

Betty made coffee and they chatted for a while.

"Gosh, I lost track of time," Felicia said looking at her watch in surprise. "I had better go, Betty. I'm running late."

"Can you hold on for a moment?" Betty exited the room before Felicia had time to reply.

She handed Felicia a photograph when she returned. It was an old black and white photograph of her husband with his grand-aunt. The child in the photograph was no more than four or five.

"Anna and Jack might like to see this photograph again when you tell them."

"What a tragic ending for such a young life, Betty." Felicia examined the old photo. "She had an exquisite face."

"Nancy Ann must have been considered a great beauty in her day."

"Sadly, she didn't get to have a heyday," Felicia said. "Not really, when you think about it. But for a brief window of time, it must have seemed that the best was yet to come."

Later that evening, Felicia told her children about Nancy Ann's suicide. They were gathered together in the TV room.

"It's incredibly romantic and yet, tragic," Anna said, enthralled. To think, that an Indian Maharaja was in love with a member of our family. Our great grand-aunt nearly became the Maharani. Doonmara could have been our ancestral home. Jack and I could have been brought up there."

Her mother thought that was stretching it a bit.

"There should have been a fairy tale ending," Felicia said. "Instead, Nancy Ann committed suicide. She killed herself and her unborn baby. That is, of course, if the rumour mill had it right, and she was pregnant."

"I definitely think she was," Anna said.

Naturally you would, thought her mother. It fed Anna's appetite for the drama of the romance.

"Isn't it weird that dad died there," Jack piped in. The doomed romance between the Maharaja and his great grand-aunt had clearly escaped him.

"I thought the same," said his mother.

"We should go back, Mum," Jack said.

"Jack's right, Mum. He's seldom right, as it is."

Jack threw her a look.

"Relax, I'm only messing." Anna flashed her brother a grin. "What do you think, Mum?"

Anna studied her mother. It was impossible to gauge what Felicia's response would be. Felicia was looking a lot better. Her mother had taken Anna's advice on board. She had an overhaul at the hairdresser and bought some fashionable new clothes.

Felicia considered their request.

"We could go in August, for your dad's anniversary," she said finally. "It would be an emotional trip," she warned, looking first at Jack, then Anna. "That might catch you both unawares. You may relive dad's death a little and that might be difficult, especially for you, Jack, because you were with your dad when he died. Why don't we sleep on it? We can make a decision tomorrow. If you're both still keen to go back, then we will do that."

"Thanks, Mum," Anna said. She gave her mother a hug.

"Your grandmother thought that you might like to see this," Felicia said, showing them the dog-eared photograph.

Jack edged closer to his sister on the couch. He looked at the photograph. Nancy Ann sat upright in a chair. Her nephew, and their grandfather, stood beside his aunt. Both figures appeared solemn. The little boy was holding his aunt's hand.

"Grandad is wearing weird clothes," Jack said.

"That's what young boys wore in those days," his mother informed him. "Don't forget this photograph is very old. It dates back to the 1920s."

"It looks like he's wearing a suit, except someone cut the pants into shorts. What's that weird tie thing? I'd have had a fit if you put that on me, Mum."

His mother laughed.

"I am sure you would," she said, looking at his navy training pants pointedly. They were emblazoned with a logo. "Your grandfather has a cravat around his neck. They were the height of fashion in those days."

Jack remained unconvinced. He shrugged his shoulders and said, "Whatever."

Nancy Ann was wearing a long-fitted dress. A single strand of pearls emphasised a swanlike neck.

Although she had her hair tied back in a bun, a few tendrils had escaped, caressing her cheeks. That softened her features. She had expressive eyes and a heart-shaped face.

"It's very staged, "Anna declared, thinking of the Instagram shots that she and her friends posted.

"A professional photographer would have taken it. That was common enough in those days."

"The photograph is worn and faded but you can see that she was really pretty,"

Anna said.

She thought of what passed for beauty among her own peer group. For starters, you had to be skinny, with fabulous long hair that was usually highlighted or coloured, or both.

Blond was definitely an advantage. Ginger was a girl's worst nightmare. Some of Anna's friends were experimenting with hair colour. Several, including Anna, had their hair highlighted.

Fake tan, and gel nails were a given. It was important that your makeup was right. And your eyebrows. Anna had hers threaded every few weeks. Most of the girls learned how to apply their makeup from tutorials on YouTube.

You had to have the 'right look' clothes-wise. And shoes mattered. If you ticked all those boxes, you were on point, which in Anna's vocabulary was the same as beautiful. Or, maybe not, she mused. As she studied the old family photo, Anna could tell that her aunt had a kind of natural beauty that didn't need to be artificially enhanced.

"She has a kind of individual beauty," Anna surmised, noting all of her friends looked more or less the same after they had 'beautified' themselves.

Anna wouldn't have been impressed that her aunt was a 'ginger'. Much of the detail that Conor's grandfather had shared got lost in the retelling of Nancy Ann's story, as it went from one person to the next. Their aunt was noted for her unusual colouring but the Russell family were unaware that Nancy Ann had auburn red hair, green eyes, and a flawless complexion.

They never knew that the Maharaja sent a bouquet of red roses to Nancy Ann's grave every year on her birthday, or that Nancy Ann liked to indulge in a secret cigarette in the fishing huts. Anna could have related to that. She indulged in a secret cigarette herself and in the past couple of months, she had begun to smoke weed. She had started drinking too, and taking pills, not often but occasionally. One her two relaxers made her mellow.

Once, she had mixed several relaxers with vodka. She had been very aggressive according to

Fiona, her best friend, who said she had popped six. Anna had blacked out and couldn't remember anything afterwards. She had been agitated the following day, craving more pills. Fiona had made her a vodka espresso first thing. She had smoked a lot of weed that day in order to mellow out.

It was a form of escape. Anna covered her tracks well and Felicia remained blissfully unaware of what her daughter was up to.

"I'll give this photograph back to your grand-mother," Felicia said, "and I'll get a copy made."

"Will you get one for me?" Anna asked. "I'd like to have one."

"Of course, I will. Would you like a copy?" Felicia asked her son.

Jack didn't really care whether he had a copy or not. But if his sister was getting one, then he was going to have one.

"Yes," he said.

"I'll have three copies made then. We'll talk about Doonmara tomorrow."

Anna and Jack were resolute in their determination to return. The following morning, it came as no surprise to their mother, that neither Jack, nor his sister, had changed their mind about visiting the castle. Later that day, Felicia made reservations.

"Will you be staying for just the one night?" the receptionist inquired.

"Yes," Felicia confirmed

One night was one night too many as far as she was concerned. Nevertheless, she would put her children first, like she had always done, as had Harvey when he was alive. She would be 'up' for Doonmara. She would pretend.

"That's one single room and a double room with two beds, checking in on Saturday, August 8th," the receptionist said.

"That's correct," Felicia said.

"I need your name and a credit card number. Can I have your name, please?"

"Felicia Russell."

The name registered with the receptionist.

"Mrs Russell, this is Maura," she said. "I was the receptionist on duty during your stay with us. I hope that you are keeping well, Mrs Russell.

"We're all well, Maura."

"That's good to hear. We look forward to having you stay with us in August, Mrs Russell."

"Thank you, Maura. The children are looking forward to it."

Maura noted that Felicia Russell didn't include herself.

"How is Jane?" Felicia said.

"She's keeping well."

"And John and Pawel?"

"John is fine but I'm afraid that Pawel has left."

"Oh, that's a shame. I know that my son would have liked to have met him again. I hope to see you all in August, Maura." And on that parting note Felicia hung up.

Maura recorded the booking on the hotel computer system. A moment or two later, Jane came by reception.

"Oh, give me peace from that man," the assistant manager exclaimed. She flung herself into the chair in the cubby hole.

"Let me have a guess," said Maura. "James?"

"Who else?" Jane said. "The man is driving me demented, Maura. He'll see me into an early grave."

"If he does, he'll have me to answer to."

"He wouldn't know what hit him," Jane said and laughed.

"You'll never guess who phoned to make a reservation."

Jane shrugged her shoulders.

"Felicia Russell. She made a reservation for herself and her two children."

Jane's jaw dropped.

Maura said, "I was surprised as well."

"I thought they might come back one day, but not this soon."

"How long has it been?" the receptionist asked.

"It will be two years in August."

"That's when they're coming. They're booked in for one night. She asked after you."

"They must be coming for the anniversary," Jane said. Reluctantly, she got up to go. "I had better get back on duty or what's his face will be on the war path. He's in a foul mood today. I think he's had a fight with his wife."

"It could be worse. Think of what she has to go through. Fancy being married to that twat."

A little later, Seán passed reception. Maura told him about the booking. Seán told John, who in turn, told Conor. Soon, most of the staff were aware that Mrs Russell, that nice lady whose husband had died under tragic and unforeseen circumstances at Doonmara, was returning with her children.

Even the general manager knew. Jane had told him. James found out most things from the assistant manager, or Seán. The porter was a fairly reliable source of information.

"Mrs Russell and her family have made a booking for August," Jane said. He looked at her blankly. "Harvey Russell's widow. He was the man who died while he was having a fishing lesson with John."

"Ah yes, I remember them. That won't be an easy trip for the family. It won't be easy for the son," James said with empathy. His own son was more or less the same age as Jack.

Jane was surprised. It was a pity James hadn't been more compassionate when Mrs Russell was checking out. The general manager had gone to Felicia in person and handed her the hotel bill. Jane had been mortified. Harvey Russell may have died during his stay at Doonmara but James made sure he paid for that privilege and with no delay. Harvey Russell's newly widowed wife would not be leaving the hotel until the account was settled. Business was business.

"August, did you say, Jane?"

"Yes, they've booked in for one night. I think it's around the date of Mr Russell's anniversary."

"I won't be here," he said.

"Oh."

Jane was confused. He was hardly going on holidays in August. It was their peak period. They were always run off their feet in August.

"There's something I intended to share with you and the rest of the staff at the end of the week but I might as well tell you now."

"What's up?" she asked with interest.

"This will come as a surprise, Jane. I'm leaving Doonmara. I've moving on to bigger and better things. I've been offered a position in a luxury hotel in Killarney and I'll be finishing up at the end of the month."

She was stunned. Mostly, she was overjoyed. Her nemesis was leaving in two weeks' time. A wave of contentment swept through her.

"Congratulations," she said, hoping her face didn't give too much away. Jane didn't say that he would be missed. That would be a travesty. She ought to say something. What could she say? That the staff would be overjoyed to see the back of him? That he had been an absolute pain in the butt to work with? That nobody had a good word to say on his behalf?

In the end, she said, "The best of luck, James," and left it at that.

"Thank you for your good wishes. It will be good to be back on home territory. Naturally, you will be deputising until they've found my replacement. That will take some time, of course. You'll see what it's like. It's not an easy job."

He had some cheek. David and Jane had been 'deputising' between them for years. Jane said nothing. Let James have his moment. He would be gone in a fortnight. She smiled sweetly.

"I can see you're pleased for me," he said, totally misreading her. "That's nice of you."

Her smile was genuine. She was genuinely pleased, if not thrilled, that James was leaving.

CHAPTER TWENTY-FIVE

Laura was standing in a queue for the toilet when a small toddler caught her eye. The child was waiting patiently at the door of the babies changing room, clutching her mother's hand. Laura couldn't see the child's face because the little girl had her back to her. Yet, there was something very familiar about her. She had the same mop of curls, the same shaped head and the same movements Rachel had at that age.

Laura felt the hairs stand up at the back of her neck. Over the years, there were occasions such as this, when Laura would see a child who reminded her of Rachel. It hadn't happened for a while.

Seconds later, the pair disappeared into the changing room.

There were over a half a dozen toilet cubicles and the queue was moving quickly. A cubicle became vacant. When Laura came out, there was no sign of the mother and child. Most likely, they were in the changing area.

Laura considered hanging round until they reappeared. She reprimanded herself: She was being ridiculous and Alex was waiting for her.

They had stopped at a motorway service area as they drove home from Dublin.

"I'd better pull in. I'm low on petrol," Alex had said as soon as the exit sign had appeared on the motorway. It was the last rest stop they would pass en route. "I wouldn't say no to a coffee either. We've a long way to go and I'm shattered."

Alex had had back to back meetings all day, and they had left Cratloe at an ungodly hour that morning.

"Why don't I drive the rest of the way? You can take a catnap."

"Are you sure?"

"Absolutely. It's not as if I've had a taxing day! We can swop round at the station."

Laura had spent an enjoyable day wandering around the shops on Grafton Street and lunching with an old school friend. Her time was her own these days. She had studied hard over the past year and was resuming her second year of studies in September. That meant she had the month of August free to enjoy at leisure.

There was much to look forward to in the weeks ahead. She and Alex were heading up to Doonmara Castle next weekend for her birthday. Later in the month, they were holidaying in the Algarve. They were joining her brother and his family for a week.

"Wouldn't it be great if we had this weather next weekend?" she said to her husband.

"Not so great for the fishing," he replied.

She laughed.

"Would you believe that we ate lunch outside?"

"Oh, that must have been nice," he said, and thought of the dried-up ham sandwich and weak coffee he'd had in between meetings. "Where did you go?"

"We went to a little restaurant on Clarendon Street. It felt very continental."

"It beats the sandwich I had!"

"Poor Alex. You must be starved."

"Famished!"

"Take out?" she asked.

"You're on."

They exited the motorway and Alex pulled into the service station. He began refuelling. Invariably, the place was busy. It housed two franchises. There was a reputable coffee outlet and a fast food outlet that was popular with families.

Moments later, Laura got out of the car.

"I need to go to the loo," she said.

"Can I get you anything?"

"No, I'm good."

Alex watched her walk towards the building. She wore a pair of white jeans in a flattering cut and a navy linen V-neck tee shirt.

Laura had told him earlier how much she was enjoying her studies. He was happy himself. Much of that he attributed to his wife's general contentment. He never thought that he would be this happy again. Not in a million years. Somehow, and against the odds, life had worked out. After all of the heartbreak and pain, they had found their way back together. That weekend in Doonmara had been the catalyst.

Alex headed inside. He was back in his car sitting in the passenger seat, and sipping his coffee, by the time Laura came out.

"Are you okay?" he asked, handing her the ignition key.

She looked shook. Laura was certainly not as composed as she had been ten minutes earlier.

"It was bedlam in the toilets," she said as she strapped herself in. She was glad that she had offered to drive. She could concentrate on the task in hand. It was bad enough that she had seen her 'white lady' in Doonmara, never mind seeing Rachel in the toilets at a service station. She needed to cop on. Alex would think she was crazy. What's more, Laura hadn't even seen the child's face.

"Damn," Alex said.

He was shifting in his seat, and searching his pockets.

Puzzled, Laura said, "What is it?"

"I left my mobile behind. I must have left it on the counter. I'll run in and see if they have it. I hope it hasn't been nicked."

He quickly made his way back to the service station. It was nearing tea time and the place was heaving with families, so busy in fact, that at first, he didn't see Caroline Cleary standing in line. He went straight to the till and enquired about his phone.

"We have it," the assistant said, and smiled.

"I'm in luck," Alex said gratefully.

She handed over his phone. He turned to go and that was when he became aware of her. "Caroline." Momentarily, he was jolted by her sudden appearance. "Of all places to bump into you."

"Alex," she greeted him, looking equally surprised. She had a bar of chocolate and a bottle of water in her hand.

"How are you?"

"I'm good. God Alex, this is so random."

He couldn't have agreed more. She looked tired and there were circles under her eyes. He remembered that she was prone to dark circles under her eyes.

"I'm cursed with them. They instantly appear when I'm tired," she had told him on more than one occasion.

The voluptuous curves had disappeared. Caroline appeared to have lost weight, too much in his opinion. She wore her hair a lot shorter these days too. He had loved her long hair. Quickly, he brushed the thought away.

"And you? How are you? she asked.

"I'm fine." He hesitated before saying a moment later, "Everything worked out. With my wife I mean."

"I'm glad for you, Alex. Really, I am."

"It's good of you to say that."

The conversation was strained. The easy informality that they had once enjoyed had gone.

"I'd better go," he said.

Caroline looked considerably relieved.

"My wife is waiting for me in the car. It was nice to see you, Caroline,"

"You too," she lied.

"Take care," he said.

She smiled a goodbye. And then he was off, off to his other life.

Caroline paid for the bar of chocolate and her drink. Then she walked over to a table in the fast food section.

"That was him, wasn't it?" said her friend Ciara, who witnessed the exchange. "He does look like George Clooney. She's the head cut off him." Ciara nodded in the direction of the small child who was sitting at the plastic table, happily eating chips. It was no exaggeration. The tiny tot resembled her half-sister, Rachel, as well. "That was close, Caroline."

"You don't have to tell me. I'm still shaking."

"What did he say?"

"He asked how I was. He told me everything had worked out between him and his wife."

"That was thoughtful. I wonder how he'd have reacted, if you said you'd like to introduce him to his daughter?"

"Forever the cynic," Caroline said, and gave a weak smile. She stole one of the little girl's chips. She dipped it in ketchup before popping it in her mouth.

"Can you imagine if you'd told him?" Ciara continued.

"For a brief second, I was tempted. It was the shock of seeing him out of the blue. But then he said that his marriage had worked out and that his wife was waiting outside in the car! Can you believe that?"

"Like I said, it was a close call. I wonder what his wife would make of it."

"They're better off not knowing. I've made my decision and I'm sticking to it."

Ciara didn't attempt to dissuade her. Ciara had tried once before. She had been met with a firm rebuttal. She tried a different tack.

"Did it ever occur to you that he might be pleased?" she said. "Clearly, he and his wife couldn't have any more children."

Caroline was rendered speechless.

"What an absurd thing to say!" she said finally. "Why would you think he'd be pleased? Can you imagine what this would do to his wife?" She looked indignant.

Ciara simply shrugged her shoulders. She drained her coffee and pushed the paper cup to one side.

"Auntie Ciara is crazy, sweetie," Caroline told the child. "She's completely bonkers."

Little Una giggled.

"Can I steal another chip, pet?"

The child nodded her head. Ketchup was splayed across her chin. Caroline took a chip, then another.

"That little girl will want to know one day, Caroline. Mark my words."

"Apart from you and me, no one knows, Ciara. That's the way I'd like to keep it. If Alex had said that he and his wife had split up, I might reconsider my decision. They haven't. I'm not going to break up their relationship. It was fragile to begin with." Caroline picked up a paper serviette and wiped her hands. Then, she had a stab at wiping the ketchup off Una's chin, before reaching for her handbag in search of baby wipes. "Anyway," she continued, "I'm not sure that I want to share Una. It's incredible that she's with me at all. We've been through so much."

"I can't argue with that," Ciara agreed, and her mind flashed back to the months of chemotherapy. "You're a little miracle, sweetheart," she said and gently caressed her goddaughter's face. Una beamed back at her.

"But she's my little miracle," her mother pointed out. "Alex and his wife have moved on with their lives and so have I with Una."

"Do you know something? You're right."

"You're telling me I made the right decision?"

"When you put it like that, I can see that no good would come from him knowing.

Besides, something else occurred to me. If this little girl resembles their daughter, she would be a constant reminder of their loss. She's not that little girl who died. She's not a replacement child. She's your daughter, Una. It would disrupt both of your lives and you've been through enough."

"Auntie Ciara has come to her senses," Caroline told her daughter. "Miracles will never cease."

Una rewarded her mum with a smile. The little girl was full of sunny smiles this afternoon. Ciara smiled too.

"Can I ask you one more thing?" said Ciara. "Then I'm done. I'm through bringing up Alex Hamilton."

"That makes two of us! Go on," Caroline said.

"Did you feel anything when you saw him? I'm curious because I know you were in love with him."

Caroline considered the question.

"Regret, certainly," she said. "But love? No. I can't say that I felt that. Not anymore. The cancer and my pregnancy changed everything. I had to go through it all without him. There was only me, my unborn baby, you and my family. Somewhere on that journey, something changed. All of my energies shifted to beating the cancer and to having my baby.

As soon as she came into this world, any feelings I had for him channelled into Una."

"There's only one thing to say then."

"What?"

"I would have."

"You would have what?" Caroline asked, confused.

"You said to me once, that if I saw Alex Hamilton in the flesh, I'd be there myself. I have and you were right."

Caroline laughed. She couldn't help but notice how happy Alex was, looking as suave and handsome as ever. Immediately, she had been conscious of her own appearance.

"I admit he did look good. I look like something the cat's dragged in! I'm surprised he even recognised me."

"You look fine, hon."

Caroline threw her friend a quizzical glance.

"Really! I was up twice during the night with this little angel. She was throwing up. Now look at her."

"They do bounce back, don't they? You're a single mum, Caroline, with a small toddler.

You haven't the time or the energy to glam up."

"I'm afraid those days are over," Caroline said. She was wearing an old pair of faded denim jeans that were hanging off her frame. The nude coloured tee-shirt that she wore did nothing for her skin tone. She was tired from a lack of sleep and it showed. "I look like crap," she said, fingering her limp hair in disgust. "I don't have a scrap of make up on and I could badly do with some war paint today."

This time, Ciara didn't disagree.

"I wouldn't have it any other way," Caroline added. "I have Una, and she's my priority now."

"Tell you what. Why don't we have a girl's night out soon? We'll don the glad rags and hit the town."

"You're on. That's a date. Mummy is taking a night off, sweetie," she told Una. "Wait till you see her! You won't recognize mummy at all." She tickled Una and the little girl giggled again. The tiny, tinkling of laughter warmed her mother's heart.

Caroline took a sip of water from the bottle. Then she broke a square of her chocolate bar before offering some to Ciara.

"Thanks," said Ciara, taking a square. "Chocolate is always good in a crisis!"

"A necessity," Caroline said.

"Better than sex."

"How would I know? That's way past my radar these days."

They both laughed. It was something the two friends did a lot of when they were together.

By this time, Laura and Alex were well into their journey home. Alex shut his eyes and attempted a cat nap. Sleep evaded him. He couldn't believe he had run into Caroline. He was fortunate Laura hadn't been there. How would he have handled that? Ought he to tell Laura? Alex didn't want to upset his wife. He didn't want to be hiding stuff from her either, not something like this. His past had come back to haunt him today.

He must have groaned aloud because Laura said, "Alex, what is it?" Are you okay?"

"I'm fine, sweetheart," he said as he opened his eyes. He looked at Laura affectionately. How he loved her. He could kick himself for his past misdemeanours. She had forgiven him but he hadn't forgiven himself.

"You were making strange noises, Al!" she joked. "You had me worried for a minute."

"Sorry, love," he mumbled and shut his eyes once more.

His thoughts shifted to the dilemma he faced. What if he told Laura? He might feel better, and it might alleviate his own guilt, but what good would it do Laura? It would stir up past hurts. Why would he do that to her? Who would pay the price for his honesty?

Their relationship had never been in better shape. These days, there was an openness and honesty to their marriage. They were friends and lovers. All told, they were a close couple. The sexual aspect of their marriage gave him a great deal of satisfaction. The sex may not have been as frantic as those first months when they had resumed intimacy, but it was good, pretty darn good in his opinion. He hoped that Laura felt the same. He thought that she did.

He missed Rachel. He would miss her till the day he died. When Rachel had been alive, he and Laura had actively tried for another baby.

"A little brother for Rachel," he had said to Laura on one of those occasions.

"Or a little sister," she'd said. "Just think, Al. More pink!"

"That's exactly what this house needs."

To the joy of both parents, Laura became pregnant again. She had lost the child after suffering an ectopic pregnancy. Soon afterwards, Laura learned that she would not be able to have another baby. They had got over that hurdle because they had Rachel.

"Would you like another baby?" he had asked her about a year ago. "Would you want a child now after Rachel?"

"If we had another baby, I'd feel as if I was replacing Rachel. We can't replace Rachel. No baby could ever replace her. This might sound strange but I'm not sure that Rachel would want me to love another child. And if I had another baby, I'd be terrified something would happen to that child. I know that I wouldn't be able to go through something like that. Not again."

"I can understand that."

"If Rachel had a sibling when she was alive, it would have been a little easier. I would have kept on going for the sake of that child. There was only Rachel. I remember standing at her graveside as her coffin was being lowered and thinking, my whole life is in that little white coffin. I can barely remember any detail of the funeral," she said, "but I can remember that."

He had placed his hand around her shoulder.

"And you? What about you?" she asked, a little apprehensively.

"When Rachel was alive, I would have loved a sister or brother for her. Rachel was a gift. A little sibling for Rachel would have been another great blessing. Now that she's gone, I don't think that I would like to have another child. I'm happy with the way we are now. I can honestly say that it's enough. I've learned to live with Rachel's death."

Alex remembered some old man coming up to him at the funeral and telling him that time would never heal you, but that it would teach you how to cope. He often thought about that. Although Alex could remember the man's face, he didn't know his identity. He'd met hundreds of people the day of Rachel's funeral and this person was the one Alex remembered, some casual stranger.

"I've learned to cope too," Laura said. "I don't want to go back to where I was. If I did, I'd go down again, Alex. I'd go down that black hole and I'd never come back. That scares me because the hurt and pain were so intense. It seemed like a physical weight on me.

"Rachel will always remain in my heart, but I think I've let her go. I've let go of what's been holding me back."

His thoughts shifted back to the present. If he hadn't left his mobile phone on the counter, he wouldn't have run into Caroline. What bad luck.

What he didn't know was this. If he had timed his stop at the station a few moments earlier, or even a little later, he might have met Una, his daughter.

One thing was certain. If Alex had seen the child, he would have known that he was her father, such was the likeness between father and daughter, and between Rachel and her half-sister. Maybe, he would have welcomed 'pink' back into his world. Now, he would never have that chance. He would never know Una.

By the end of the car journey home, Alex reached a decision. He wasn't going to tell Laura about his encounter with Caroline.

Later that night, as Caroline lay in her bed, unable to sleep, she thought about the past. Una had been a miracle. Her miracle. A miracle that her she was loathe to share. It was just her and Una. Caroline didn't want that to change.

Caroline had conflicting thoughts. She could get sick again. If she died, who would provide for Una? What would happen to the child? Thoughts like this crept up at night.

She was cancer free. At first, she had check-ups every three months. Soon, it became every six months. All of her check-ups were clear. She needed to forget about the cancer. She wasn't going to get sick again. That wasn't going to happen.

When all was said and done, what it really boiled down to was this. Caroline didn't want to share Una, certainly not with Una's father or his wife. Her daughter would not be a replacement for their dead child. Una was not going to be a surrogate for Rachel no matter how sorry Caroline felt for Alex.

It was a tragedy that Rachel had died, a dreadful tragedy. He had shared his pain with her.

"No other grief comes near it," Alex had told Caroline. "The first few weeks went by in a haze of love and support from family and friends, and then the grim reality of life after Rachel set in. The pain never goes away completely, nor does time heal. The grief morphs into something else and you become a different person.

"I used to worry about things. I'd remember slights from the past. None of these things really matter anymore. I'm more forgiving."

"Why didn't you tell me before today?" she had asked.

"I think I became unable to keep repeating my sad story," he'd said. "There were times when I was unable to hold back the tears and hide how devastated I was. I didn't want your pity, and I didn't want to immerse myself in self-pity and grief."

What a nightmare he had gone through. Poor Alex. And in the dead of the night, Caroline remembered what Ciara had said earlier.

"Did it ever occur to you that he might be pleased?" her friend had asked. "Clearly, he and his wife couldn't have any more children."

Una was a link to their dead daughter. Ciara hadn't said so but it was what Caroline was thinking now.

Very quickly, she dismissed the thought. She told herself that Laura Hamilton would be devastated at the news of Una's existence. Alex Hamilton had said that he and his wife had worked things out. They were happy. Caroline and Una were happy too. It was best for everyone if Una's identity remained hidden.

CHAPTER TWENTY-SIX

"Mum, I've been thinking…..," Anna paused, leaving the sentence unfinished.

Her daughter shifted her weight from one foot to the other. She was wearing a pair of denim shorts. They were very short her mother noted. She must have cut them up herself. Anna had rimmed her lower eye lids with a black pencil. She thought it made her eyes look bigger but it had the opposite effect. Her daughter had been experimenting a lot recently with eye makeup. Felicia didn't comment on the shorts or the makeup. Anna was at a sensitive age.

Her children were standing side by side in the lounge. Anna seemed uneasy. Jack was anxious too.

Felicia had been watching the six o'clock news. She liked to catch the headlines at that time.

"Yes, darling," Felicia said. "What is it?"

"We've decided," Anna said, looking to her brother for support, "that it's not the best idea to stay in Doonmara.

Felicia was more than a little surprised. The children seldom backtracked, especially Anna, once they had made up their minds to do something.

"We'd still like to go to Doonmara next week," said Anna.

"But not to stay there, Mum," Jack chimed in.

Felicia switched down the volume on the TV.

"Thank God," she said and gave an audible sigh of relief. "I was dreading it."

It was Jack and Anna's turn to be surprised.

"We thought you'd be cross, Mum," Jack ventured.

"Why would you think that?" their mother asked.

"We pushed you into going. You booked the hotel and everything," Anna said.

"I'm sure that won't be a problem. We'll go as planned but we won't stay over. The three of us can take a walk down to Beat Two. We can have lunch in the bar beforehand. How does that sound?"

"I'd like that," said Jack.

"Me too," confirmed Anna.

"Mum, do you think the same staff will be there?" Jack asked. "I'd like to see John and Pawel."

"The receptionist mentioned that Pawel had left."

Her son looked disappointed.

"I'm pretty sure the rest of the staff are working in the hotel," Felicia said. "We can time it so that we have lunch at one. That's when the gillies and the fishermen come in."

A thought occurred to his mother.

"Would you like a fishing lesson, Jack? I could book one with John if you like."

"Not this time, Mum."

"It's early days." Felicia said, understanding that it would bring back too many difficult memories for Jack. "What made you two change your minds?" she asked.

Anna took the lead.

"I've been feeling kind of weird for the last few days," her daughter said. "The closer we were getting to dad's anniversary, the more I realized how hard it would be to stay in the hotel. I asked Jack did he still want to go."

"I didn't want to stay there either," Jack said. "I know what you mean, Mum, when you said it was too soon."

He thought back to his conversation with Laura Hamilton the morning after his father had died. She had been right when she said that grief was sometimes triggered by reminders such as anniversaries or places. He remembered what she had advised: rather than forget, he should attempt to remember. He should remember what he had learned from his father and remember what they had enjoyed doing together. And he should cry, if he felt like it.

"Come here you two and give me a hug," his mum said now.

Jack gave his mother a half-hearted hug.

"You've got too old to hug your mother," Felicia said. "You'll never make a diplomat. It's all hugs and kisses, Jack."

Her son looked suitably embarrassed. He mumbled something unintelligible and quickly disappeared. Anna and Felicia laughed. Anna gave her mother a warm embrace and plonked herself down on the couch. Her shorts rode even higher up her thighs.

"Mum, it's a long drive up and down to Connemara on the one day," she said.

"We could stay in Galway for the night and break up the journey," her mother suggested.

"Cool. Galway's brilliant. I'd love to go to University there. Fiona's sister is in college in Galway. Fiona is thinking of going there next year."

After her dad's death, Anna's friends had been a main source of emotional support for Anna. Little did Felicia know that Fiona borrowed her sister's ID to buy booze for herself and Anna. Fiona also bought the pills, innocuous looking relaxers in trays of ten or twenty. Anna was living a whole other life that her mother knew nothing about.

It was at her friend's house that Anna smoked weed, drank vodka, and popped relaxers. Fiona's parents were never at home. Anna would stay over and Felicia was none the wiser as to what she got up to.

Her father's death had come like a swift wind. Loss had ripped something out of her and Anna was filling the void left behind with alcohol and drugs. The drugs didn't work. They didn't end the pain.

Recently, Fiona had unprotected sex with a boy at the house, a much older boy, and a friend of her sister. She was off her head at the time. Anna went with her to the family planning clinic for the morning after pill. They had both bunked off school that day.

Then Fiona discovered she had picked up an STD. She had found a lump of sorts and panicked, thinking she had cancer, fearing the worst. She confided in her mother who made an appointment with the family doctor. He diagnosed genital warts. That was nearly as bad as far as Fiona was concerned. She thought her life was over. Fiona's mother went ballistic.

Fiona had been mortified when she had to attend the STD clinic in the general hospital. The treatment was going to take forever. Fiona had been afraid to confront the boy in case he might post something about her on Facebook. She'd be called a skank, or worse.

It was harder for boys to talk about their feelings. Felicia knew that. Maybe that was why her son had thrown himself into his rugby with a passion. It was a coping mechanism and kept him busy, kept him close to his father.

"We can look around the campus on Monday, if you like," Felicia said to Anna now.

"Really? Great."

"We can also pay a visit to the graveyard in Roundstone. It's only a few kilometres from Doonmara."

"I'd like that."

"So would your father," Felicia said, remembering how Harvey had planned to visit the cemetery that fateful weekend.

"Jack will be keen too, seeing how it was he who found Fred and Nancy Ann's names in the fishing log."

"Then, we'll do that. I'll phone the hotel and let them know that we are cancelling our booking."

"We'll have a busy weekend,"

"We certainly will," her mother agreed.

That was precisely what Felicia intended. Revisiting Doonmara was going to be difficult, even if they were not staying in the hotel. Felicia was under no illusions about that. The more activities Felicia planned, the less likely it was that she would fall apart.

The doorbell rang.

"It's Richard", said Anna, leaping up from the couch. "He's taking me for a driving lesson."

Her daughter answered the front door. Two months previously, when Anna had turned seventeen, she had applied for and passed the theory test for her provisional license. Richard had kindly offered to take her out for a couple of driving lessons.

"Hi there," Richard said to Felicia.

"Richard, Hello! Come in"

Richard sat himself down.

"Can I get you a cup of tea or something to drink?" Felicia said.

Anna threw her eyes up to heaven. She remained standing.

"I won't dawdle too long, Felicia. I'd better take this young lady out for her lesson or I'll be in trouble."

Felicia smiled.

"Anna's impatient to get on the road," she said, sensing Anna's restlessness. "Thanks for taking her out, Richard. It's good of you."

"It's my pleasure."

"I'll be back in a minute," Anna told Richard. "I need to get my phone."

"Why she needs her phone for a driving lesson is beyond me," Felicia said once she had left the room.

"Different generation, Felicia. Now tell me. How's your new career going?"

"Its early days but I'm enjoying it. The extra bit of cash is nice."

Felicia had begun some interpretive work for one of the embassies. An old colleague of Harvey's had recommended her for the job. Fluent in Portuguese and German, Felicia had been an interpreter before she married. She and Harvey had first met through work. They had been introduced at a function in the Portuguese embassy. She had liked him on sight and the romance had blossomed from there.

When Harvey had received his first overseas embassy posting, Felicia had no option but to give up her job. Then, the children had come along.

"Do you miss embassy life?" Richard said.

"A little."

"I'm imagining a constant round of cocktail parties and dinners out."

"We were always attending one function or another. Harvey loved that side of things. He was such a social animal. He enjoyed meeting new people."

"Harvey was a genial man," said Richard reminiscing. "He was great fun to be around. Everyone loved Harvey."

"I miss that side of him. He was great company. I live like a hermit these days by comparison. It's not as if I come from Dublin. Apart from you, Alice and the girls, I don't have a core network here. Besides, we Brits are a lot more reserved than you lot."

"Just a touch! Do you regret having moved back here?"

"No. It was the best option for the kids. I didn't want to pull them out of their schools. That would have only meant more disruption in their lives. I miss my family of course. But my parents have been very supportive."

Maybe you'll meet some new people through work."

"Actually, I have been invited to attend a drinks do at the embassy next week. It will be a little awkward going on my own."

"You'll be fine, Felicia."

She told him about the up and coming trip to Connemara.

"It's extraordinary that none of you knew Nancy Ann's story," she said.

"The Russell family were a strange bunch," he said.

"Your mother must have known."

"She never mentioned Nancy Ann. I was never aware of her existence," he lied. Richard didn't like deceiving Felicia, but decided he had no option.

Anna came in to the room. She was a bit jittery today. She had been drinking at Fiona's house the night before.

"All set?" Richard said keen to leave before any more questions were asked.

"Yep."

"Let's hit the road then."

"Good luck!" Felicia said.

"To whom?" Richard asked.

Felicia laughed and said, "Off with the pair of you."

Felicia walked them to the door and watched as the pair drove away. If Anna's father was alive, he would be doing what Richard was doing. Harvey would be taking his daughter for driving lessons. That's what she was thinking.

Later that evening, Felicia contacted Doonmara Castle to cancel the reservation. Maura wasn't on duty, but the receptionist who handled the call was very pleasant.

"We'll have no trouble filling the rooms," she informed Felicia. "As a matter of fact, we have a waiting list."

"That's good to hear. I don't feel too bad now."

"I've cancelled your reservation, Mrs Russell. And I've booked a table for three in the bar. To confirm, that's next Saturday, August the eighth, for one o'clock."

As soon as Felicia had hung up, the receptionist put a call through to Jean-Pierre's mobile. She heard the international ring tone.

"Hello," the Frenchman answered. He had seen the international code for Ireland flash on his mobile screen.

"Good evening," the receptionist said. "Monsieur Bert, I'm calling from Doonmara Castle in relation to your reservation with us next weekend. We've had a cancellation, and we have a room available should you still wish to extend your stay on Saturday night."

"*Parfait.* He corrected himself. "Perfect. I would like to do that. Will we have to switch rooms?"

He had booked one of the luxury river suites.

"You're in luck, Monsieur Bert. A river suite was cancelled," she said.

Mrs Russell had booked a superior room, but Jane had seen to it that Felicia had been given an upgrade to one of the river suites.

"We will send you an email confirming your new reservation," the receptionist continued. "We look forward to having you and Madame Bert stay."

"Thank you," he said. "We had our wedding reception in the hotel. We're looking forward to our visit."

He wondered which receptionist was on duty. It wasn't Maura. He would have recognized Maura's voice straight away. Besides, Maura would have addressed him by his first name. All of the old staff called him Jean-Pierre and it annoyed him. In his opinion, it was too familiar. A person of his standing deserved more deference.

Jean-Pierre had lied to the receptionist. He had no desire whatsoever to return to Doonmara. He remained concerned that Pawel would spill the beans. Pawel could wreak havoc on his marriage. To date, Jean Pierre had managed to stall any plans to return to the hotel. This time, Marie had got her way.

"Please, Jean-Pierre," she had pleaded. "I'd like to go back. Why don't we?"

How could he refuse? What could he say? In the end, he gave way.

"I remember you, Monsieur Bert," said the receptionist, interrupting his thought flow. "I remember the wedding. It was the biggest wedding we've held in Doonmara."

"Can I ask you one more thing before I go?" he said.

"What can I help you with, sir?"

"Are all of the same staff with you?"

"Most of them are, yes."

He cursed silently.

"Of course," she added, handing a much-welcomed life line to Jean-Pierre, "Quite a number of the restaurant staff come and go every summer."

Jean-Pierre took it.

"Is Pawel still in the restaurant?" he asked.

"I'm afraid Pawel is no longer with us, Monsieur Bert. He left some time ago."

"He was engaged to the Slovakian chambermaid."

"That's right. Lucy is with us but Pawel has gone home to Poland."

"Quel dommage!" he said.

The receptionist didn't speak French but she caught his drift.

"Pawel is missed by us all," she said. "Is there anything else I can help you with, Monsieur Bert?" she asked.

"No. Thank you for the call and I look forward to our visit."

With that, Jean-Pierre bid the receptionist adieu. The news that Pawel had left Doonmara was music to his ears. With relief, he put down his mobile.

Marie would be pleased about the change in reservation, as their return flight was leaving on the Sunday. She was looking forward to their short break in Connemara and now, he was too. Lucy might be there but she wouldn't present a problem. She had a good heart. And beautiful breasts. He closed his eyes for a moment picturing Lucy naked.

He didn't regret his encounter with the pretty chambermaid on his stag weekend. She had looked fetching in that chambermaid outfit. It had appealed to his fantasies. He did regret being caught.

Jean-Pierre hadn't changed. Only two years into his marriage, he was already seeing someone else on the side. Marie was clueless. She would be heartbroken were she to find out. But Jean-Pierre was a master at deception. It was easily his best quality.

That same night, Caroline Cleary tossed and turned in her bed, unable to sleep, again. Caroline was anxious. She had every reason to be.

She had collapsed with an acute pain in her right side three days previously. Her doctor immediately sent her to the oncology department in the hospital. They had ruled out a gall bladder problem or a possible appendicitis. Although she had been released several hours later, an appointment had been made for Caroline to undergo an endoscopy tomorrow morning.

Once again, Ciara had stepped in to help. Ciara was collecting Caroline and taking her to the hospital. Una was accompanying them. Ciara was going to look after her goddaughter while Caroline underwent the endoscopy.

Caroline had told herself to forget about the cancer. After all, the prognosis had been optimistic. She had told herself that she was not living in fear of a recurrence. She wanted to believe it.

The reality was different.

I don't think you ever quite forget you've had cancer," she had admitted to Ciara recently.

In the early hours of the morning, her imminent death seemed a distinct possibility and fear played on Caroline's mind. The cancer was back. She was sure of it.

Caroline had appointed Ciara as Una's legal guardian in the event of Caroline's premature death. She couldn't levy such a heavy weight on her friend. It wasn't fair to Ciara. Her friend was entitled to have a life of her own. And what would happen if Ciara met someone and wanted her own family?

It was a huge responsibility and a financial burden too. Was it fair to expect Ciara to provide for Una? Was Ciara in a position to do so? She was sharing a house with two other girls. It wasn't as if Caroline had any assets to leave Una. As it was, Caroline was struggling to make ends meet.

As dawn broke, Caroline considered contacting Alex Hamilton. She would have to put Una's welfare first. If Caroline died, Una would have no mother or father. What would that do to the child? Surely Alex Hamilton and his wife were better than having no parents at all. Ciara would back her. Ciara had wanted her to tell Alex Hamilton.

By the time Ciara had arrived to collect her and Una, Caroline had make up her mind. She was going to tell Alex Hamilton that he had a daughter.

CHAPTER TWENTY-SEVEN

August 2013

Alex and Laura arrived early Friday afternoon. The cattle grid rattled as the car drove through the entrance.

Laura stifled a yawn. She had slept fitfully. In the deep of the night, she had awoken from a dream. She was standing on the shoreline. In the distance, she could see a woman and a small child running. Something about the child looked familiar. At first, she thought it was Rachel.

It wasn't because Laura heard Rachel calling out to her. Turning to face her daughter, Laura's heart was filled with joy at the sight of Rachel walking towards her.

"Find her, Mummy. You have to find her," Rachel implored. With reluctance, Laura looked back but the two figures had disappeared from view. When she turned round, Rachel was no longer there. Laura woke up. It was hours before she fell asleep again. Beside her, with his back turned, Alex was lightly snoring. She kept replaying Rachel's voice in her head. If she kept replaying the sound, she might remember Rachel's voice.

Now, Laura took in her surroundings. The hydrangeas were in full bloom. The front garden had erupted into a sea of mauve, purple, blue, and pink. Marshmallow clouds floated over the mountains. Today, the mountains had been painted a slate grey.

Alex parked the car.

"The hydrangeas are spectacular," he said as they approached the garden. They stopped for a moment to admire the flowers.

"Especially the blue," Laura said.

Her husband smiled. He turned to her and said, "The last two years have been kind of magical."

"They've been our best years. After Rachel, that is." She hesitated and said, "You gave me reason to go on. I love you, and more now than I ever did."

His heart lifted.

"Thank you for that," he said.

"I had completely lost myself, Alex. You could have left me and no one would have blamed you."

"I don't know about that, Laura. I wasn't exactly a saint."

"I don't mean to make you out to be. But I feel very close to you."

"And I to you," he said.

Reaching for her hand, they walked into the hotel together. Seán spotted them immediately in the foyer. He made a bee line for Alex. Seán had news he wanted to share. Laura went straight to reception.

"Changes at the Castle, Mr Hamilton," the porter announced.

"Oh. That sounds ominous, Seán," Alex said as he handed the porter his car keys.

"On the contrary, Mr Hamilton. Things are looking up. His lordship has left."

Alex knew immediately to whom Seán was referring.

"How did you manage that?" he said. "I never thought you'd be capable of orchestrating Jame's departure.

The porter laughed heartily.

"He's 'emigrated' back to Kerry, so he has. He told the staff that he was moving on to bigger and better things."

It was Alex's turn to laugh.

"I gather you're not too dismayed."

"What do you think?" Sean said, and winked.

"I assume Jane is delighted."

"She's not alone but she'd be at the top of the list all right. She's deputising till the new man comes on board."

"If you ask me, that woman has been deputising for years. When will you have your replacement?"

"The new recruit will be arriving at the start of September. It's a Dublin man by the name of Michael Wood. He was general manager of The Portland Hotel in Cork."

"That's a reputable hotel."

"Indeed it is. Mr Wood is a family man, with a wife and two small children."

"You'd have made a fine investigative journalist, Seán. You always have the latest scoop."

"I'll take that as a compliment, so I will, Mr Hamilton. Now then, I had better get your luggage up to the room or there will be uproar. We're busy. We've a full house this weekend."

"Before you go, Seán, is there any word on Conor's grandfather?"

Maura had contacted Alex earlier in the day.

"Conor's grandfather has taken a bad turn," the receptionist had informed Alex. "I'm afraid Conor won't be available this afternoon.

"It's not looking good," the porter said now. "He's nearing the end. He's had a good innings though."

Seán headed out to the car and Alex joined his wife at the reception desk.

"I hear you'll have a new man at the helm," he said to Maura.

"That's right, Mr Hamilton."

They chatted amongst themselves for a moment.

"Excuse me, may I have the key for Room 27," someone interrupted in a heavy French accent.

"Certainly, Jean-Pierre," Maura said. "Here you are."

Alex and Laura greeted him politely.

"Hello," Jean-Pierre said. He remembered Alex Hamilton straight away. His was not a face you could forget easily. Jean-Pierre hadn't noticed the wife till that afternoon.

"I believe you got married here since we last met," Alex said.

"Yes, I did. This is the first time that my wife and I have been back since our wedding."

Marie was standing by the fire, waiting for her husband to get the room key. He called her over and introductions were made all round.

"I hope you have a wonderful few days," Laura said. "The hotel must hold special memories for you both."

"It does," Marie agreed.

She was very polished, thought Laura, admiring the camel leather handbag that Marie carried.

Everything about Jean-Pierre's wife was flawless: the hair, her makeup, her jewellery and the clothes she wore.

Marie sported immaculate white jeans and a fitted white shirt, both pressed to perfection. Her shirt was tucked underneath the cornflower blue Hermés belt that looped her jeans. A lightweight cashmere jumper in matching blue was casually draped over her shoulders.

The look was effortless and chic, and very Parisian. Several rows of delicate gold chains hung around the French woman's neck. One chain had an oval gold disk engraved with the initial M set in pavé diamonds.

The hall door opened. Seán came in laden down with baggage. The porter observed the two couples chatting as he passed through reception. He glanced at the French man. Seán didn't think that marriage and a wife had changed Jean-Pierre. Not one iota. He was still a pup.

The Hamiltons and the Berts made their way to their respective quarters. As it happened, they found themselves only a few rooms apart. The Hamiltons had been given their usual room and Jean-Pierre was back in the suite he had been allocated for his stag weekend.

As they made their way, Lucy Sukova carried out the final touches to Room 27.

Lucy left the room and returned momentarily, armed with two bottles of water, and a box of tissues, taken from a service trolley parked outside the door.

She placed the tissue box on the dressing table in the walk-in dressing room. An assortment of clothes hung in the wardrobe. She flicked through the hangers admiringly.

Lucy recognized some of the labels from the magazines she read, generally magazines that the guests left behind. Lucy was allowed to keep those.

"A perk of the job," she had once told Pawel.

She spotted a pair of delicate strappy gold sandals. Lucy picked one up, noting she and Marie were the same shoe size. The heel was cigarette thin, at least five inches, and the sole was stamped with a designer label. Lucy was sorely tempted to try it on and have her Cinderella moment. However, Lucy did not envy Jean-Pierre's wife, not when she had Jean-Pierre for a husband. Jean-Pierre was no Prince Charming.

Lucy's wages were minimal and she scraped by. The chambermaid was saving up for a car. It would be a while yet before she reached her target.

She checked to see that everything was pristine in the bedroom. She plumped up the pillows on the bed, the same bed that she and Jean-Pierre had made love in two years previously, almost to the day, and she straightened the eiderdown. The Frenchman was now sharing this bed with his wife and Lucy felt uncomfortable at the thought.

Lucy wheeled her trolley down the corridor and spotted the foursome. She pulled her trolley to the side and stopped to allow the guests walk by.

Jean-Pierre smirked when he saw the chambermaid. Lucy looked very cute in that uniform. Could he still seduce her? He'd be game. She wouldn't be able to resist him, he decided.

Laura and Alex Hamilton paused for a moment to chat. Madame and Monsieur Bert walked on.

"How are you Lucy?" Laura asked. "How's the romance going?"

"It's all good. He's a keeper, Mrs Hamilton."

"I'm glad, Lucy. It's nice to see you so happy."

"He's a lucky man," Alex said.

Lucy smiled before heading off with her trolley. Almost 1.30, it was time for her break. After lunch, she would be helping Jane to hang pictures. Some old black and white photographs, dating back to the Maharaja's time, had been discovered by Jane, now the acting manager.

Jane had shown James the pictures.

"I found these in that desk we brought down from the attic," Jane had informed him. "We could have them enlarged and framed."

"Whatever you think, Jane," he had said, uninterested. "You can make your first executive decision."

She had bit her lip and refrained from making any comment. He'd be gone in a week. She had the photographs enlarged and framed in Clifden. They had been delivered to the castle earlier that morning.

"I'd like to hang the photographs along the stairwell near the river suites." Jane had said to the housekeeper. "I never liked the floral prints there. These are more in keeping with Doonmara and its history."

"That's for sure, Jane. Besides, that back entrance is looking a bit tired. It could do with a revamp."

"That's what I thought," Jane said.

"I won't be on duty but Lucy can give you a hand," the housekeeper said. "Leave it with me."

Lucy and Jane stood in the stairwell. Jane had commandeered extra help. One of the young lads who worked in the restaurant was assisting her. Following Jane's instructions, the waiter removed the four floral prints that were hanging. Next, he was asked to hammer four additional picture hooks along the wall.

"You need to place each hook at an equal distance between the old ones," Jane instructed. "You'll need to align them carefully so take your time."

He was precise.

"That's great. Job done," she said. "Now, can you take these pictures straight to the storage room and stack them there."

Floral prints in hand, off the young lad went.

Lucy dusted the frames. She looked with interest at the old black and white photographs lined up in front of her.

"What do you think?" Jane asked. "Do you like them?"

"They are very old," Lucy said.

"They date back to the 1920s, to the time the Maharaja lived in Doonmara. See this one here," Jane said, pointing to one of the frames.

Lucy looked at the old photograph.

"That's one of the old station house. That's the red house, next door to the hotel. The Maharaja used to descend from the train there."

"I recognize the house. The old railway track is behind the river walk."

"That's right," Jane said, and moved on the next frame. "This one is of the Maharaja's two nieces. They went to boarding school near here."

Lucy studied the picture. Two young Indian women, traditionally dressed in long robes, with their heads covered, smiled shyly at the photographer.

"They are very young," Lucy said. "They were a long way from home." Lucy could relate to that. She had left the Slovakia when she was nineteen.

"They can't have been more than fifteen or sixteen when this photograph was taken," Jane told her. "The Maharaja was particularly fond of them. He had no children of his own."

Another photograph featured a hunt gathered outside Doonmara Castle. Drinks were being served to the huntsmen. Jane had to explain to Lucy what a hunt was.

"I've never seen a photograph of a hunt before," Lucy remarked. "It's interesting to see what the place looked like in those times, and to see pictures of the people back then."

There were three photographs of various fishermen fishing at the beats, including one of the Maharaja with his gillie. The Maharaja was wearing tweeds.

"That's a strange outfit," Lucy said. "The pants look like a pair of jodhpurs that have been cut off at the knee."

"That's what the gentry wore in those days," Jane informed her. Lucy remained puzzled. She wasn't quite sure what or who the gentry were.

Jane studied the final two frames: one of the Maharaja with his staff, the other a photograph of a woman in her late twenties.

"That was taken at the luncheon party that the Maharaja gave his staff every year," she said. "He would serve the staff himself. Imagine that."

Lucy looked at the photograph. A few dozen people were seated at long, rectangular banquet tables that had been set up outside the hotel entrance.

"That doesn't happen anymore!" Lucy said.

Jane laughed. Turning her attention to the remaining picture she said, "She's beautiful."

The two women looked admiringly at the woman in the photograph. She was dressed in a long white dress. Her hair was pinned up in what looked like an elaborate style.

"Her dress is very fancy," Lucy said.

"Maybe she was attending a party at Doonmara," Jane said. "She looks happy. There's a glow about her."

"I know where that photograph was taken."

"Oh. Where?"

"In the front garden," Lucy said.

Jane took a closer look.

"Do you know what, Lucy? You're right. Even though it's in black and white, I recognize the hydrangeas. She's standing where the bench is now, and next to the blue hydrangea."

"Is she someone important?" the chambermaid asked.

"I have no idea," said Jane. "Mind you, some of the photographs are signed. As a matter of fact, they're signed in the Maharaja's own hand. Let's see if this one is signed at the back."

Jane turned the frame around.

"Oh dear, they're sealed at the back," she said, disappointed. "What a shame. We'll never know who she is."

Lucy and Jane hung the framed photographs. The mysterious white lady was placed on the wall, at the bottom of the stairwell, next to the exit door.

Sunday arrived. It was a windy day. Alex had two missed calls on his mobile. The number had been withheld. Briefly, he wondered who was looking for him.

The Russells will be here soon," he said to Laura. They were standing in reception and planned to lunch in Roundstone. "Will we wait to say hello? We could catch up with them later."

Over a pint the previous evening, John had informed Alex that Mrs Russell and her two children were arriving for lunch the next day.

"Let's stay put in case we miss them later on," she said.

"Coming back will be tough."

"I'd say they'll have mixed emotions. Today is Harvey Russell's anniversary."

He reflected on what she said.

"Is there any update on Conor's grandfather?" Laura asked.

"He's hanging in there."

Before long, Felicia, Anna and Jack arrived. Laura and Alex greeted the family warmly.

"Laura, this is a surprise," Felicia said. "I wasn't expecting to see you here. How lovely to bump into you like this."

"I'm delighted to meet you all again," Laura said, looking at the three of them. "I know that today is your husband's anniversary, Felicia. It must be a poignant day for you and the children."

"Yes, but we're glad we came. What a coincidence that you're here this weekend."

Laura didn't like to say that it was her birthday weekend and that she came to Doonmara every year to celebrate, not when Felicia's husband had died so tragically the day after Laura's birthday. It didn't sit right with Laura. Felicia was mourning and Laura was celebrating.

The women exchanged pleasantries while Alex engaged the children.

"You look marvellous," Felicia said. The change was extraordinary. Laura was animated. The faded flower had found its bloom. "I'd love to see the famous ring? Are you wearing it by any chance?"

"I'm afraid I don't have it with me," Laura said. "It's far too valuable to wear. We had to install a safe to keep it in. I've sent the ring to Sotheby's in London to be appraised. They're auctioning it in the autumn."

Alex and Laura had discussed her decision to put the ring up for auction. They spoke about what Laura might do with her windfall.

"I'd like to give a chunk of the money to a children's charity," she had said to Alex. "What do you think?"

"That's a great idea," said her husband. "It would be wonderful if a child somewhere benefits."

Felicia never saw the ring. If she had, she might have tried it on. She might have seen the inscription. Preoccupied, Felicia she didn't ask Laura any more questions regarding her find.

The women touched on the subject of the Russell family connection to Doonmara.

"It's a fascinating story," Laura said.

"And a very sad one," Felicia said. "We're visiting the family graves later this afternoon. Harvey's grandparents are buried in the old Protestant cemetery in Roundstone, as is his great aunt Nancy Ann."

"That will take you a step back in time," Laura said.

Eventually, Laura and Alex bid the Russell family farewell. As they did, Jane appeared and welcomed the family. The small group moved into the bar where John was waiting for their arrival. Before long, Seán dropped by to say hello.

After lunch, the family made their way to Beat Two. It was with some trepidation that Felicia and her children walked along the river path. Although a short walk, it was an emotional minefield. Felicia retraced Harvey's final steps on that fateful afternoon. By the time they reached Beat Two, Jack was shaking like a leaf and Felicia was in tears. Anna comforted her mother and brother but it was Anna who needed minding.

Seán and John watched as the family set off.

"Not easy," John said.

"No, not easy at all," agreed the porter.

Seán had enjoyed a pleasant conversation with Mrs Russell. He heard that Laura Hamilton was having her ring put up for auction in London. *That will make her a nice few bob*, he thought. He remembered the name that had been inscribed on the band - *Suri*.

"That's a very odd name," he had said to Laura on her last visit. "Did you ever find out where it originates from?"

"I did, as a matter of fact," she'd said. "It's Persian in origin. It means my red rose."

"Fancy that," said the porter.

En route, the Russell family passed Madame Bert. She was walking along the river path and appeared lost in thought. From his bedroom window, her husband watched her approach.

As he did, he heard a ping.

He picked up the mobile phone on the table. Absently, he clicked on the text message. Only then, did he realize that he had mistaken his wife's phone for his own. After reading the text, Jean-Pierre began to click on others.

The French man made an unpleasant discovery that afternoon. It appeared that Marie, his wife, was in the throes of a passionate affair with Olivier, his best friend. Jean-Pierre had been cheated on by the two people he trusted most. Olivier knew about Jean-Pierre's infidelities, past and present. And Marie? Jean-Pierre assumed that she knew too.

Olivier had a weakness where Marie was concerned. Jean-Pierre was aware of that. His old pal had taken Marie out a couple of times before Jean-Pierre had ever met his future wife. In fact, it was Olivier who introduced Marie to Jean-Pierre, his best friend – that same best friend who then stole his girlfriend.

"Why did you ask Marie out?" he had said to Jean-Pierre at the time. "We're seeing each other.

I like her. You know that." Olivier had sounded aggrieved.

"Don't be silly. You hardly know each other," Jean-Pierre had said dismissively.

He thought Olivier was cool about it. Apparently not. Jean-Pierre had got that wrong.

It seemed Olivier had got his own back now.

What was he going to do? That was the question that needed answering. There were several factors to be considered. First and foremost, there was Marie's father. That could be tricky. Henri Leclair was his boss now.

Then there was the money factor. Marie was an heiress in her own right from a family trust that had been set up, but Jean-Pierre had been persuaded to sign a prenuptial. He had signed away his right to everything. In his wife's case, everything was an awful lot.

"It's a formality," Marie's father had said. "I trust you'll both be very happy together.

She's my only daughter. Look after her for me, Jean-Pierre. Or you will have me to answer to!"

Henri Leclair was warning him, a warning that could be perceived as a threat. If he left his wife, Jean-Pierre would be jobless. Moreover, he would leave without a penny. And Marie's father would make sure that Jean-Pierre never worked again in the financial sector. Henri Leclair had the power and influence to do that should he so wish. Jean-Pierre didn't intend to incur the wrath of his father-in-law.

Fifteen minutes later, Marie was back in the suite. She came in through the back entrance, stopping to admire the photographs hanging along the stairwell. Intrigued by the elegant lady in the white dress, Marie stared at the photograph for a long time.

Marie remembered wearing a long white dress in this very place not so long ago. Did she look as radiant on her wedding day? Marie had been very happy that day. But life had not unfolded the way Marie had thought it would, and neither had this weekend.

She had been disappointed in her marriage. Early on, she realized that Jean-Pierre was unfaithful. Olivier had confirmed her suspicions and they had drifted into an affair. Initially, it had been about getting her own back on her husband. Olivier was particularly attentive. He was the polar opposite to her husband. Before long, she began to develop feelings for Olivier. That frightened her. She wasn't ready to call time on her marriage yet. She had decided to give it another shot.

Marie had suggested coming to Doonmara because she thought it might help mend her marriage.

She had ended the relationship with Olivier before she left and he had not taken it well.

Then, Olivier had phoned her yesterday with a new revelation. He informed Marie of what had occurred between that pretty Slovakian chambermaid and her husband, and in the very room she was now staying. Jean-Pierre had told his wife that he had stayed in the suite on his stag weekend. It was the final straw for Marie. She was looking forward to going home to Paris, back into the arms of Olivier.

Marie made her way back to the bedroom. Jean-Pierre gave nothing away. He said nothing about the discovery he'd made. He noted that Marie checked her phone immediately. He was completely shocked at the betrayal. He didn't know who had surprised him most, Olivier or Marie? He wondered how long the affair had been going on and if Marie intended to leave him.

He didn't intend to lose his wife. He would win her back. He would beat Olivier. There and then, Jean-Pierre began a charm offensive.

Spotting the oncoming car, Alex Hamilton beeped his horn and Felicia flashed her lights.

Felicia and her children were heading to Roundstone.

The car journey had been quiet, each alone in their own thoughts. Anna was remembering how close she had been to her dad. She had felt her father's presence today at Beat Two. She missed having him in her life. Harvey had often told Anna how proud he was of her. He wouldn't be so proud of her now. There and then, she made a silent promise to stop smoking weed. She'd never touch another joint.

Almost immediately, she became uneasy at the thought, anxious even. It was going to be difficult, very tricky indeed. She wondered if that made her an addict.

Maybe she wouldn't be able to quit altogether. At the very least, she would cut down on her drug habit. And all was not lost because she got a buzz when she drank. She'd still have the booze, and she'd have her ciggies. She'd smoke the occasional bit of weed, that's all. She'd stop taking Vicodin too. What's more, she would never take coke again. She'd stick to that promise. Definitely.

She had loved the buzz she got from cocaine; awake all night, euphoric and in party mood, with too much energy. But the come down the following day had been horrendous. She had taken two relaxers as well as weed to even out.

Oblivious to what was going on his sister's head, Jack was thinking how influential his father had been on his beliefs, likes and dislikes. And Felicia was thinking that a happy future would be impossible without Harvey beside her. When she looked in the mirror, Felicia didn't recognise the woman staring back at her. She seemed older and infinitely sadder.

Felicia parked her car on the main street. She glanced over at Anna, her strong, dependable daughter. Anna was in a world of her own. She shouldn't rely on Anna so much. She was only a teenager. Her daughter had taken being selfless and responsible to a worrying degree.

Anna had been tetchy recently. She was grieving for her father Felicia concluded. That could be why her daughter hadn't done as well as expected in her end of term exams. Anna's grades had dipped this year.

The Russell family found their way to the graveyard. Seán had given Felicia explicit directions. "It's easy to miss because the entrance is hidden off the street," he had said.

In between two village houses lay a narrow flight of steps. Felicia, followed by her two children, walked up the steps and came to a laneway entrance. From this vantage point, the church was not visible.

They walked along the leafy laneway until they arrived at the cemetery and a small stone church with stained glass windows. Felicia could hear birds chirping. She admired an ancient yew tree, conical in shape, but broad. They walked about the grave-yard looking for Fred Russell's grave.

"Here he is," said Jack. "I've found him. I've found both of them."

All three of them immediately perked up. Anna and Felicia walked over to where Jack was standing. Harvey's grandfather and Jack's great grand-aunt Nancy Ann had been buried side by side.

"Where is Bride buried? Anna asked her moth-er. "Why isn't she buried with her husband?"

"I have no idea, Anna. I have to say, it's very strange."

"It must be another Russell family mystery," Anna said.

Felicia looked at the headstones.

Nancy Ann's headstone read:

In loving memory of my beloved sister Nancy Ann, born 8th August 1900, died December 20th, 1929.

Erected by her loving brother.

Her brother's headstone read:

In loving memory of Dr Fred Russell, beloved brother of Nancy Ann, born 18th January, 1891, died November, 10th 1954.

"Fred and Nancy Ann," Anna said. "We know so little about them. Dad is with them now."

Felicia and her children stood for a few moments by the graves.

"I think we should make tracks," Felicia said. "What do you think?"

"I suppose we should," Anna said. "It's been emotional, Mum. But I'm glad we came."

"So am I," Jack said.

"That makes the three of us," Felicia said. Like her daughter, she had felt Harvey's presence at Beat Two. And she had found comfort in the stillness and beauty of her surroundings. This was a journey that she'd had to make.

"It was harder than I thought it was going to be," Jack continued. "I feel sad, Mum. I don't think I'll be fishing in Doonmara for a long time."

Felicia put her arm around his shoulder.

"Let's give your gran a quick call. It would mean a lot to her."

Laura and Alex hadn't visited the graveyard. If they had, Laura might have made the connection between Nancy Ann's birthday and the date that was engraved on the ring.

⇥✢⇤

Alex and Laura were home by eight. His phone rang half an hour later. At the time, Laura was upstairs in the bedroom. The number had been withheld again. The same person was calling.

He had no difficulty in recognising the voice. It was Caroline Cleary. His immediate thought was: What the hell did she want? He had to get her off the phone fast.

"Don't hang up," she said. "I wouldn't be phoning unless it was absolutely necessary. Believe me, Alex."

Then she told him, and his whole world collapsed, again. It was as if he had aged a thousand years.

The results from Caroline's endoscopy had come back. The cancer hadn't returned. She had a stomach infection, a bacterial infection that was treatable with a triple course of antibiotics.

Nevertheless, she had been scared enough to finally contact Alex. It was possible that the cancer would return at some stage in the future. She didn't intend to go through the same agony, worrying about her child's future. Caroline Cleary finally told Alex Hamilton about the child they had conceived together.

It had been an emotional conversation. A very difficult conversation.

Conor sat beside his grandfather's bed.

"It won't be long now," a nurse had whispered into his ear earlier.

His grandfather was breathing heavily. Conor held his hand. The old man looked peaceful. Conor was grateful because his grandfather had been agitated that morning. He had been rambling.

"His mind has been drifting in and out of the past all morning," the nurse had observed.

"It often happens towards the end."

The old man's mind drifted again but to happier times. Now, he was remembering his time as a boy at the Castle. He recalled a story his father had told him about the Maharaja. It was a story that Conor had heard many times.

The first time the old man's father had taken the Maharaja out fishing, he had been dubious about the fishing skills of his new employer. The gillie hadn't been sure how to address his new boss.

"I called him your worship, and your lordship, and any number of things," he'd told his son. "And to my surprise didn't he hook a salmon, and a big one at that. I was gobsmacked. I didn't think he had it in him. I instructed him in what to do but he didn't listen to me. His line snapped and the salmon escaped. I was disgusted, and before I knew it, I said to him, 'Ye bloody black bastard, ye lost him, so ye did.'

"I thought I had lost my job but the Maharaja only laughed. And the Maharaja told that story till the day he died. The man had a good sense of humour. I'll say that about him. I didn't mean any offense and I told him that to his face. 'None taken, my good man.' That's what he said to me."

The old man's father had laughed heartedly when he told the story, and so did Conor's grandfather when he, in turn, had retold the tale to Conor.

The old man himself had been fond of the Maharaja. He recalled that Gai Singh had been a handsome man. He and Nancy Ann had made a striking couple. Conor's grandfather remembered the pair of them sneaking a cigarette in the fishing huts. He could hear Nancy Ann laughing. She had a lovely laugh.

She was a beautiful woman and a gentle soul. The doctor's sister was a real lady. What was it the Maharaja used to call her? He struggled to remember. A moment later, it came to him. His red rose. Gai Singh often called Nancy Ann his red rose. It was on account of her waist-length red hair. The old man smiled.

Conor took notice of that smile now. And then the old man died.

⚔+⚔

Harvey's mother had spoken to Felicia. Betty was touched that Felicia had phoned from the graveyard. Felicia and her grandchildren were all the family she had left now. She missed her son beyond measure.

After the phone call, Betty went to the study and opened the desk drawer. She took out a large brown envelope. Inside the envelope was the photograph of her husband Kirk and Nancy Ann, as well as Kirk's birth certificate. Betty looked at the photograph now. It was hard to believe that the small child in the photograph was her husband. It was the only photograph she had ever seen of Kirk as a child.

Betty was delighted that her daughter-in-law and grandchildren had found the two graves. Nonetheless, she had been very surprised that Kirk's mother hadn't been buried alongside Kirk's father. Instead, Dr Fred lay next to his sister, Nancy Ann.

That's odd," Betty had said to Felicia. "I find that most peculiar. Where has his mother Bride been buried?"

"Bride wasn't buried here, Betty. That's for certain."

Betty put the photograph back in the envelope. Then, without giving much thought to what she was doing, she took out the birth certificate and opened it up. She had never had a proper look at Kirk's birth certificate before. This time she studied it in detail.

It read:

Mother Nancy Ann Russell. Father unknown.

That threw her completely. Betty had an ominous feeling, one she couldn't shake off.

The doorbell rang. Betty was expecting Richard. She drew a breath. Surely he could shed some light on this bombshell. It was Harvey's anniversary, and Richard had said he'd drop by for a chat. Betty looked forward to Richard's visits. These days she had few visitors.

She told Richard immediately. His facial expression was proof enough that he had been aware all along.

"I know," he admitted. "I've always known. Close to the end of her life, my grandmother spoke about Nancy Ann to my mother. She made my mother swear that she'd never tell Harvey."

"But why?" Betty asked, puzzled. Something was wrong. Harvey hadn't told Betty, and he must have known that he was illegitimate. He'd seen the birth certificate. Why would he have hidden that from her? It would have made not one bit of a difference to Betty. There was something more to it. There must be.

"Betty," Richard began, "I'm afraid there's a major skeleton in the Russell family closet and what I'm about to reveal is incredibly scandalous. There's no easy way of telling you this but the fact of the matter is that Nancy Ann and Fred were Kirk's biological parents.

"Oh my God," she said, absolutely shocked. At the news, Betty felt sick to her stomach. She sank back into the chair. Richard gave her a moment to compose herself before continuing.

"Nancy Ann and Fred were brother and sister but they were half-siblings. They had the same father but different mothers."

"That's something I suppose," Betty murmured. "But it's still terrible."

"Yes, dreadful," Richard agreed. "Fred's mother was named Bride and she died in childbirth when Fred was born," he explained. "Fred's father remarried a few years later and his step-mother had a baby girl, Nancy Ann. Fred was sent away to school in England at a very young age. He was seven or eight. He didn't really see his half-sister, Nancy Ann for years. They didn't grow up together. He was nine years older."

"So Fred never actually married a woman called Bride?" Betty asked.

"That's correct," Richard said. "Bride was his mother. After university, Fred came home as a newly qualified doctor. And that's when it started. He became obsessed with Nancy Ann. At seventeen, to the shock and horror of the family, she became pregnant. She was ostracized. Her father was a rector so you can imagine the outrage.

"She was sent away to have the baby. She ended up in one of the mother and baby homes. Nancy Ann wouldn't say who the father was. There were no likely candidates. Nancy Anne lived a very sheltered life. My grandmother was aware of Fred's obsession with Nancy Ann. Their relationship made my grandmother very uneasy. The thought that the two siblings might be having a relationship was sickening, and my grandmother never articulated her suspicions.

"Incest wouldn't have been discussed openly in those days, and she thought no one would have believed her. In time, it emerged that other family members knew, and the truth trickled out. But it was never spoken about openly.

"Somehow or other, Fred got custody the baby. He was a doctor and a respected member of the community. It can't have been too difficult.

"Fred moved to Roundstone and presented himself as a recently bereaved widower and before long his younger sister arrived to take care of the infant. Neither of them had contact with the family again. None of the family would have had anything to do with them anyway.

"Years passed and then my grandmother had a letter from Nancy Ann. She had always been close to my mother. They were first cousins and had known each other forever. My grandmother had been very fond of her as a child. Nancy Ann promised my grandmother that the relationship with Fred finished before the child was born. She told her that she had stayed only because of the child. She begged for forgiveness. To my grandmother's great shame, she never replied to the letter. My grandfather wouldn't allow her to correspond with Nancy Ann. And when Nancy Ann killed herself, my grandmother felt dreadful remorse. When she was close to death, she felt the need to unburden herself, and that was why she told my mother the truth.

"My grandmother believed that Fred used the child to control Nancy Ann. She said that she had been a complete innocent and impressionable. But he was an adult. He had taken full advantage of Nancy Ann.

"And then Kirk went away to boarding school and Fred couldn't control his half-sister anymore. Worse still, Nancy Ann had fallen in love with the Maharaja. Finally, she could get away from her brother."

"I hardly know what to say," Betty told him. "It's beyond belief."

"Nancy Ann's secret stays between us," Richard said.

Betty nodded vigorously. Felicia and the children could never know.

"How much did Kirk know?" she asked.

"Kirk found out everything. That was the reason for the fall out with his father."

Betty heaved a deep sigh. She could still feel the knot in her stomach. She hated to think that her husband had carried the secret to his grave.

"I understand why he couldn't tell me," she said to Richard. "The shame of it would have been too much to bear. And he would have wanted to protect Harvey. He would have wanted to protect us both. I'm glad that Harvey never knew. That's of some comfort."

Betty handed the birth certificate to Richard. He tore it up into tiny fragments.

"You have a daughter," Caroline said. "Her name is Una."

Alex was in deep shock. It was too much to take in. He found it impossible to continue the conversation. He told Caroline that he would phone her back in the morning.

As soon as he put the phone down, he was engulfed with panic, and then disbelief. He could hear his heart beating, and his hands were shaking. He thought he was about to have a panic attack.

Laura would have to be told. It would mark the end of his marriage. He knew that. He would be a father again. What would that do to his wife? Laura was the person he loved the most. He had failed her once more. He could offer her no comfort. He had lost Laura and somehow, they had found their way back together. They had been through so much hurt and pain. He was about to lose her for a second time and the pain of that hit him forcibly. His mobile bleeped and he opened a message from Caroline. He had asked her to text her phone number. When the affair was over, he had deleted Caroline's number from his phone. If she had been surprised by that, she didn't show it.

Not long afterwards, Laura had come downstairs. She knew by the look on his face that something was dreadfully wrong.

"What is it, Alex? What's happened?" she asked, concerned, and unaware of the turmoil he'd created.

And then he told her. He told her about Caroline Cleary and the child that he had fathered. *I have a daughter*, he thought. He found it too hard to say out loud. It seemed too bruising to Laura. He referred to Una as a child he had fathered.

"No, it's impossible," Laura insisted. "That's ridiculous. This can't be. That woman is lying to you."

"It's true, Laura," he said.

"Why would you believe her? Why?"

"She texted a picture of the child."

"And from one photograph, you can positively say that this child is yours? That's ludicrous."

"She's my daughter, Laura. There's no doubt about that," he said, and his voice faltered.

Caroline had texted a photograph along with her number. When Alex saw Una's picture, he wept. He had gripped the phone tightly, mesmerized by the face of the little girl in the picture who closely resembled Rachel. Memories of Rachel came flooding back. All sorts of emotions stirred within him, including one of deep paternal love. He had bonded to the little girl straight away.

"How could you do this to me?" Laura screamed, enraged.

He had no answers for Laura. He reached for her.

"Take your hands off me. Leave me alone. Get out, Alex. I want you to leave now." Laura felt herself edging towards that black hole again.

Alex thought it best to do as she said. He went upstairs to pack a bag. He paced the room, backwards and forwards, in constant movement. He would have to go but he wanted to stay. He couldn't envisage a life without Laura.

He considered phoning her brother because he feared for his wife. Maybe Peter could help to calm her down. Someone should be with Laura but there was no doubt about it, that person was not him. Alex's very presence was driving her crazy. He wanted to do what was best for Laura. He didn't know what that was.

Alex had left his mobile on the table downstairs. In a rage, Laura picked up the phone. She opened the text. There was a picture of a young child. That picture changed everything.

She ran upstairs and found him in the bedroom. Laura flung herself into his arms. "Don't leave me," she said. "I love you, no matter what has happened."

"But, Laura," he began.

"Shhh," she said, like she had said that night in Doonmara. "I've seen her picture, Alex. She's a part of Rachel. She's Rachel's sister. She's not our daughter but she is a part of Rachel. She's a little piece of Rachel, a connection to Rachel. In a million years, I never thought I'd have that. We had nothing. Now, we have something. I should be joyous. We should be joyous. I understand that now. Rachel has sent her to us. I know she has."

Laura was certain of it. She had seen it in her dreams.

EPILOGUE

Nancy Ann sat in the shed smoking a final cigarette. Briefly, she considered her predicament. The Maharaja had forsaken her. She loved him dearly, and she thought he had loved her. She had been mistaken. Now, she was pregnant again, and alone. The first pregnancy had been unwanted, but she wanted this child.

She was not going back to her brother's house; of that she was certain. There was nowhere she could go. There was no one who could help her. Her situation was hopeless. She had never felt so isolated. When all was said and done, only one choice remained for Nancy Ann.

She walked to the river's edge at Beat Two. The Maharaja had proposed to her here. He had promised to love and to cherish her forever and had presented Nancy Ann with a beautiful diamond ring as a symbol of their love. He had bought the ring at Cartier. He had gone to Paris solely for that purpose because he wanted a diamond that was rare and precious, like she was to him. He had promised to bring her to Paris on their honeymoon. But the Maharaja had abandoned her.

She threw the engagement ring into the water. The night was silent and she heard the small splash.

Nancy Ann asked God for forgiveness for what she was about to do next. A part of Nancy Ann thought her soul was eternally damned anyway. The sins of her past remained with her. She had never been absolved. Her sin had been too great.

She headed in the direction of Sná Beg. A full moon guided her. The river path was mucky here and the hem of her white dress became heavily soiled.

She arrived and found the boat that would take her on a final journey. She stopped rowing when she had reached the middle of the lake. Her plan was fool proof because she was unable to swim.

Already, she mourned the death of her unborn child and of what might have been. She lowered herself into the freezing water. Her final thoughts were of her son, Kirk. He may have been an unwanted child, but she had loved him with all of her heart.

The End

THE AUTHOR

Mirette Hanley studied English, Psychology and History at Trinity College Dublin, beginning her working life as a journalist, working as a features writer for The Irish Times and in broadcasting. She has also been published in a number of magazines. She later worked in the education sector, working as an advocate with adolescents in second chance education.

These days she divides her time between writing and working as an advocate. She lives in Limerick with her husband.

19715318R00305

Printed in Poland
by Amazon Fulfillment
Poland Sp. z o.o., Wrocław